T0279330

BENEATH THESE CURSED STARS

BENEATH THESE
CURSED
STARS

LEXI RYAN

An Imprint of HarperCollinsPublishers

HarperTeen is an imprint of HarperCollins Publishers.

Library of Congress Control Number: 2023943947
ISBN 978-0-06-331190-9

Typography by Chris Kwon
24 25 26 27 28 LBC 5 4 3 2 1

First Edition

For Heather, who indulged me by reading my favorite books and horrified me by demanding spoilers. We miss you. I would gladly give you all the spoilers for just one more family dinner with you at the table.

WILD FAE
LANDS

GOLDEN
PALACE

CEMETERY

SEELIE
COURT

SERENITY
PALACE

UNSEELIE
COURT

UNSEELIE
PALACE

CHAPTER ONE

◈

JASALYN

THE MALE I CAME TO kill is drunk when I find him. He's lounging on a chesterfield sofa at the back of a crowded underground alehouse, his elven ears poking up through his mop of dirty-blond curls.

I weave through the crowd and sit on his knee as if we're old friends.

"Hey there, beautiful," he says, head lolling to the side, his smile as sloppy as his words.

Disappointment is an unexpected sharp pain in my otherwise numb heart. It's a pity—the drunkenness. Killing him while he's this inebriated won't feel like the triumph I'm after. I'm tempted to come back another time, but I won't risk losing my opportunity.

I tilt his face toward mine, remembering every nasty word he once hurled from his too-pretty fae lips. "I've been looking for you, Vahmer."

"Are you real or a dream?" he asks. His gaze is fixed on my mouth.

I give him my most wicked smile. "What do you think?"

"I think if this is a dream, I don't want to wake up."

I cup his jaw and stroke my thumb across his cheek. "Don't worry," I whisper. "You won't."

A mere three years ago, the faeries in this room—the nastiest, greediest citizens of the Unseelie Court—were enjoying ill-gotten wealth under Mordeus's rule. When he died and my sister took the throne, they scrambled like rats from the sun, hiding away and hoarding their riches, scheming to overthrow the rightful queen.

Here, in the deepest caverns of the darkest mountains, they live like kings. Throwing parties where pleasure is the purpose and cruelty is the side act.

"Tell me what you want," he says, attention still fixed on my lips. "Anything I have is yours. Anything I don't, I'll get for you."

Such sweet words from a mouth that spit in my water just to see me cry. Such a hungry gaze from eyes that danced in amusement as my cellmate drew bloody pictures into my flesh with a knife.

Without the moonstone ring on my finger, I'd never be able to tolerate having him so close, but this ring puts as much of a spell on me as it does on those in my presence.

I rise from his lap and back away. "The only thing I want is for you to come with me."

He follows, and the other revelers watch with stars in their eyes, wishing *they* were so lucky.

Like every night I seek out my enemies, my lips are bloodred. I painted them before I left my chambers—a reminder to myself of their deadly power. Neither the makeup nor my hooded cloak hides my appearance. They don't need to. The magical ring on my finger enchants everyone around me. They won't recognize me.

They'll be too bewitched to consider why my face looks familiar.

"I'll go with you," a barrel-chested dwarf barks. "He can't give you anything worth having."

A beautiful white-haired female reaches a delicate, pale hand my way. "No, take me instead."

The crowd surges toward us.

They won't touch me. They want to, but they wouldn't dare without my command.

"You all stay here," I say sweetly. "I'll be back later." It's so tempting to poison their wine and command them all to drink, but I've never seen them before. I don't know the atrocities they've committed. Anyone who's part of this crowd is no doubt guilty of many, but even with this cold heart, I won't execute without cause. *I won't be like them.*

I lead my captive up the stairs and aboveground to the rain-slicked street. The air is crisp tonight, promising an early winter. I *crave* winter. Crave the bitter cold. The ice. The numbness that creeps into my fingers and toes.

This winter, thanks to the ring on my finger, I'll have a heart to match.

"I'm very strong," my newest victim tells me. "Strong and important. I could take good care of you."

I spin on him. "You didn't take care of Crissa when she was a prisoner in Mordeus's dungeon." I curl my lip and narrow my eyes. "You hurt her."

"Who's Crissa?"

Of course he doesn't remember her. Humans are inconsequential to the fae. "She was the girl who shared my cell."

"Why are you so worried about a *human*?" He says it like

someone might ask why I'm worried about a piece of trash.

We were all cheap toys to him, and using his magic to control her, making her cut me up with no way to stop herself, that was nothing more than a game. "She was my *friend*."

He shakes his head. "There were a lot of prisoners in that dungeon. I wouldn't have hurt anyone if I knew they were friends with *you*."

"You did hurt her. You made her cry and then you took her away."

His brow creases, and his lower lip trembles. "I was doing my job, but if I'd known you wanted her safe, I never would have handed her over to the king. I would've been punished, but I'd take any punishment for you."

"Where did Mordeus take her? Did he kill her?" She told me he wouldn't. Told me she was worth more to him alive than dead. She was so sure she'd be rescued. "I need to know if she lives and where I can find her." The green-eyed faerie before me isn't the first guard I've found since acquiring this ring, and he won't be the first or last to know my wrath, but he's the one who took my friend away. He's the one who can tell me where she is.

"I took her to the king. Perhaps he can tell you where she is."

I frown. "The king is dead." My sister killed him herself after she freed me from his dungeons.

His eyes flare bright. "You do not know! Our king lives! The gods have listened and given him back to us!"

"That's not possible." My words snap in the quiet night.

"But it is. Mordeus was wise, and he prepared for all eventualities. We never should have doubted."

4

Fear is a chisel chipping at my icy heart.

I yank my heart back and lock it away where it belongs.

The faerie reaches for me but stops, his hand just short of my shoulder. "Are you mad at me?"

"I am. *You* are the reason my friend cried and shook in the dark. And you are the reason she is lost to me."

His face crumples. "I'm sorry. So sorry. I didn't know," he blubbers, tears sneaking out the corners of his eyes.

I wish I could've seen him like this in the dungeons—could've seen him begging. My disapproval *hurts him.* While I wear this ring, he would do anything to be in my good favor.

"Tell me what you want," he pleads. *"Anything."*

It's getting late. Too soon the sun will rise, and my sister will be looking for me—looking for the weak and frightened little girl she expects to live inside this skin. So I don't draw this out the way I prefer. I bat my lashes and fist the fabric at the front of his tunic.

I curl my lips and watch his heartache wash away. My smile makes him happy. My smile makes him believe he's done something right. "There's only one thing I want," I say, leaning closer.

"It's yours." He's breathless. Desperate for my command. "What is it?"

"A kiss."

"Thank you." He exhales—relieved and grateful. I've given him permission to take what he's wanted since he set eyes on me.

This is where the magic truly is. The moment these red lips touch his.

His breath hitches. His lips part in horror, and life leaves his eyes. He becomes a heavy weight—death leaning against me. I smile in earnest now. He can no longer torment those weaker than him. He can no longer find pleasure in others' pain.

Once I release his shirt, his lifeless body falls to the ground.

I slice off a handful of his curls with my dagger, then slip away as quietly as I arrived, knowing the faeries in the alehouse below will have no memory of my visit, no memory of the chestnut-haired woman with the face of the shadow princess.

My chambers are warded against goblin travel, so I have my goblin bring me to a remote area at the back edge of the palace grounds. The sun hasn't yet begun to rise, but the palace is lined with paths lit by torches that illuminate my companion's pimpled face.

Gommid is two feet shorter than me with a big belly, a bulbous nose, and a tongue he can't quite keep inside his toothy mouth. He eyes my magic ring and shakes his head. "Perhaps you should learn to face your enemies without that wicked crutch," he says.

I ignore this. I don't know why the ring doesn't affect goblins, but I know Gommid well enough to know my secrets are safe with him, so I don't worry about it.

I reach into my pocket and retrieve the handful of my victim's curls—Gommid's payment—but hold them away from his grasp. "A male I spoke with tonight told me Mordeus is back. Did he speak the truth?"

"You ask about the honesty of the male you *killed*?" He sniffs and flicks at the tip of his nose with his long tongue.

I shouldn't be surprised that he knows how I spent my night. Goblins are the keepers of secrets in this realm, and they always know more than they'll share. My sister told me their knowledge is collective. What one knows, they all know. She wasn't warning me so much as letting me know they are a useful resource, but I've always wondered what they do with all that information. No one really knows where goblins' loyalty lies.

I shrug. "Is it true?"

"Your sister's claim to the throne is secure. Do not fret."

I scowl. "I'm not *afraid*."

"Oh? Is that why you wear that ring and hunt your enemies in the dead of night? Need I warn you again? You must be yourself more than the Enchanting Lady, or she will control you."

I retreat a step, backing toward the palace. "I'm in no mood to be lectured by a creature who does favors for fingernails and locks of hair."

Grunting, he snatches the tangle of curls from my hand and disappears.

I don't bother sneaking into the Midnight Palace. There's no need when I'm wearing the ring. I walk right in through the doors off the gardens and into the east hall, where servants have already begun to prepare for the day. I feel their eyes on me as I stroll through the kitchen and up the narrow servants' stairs.

"I would consider it a personal favor."

I pause at the sound of my sister's voice coming from one of the small meeting rooms on the second floor.

"You don't need to ask," someone replies—a familiar male voice.

I turn out of the stairwell and stand just outside the cracked-open door. I spot the dark head of the Wild Fae king. He's seated at an oblong wooden table, his back to me. My sister paces the opposite side of the room, her fiery red curls flowing down her back.

"You're going to wear a trench in the floor if you keep that up," Misha tells her. "Sit and take a breath."

She spins to face him, and I step out of view—just in case her eyes stray to the door. "I cannot focus on my duties when I am so consumed with worry over my sister."

I flinch. She's *always* worried for me, and I hate that. I hate that I've brought her so much grief and pain in her short years.

"It's been *three years*," my sister says, her desperation drawing out the words, "but she walks around with the same terror that was in her eyes right after she was freed from Mordeus."

"Your sister is always welcome in my court," Misha says. "She can stay as long as she likes."

Stay in the Wild Fae Lands? Is my sister planning to send me away?

Brie crosses her arms. "She won't want to stay. All she ever wants is to sit in her room and hide and sleep and pretend that she isn't months away from becoming fae."

A light brown hand reaches toward her, and I realize my sister's partner, King Consort Finnian, must be at the end of the table I can't see. He brushes his fingers against her wrist. My sister looks his way and nods. I can see the calm wash over her. Finn steadies her, brings her comfort and peace and, when needed, his own strength. I love him for that. Even if he is fae.

"She'll need to agree to it," Misha says. "I'm not interested in holding her captive."

8

"She will," Finn says. "If Brie makes it clear that's what she wants."

"She'll let it be known that she's displeased about it," Brie tells Misha. "But I think you could win her over." She flashes a weak smile. "As you did with me not so long ago."

"I'll do what I can, but you know your sister. She isn't very . . . *open* to friendships. But I will try."

"I'm afraid I must ask you for more than your friendship, Misha. I need you to give her a purpose. Otherwise, she'll do the same at Castle Craige as she's done here for three years."

Misha leans back in his chair. "And what makes you think my efforts to make her live her life will go over any better than yours?"

Brie grimaces. "She's too gentle to tell you no."

Gentle. It's all I can do to stifle my scoff. I just watched the life leave a male's eyes, and it was the best part of my week by far. That they think I'm *gentle* proves they don't know me at all.

"What do you have in mind?" Misha asks.

"It can be anything. Just get her involved with the day-to-day of running the territory. Take her with you when you travel. Get her outside. *Anything.*"

"And you're sure she wouldn't be safer locked in her chambers here?"

"If the rumors are even true," Brie says, "I suspect Mordeus will stay in the Unseelie Court, where he can gather his followers and pull power from the land. He knows this court and this palace better than anyone, and he knows too well what I would do to protect her. I can't risk being the reason she's hurt again, and

I can't risk this court being in danger if the worst happens and Mordeus is able to get his hands on her again."

Mordeus? Am I the last to know these rumors?

I must make some sound, because Misha and Brie swing their heads toward me.

"Jas!" my sister squeaks, rushing around the table to swing the door open and greet me. Her pale skin flushes at the sight of me. "Why aren't you in bed?"

I rub my thumb against the ring still firmly in place on my middle finger, a reminder that none of them will remember this interaction. "I couldn't sleep."

"I'll call for your handmaid. She can get you more—"

"Please don't. Mordeus is back?"

"There are rumors," Misha says, standing and coming closer. "You are stunning," he says, sweeping his gaze over me. "May I be so bold as to ask you to walk with me?"

Brie shoots him a puzzled look. "I'll handle this."

I roll my eyes. The ring is effective, but sometimes the results are . . . absurd. "Focus," I tell them. "Tell me what you know about Mordeus."

Brie looks to both Misha and Finn, who's pushed to his feet to come closer, but they're both under the spell of my ring and offer her no help. She sighs. "My sources tell me that his followers have been chattering about his return—a supposed resurrection," she says. "We have spies in the field as we speak, trying to find out more, but I don't want you to worry about it."

I cock my head and study her. She seems her normal self. Almost as if she's unaffected by the ring.

I don't have time to worry about what that could mean. Finn comes toward us, and when I meet his silver eyes, a shiver of revulsion goes down my spine.

I shift my gaze and focus on his dark curls, so different from the straight, silver-streaked hair of his wicked uncle Mordeus.

Finn gestures to his chair. "Please, take my seat. Let me get you some tea."

"No, thank you," I say. "I'm tired and want to go back to bed."

"I'll walk you," Misha says, eyes bright. "I want to make sure everything in your room is as you like it."

"You all stay here and finish your meeting." I step back toward the stairwell. "You never saw me anyway."

I turn away from the doe-eyed affection on their faces and walk quickly to the stairs. Behind me, I hear my sister ask, "What is wrong with you two?"

I bite back a laugh and go to my chambers.

The sentry who stands outside my door beams when he spots me, his eyes bright, his smile comically wide.

"What can I do for milady?" he asks. Dryus is a distant cousin of Finn's, with the same silver eyes, light brown skin, and dark hair. He's young and kind and has been nothing but good to me in the three years he's been charged with my protection, but his pointed, elven ears are a reminder than he can't be trusted. My once-human sister excepted, no faeries can. I was a stupid little girl for ever believing otherwise.

I cock my head to the side. "Do you tire of babysitting a human girl?" I ask.

"It is both tedious and a privilege, milady. But what of you?

11

Are you tired? May I help you in any way?"

I sigh. His honesty is boring. I was hoping for evidence of an ugly heart beneath that pretty face. Perhaps it's the ring that makes me crave a reason to hate him. "Remember, the princess was in her room all night. She passed the hours reading because she couldn't sleep."

"Of course, milady."

I step around him and through the door, hanging my cloak and stripping out of my dress. I pull on the sleeping gown my maid helped me into eight hours ago. It seems like a lifetime.

Mordeus is back.

I stare at my magic ring, at the smooth moonstone framed on either side with a silver crescent moon. It's time to take it off, but I dread the brutal *humanity* that will follow. Maybe this time it won't. Maybe I can block out the pain the same way my tutors have taught me to block faeries from my thoughts.

The second I slide the silver band from my finger, my terror hits me like a tidal wave, and I collapse onto the bed.

Mordeus is back. Mordeus is looking for a way to destroy my sister.

I know I should care about what he wants beyond that—the part where he intends to steal back the throne and rule this kingdom, but I don't. I want no part of it, royal fae blood and destiny be damned.

I drag myself to my pillow and bury my face, muffling sobs. I have my own wing in this palace, but no privacy. In addition to the sentry outside my door, there are two more at the top of the main stairs and another standing at the servants' stairs. If they hear me cry, my sister will know about it by morning.

I grip the ring so hard it bites into my palm. I want to put it back on. It will ease this ache in my chest—turn it to ice, numb my heart, and cool my anger. It will transform this nightmare I've found myself living into a plan for vengeance.

I could. I could slide it on my finger and slip right past the guards. Let them greet me and forget me just as quickly. But Gommid's warning chimes in my head. *You must be yourself more than the Enchanting Lady, or she will control you.*

Would that be so bad? To never feel so deeply again? To never fear? To never hurt like this? To spend my days and nights ending the most wicked creatures in this land?

Across the room, the first fingers of dawn stretch into the window, reminding me that my ring has a magic meant for darkness and using it during the day comes at a cost.

Sleep. Just sleep.

After tucking the ring into the hidden pocket I sewed into the back of my mattress, I find my herbs from the apothecary. If my heart can't be numb, I'll hide in deep, dreamless sleep.

I take a double dose.

CHAPTER TWO

◆

JASALYN

"Good morning, sleepyhead!"

My sister's cheerful voice cuts through the thick blanket of sleep and drags me from my nightmare with a gasp. For a moment I expect to find myself in a dark cell, the scent of urine filling my nose, the icy cold of the stone floor seeping into my bones.

But the bed is soft and my blankets are warm. Day has come and, with it, the honey glow of light through the cracks in the curtains.

The bed shifts and I smell Brie's cinnamon and vanilla soap, sense her warmth. And her worry. *Always* her worry.

"I'm sorry to wake you," she says softly, knuckles brushing the back of my hand. "But I have a meeting in the northern mountains in a couple of hours, and we need to talk first."

Before I was sold to Mordeus and dragged to Faerie from my home realm, the human realm of Elora, I never wasted much time imagining what it might be like to be queen of a faerie court, but I would've guessed it involved decadence and balls and . . . I don't know, appearing before your subjects like some beneficent goddess. But judging from my sister's experience in the last

14

three years, it's mostly meetings and more meetings. When she's not convincing the lords of the court to assist in her rebuilding efforts, she's mediating petty squabbles between shadow fae, like a schoolmistress teaching children to play nice.

As if dealing with the politics within the court isn't bad enough, she's also left to navigate the politics between courts. While she calls the king of the Seelie Court and the king of the Wild Fae Lands both friends, the subjects of the three main territories of Faerie aren't keen to follow her lead. The Seelie and Unseelie fae were enemies for centuries before Abriella took the throne, and though historically neutral, the Wild Fae were reluctant allies at best.

"Jas?" Brie says, taking my wrist in her hand.

I force my eyes open before I fall back to sleep.

Brie's wearing her riding clothes—brown leather pants with knee-high boots, a soft white cotton blouse beneath a leather riding vest. I catch her frowning at the puddles of dried wax on my bedside table from all the nights I've left candles burning while I sleep. She knows I hate the dark, but I don't talk to her about it because she gets that crease between her brows and guilt fills her eyes.

It's not her fault our aunt sold me to an evil faerie. It's not her fault the darkness reminds me of those long nights in Mordeus's dungeons and the horrible things I endured there.

She gently strokes her thumb over the circular scar on my wrist. It's as wide as a plum and gnarled like a knot on an old tree. I hate the pain and worry that contorts her face when she looks at my scars, and I yank my wrist from her grasp and pull down the sleeve of my sleeping gown.

"Any new marks this morning?" she asks, eyes searching my face.

"I don't know." I yank up my blankets, tucking them under my arms before she gets any ideas and tries to look for herself. There are already more than she knows about, though I'm guessing my maids have told her about the game board of puffy scar tissue that's appeared across my abdomen.

"Perhaps next time Finn and I visit Juliana in Staraelia, you could—"

"Is my appearance so disturbing to you that you need your High Priestess to fix me?" I snap.

She flinches, and I wish I could take the words back. The scars began appearing at random intervals shortly after my birthday. Once Abriella found out about them, I agreed to let her healers look at me, but their salves do nothing to make the marks fade, and they haven't had any answers for their queen about my mysterious scarring. But I fear the High Priestess and whatever magic she has would tell my sister too much.

Abriella is a powerful queen, but with me she acts like a nervous child. And that's all my fault. It's all my fault because I'm broken. It's all my fault because while this life in this world has made Brie grow and thrive, for me it feels like trying to breathe underwater.

I don't need Brie knowing that though the timing of the marks' appearance is random, the scars themselves are not. Each corresponds to an injury inflicted on me in Mordeus's dungeons.

I don't want her knowing about what happened to me during

those weeks. What good would it do, anyway?

At least now I have the ring and my nights tracking down my enemies. At least when my heart is cold, I feel like I can breathe.

On the other side of the room, my handmaid draws the curtains, and the streams of golden sunlight turn to swaths that fill the room.

I squint, push myself up, and lean against my velvet headboard.

"It's nearly lunchtime," my sister says. There's no censure in her tone, only concern.

"I had trouble falling asleep." A lie. Once I took my herbs at sunrise, sleep came hard and fast. *And the nightmares with it.*

The dreams of my days in Mordeus's dungeons haunt me, but worse than those are the dreams where I'm in his body. My mind twists my worst memories until my dreams show our "visits" from his eyes. In those dreams, I have to see the terror in my eyes as he steals all my control. I have to see myself writhing in pain from his brutal torture. But the worst part is how I feel in those dreams. How much I relish the power. How satisfying it is to see myself suffer.

Brie stares down at her hands. Her red hair falls forward, a curtain hiding her face. I always loved her hair—an orange red like the lilies in the Court of the Sun. It's grown long again in these last few years, and now the waves flow down to the middle of her back. Once upon a time, I'd sit behind her and weave it into braids.

But that was before. Before the dungeons. Before the Throne of Shadows. Before the person I loved most in the world became

17

what I hate most: a faerie.

"It's normal, you know," she says. "Excessive sleeping is a symptom of depression and—"

"I'm not depressed."

When she lifts her head, I flinch at the pain I see in her eyes. "I know you're not happy here. You can talk to me." Her desperation hurts worse than the many daggers twisted into my flesh while I was Mordeus's captive. "I fight every day for the people in this court, and all the while I feel like I'm losing you. I can't do this if you are the cost."

Then don't. But I can't ask that. Not when leading these people means everything to her. Not when, if it weren't for me, Brie would be happier now than she's ever been in her life.

And besides, what's the alternative? Brie uses her magic to glamour herself so we can go home again? I miss the realm of Elora, the land where we were born and raised, the way I miss the innocence of my childhood. There's no going back, and we both know it.

"You've suffered through so much," she says. "Two major traumas that you never speak of. If you needed to talk—"

"I don't." I tear my gaze from hers and stare at my lap, counting down the seconds until she leaves me alone.

"You don't even want to sew anymore."

"This again? Why are you so fixated on me sewing? You probably have a hundred servants capable of the job." I give her a smile. Not the seductive smile of the Enchanting Lady, and not the satisfied smile that curves my lips when death takes my victims. No, I give her my Princess Jasalyn smile. This is the expression of the

18

girl I'm supposed to be. Meek and scared, but grateful. "I'm truly fine. You've given me a home, and I am content here." Another lie. I've gotten too good at this.

"Nevertheless, I would like you to go stay with Misha for a time."

Everything from last night comes back in a rush. *Mordeus is back, and my sister wants to send me away.*

But I'm not supposed to know any of that and she doesn't seem to remember, so I cough out a laugh. "I'll pass, thanks." Misha is my sister's best friend. He's a nice enough male, but when he visits, I always feel him poking around in my head. Luckily, he's also the one who taught me how to guard against such mental exploitations. He taught me well, but I find it unnerving nevertheless. I always fear slipping in his presence. What would he do if he knew my secrets? Tell my sister, surely, and then what?

What would Abriella do if she knew her terrified little sister was leaving a trail of her enemies' bodies throughout the mountains?

What would she do if she knew what I traded for that power?

"The Wild Fae territory is beautiful," Brie says.

"I'm sure it is, but I don't want to go."

"You could go riding and explore the village."

"I could go riding here."

"You could start fresh—away from the court where so many terrible things happened to you." She tucks a strand of hair behind my ear, and I flinch before catching myself. She yanks her hand away as if she's been burned. "You could make new friends. New memories."

19

My heart pinches. She doesn't just want me to *visit* her friend. When they were talking last night, I thought she meant a few days, maybe a week. "You want me to *live* there?"

"I think it would be good for you."

"Is it that bad?" The words are out before I can stop them. "Having me here? Knowing that I struggle a little? Is it so terrible that you must send me away?"

My sister's beautiful hazel eyes go wide. "No!" She shakes her head, panic all over her face. "Jas, it's not that at all. I *love* having you here. Love it so much I wonder if I've been selfish to keep you in the palace when perhaps you'd heal better . . . elsewhere."

Elsewhere. Further from my mission. Somewhere I will be expected to act as the shadow princess. At least here I'm left alone. At least here I can hunt those who hurt me and feel some sort of purpose. "Well, I won't, so forget it."

She bites her bottom lip—Abriella, fierce and feared queen of the shadow fae—cowering because she's scared of hurting her human baby sister. I'm not sure whether to laugh or cry.

"It's not just that," she says. "There are things happening in this court. Unexplained deaths and rumors that give me pause."

Mordeus. "What rumors?"

"Nothing I want you worrying about. Until I figure out what's happening," she continues, "I'd like you to be with Misha. Away from any potential danger."

My mind skips back to the other piece I didn't hear them talk about last night. "Unexplained deaths? Surely that's nothing new." I can't imagine the few faeries I've killed myself are enough to raise the alarm—especially since these vile creatures were already in hiding.

"This is different. We're talking trails of bodies. Death with no obvious cause."

My pulse stutters into a run. "Where?"

"All over the court." Abriella frowns. "It's been happening for weeks, maybe months—though it's hard to know when it started because not every death is reported to me. It's hard to identify a pattern without all the information, but we're hearing reports of groups of dead fae—from a few to as many as a dozen at once. Every sign indicates that their deaths are magical, as most are uninjured and showed no sign of illness before they were found dead. It seems I'm getting another report every few days, and the numbers just keep growing."

"And you think *I* might be targeted?"

With a heavy sigh, she pushes off my bed and paces. "I think I will worry unless I know you are safe."

"I'll be fine, sister. You've had me trained by the best. Self-defense, mental shields, sword fighting, archery."

"I don't want you to *need* any of those skills." She peers out my windows, but her eyes are distant, as if she's envisioning an entirely different time and place. "We should never have been so honest with the court. We should have led them to believe that Mab already made you fae."

For months after Abriella took the throne, she and her advisors went round and round about what I thought of as "the human problem." Mab had told Abriella that I would turn fae on my eighteenth birthday, so they had to decide whether to pretend I was already fae in the meantime or to potentially allow Abriella's enemies to know my weakness: mortality.

No one ever pushed me to take the Potion of Life that can

turn a mortal fae. Maybe because Abriella experienced it and it really is so excruciating that she didn't want me to go through that. Or maybe because they already knew, on some level, that I dread becoming that which I loathe. I didn't ask, and neither did they.

"Honesty seemed like the best way to begin my reign, but now I wonder if I've left you too vulnerable."

"I'm always at the palace," I say. Which is true, unless I'm wearing my ring, but given the powers that come with that, I'm not too concerned something could happen to me with it on. "Where could I possibly be safer?"

She folds her arms. "You aren't safe in the palace if our enemy knows it as well as we do."

I throw off my covers and stride across the room to stand next to her at the big windows that overlook the palace's midnight gardens. They're filled with flowers that blossom in the moonlight and are rather nondescript during the day. Like me with my ring and me without.

"It is only out of an abundance of caution that I want you to stay with Misha," Brie says. "Not forever, but for now. Once we figure out these deaths and investigate this rumor . . ."

"Mordeus?" I ask, not looking at her.

She's quiet for a long time before replying. I can feel the tension rolling off her, can feel her stress. "They're saying he's been resurrected. Finn and I are meeting with the palace sentinels today to add extra security to the gates and doors. But these rumors might not even be true."

My jaw aches. I focus on relaxing it before I break a tooth.

"Queen Mab was resurrected," I say. The resurrection of the first Unseelie queen is a story Abriella drills into me. In this court, our great-great-who-knows-how-many-greats-grandmother is honored as much as any god. Her blood is the reason Brie sits on the Throne of Shadows and the reason I, born human, am destined to become fae on my eighteenth birthday. For generations before my sister and I were born, the children from Mab's bloodline were born and lived as humans in Elora, their royal, magical blood hidden from everyone—even themselves. It was the best way Mab could protect her progeny from the wrath of her enemies, but it seems that mercy ended with us. "If Mab can return from the dead, why not Mordeus?"

"The gods favored Mab and rewarded her for her selfless love," Brie says. "It is not the same."

I flash her a skeptical glance. If I've learned anything during my time with the fae, it's that they are as clever as they are evil. I have little doubt that Mordeus could've had a plan in place that would've allowed his people to bring him back in the event of an assassination. "What happened to his body—after you killed him?"

Brie draws in a long, measured breath and holds my gaze. "I don't know. But if I could do it again, I would've stayed and watched him burn. If he's back, it's my fault, and I will not let you be a consequence of that failure."

"I want to stay here." I want to find him myself. I want to *end him* myself.

"I promise that I'll have you back here in time for your eighteenth birthday."

I flinch at the mention of that looming date. When I got the ring, a year seemed like so much time. Now I only have nine months left, and I fear it won't be nearly enough.

Her boots scuff the stone floors as she turns to me. The hand she places on my shoulder is warm and tentative. "Sooner if possible."

Hot, angry tears fill my eyes.

"Don't be scared," Brie says, misinterpreting my emotion. "I promise I'll keep you safe."

She doesn't understand that feeling safe isn't my problem. I'm used to the endless fear. But I'm not scared of Mordeus hurting me. I'm scared that my sister will send me away before I can finish what I started. I only have until my eighteenth birthday. I forfeit any days beyond that when I traded my immortality for a magical ring.

The swamps in the north of my sister's territory smell of rot and festering filth that makes my eyes water.

Gommid curls his skinny lip as he surveys the bubbling greenish muck surrounding the sparse trees. "The human faerie uses her favors in strange ways."

I can't risk my sister sending me to the Wild Fae Lands before I track down Mordeus, so as soon as she and Finn left for their meeting, I donned my magical ring and summoned Gommid.

"The human is not a faerie," I remind him. I hate when he calls me that. *Human faerie.* That's not even a thing. I pat the pockets of my cloak, reassuring myself that my ring is secure in the hidden pocket where I tucked it away to use when darkness falls. Wearing the ring even for the brief minutes it took me to escape the watchful eyes of my sister's sentries left me feeling weak and queasy.

When the witch I bought it from warned me to only use it at night, her explanation was that all magic must be balanced. Apparently, my ring's magic is balanced by making me ill if I try to use its power in the daylight.

The swamp belches, sending a putrid breeze my way, and the lingering nausea surges in my throat.

Gommid extends a hand. "I do not work for free, Princess."

I dig a tooth from the pocket of my cloak and drop it into his waiting palm.

His already bulging eyes widen. "A fine incisor from an Unseelie sentinel. You did not remove this yourself." It's not a question.

I shrug. "The guards who were sparring on the practice mats next to me this afternoon were a little aggressive. When one spit out a bloody tooth, I claimed it as my own."

He tucks it into his pocket. "Mine now."

"What do you do with them?"

He grins, showing off his own mouthful of pointy teeth. "What will you give me for that information?"

"Never mind. Thank—" He's already gone. I sigh. "You."

I survey the rancid swamp. There's not a soul in sight, but I've spent enough time in the company of Mordeus's followers and heard enough chatter to know they have a training outpost near here. When night falls, I'll put on my ring and ask every one of his disgusting sycophants where I can find the resurrected king.

The wind rustles through the trees, and the sun sinks toward the horizon. I don't have much daylight left to find what I'm looking for, so I hike up my cloak and start walking.

The farther I walk from the swamp, the more the rancid smell fades and is replaced by the scent of the forest.

I love this time of year in the mortal realm—the changing colors of the leaves on the trees and the crunch of the dry grass beneath my boots as I walk. I ache for it—ache to return to Elora and stay.

But I don't belong there anymore. While the truth of my ancestry might not be known among the mortals of Elora, *I* know, and I feel like a fraud when I'm there. As if the humans of my home realm can see the faerie lurking beneath my skin. My sister's station comes with so many rules, and while I've resented many of them, resented this world and the way we were shoved into it, the Midnight Palace is the closest thing I have to a home.

And she wants to send me away.

I lean back against a thick oak and close my eyes, enjoying my reprieve from the watchful stares of my sister's sentinels.

I wonder if they're noting my absence back at the palace. I hope the words the Enchanting Lady whispered to my guards will keep anyone from checking my chambers until morning.

I won't let myself think about what I will do if I don't find Mordeus tonight. I can't.

A hand slaps over my mouth, and hot breath hisses in my ear. "Silence." A masculine voice, low and rough. He's too strong, too big for me to escape, and I feel myself shutting down, feel the panic making me freeze when I need to fight.

I throw my elbow into my captor's gut, and he grunts softly

before tightening his hold and pinning down my arms.

I open my mouth to scream, but no sound comes out.

Rough fabric is shoved over my head, and horrible darkness envelops me. I try to scream—*try and try and try*—but there's nothing. As if I never had a voice.

Then I'm flying through the air. My breath rushes out of me with an *oomph* as I'm thrown over a shoulder.

"Easy," a feminine voice says. "He said to be careful with her."

"I'll be easy when we're out of here."

I'm jostled more, like an inconvenient sack he's forced to carry, and then we're running—the crunch of crisp leaves underfoot and air winding around my legs, cool even through my riding leathers. I want to flail, to struggle, to injure with all the maneuvers my trainers taught me, but I can't move. My arms and legs are as paralyzed as my voice.

There's a low braying, and I'm hoisted up and over—a horse?

"Let's go!" Then we're off. Flying. My stomach pummeled by the jostling of the horse.

I thrash violently. Or *try*. I can't move my limbs, but if I squirm enough, perhaps I'll fall off.

This is why Brie wanted to keep me locked up. *This* is why she has her rules. Because she knows. How many times did she tell me that they would come for me, that there was always a risk of someone wanting to hurt me?

And here I brought myself to our enemy's doorstep during hours not fit for my ring, and now some sort of wicked faerie magic is stealing my voice and strength.

What if they're taking me to Mordeus?

My heartbeat stutters, and bile surges up my throat. I can already feel his hot breath in my face as he taunts me. Can already imagine the wicked curl of his lips as he draws out my torture.

"Would you *please* make her still before she falls off?" the male says.

"Fine," his female companion says.

Panic has me by the chest. I can't breathe. I can't—

I hear a *puff* and then . . . sleepiness falls over me. So heavy. I fight it. Try to keep my eyes open. I can't be weak if I'm to face him again.

I focus on the sound of the hooves on the path, the feel of the wind snapping the exposed skin at the back of my neck, and the smell of the swamp in the distance. I make myself describe each of these things in my mind as I cling to consciousness, but it's too late. I'm pulled deeper.

CHAPTER THREE

―――◆―――

FELICITY

"THREE DROPS EACH MORNING AND no more," I say, my wrinkled fingers gripping the pipette to fill the small bottle with the healing tincture. "If her cough doesn't get better in two days, come back. But this should be an improvement over the thyme and honey variation you tried last week." I stride to the front counter and pass the bottle to the pale-faced young mother.

Worry is etched across her forehead, and the dark circles under her eyes tell me she hasn't slept in days. "Thank you so much." She digs in her tattered purse, no doubt looking for the coin to pay. I wonder how many times she's had to choose between food for herself and a visit to the apothecary.

I glance over my shoulder to make sure the little shop's proprietor—my boss—hasn't made it in yet. "No charge," I say quickly. "Since the original tincture didn't help."

Her brown eyes fill with tears. "Thank you," she whispers, voice hoarse. "Thank you so much."

I hear the creak of the back door and stiffen. "Hurry on, now."

"Felicity!" Estella barks. "We need to talk."

The young mother's eyes widen for a beat, but then she wisely hurries out the door before Estella can make it to the front.

I busy myself with straightening my station, moving with the steady grace of the gray-haired faerie whose form I've been taking since I got this job two months ago.

Estella pushes into the front of the shop, letting the door swing wildly behind her. She's as physically beautiful today as she was the day I came here looking for a job—silky blond hair that falls past her shoulders, bright violet eyes, with a regal face and long, graceful limbs—but all I can see when I look at her now is ugliness. She's a terrible apothecary who uses the cheapest ingredients over the most effective. Half of her tinctures are little more than soaked herbs.

"I had a young male come into the shop last night who wanted me to refund the continence tincture I sold to his father. He said when he tried to buy some for himself, *you* told him it wouldn't protect them against the faceless plague." She lifts her pointed chin, nostrils flared. "Do you know what happens when you say things like that?"

That young male was begging on the street before coming to see me. I couldn't take his money in exchange for a tiny vial of useless drops. "We should be selling products that *help* people, not—"

"When you spread lies about our products, people talk, and soon no one buys from me."

"But those continence drops can't protect anyone from—"

"None of my customers have fallen to the faceless plague yet," she snaps before I can finish.

Only because it hasn't torn through our village yet. But I don't

30

dare say it out loud. It seems like nearly every week for the last few months there's a story about another group of fae found dead with no sign of the cause, so the people have begun to call it the faceless plague. The victims are always found in groups, pale but uninjured. Most, if the rumors are to be believed, had no prior signs of illness. It's as if Death himself is showing up to gatherings uninvited and taking the attendees without reason.

"People are scared." Frowning, I twist my hands. Too many people in this village lost everything during the years of Mordeus's rule. After he stole the throne, all it took was a whisper of an alliance with the rightful king, and Mordeus would send his personal army to destroy their businesses and their homes. While I don't know what it was like to live here during those times, I know what it's like to have nothing, know what it's like to wonder where your next meal will come from. "We shouldn't exploit that. We should—"

"How *dare* you, you ungrateful crone," Estella says, seething. "The only reason I hired you was because people trust your wrinkly face and spend more money when you're behind the counter. But you do me no good when you convince them not to buy! Get out of my shop, and don't come back."

I squeeze my eyes shut. Jobs are hard to come by, and if I've ruined this . . . "Please reconsider."

She points one long, manicured finger toward the door. "Go. Before I decide to take what you've cost me from your hide."

Lowering my head, I fist my hands at my sides and make toward the door. I went too many months without steady work before Estella agreed to hire me, and now I have to start over.

31

Maybe it's for the best. I couldn't endure her greed and lies.

The day is bright. I squint against the afternoon light as I emerge onto the bustling streets—and freeze when I spy a familiar face watching me from across the road.

In riding leathers with white tattoos all over his forearms and glasses perched on his nose, Natan still appears to be no more than a harmless scholar.

My pulse skips a beat—stuttering from a heady mix of hope and heartache. I immediately scan the streets for my brother, who's never far from his side. I haven't seen him in three years. Not since before my mother sent me away.

I'm still looking when someone grabs my arm and drags me into an empty storefront by Estella's apothecary.

"Hello, Felicity," my brother says, his grin wolfish as Natan slips in behind us.

Hale Kendrick's long light brown hair is tied back at the base of his neck, and his ice-blue eyes bore into me, seeing every fault and failure. Every moment of cowardice.

The door clangs shut, and my throat goes tight.

Natan dips his head in greeting. There's so much in that simple gesture—awareness of who I am beneath this form I've taken, acknowledgment of the adventures we shared as children, and a reminder that he's here to protect Hale, all rolled into one.

Instead of lying, instead of pretending I'm the elderly faerie everyone sees when they look at me, I give my own nod of acknowledgment before glancing around the empty store. "What brings you to this part of the world?" I ask, as if I haven't ached from missing them every single day of my three years away.

"The usual," my brother says, his blue eyes bright. "Rebellion. Treason. Sedition. Plans of world domination."

I nod and wipe my wrinkled hands on my skirts. "How did you find me?"

"It's cute that you think I ever lost you," Hale says. He's my brother in every way that counts. We might not share blood, but we were raised side by side, and he would never just let me run away without bothering to keep tabs on me.

"And how is Mother?" My voice hitches on the word and Hale's face softens.

"Why don't you go home and find out for yourself?"

My stomach twists painfully at the thought. It's like seeing a warm bed after days in the cold and knowing you can't climb in. "Did you come here to be cruel?"

Hale sighs. "Never, Lis. I came because I need you."

Guilt swamps me. Hale wants me to save our home realm, Elora, and all I've ever wanted was to save him.

He sweeps his hand up and down my form. "Who's this? Tell me, does living in a body that can't even fight make you feel safe?"

I can fight just fine but won't bother trying to convince him. I lift my chin. "Why do you care?"

"Because I'm going to need you to leave behind the elderly faerie act. Immediately. It's time to slip into your other favorite skin."

"You're being obnoxiously vague, Hale."

"You're being deliberately obtuse, Lis." When I narrow my eyes, he laughs. "Gods above and below, when you look at me like that, I can almost see the real you in there."

"What's she look like?" I ask. "Just curious, since it's been over three years since I last got a glimpse of myself."

He shrugs. "That was the choice you made when you decided you'd rather hide for the rest of your life than fulfill your own destiny."

"Hale . . ."

"I'm not here to try to change your mind about that." His hard eyes soften, and so does his tone. He reaches into the satchel hanging at his side and withdraws a tattered, leather-bound notebook. "I'm here about this."

I gape at the journal—*my* journal. Inside, next to a small envelope of the princess's hair I bought from a palace maid, I've been keeping notes about the shadow court's princess, documenting every detail I've learned from taking her form, hoping to figure out what the oracle meant when she told me the shadow princess could save Hale from an early death.

"It seems you've been taking Princess Jasalyn's form for months."

I huff out a laugh to hide my grimace. *No one* knows that I've been taking the princess's form, because I never leave my house as her. But Hale only had to see those hairs and read a few pages of my scribbled notes to know. Every memory from every transformation is documented in there, spanning between the most uneventful moments from her childhood to the darkest days as the shadow princess.

"You know something, don't you?" he asks. "You knew, even before me, that she can help us save Elora."

I frown. I don't know anything about that, but maybe if she

really can save Hale, she can help us both. "What do you mean?"

"I need you to take the princess's form—but not just in the privacy of your own chambers this time."

"Right." I glare when what I really want to do is yank my journal from his grasp. "And have a target on my back for impersonating royalty? I'll pass."

"You can't *pass*, sister. If you don't help, the streets will be flooded with shadow court sentinels searching for her."

I stare at him, confused for a beat until I realize—

"You took her? You kidnapped *the princess*?" I spin to Natan, hoping this is their idea of a joke, then squeeze the bridge of my nose when I catch his hard stare.

"I did," Hale says. "And since I'm putting my entire team at risk if the queen is looking for her, I need you to go to the palace and *be her*. As soon as possible."

"The palace?" I shake my head. He's always thought me braver than I am, from the first time he taught me to climb a tree and I got stuck fifteen feet off the ground. Now, once again, he's asking too much. "No way."

"Yes."

"Absolutely not. I can't do that."

"You always underestimate yourself," he says, glancing over his shoulder and toward the busy street beyond. "I've left you alone for three years, let you deny your destiny, let you abandon your realm. Now it's time to step up. You *know* her. You have, what"—he waves the book between us—"a dozen memories by now?"

I fold my arms. "You're going to get me killed. You're asking me to take her form and then live with her sister. Her handmaids. All the people who know her best."

"A day at most with her sister and then you'll be sent to stay with King Misha. The queen wants the princess away from the shadow court for a while."

Pretending to be the princess would be much simpler in the Wild Fae territory, where I wouldn't be surrounded by the people who know the princess so intimately. But why would the queen send her away when she's been so protective of her up to now? "Because of the faceless plague?"

Hale shrugs, but I'm sure he knows more than he's saying. Hale always knows more than he lets on. He also cares for me more than he lets on, and I know he wouldn't ask without good reason.

"It's too dangerous. If they found me out—"

"I have faith in you." These words, spoken with absolute sincerity, make me more homesick than I've felt in months. They make me miss the relationship Hale and I had before he *lost* faith in me.

"This is your out, Felicity," he says softly, as if he can see my thoughts on my face. "This is our way back home for good."

My chest aches. I'm not the only one who's desperate to go back to Elora. Hale was fifteen when he dedicated his life to bringing down the Elora Seven and returning the realm to the rightful monarchy. While I can't return to Elora so long as I'm hunted, my brother won't let himself go so long as his quest is unfulfilled.

"How?" I ask, voice cracking. "How does Jasalyn figure into this?"

"I visited the oracle."

My stomach flips, then plummets. The Oracle of Light is sacred and revered, and I hate her with every fiber of my being. Knowing your destiny can be more of a curse than a gift. "Not everything the oracle foretells is so simple," I say to my hands. But if she showed me Jasalyn as a way to save Hale and showed Hale Jasalyn as a way to save the realm . . .

I shove away the temptation of hope before I can pull its poison into my lungs.

"Regardless of what you think of the oracle, you might want to know what she showed me this time," he says. He's quiet for a few long moments, probably waiting for me to meet his eyes, but I can't. "The princess, Felicity. She showed me the princess slaying your father." He tilts his head and hoists the journal in the air. "But maybe you already suspected she'd play a role, and that's what's behind your little research project."

I draw a ragged breath, suddenly lightheaded with the possibility of a better future. *Dangerous.*

"You told me years ago that you won't kill Erith," Hale says, and I flinch.

"It's not that simple."

"Listen to me, Lis. I've found an alternative. I was *shown* the alternative. Will you help us take it or not?"

My heart is racing. My birth father has grown too powerful, and the consequence of that power has been horrific for the majority of the Eloran citizens. Even if I didn't have my own reasons for needing him gone, I would want to help my brother with his mission. Hale has never been able to understand why I wouldn't slay my father myself. He's never known what the oracle showed *me*. But I'm haunted by the memory of that vision, by the sight of death creeping into my brother's eyes as his blood pools around him.

If I kill Erith, as was foretold, Hale will die too. I don't know how one leads to the other, but I know what the oracle showed me.

And I could never tell Hale, because he would've told me to do it anyway.

But now we've both been shown the shadow princess as the key to an alternate path.

"What do you need me to do?" I ask. My hands are shaking. I can't believe I'm agreeing to this. It's insanity. It's a death wish. *It might be the only way to save Hale.*

"Be the princess. Then once you're sent to Castle Craige, I need you to get as close to King Misha as you can."

"Why?"

"So he'll fall in love with you, of course," he says.

I grunt. "You overestimate me."

Hale grins. "You underestimate the allure of a beautiful human girl. I need him to show you his Hall of Doors. If we can't find the sword, the Hall is our only way to give Jasalyn a direct portal to the Eloran Palace."

I frown. "We don't even know if the Hall of Doors is more than a legend."

"The Halls are real. The Unseelie Court lost theirs when the queen took the crown from Mordeus, which leaves the Seelie and the Wild Fae."

In which case, the choice is obvious. "How do you know this?"

"While you've been hiding in the shadow court, Shae's been

investigating. We've learned a lot since you left."

I flinch at the name of my old crush. He was always by my brother's side and yet always out of reach. Then I was sent to the oracle, and for a moment after I returned, I thought maybe he might feel something for me too. But then I had to run—had to hide to protect my family—and Shae never came to find me.

I fold my arms in front of my chest, as if I can hold my heart together. "Okay, so assuming he's right, even the legend says that the courts hold the locations of their Halls as sacred. King Misha wouldn't hand it over to a human princess—no matter what good ties he holds with her court."

Hale smirks. "Then I guess you have some work to do."

"Please tell me you're not resting the future of the realm on my ability to seduce a faerie king."

This earns me a crooked smile from Natan.

"We'll be looking for the sword," Hale says. "I know what the oracle showed me and have every faith we'll find our way to where we need to be. That said"—he waves up and down to indicate my general form—"the princess has been missing from the palace for several hours now, and the longer she's gone, the more closely they'll investigate her on her return."

I scowl at him. "Then maybe you should take her back." Of course he waited until he'd already captured her to tell me his plan.

"Wrap up any business you need to this afternoon and then get some sleep." He presses several strands of hair into my open palm. "We'll be back tomorrow to take you to meet the princess. If you have any questions before making your grand return to the palace, that will be your chance."

39

"She's truly agreed to help you?" I ask. Jasalyn was a human from Elora before she was the shadow princess, so she would've been raised to believe the Elora Seven were the saviors nearly everyone else in the realm believes they are. "She's agreed to slay the leader of the Seven just because you asked?"

"She doesn't know all the details yet." He shrugs. "But she will, and when she does, I'm confident she'll get on board."

Typical Hale. "And if she refuses?"

He leans over and flicks my nose. "Don't worry so much, sister. The oracle has been asked, and she has answered." He turns for the door, Natan his silent shadow. "See you in the morning."

After the door clangs closed behind them, I can only stare at the strands of hair in my palm.

I'm not like my brother. He rushes in to save the day because he believes the hero wins and fate is the reward the good guy gets at the end. I used to believe that too—until my biological father found out I was alive and the soldiers he sent looking for me slaughtered the man who raised me. I've seen the cost of *fate* and know it's not always worth paying.

But if Hale is working with Jasalyn, maybe the tides have finally turned.

Could Jasalyn truly have the power to take out Erith, Patriarch of the Seven? Could she be my way home and prevent Hale's life from being cut far too short?

I wish I could have a fraction of Hale's optimism, but it doesn't come that easily to me. I'll do this anyway, because I owe it to my brother to try. I owe it to the whole realm.

CHAPTER FOUR

—◆—

JASALYN

I WAKE TO THE SOUND of a crackling fire and the soft scuff of footsteps. The smell of something sweet and spicy hangs in the air and reminds me of my childhood, like Sunday mornings before Mom left. I can almost imagine her standing at the stove stirring porridge for our breakfast and telling Abriella a story.

I'm scared to open my eyes. I'm warm and the bed beneath me is so soft. But no amount of denial is going to return me to a house we lost, and no amount of wishing is going to bring my mom back.

When I open my eyes, I find myself in a cozy cabin. A trio of males sit with their backs to me, facing the glow of the fire, each with a mug in his hand. They're speaking in low murmurs I can't make out. In the corner opposite this bed, there's a window over a washing basin. But no light streams in.

How long was I sleeping?

One of the males turns and—*no. Men.*

I was captured by *humans*?

I push myself up and am surprised to find my arms work again. Perhaps if I move quietly enough, I can slip out before they notice me. *My ring.*

My stomach sinks past the floorboards. *My cloak is gone.*

If I had my ring, I could sweet-talk them into anything I wanted and walk out the door. They'd never remember they had me here.

I ease up as slowly as possible. If they are human, they won't have the same keen hearing as the fae. If I'm very careful—

The mattress groans beneath me, and a man whips his head around. When his eyes meet mine, I can't breathe.

Those eyes.

So icy blue they're nearly transparent, like I could see all the way to his soul.

I know those eyes, know those thick, dark lashes. Between the eyes and his long light brown hair, someone might mistake him for *pretty*—if it weren't for the absolute masculine angles of his jaw and the scruff lining it. If it weren't for the sheer strength and power so obvious in the way he stands.

There were nights in Mordeus's dungeons that the fear alone was enough to drive me over the edge. There were nights when the darkness threatened to swallow me, and I wished for death. Until Kendrick was thrown into the cell across from mine and he realized how much I needed a friend. Until Kendrick talked me through the darkest nights.

Close your eyes, Slayer. The sun will rise again tomorrow.

"Kendrick?" I say before I think better of it. Why is he here? Why am I here? Did he rescue me from my captors? But why would he be in Faerie? Wasn't he freed after Mordeus was killed? Why didn't he go home?

Kendrick eases to his feet, hands up, palms toward me as if

42

I'm some wild animal he's trying not to spook.

"What are you doing here?" I ask. But I should ask something altogether different. *What am I doing here? Who were those people in the woods?*

"Careful. She's not restrained," one of the other men says. His voice is vaguely familiar. He sounds like the male who captured me, but that doesn't make sense. My captors had to be fae—they used magic on me—and this guy is with Kendrick, who would never let anyone hurt me. If Kendrick is here, it's because he saved me.

"She won't hurt me," Kendrick says, eyes never leaving mine. "Jas, we need to talk."

I look back and forth between him and his friends. Both face me now. One is thin with big wire-rimmed glasses, a messy ponytail, and a gold hoop in one ear. The other is stocky with long dark hair, a trim beard, and hard eyes. He's acting like he's Kendrick's friend but looking at me like I'm a snake that might strike.

"What's going on?" I ask. "How did I get here?"

"By *horse*," the bearded one snarks.

I *do* recognize his voice. "It was *you*. *You're* the one who captured me." I swing my gaze back to Kendrick. "Why?"

"You could've been seen by any number of rebels in that camp if we hadn't grabbed you," Kendrick says. "We needed to talk to you anyway, but your whereabouts required us to"—he exchanges a look with his friends before turning back to me—"*expedite* the situation. So you didn't end up hurt."

I shove off the bed, and the second my feet touch the floor, I realize they took my damned boots as well as my cloak. I stomp toward him. "I didn't ask for your help." I poke his chest with each word.

He glances down at my finger.

"Don't try to use your magic on him," the bearded guy says. "We will restrain you again if we have to."

I whip my gaze to him. "*What* magic?" I blurt, then cringe at my inadvertent admission. Even though the whole realm knows I'm human, my sister's advisors told me to never reveal my lack of power. There's strength in their assumptions, strength in keeping them guessing.

We don't want the world to know anything more about you that they might perceive as a weakness. And besides, your powers will come to light anytime now.

By the time my sister was seventeen, she could wield shadows. Even as a human. But the only magic I have comes from my ring—and that was forged by a witch in the human realm and is currently either lost in the swamps or wherever Kendrick's men have my cloak hidden away.

"*What magic?*" the bearded guy scoffs. "You think humans are stupid, Princess?"

Kendrick shoots him a look. "You're not helping."

"Ignore Remme," the other guy says. His voice is soft, soothing. A low murmur more suited to libraries and classrooms than the battlefields and barrooms his companion was built for. "He missed his nap today."

I fold my arms, staring them down, one by one. I should let them think I have magic. Let them fear me.

Kendrick cocks his head. "You never told me you had faerie

44

blood." There's no anger in his voice, just . . . disappointment?

"You never told me you were a kidnapper," I snap back.

He smiles. "So, we're even?"

I'm almost knocked over by the sight of those dimples peeking out through the scruff on his cheeks, and I have to swallow hard. There were so few times in Mordeus's dungeons that warranted a smile, but Kendrick found ways and reasons to smile at me just to help me through.

"Give me my cloak and my boots." I glance around the cottage again but see no sign of either. "I need to go home."

He shakes his head. "I'm afraid we can't do that."

I release a sound that's way too close to a squeak. "You can't just . . . just *take* someone."

"And yet we did," Remme says.

I could run, but they've already demonstrated that they're faster and stronger than me, and how far would I get without shoes? *And how long could I handle the darkness of the night without the magic of my ring to protect me?*

"You're *lucky* we grabbed you when we did," Kendrick says. "Those insurgents would've taken you and used you to manipulate your sister, *the queen*. Is that what you want?"

"And how will *you* use me?"

Kendrick scrapes a hand over his jaw. "We need your help."

It's like they aren't even listening to me. "I *respectfully* decline."

"Not until we talk," Kendrick says. He looks at his friends. "Leave us, please."

Remme folds his arms. "Hale, you can't—"

Kendrick snaps his fingers, and the door to my left flies open.

45

I gape. *He has magic.*

Kendrick points to the open door. "Get out."

The quiet one winces. "I don't love that idea, Hale."

"Out," Kendrick repeats. He shifts his gaze between his friends. "Both of you. I need to talk to the *princess*." He says the word like it has a bitter taste and he needs it off his tongue as fast as possible.

The quiet one frowns. "I'm advising you not to be alone with her. You don't know what she's capable of."

"Do you see the door?" Kendrick asks, nodding to the door he's still pointing to.

The men listen, taking a second to glance over their shoulders a final time before pulling the door shut behind them, and then I'm left alone.

With Kendrick.

"They call you Hale."

He nods sharply, still watching the door as if he expects them to barge back in. "That's my name."

"I thought it was Kendrick."

Slowly, he slides those eyes back to me, and a warm shiver shimmies down my spine. "Kendrick is my family name."

I never asked. They called him Kendrick in the dungeons, and I assumed that was his given name. I guess it serves to prove I never knew him that well after all.

I look at the door—the one he opened with a snap of his fingers. "You have magic."

There's a challenge in the way he raises his brows. "Trained since birth."

46

"I don't know what you want from me, but I'm sure I can't help you." I don't say, *I thought you were my friend,* but his expression softens like he sees the accusation in my eyes.

"Just hear me out," he says.

I hold his gaze for a long time. I know those eyes. I was saved by those eyes—their tenderness, their compassion. When a guard broke my fingers one by one only to heal them and do it all over again, Kendrick lured him into his cell and broke his neck. When my fear and misery threatened to drown me, Kendrick reminded me I wasn't alone.

"And if I hear you out and I still want to leave," I ask, "will you let me go back to the palace tonight?"

Closing his eyes for a beat, he draws in a slow breath. "I hope once you hear me out, you'll understand why I can't do that."

My chest feels too tight. "You've changed."

Kendrick's eyes darken, and he looks me over from my lips all the way down to my stocking feet. When his eyes make their way back up, they linger on all the curves in between. "So have you."

My cheeks flame with heat. It was never like that between us—never about romance or sex. I was too young and too preoccupied with trying to survive, and Kendrick was, well, he wasn't the kind of guy who'd see a malnourished fourteen-year-old in that light.

Luckily, he turns away from me and I'm spared from him seeing my embarrassment. He goes to a small table by the fireplace and fills a pewter mug before offering it to me.

My mouth is so dry I want to yank the mug from his hand and gulp it down, but I only stare at him, even though its contents smell so good. It's the delicious cinnamon and spice scent that I woke up to. "Poisoning me so soon?"

"Come on, Jas. You're smarter than that. If we wanted you dead, would you have woken up?"

A sudden burst of feminine laughter from outside draws our attention to the door. I wonder if it's the same person I heard when I was taken. Is she involved with Kendrick somehow?

"We both know death is hardly the worst thing our enemies can do to us," I say, pulling my gaze back to his.

"You could trust me then, and you can trust me now," he says softly.

"How do I even know it's you?" I ask. "You could be someone imitating him. This could be a trick."

"Because you know me," he says. He extends a hand toward my face, and I retreat on instinct.

The backs of my thighs hit the bed, and I scramble into the corner, pulling my knees into my chest.

He sighs and resignation pulls down the corners of his mouth as he lowers himself to the edge of the bed.

He's so close.

How many nights in that dungeon did I struggle to sleep and wish he could be this close? How many nights since have I thought of him and wished for just one chance to say thank you? I never thought this was how I'd get it.

He extends the steaming mug toward me again. "Please. Your mouth is dry from the magic Remme used to restrain you. Drink this and I'll tell you everything you need to know."

I take the mug because the spices smell so delicious, and

he's right. My mouth is so dry I can barely swallow. I sniff the contents, trying to detect any of the odiferous poisons I learned about. I smell nothing concerning, but there are any number of odorless poisons—

Kendrick takes the mug back and drinks from it, watching me as he swallows. "It's safe." He hands it back.

I will not think about my lips touching where his lips just touched. I will not wonder what those lips would feel like on mine.

Too late.

I take a tentative sip, as desperate to change my line of thinking as to get rid of this desert in my mouth. It's mulled cider and tastes even better than it smells. I force myself to wait before taking another drink, just in case, but feel no ill effects, only soothing warmth.

"Why aren't you home?" I ask. Because I'm ridiculous. He kidnapped me. I shouldn't care whether he was reunited with the family he missed so much.

He turns sideways on the edge of the bed, his gaze scraping over my face and analyzing every feature. "I went home for a while. But what I need to protect my family and the people in my charge can only be found here. So I'm back to get what Mordeus stole."

"The Sword of Fire?" I ask. When we were in the dungeons together, he admitted that he'd been captured while searching for it.

"Yes. I need it if I'm going to make any sort of lasting change in Elora."

Three years ago, he believed himself a failure for having been unable to retrieve it.

"I'm sorry you haven't found it yet."

"Me too. I've been searching this realm for a year, and I have nothing to show for it."

My stomach constricts like one of Mordeus's guards kicked it. He's been here for a year, and he never came looking for me. Never came to so much as say hello. *It shouldn't matter.*

"That's why I need your help," Kendrick says, oblivious to the ridiculous ache in my spurned heart.

"They say Mordeus is back," I say.

He nods. "I've heard the rumors."

"It's not safe for you here. You're mortal, and his magic is great—"

"There are mortals who have magic too, Princess." He shifts on the bed and leans his weight on one palm in the center of the mattress. "You never met a single mage in your fourteen years in Elora?"

"Of course I did, but—"

He arches a brow, as if to say, *There you go.*

"You're not that foolish. You've been captured by Mordeus before. Why would you think you wouldn't be vulnerable now?"

"I never said I'm not vulnerable. I said I need what Mordeus stole if I am to protect my family and deal with the mess happening back home."

"And *I'm* supposed to help you with that somehow?"

"Exactly." He toys with a loose thread on the sheet. "Our enemies are growing stronger by the day—and they're using their power to increase the gap between the wealthy and the poor. Between the magically trained and the magically ignorant."

"What does that have to do with me?" I shake my head. "I don't belong there anymore."

"Because when you turn eighteen, you become fae?"

I frown. "Why do you know so much about my life?"

His lips twitch into a smile. "You think I missed that you're not just the princess of the shadow court but a descendant of Mab? Do you think I've been hiding under a rock the last three years?" He nods toward the door. "Why do you think my friends are so convinced you have magical abilities and may harm me at any moment just for the thrill of it?"

I open my mouth to lie, to pretend I'm powerful and hint that they *should* fear me, but then I meet his gaze and know I can't. I can't lie to Kendrick. Not after everything we went through. "Well, they're wrong." I shrug, then because I can't help myself, the corner of my mouth twitches into a smile. "About the magical abilities at least."

This earns me a full grin, complete with both dimples. That grin could get me into trouble. "You've changed more than physically, Slayer. Gotten a little fierce in the last few years." He nods. "I like it."

"As you've pointed out, when you're princess, there's always someone hunting you. I've had to learn to protect myself." *Even though I failed today.* I push that thought away and return to the topic at hand. "As admirable as I think it is, I don't know what you think I can do about the inequities in Elora. It's been a problem for longer than I've been alive and will continue to be long after I've died."

His gaze dips to my mouth. "Since you're soon to be immortal, let's hope that's not the case."

I dodge his piercing gaze and study what remains of my cider. "Do you have a plan? To help the less fortunate in Elora?" So many in my home realm get roped into impossible contracts that result in a lifetime of servitude. After our mother left, Brie and I were among them. We were only freed from ours because our aunt sold me to Mordeus, and that would never have happened if my sister's fate hadn't been tangled up with the future of the Unseelie Court. It's hard to imagine the human realm being kinder to unfortunate souls like my sister and me, though I admit I love the sound of it.

"I do," Kendrick says, his gaze distant. "I went home and to visit the oracle. Now I have hope, even if we never find the sword."

I straighten. "I didn't think anyone but the Magical Seven of Elora were allowed to access the Oracle of Light." The Magical Seven are benevolent leaders of my home realm. Centuries ago, when the fae stole humans from Elora to fight in their wars, the Magical Seven came together to protect us. They closed the portals and forbade the fae from taking humans without their consent.

"That's what they want you to think, but only the oracle can choose who she'll speak with." He shrugs. "The oracle showed me someone who could tip the scales in this revolution."

My stomach knots. "Who?"

"The vision she showed me, Jasalyn, shadow princess, child of Mab, was of *you*."

Someone pounds on the door. "Hale?" Remme shouts. "You dumb bastard, are you still alive?"

"I'm fine," he calls. "Stay outside, or I swear you're doing

52

Skylar's wash for a week."

I hear female laughter and unhappy muttering that I can't make out.

"There has to be some mistake," I whisper. I hate being stuck in Faerie, but I have no part to play in a revolution. How could I?

"Do you have an identical twin?" He stands and makes a move, as if he's ready to head out the door. "Because I'll go grab her now. Tell me where to find her. Time is of the essence."

I roll my eyes. "Shut up. I just don't understand. Why me? I don't want to be part of this fight. In nine months, I will be as unwelcome in the human realm as my sister is now. Why would the oracle name me as the key to fixing it?" His words click in my mind, and I frown up at him. "You said I'm the hope if you never find the sword. Who is it you need me to kill, Kendrick?"

He holds my gaze. "His name is Erith."

"He's from Elora?"

"Yes. And I'll tell you all you need to know about him, but first I need you to agree to work with us. We'll keep looking for the sword because it can open a portal directly to Erith, wherever he may be, but even if we don't find it, we still have a chance if we have *you*. Help us. This is for the good of your homeland, Jas. It's your *destiny*."

I nod to the door. "And yet your friends don't trust me."

"Whether you're officially fae now or months from now, Unseelie blood flows through your veins. We don't yet know or understand your loyalties." He sinks back to the edge of the bed. "But I believe in my heart that you want to protect those weaker than you. You're not just some Faerie princess to me. You're my

53

friend. You're my *Slayer*, and when the oracle showed me your face, I believed there was finally hope again."

"You abducted me for a lot of *maybe*s. And if you ask me, all those *maybe*s sound unlikely. I don't know where this sword is or how to get to your Erith without it." I shake my head. "And I can't just disappear from the palace. My sister will come for me. She's probably already looking for me."

Kendrick cocks his head to the side. "I doubt that. Not when your guard is telling anyone who comes to your door that you've asked to be left alone in your chambers today. Anyone who asks to see you is told you aren't to be bothered until morning."

My chest tightens. He has connections inside the palace. "How do you know that?"

"Do you think that we nabbed you the first time we saw you? You are royalty. The Unseelie princess, next in line for the Throne of Shadows. You think my people would be foolish enough to take you from the woods when someone would be keeping an eye on you? We've been plotting for weeks on how to get to you."

"I thought you said you took me because I was in danger?"

He shrugs. "We were *able* to take you because you *put yourself* in danger. You made it easy—too easy." His jaw hardens. "What were you doing in those swamps? Do you realize what kind of people reside in that area?"

"So I'm supposed to be grateful to be your captive?"

"Grateful to be *ours* instead of *theirs,* yes. We won't hurt you or use you against your sister's court. I can't say as much for others who would've liked to get their hands on you today."

"And what about after today? My excuses only buy me so

much time. They will expect to see me tomorrow."

"Leave that to us." He walks across the room, grabs his mug, and refills it from the steaming pitcher.

The door rattles as someone pounds on it again. "Are you going to make us sleep out here, Hale?"

Kendrick ignores Remme. "What else do you need to know?"

"Can I sleep on it?" I ask, already thinking through my escape. I don't want to leave without my ring, but I don't see my cloak anywhere, so I might not have a choice.

Kendrick comes to stand before me and sinks to his haunches so we're eye to eye. "You can sleep, but nothing will change. I *need* you, Jas."

Of all people, I never would've believed Kendrick would betray me in any way. Once, he was helping me plot my escape from Mordeus, and here I am, plotting my escape from him.

As soon as they're all sleeping, I'll call for my goblin.

CHAPTER FIVE

◇

JASALYN

"You can keep staring at that door, but even your glare isn't going to put you on the other side of it," Remme says the next morning. I turn said glare on him, and he chuckles and offers me a mug of coffee. "You might feel a little less like something from the bottom of my boot if you hadn't been so determined to sneak away last night."

I snag the mug from his hand. "I don't know what you mean," I mutter into the cup.

"Sure you don't. I saw you watching me and Natan. What were you planning to do? Run back to the palace on foot? Or maybe you were planning to steal one of our horses?" He gulps from his own mug. "Do you even know where we are? Would you have known which way to go?"

I wouldn't have had a clue, which is why I'd planned to use my bracelet to call my goblin, but goblin bracelets are invisible to everyone but their owner and I'm not planning to reveal the only advantage I have in this mess.

Not that it mattered. There was always someone awake. Always someone watching. Kendrick's clearly more adept at dealing with a captive than I ever would've imagined.

The coffee is rich and like an answered prayer. Brie says I drink too much of it, but dark black coffee is one of the few things that inspires me to get out of bed in the morning. Thank goodness this isn't a tea-drinking group. "Where are Kendrick and Natan?"

"They had someone they needed to see this morning," Remme says. "They'll be back soon."

I frown at the four packs piled by the door. They weren't there last night. "Going somewhere?"

"We're always going somewhere, Princess. We're not in this godsforsaken realm because we're looking to settle down."

I roll my eyes. "*Where* are you going?"

"Feegus Keep. It's a few days' ride from here and is the primary stronghold for Mordeus's remaining followers."

"You think Mordeus is there?"

"The dead king?" Remme snorts. "Unlikely."

"The sword?"

"If we're lucky." He takes another gulp of his coffee. "We're looking for Mordeus's son. If he's there, then Mordeus's most prized spoils will be there too."

I've been so focused on getting away from Kendrick and his friends that I never considered the benefits of staying. If I go back to the palace, my sister will send me away to Misha's court. There, it would be difficult to hunt for the remaining guards from the dungeons, even with my ring, and it would be impossible without it. If I stay with Kendrick while they search for their special sword, they would take me to the doorstep of my enemies.

Do I have the courage to end them without the Enchanting Lady?

The cottage door opens and Kendrick strolls in. The cottage seems smaller the moment he walks through the door—or everything else seems less significant.

How did I forget how tall and commanding he is? How piercing his eyes are?

He looks me over with a calculating sweep of his eyes. "Good morning, Princess. I wish I could say you look rested, but you don't."

"Is that the kind of sweet talk you're using to get me to kill your Eloran bad guy?"

"Don't mind him," a feminine voice says behind Kendrick. "He wouldn't know charm if it smacked him in the face."

A woman peeks out from behind Kendrick. She's as short as I am, but unlike me, no one would ever mistake her for weak or fragile. She has fierce written all over her. It's no one thing—not the sword strapped to her back or the miscellany of knives at her hips. It's not just the tattoos that cover her ivory skin or the fact that her light brown hair is shorn close to her scalp. No, this woman's ferocity comes from within. It's the look in her eyes and the instinctive way she balls her fist and scans the room, as if she's sure her next foe is going to jump out from a dark corner at any moment.

And flowing down the middle of her back—

"That's my cloak." I hop off the bed. "And my *boots*."

She grins. "Turns out, we're the same size."

Kendrick sighs heavily. "Skylar, take them off."

"What? I wanted to know what it was like to walk in a princess's shoes." She unties the cloak and lets it fall to the floor. It's all I can do to keep my feet rooted where they are. If I scramble to check for my ring, they'll know it's something they should keep from me.

It has to be there. She never would've found the pocket, not with the way I disguised it.

If I have my cloak, then I have my ring.

"And my boots?" I say, not that I care much about the shoes, aside from having something on my feet.

"Nice to meet you too," she says. She lifts one foot at a time as she loosens the laces and lets them fall to the ground. She winks at me before she turns to pour herself some coffee from the pot sitting by the fire.

"What'd you find out at the palace?" Remme asks her.

"Inside? Total chaos," Skylar says. "Lots of infighting and finger pointing."

My stomach clenches as I imagine what my sister must be feeling this morning. I promised myself she'd never have to rescue me again, and now she thinks I'm missing.

"Outside, they're keeping it quiet," Skylar says. "They don't want anyone to know she's missing. But why wouldn't they sound the alarm? Get everyone looking?"

"Because they don't think she was taken," Kendrick says, sneaking a glance at me. "They think she ran away with her secret lover."

"My *what*?" I squeak.

"Oh, look who's so pious," Skylar says, wrapping her hands

59

around her mug. "Saving yourself for your future prince?"

I don't even have a boyfriend, and the only males I've ever kissed have fallen dead at my feet. The idea of my having some secret lover is beyond ridiculous. "Why in the name of the gods would my sister believe that?"

"It's a long story," Kendrick says, "but one that bought us some time."

"Enlighten me."

Kendrick and Natan exchange a look before Natan nods and heads toward the door, waving to the others to follow him.

Skylar groans. "I literally just got back from doing *your* scouting," she mutters. She turns toward my boots, but I snatch them up with my cloak before she can grab them. "I wasn't going to use yours," she says, spinning to grab a pair from a small closet.

When the others leave and pull the cottage door shut behind them, I tuck my cloak against me and return to my perch on the edge of the bed. I knead the fabric until my fingers connect with the ridge of the ring between layers of cloth. I release a breath.

Kendrick grabs a chair and swings it around to face me before taking a seat. He leans forward, resting his elbows on his thighs. "We had someone plant some things in your room," he says. "It doesn't take much. A piece of jewelry, some dried rose petals, a love note—all hidden in places a simple search would turn up."

I shake my head. "That won't keep her from looking for me."

"Which is why we need to send someone back to the palace in your place."

"That would never work. My sister would see through them."

"But your sister plans to send you away to the Wild Fae

territory, does she not?"

I frown. "How do you know that?"

He shrugs. "We have informants."

"It's one thing to take someone's form and quite another to convincingly become them." Then again, I've pushed everyone away so aggressively, maybe Misha truly doesn't know me.

Does *anyone* anymore? The true me? All that I am on the inside? Broken bits and grotesque scars and all?

"Felicity is very good at what she does," Kendrick says. His voice is gentler now, as if he can see the heartache in my eyes. "I've known her for a long time. She's agreed to take your form and go to the palace as you. She'll stand in for you so your sister doesn't worry and so we can search for the sword without the queen tearing her kingdom apart."

I have to force words out past the thickness in my throat. "And you trust her? No one gets that close to the queen. She could take advantage of the situation and—"

"I trust her like family," he says, eyes solemn. "In fact, she would like to meet you before going to the palace. She has some questions, and I think it might make you feel better as well."

I bite my bottom lip and stare into the fire as I think. The flickering and snapping is a balm to my nerves.

I don't like this, but I can't go back to the palace and be sent off with Misha like a child in need of a nanny. Sure, I could spend my days there and use my ring and my goblin bracelet to return to the shadow court each night. In theory, I could deny Kendrick everything he's asking and still search for Mordeus on my own, but my knowledge of the court is too limited. I'm running out of places to search, and I still have a list of males I'd like to introduce to the Enchanting Lady. Wouldn't it be easier to stay with Kendrick and take advantage of their knowledge?

"What will it be, Princess?" He arches a brow. "Are you in?"

"You're so sure you want me to kill this Erith?"

He wraps his arms around me and lifts me from where I sit, spinning me around and laughing. When he lowers me so my feet touch the floor, he's grinning, both of his dimples showing through the rugged scruff on his cheeks. We're still so close, barely a breath apart. He's strong and warm, and instead of wanting to flee his touch, I lean into it. Crave more. His ice-blue eyes search my face, and it's all I can do to keep myself from reaching up and touching him. "Gods above, woman. I could kiss you," he says, shaking his head.

I freeze. "Don't kiss me." I step back, letting his hands fall to his sides. "Promise me you won't kiss me."

He flinches. "It's a figure of speech. I wouldn't—of course." He searches my face and must see my fear there. "I promise. I just mean you'll be the hero of Elora."

"I can't believe you're really here," I hear myself say. The wonder in my voice is beyond ridiculous, considering the circumstances. I should step away from him. I never let anyone stand this close to me. But I can't. Because if there's anyone I wished I could have close in the last few years, if there's anyone who could understand how twisted I became inside during my weeks as Mordeus's captive, it's Kendrick.

His eyes crinkle in the corners with his smile. "Were you worried about me?"

"I never doubted you'd get out of there and make it home. I just didn't think I'd get to see you again."

He plucks a loose lock of my hair from my shoulder and toys with it between two fingers. "I didn't think I'd see you again either."

"Why not? It would've been much easier for you to find me than the other way around." Once again, I've said too much and wish I could take the words back.

He huffs out a breath. "What reason would I have to bother the shadow princess, child of Mab?"

My blood cools at the reminder, and I step back. He drops his hand and something flickers in his eyes I can't quite identify. Disappointment? "I can't help who my ancestors were or that my sister took that crown," I say. "No one asked me if I wanted the title of princess."

He shakes his head slowly. "We don't get to choose the burdens we bear, only how we bear them."

The cottage door creaks open, and Remme sticks his head in. "Should we prepare the horses while we're out here?" he asks.

"Not just yet." Kendrick waves them in. "Jasalyn's agreed to work with us."

Remme raises a brow. "Really? Just like that?"

"What's that supposed to mean?" I ask.

"It means he doesn't trust that some spoiled Faerie princess is going to go out of her way to help Eloran rebels," Skylar says.

I scowl. So much for female solidarity. "I'm not a faerie, and if you've forgotten, I'm from Elora too."

She scoffs. "I'm sure you've thought about your homeland a

63

lot in the past three years while you've been being pampered in that palace."

I take a step toward her. "You have no idea what my life's been like."

"And *you* have no idea what ours has been like in Elora."

"Enough," Kendrick says, throwing an arm between us. "We all have stories to tell, and there will be time to tell them. That time is not now."

"What's the plan, Hale?" Natan asks.

Kendrick steadies his gaze on the window and narrows his eyes. "Felicity should be awake by now. Bring her straight here. I want her at the palace before nightfall."

"You're sure she can pull this off?" I ask.

"We're sure," Skylar says, stepping up beside me and messing with my hair. I bat her hands away, but before I realize what she's doing, she's cut off a lock from the back.

"Hey!" I grab for the hair.

"Calm down." She wraps the lock in a leather tie and smirks at me. "It matches the other patch you already cut. Got yourself a nice little goblin bracelet, do ya?"

My gaze snaps to my wrist and the goblin bracelet I wear there. The bracelet that's supposed to be invisible to anyone but me.

Skylar chuckles. "Guess so."

I fell right into that trap, but I shrug. "Foolish not to have the tools I can."

"Gotta be careful who you give your hair to," she says, before transferring my hair to a silk bag. "Never know what they're gonna do with it."

"What are *you* going to do with it?" I ask.

"Brew a potion to make your own blood devour you from the inside if you turn on us."

"Skylar." Kendrick mutters something under his breath about needing patience, then shakes his head. "Next, we head south, just like we planned."

"Perfect," Skylar says, smacking the sides of her thighs. "Let's leave tonight. Traveling in the dark will save us all kinds of trouble."

Natan shoots her a look. "Not a great idea, Sky."

"Why not?"

"You're so sure we're immune to whatever or whoever is going around, sucking the life out of fae, that you're willing to risk crossing the court at night?"

She grins, showing teeth. "Let 'em come at me."

"Natan's right," Kendrick says. "We can't risk traveling at night. We leave in the morning." He opens the cupboard and removes a bag of supplies. He pulls out long, crusty baguettes and apples. I watch his forearms flex as he slices them.

"And then there's the matter of deciding who stays back with the girl," Remme says.

"Not it," Skylar says.

"Wait—what?" I snap my attention off Kendrick's hands and to Remme. "I can't stay here if I'm supposed to use the sword."

"If we're right and it's hidden at Feegus Keep," Remme says, "we'll come get you."

This isn't what I agreed to.

My heart rate accelerates and the walls of the cottage creep in closer. "I won't be a prisoner again."

Kendrick shakes his head. "She comes with us," he says without looking my way.

"The hell she does," Skylar says.

"Come on," Remme says, "I don't care if she says she's going to cooperate. That doesn't suddenly make her part of the team. She stays here until we're ready for her."

"I'm not staying here," I snap without thinking. But I'm not. *I can't.* "I'm agreeing to work with you because I want to. *Not* because you took me. That needs to be clear *right now*." The idea of being locked in this tiny cabin . . . My breathing quickens and my stomach tightens and—

Kendrick rests his hand on my shoulder. I didn't even notice him cross the room. He holds my gaze as he murmurs, "Easy, Slayer." Then to the others, "Jasalyn travels with us."

My heart slows.

"That's reckless, Kendrick," Skylar says.

"We aren't jailers," Natan says softly.

I'm still looking at Kendrick, still soaking in the reassurance in those blue eyes.

Close your eyes, Slayer. The sun will rise again tomorrow.

Remme scoffs. "So we just run around the court with the *princess* in tow. Yes, that will definitely keep us from turning any heads. Discretion, thy name is Kendrick!"

Kendrick ignores this and turns to Natan. "You'll glamour her?"

He gives a sharp nod. "Of course. Though it would be wise to take additional measures as well. For anyone who might be powerful enough to look beyond the glamour."

"Are there *any* faeries who couldn't see beyond your magic?" I ask. I know human mages can glamour with potions, but Eloran magic doesn't compare to faerie magic.

"Them's fightin' words," Skylar mutters.

"Most of them." Natan shrugs, unbothered. "I'm good."

Kendrick looks me over. "We could dye her hair?"

"Or shave her head," Remme suggests.

"So your girlfriend and I could be twins?" I ask him.

Remme arches a brow. "Skylar? My girlfriend?"

Natan bows his head and chuckles.

"In his dreams," Skylar mutters before turning her scowl on me. "She'd look like an idiot if she tried to pull this off. And anyway, doesn't she have some sort of special blood? Child of Mab or whatever? I bet they can smell her coming from a mile away."

I fold my arms and set my jaw. "Are you always this charming or only when you make new friends?"

Kendrick turns to me and cocks his head. "I don't know, Slayer, Skylar seems to bring out a side of you that's an awful lot of fun."

Natan hums and taps his lips with his index finger. "Her appearance isn't truly that well known," he says. "The queen hasn't allowed any paintings of her to be distributed, so the depictions floating around are based on rumor and hearsay."

"We'll just focus on what's most recognizable about her and make her look the opposite," Kendrick says. "The whole court will believe she's staying at Castle Craige with King Misha, so they won't be looking for her."

"What do you think of when you think of the shadow princess?" Natan asks.

"Quiet, meek, and virginal," Skylar says, but the words are snapped like barbed insults.

I turn to Kendrick. "What if I wear a wig and something under my dress to make me look pregnant?"

"But we're traveling as fae," Natan says. "And any faerie who's with child is something special. That in itself would attract too much attention."

"No one will try to detect a glamour if we don't give them a reason to suspect one," Kendrick says. "Let's keep this simple."

Skylar chuckles, pulling all eyes her way. "I have a plan," she says.

CHAPTER SIX

FELICITY

IT'S DARK IN THE DUNGEON. *Always so dark. And tonight the darkness is joined by rare silence. Usually there's a cacophony of horrific sounds coming from the other cells—wailing from the woman whose child was ripped from her arms, mad screams from the male down the corridor who was threatening death to his captors then howling because they took his hands.*

In some ways, the silence is worse. At least the screams of the other prisoners remind her that she's not alone. But when it goes silent, the sound of nothingness fills her ears, her head, her whole body. In this dark so deep she can't see her own hand in front of her face, she wonders if she's ceased to exist entirely. If this is the nothingness that comes after.

When she first arrived, she cried for hours. Or was it days? Time has no meaning in this godsforsaken place. She cried until her eyes burned like white-hot embers at the bottom of a fire, sobbed until her chest ached from the exertion.

Tonight, she has no tears, and when the guard drags her from her cell and places her in front of the silver-eyed king, she doesn't sob. When he slices open her palm and presses it to his lips to drink, she doesn't cry out for her dead mother. When he reveals he is among the fae who drink the blood of their captives to learn their secrets, she doesn't cower.

Now she only wishes for death.

And when he cuts her wrists and she watches numbly as he fills a goblet with her blood, she hopes it comes quickly.

My heart swells at the sight of my old friends gathered in front of a small cottage. This might not be the same as going home, but it's the closest I've been in years.

I'd been awake for hours when Natan finally arrived at my cottage to lead me back to Hale. My earlier anxiety at the idea of going out in public in the princess's form eases as we join the others. I'm just thankful I can be part of this.

Part of ending Erith. Part of saving Elora. Finally.

Hale's busy talking to Skylar, so he doesn't notice I've arrived, but when I hop off my horse, Remme wraps me in a tight embrace. "I could just knock you out for running away the way you did," he grumbles into my hair.

"I know. But I couldn't be who you needed me to be."

He grunts in understanding, then steps back, chucking me on the chin. "You were just a girl. Don't be too hard on yourself."

Natan, Remme, Skylar, and Shae were always Hale's people—his friends and protectors who simply tolerated his pest of a little sister—but at some point they became something to me too.

I've missed them.

I scan the faces around us again, but I already know Shae's not here. I'm not sure I'd want to face him if he were. Would it still hurt? Would I still feel that twist in my chest that comes from wanting someone who doesn't want you back?

I push those thoughts of adolescent infatuation to the side and drop my hood, adjusting my posture. Princess Jasalyn, sister to the Unseelie queen, child of Mab, is small in almost every way. Slight in stature, standing just over five feet, with tiny hands, a soft voice, and a small waist. Even the way she carries herself is small. Chin tucked, eyes downcast, smile tentative. She moves through the world like she wants to disappear.

Remme nods in approval. "Not bad, kiddo."

My brother spots me from his periphery and does a double take.

A cackle bursts from my lips before I can stop it. I know that reaction. It's the discomfort of a male who's looking at someone who is the spitting image of the female he adores.

"Is something amusing to you?" he asks, eyes narrowing.

"Nothing." My lips twitch. Every time I take another's form, I am given a memory through a dream. About a month ago, my dream was a memory of Hale in the cell across from Jasalyn in Mordeus's dungeons. He protected her when the guards thought to torture her. I know him, so if he had told me, I wouldn't have been surprised, but seeing it for myself, living Jasalyn's memory in my dream, was something altogether different.

Hale folds his arms. "Lis. Don't bullshit me."

I shake my head. "It's not like you, that's all. To let a girl distract you from your mission."

His brows fly up. "Do I look distracted?"

Remme chuckles, but doesn't turn our way. I glare at his back. *Coward.*

71

Hale's frown turns to a scowl. "What'd you see?"

"Enough," I say, smoothing my skirts.

"Tell me," he presses.

I lift my gaze to his. "You saved her, being there for her like that."

He sets his jaw. "And your point?"

"My point is that you might've felt nothing more than protective of her then, but I'd bet my favorite sword your feelings are a little less innocent now that your princess is all grown up."

"You haven't even seen the way he looks at her," Remme mutters.

But I have. I saw it in that split second before his rational mind reminded him that I'm not her.

"Butt out, Remme," Hale says.

Skylar scowls, arms folded. "I don't know why you're all playing matchmaker, as if there can be any future there."

My brother's expression goes blank, and he drops his gaze to the ground. I'm not the only one who's not keen on the whole of my fate. But unlike me, Hale would never dodge his destiny. *And therein lies the problem.*

"We should get you inside to meet the princess," Natan says, appearing from the shadows between the cottage and its neighbor.

"I'll take her in," Hale says, waving for me to follow him up the set of wooden stairs into the tiny thatched-roof cottage.

I frown at his rounded ears as we head to the door. "Will you be traveling as humans or fae?" I ask.

"Fae," he says, not bothering to look back at me. "It's safer."

"The princess too?"

He nods. "I don't intend to travel around with her being recognizable."

I don't doubt it. And now I realize, more than ever, that protecting her *isn't* just about his mission. It's not just about destiny and the future of Elora. It's about the princess. It's about whatever connection grew between them during those weeks he was locked away in Mordeus's dungeons.

The house is small and dim, warmed by a blazing fire.

The princess sits in front of the hearth, staring into the flames as if they hold the solution to all her problems. I've seen that face in the mirror many times after taking her form, but seeing her in front of me is different.

I know from Jas's memories that her days in captivity changed her irreparably. She doesn't like attention, and she *hates* the fae, especially the Unseelie.

The princess is a conundrum. She's fragile and angry. She's delicate and sharp. She was once so soft and hopeful, and now she's hardened and bitter.

This princess radiates a certain something that goes beyond the smallness I've mimicked in her features. It's a sadness. A deep-seated melancholy I can only hope I'm never able to truly duplicate. And something else as well. Something ethereal perhaps. Something that can only be gifted by the gods.

Princess Jasalyn, the human heir to the Unseelie throne, has the presence of a queen.

When Hale clicks the door closed behind me, her attention snaps to us, and she jumps up from her chair. "Oh. Hello. You *do* look . . ." She swallows, but as she takes me in, I can't help but notice that her eyes aren't wide with shock so much as furrowed in concentration. *She wants this to work.*

"Jas," my brother says, guiding me deeper into the cottage to join the princess in front of the fire, "this is Felicity. My . . ." We exchange a look, and I realize he won't be claiming me as his family. We share no blood, but it stings. "We are old friends."

The princess frowns. "How did you come to know a fae shifter in Elora?"

He said he hadn't told her everything yet, but it seems he hasn't told her much at all.

"It's a long story that I'm sure I'll have a chance to tell you on our journey."

"I look forward to that," she says, gaze still fixed on me. "Would you mind giving us some privacy, Kendrick?"

"Of course." He slips out the door quietly, leaving twin princesses studying each other before the fire.

She cocks her head to the side. I know what she sees. Everything about my form in this moment is identical to her—or at least identical to her as she was when she shed the hair I wrapped around my finger and pressed to my heart before I went to sleep last night.

She reaches for my hand, hesitating before her fingers connect with my skin. "May I?"

I draw in a sharp breath, half shocked that she's bothering to ask permission and half miserable that I understand why she does. The princess hates being touched. I learned that the second time I took her form. In the memory I was given that time, she

74

was sitting at a table with her sister. She sipped tea as the queen spoke, but she wasn't really listening. She was staring into the swirling eddies of her tea and wishing her sister would take her hand from her shoulder. *How is it that I cannot even tolerate my sister's touch?* she wondered in that moment, followed quickly by a fleeting thought—more impression than words—of *I will never be whole again.*

The memory was short, but so full of desolation that I've not let myself think about it much until now.

I turn my hand up for her and nod curtly.

Jasalyn's touch is gentle as she nudges my sleeve to my elbow, exposing the gnarled circle of scars on the inside of my forearm.

"Your ankles?" she asks, nodding to the floor.

"Scarred as well," I say.

"Show me." Her command is still somehow gentle.

I make quick work of the laces on my boots and pull them off, followed by my stockings, until she's staring at the scars that I already know match hers precisely.

"Before you ask," I say, clearing my throat, "I also have them on my hips and a patchwork of scars on my stomach."

"Always? Or only when you're in this form?"

"Only when I'm in this form. Are they from your time in Mordeus's dungeons?"

She swallows, and her eyes are haunted. "I don't know where they're from."

"Lying to me won't make this more successful."

I can't imagine what terrible things Mordeus and his cronies did to her just because they could.

"Don't." Her voice is hard.

"What?"

"That pity. Don't. There is a reason I agreed to go with Kendrick. I plan to find Mordeus and kill him myself this time."

My heart aches for her. For this broken shell of a girl. *I will never be whole again.* "Mordeus is dead."

She straightens. "You haven't heard. He's been resurrected."

A cold chill races up my spine, nausea following quickly after. If it's true, I'm in trouble. Mordeus was the one who discovered that I was alive and shared the truth with my birth father. If he's back, he will find me and use me as political leverage again. My mind is spinning with questions. And fear. Now I want nothing more than to stay in Jasalyn's skin and run off to the Wild Fae Lands, far from the silver-eyed wicked king.

"How?" I ask.

She shrugs limply. "What do I know of the fae and their magic? But I think rather than find the answer, I'll end him."

My insides tremble at the thought of him even breathing. But the idea of getting close enough to kill him? "How are you so brave?" I ask, but what I want to know is *how do you think you can do something so courageous when you are so very scared all the time?*

She smiles. "Magic."

"I thought you didn't have any."

"Not of my own. But I'll let others' magic help me when needed."

I'm not sure what that means, and I want nothing more than some reassurance that this girl is capable of saving my brother

76

from an early death, but I get the feeling she'll only be more vague if I push.

"How do you do it?" she asks. "I know shifters. One of my sister's advisors is a shifter, but this . . ." Her eyes scan me again, like a particularly interesting puzzle. "This is different."

"How so?" I ask. I would always rather ask a question than tell a lie.

"I can't put my finger on it. You . . ." She shakes her head in wonder. "Perhaps I do not know any shifters as skilled as you."

I lift my chin. "I appreciate the compliment, Your Highness."

Something flashes in her eyes. "Please call me Jas. The only princess in this room for the next long while is *you*."

I shiver at that sobering thought.

"Do you know how to shield your mind?" she asks. "Do you have any training?"

"Of course. This task would be impossible if I didn't."

She lifts her chin. "Misha will try to get into your mind. He's the one who taught me to shield, and he pokes to make sure I keep my defenses strong. You cannot be lax. Even for a moment."

"I was trained from a very young age," I assure her. "It's an essential skill for one with my gifts."

"Okay." She releases a breath. "I'm giving you access to the queen. To my sister. I'm trusting you because Kendrick trusts you. But if you touch one hair on her head, I will make the things Mordeus did to his prisoners look like a holiday, and you will wish he'd found you instead of me."

I know I'm supposed to be intimidated, but the princess's words only make me respect her. More importantly, they help me understand her. "I will protect your sister as if she were my own. She is a good queen."

Jas nods sharply. "Then tell me what you need to know."

"Everything."

Hale and his friends are in a circle discussing something in low murmurs when I exit the cottage in Jasalyn's riding leathers. I can't return to the palace wearing a castoff gown without raising suspicions, and she agreed to trade clothes.

I pull the door shut behind me and fold my arms, frowning at my brother. "Is it true? Mordeus lives?"

Natan blows out a breath. "Is that what you two talked about for so long?"

Hale is just looking at me, eyes worried.

"You didn't think I'd want to know that?"

Skylar scoffs. "We don't know anything for sure. You want us to debrief you on all the rumors flying around Faerie? You should hear what they're saying about this so-called plague. Some believe Mab is punishing descendants of her enemies from the Twilight. Others believe those fire gems they all wear to amplify their magic have turned toxic. Nothing more than superstitious hogwash."

I hold my brother's gaze. He knows what's at stake for me. I'm merely a pawn to Mordeus. If he thought that he could deliver me to my father to restore even an ounce of his power in this realm, he'd do it. Hale might threaten, but he's sacrificed too much to keep me alive, and I've always seen his threats for the bluster they are.

"You're still worth more to him alive than dead," Natan says.

I cough out a laugh. "Really? That's how you're going to comfort me?" I stomp toward them to untie my mare. "Thanks for nothing, Nate."

"Hey." Hale tugs on the long braid I twisted my—Jasalyn's—hair into before riding here, and I turn to him. "Try not to worry about it."

"Mordeus is the reason I barely remember my own face," I say. "He's the reason your father—*our* father—is dead."

"And if he really is back, you'll be safe in the Wild Fae Lands," Hale says.

My eyes burn with unshed tears, and my vision goes blurry. "And what about you? Am I not supposed to worry about you either?"

He cocks a brow. "Thought you hated me, little sis."

I sniff. "Just because I don't want you to rot in his dungeons doesn't mean I don't hate you."

"Gods, so much mushy gushy crap," Skylar groans. "Pull it together."

Hale pulls me into a hug, and I hear the scuff of Sky's boots on the gravel as she walks away.

I hug my brother back, my chest already aching with the loneliness I know will hit once I leave. "Three years is too long," I whisper against his chest.

"I was thinking the same thing. Mom misses you," he murmurs. "Find us that doorway so we can go home, okay?"

I pull back and nod, swiping at my cheeks. "I should get to the palace before nightfall."

Hale's gaze flicks toward the door. "Did she tell you every-thing you need to know?"

I huff. "Not even close, but I'll manage. She keeps herself iso-lated, so that will help."

"Don't be too isolated," he says. "You have a king to woo."

I shake my head and mount my horse. "I asked. Their relation-ship isn't like that."

"Make it like that."

I arch a brow. "And when we switch back? You'll be fine with the princess becoming the new Wild Fae queen?"

He backs away from my horse. "I'll be fine with the princess doing whatever it is she needs to do to be happy."

I don't even think he knows he's full of it. "You know she's only going with you so she can kill Mordeus, right?"

Skylar barks out a laugh from ten feet away, where she's obvi-ously been listening while pretending to groom her horse. "She's scared of her own shadow. How's she going to kill a resurrected wicked king?"

Hale's broad chest expands as he draws in a long breath. "I suspected something like that might be involved." He pats my mare on her hind quarters. "Let me worry about the princess. You have enough on your plate."

I flip up the hood on my cloak, and he frowns. "That's not her cloak."

"She refused to part with it."

"She gave you the boots, though," Skylar says. "She wouldn't let *me* wear the boots."

"Get over it already," Remme mutters. He snags a silky bag

from Skylar's hands and tosses it to me.

I snatch it from the air. I know its contents without opening it. More than enough hair for many months as the princess.

If I'm lucky, when this is all over, I might be able to see my own face in the mirror.

CHAPTER SEVEN

◇

FELICITY

THE MIDNIGHT PALACE IS HAUNTINGLY beautiful, as if the Unseelie ancestors who built it centuries ago were trying to play on the rumors their enemy court had spread about them. That the Unseelie were darkness and nightmares. They were wicked and cruel. So they built a palace that would meld with the night sky, the crushed black quartz walls shimmering alongside the stars when the moon shines.

I half expected to be spotted by sentinels on my way here, but they must be searching for the princess elsewhere, because I don't catch any attention until I arrive at the gates. I lower my hood and meet the gaze of the males positioned there. Jasalyn gave me the names and descriptions of half a dozen sentinels who might be positioned at the gates at this hour, and I hold my breath as I nod to each of them. "Horice. Gilberd," I say. "Good to see you both."

Their eyes go wide, and they exchange a look. "Princess, what are you doing beyond the gates?"

Princess Jasalyn, the human girl who ranks second only to the great shadow queen, is missing, and the palace hasn't told a soul, not even their own sentinels.

I dismount and hand Horice the reins to my horse. "I needed a change of scenery."

He clears his throat, and they step aside for me. "Yes. Of course. We'll get a stable hand to take care of this mare for you."

I've never been to the Midnight Palace before, and I'm surprised to find how stunning the grounds are. I follow cobblestone paths through manicured gardens interspersed with torches I can easily imagine glowing after dark.

When I reach the palace, I enter through the servants' quarters, just as Jas instructed me to do, my boots thudding softly on the black-veined marble floor as I make my way deeper into the palace—past a bustling kitchen and a steaming laundry.

I continue down the hall and hesitate outside the small family dining room, where I was told I'd find the queen with King Consort Finnian. They're there with a female I don't know but who favors the Wild Fae king in coloring and bone structure. From the information Jas gave me, I'd have to guess she's Pretha, sister to Misha and one of the shadow queen's advisors and closest friends.

I hesitate at the door, taking a moment to register the tension in the room.

I can sense the queen's anguish. Her desperation.

She grips her fork, but her food is untouched, and there are dark circles under her eyes, as if she hasn't slept in the day and a half since her sister left the palace.

If I weren't so desperate for Jasalyn to do what my brother believes she can, I wouldn't be here. I wouldn't take this risk. I am physically the princess, but with only a handful of her memories and the hour or so of information she gave me this afternoon, I fear her sister will see right through me.

I take a deep breath. "Abriella," I say softly, taking a step into the room.

Her fork clatters to the table, and chaos erupts in the room. Chairs groan against the stone floors as they're shoved back. Finnian stands, and Pretha presses a hand to her chest, relief washing over her fine features.

It's tempting to study the room, to stare in wonder at these people tapped to be the queen's inner circle, but I keep my focus on the queen. She has tears in her eyes, and her bottom lip trembles. "I'm sorry," I whisper.

The queen stands. "Leave us. I need to speak with my sister alone."

Pretha gives me a pitying smile. "I'm glad you're safe," she says before gracefully floating from the room.

Finnian whispers something in the queen's ear.

She nods and whispers, "I know," squeezing both of his hands.

When he leaves, he doesn't give me the pitying smile that Pretha did, and he doesn't scowl the way I sense he'd like to, but the look in his eyes is somehow a combination of pity and anger. I'm grateful that Jasalyn is the type that would bow her head to avoid holding his gaze, because dropping my eyes to the floor is a relief.

While the tap of their steps grows ever more distant, I wander to a small sitting area by the windows and lower myself onto a settee, looking out at the gardens glowing in the evening sun.

Only when the queen's ragged sob rips into the silence do I turn. She's kneeling at my feet, head bowed.

The shadow queen is on her knees, bowing before me.

My insides quiver with nerves.

"I should have listened to you," she says, her voice small, even though her presence remains so powerful, "and I didn't. I need so badly for you to see things from my perspective that sometimes I forget that you need me to see them from yours."

When she lifts her head, tears roll down her pink cheeks. I don't know this female save for the few memories I have of Jasalyn's that she's been in, but the raw hope in her eyes cuts through me. *This* is why this once-human queen has become so quickly beloved by so many of her subjects. That unconditional love she feels for her sister is the same she gives to her court. I can see how easy it would be to follow her, and I'm a little envious of the shadow fae for having such a leader. Elora has a long way to go before we can even hope to have anyone this honorable leading us.

"I was so afraid I'd lost you for good this time," she says, her voice shaking.

I draw in a ragged breath. All I have to go on is the story Hale and his friends planted. I cling to it, but it's tricky to navigate. The truth is, there's no way to answer questions about the princess's secret faerie lover in a convincing way, because the princess would never have found herself with a secret faerie lover. "I'm sorry. I was . . . selfish. I panicked at the idea of not seeing him again."

"You didn't tell me you'd met someone." There's no accusation in her voice. Just sadness.

"I didn't want you to think you needed to protect me from him. He's not royalty, only a baker's son."

She squeezes her eyes shut. "You've fallen for him," she says matter-of-factly.

I flick my gaze up to meet hers for a beat, trying to imagine what it would be like to be a malcontent princess who's fallen in love with a commoner. "I didn't expect to. It just happened." I search the dozen or so of the princess's memories I've collected since first taking her form. I need to offer the queen something authentically Jasalyn. Something that will make sure she doesn't question my story. I swallow hard before I say it. I don't know the princess, but saying the words out loud feels like a betrayal of a girl I've only met once. "He's the first person since the dungeons whose touch didn't make my skin crawl."

She's quiet for so long that I lift my head. She's looking out the window, her face contorted in anger. "It's not that I didn't suspect you were struggling with physical affection, but I wish you had talked to me about it."

"And have you feel even guiltier for something that wasn't your fault?"

She lifts her hand to my cheek slowly enough that my heart aches for her. She's had to learn to withhold her touch from Jas, had to learn that it isn't welcome. "You are forgiven," she whispers.

When she finally touches my cheek, I close my eyes but make sure not to lean into it, and after a beat, I pull away and focus on my hands in my lap again.

"There are days that I want to go to the underworld and beg Mab to turn you fae now so you won't be so vulnerable," the queen says. "The only thing that stops me is knowing how much you dread the day you become what I already am."

I can't look at her. This is like eavesdropping on the most inti-mate conversation. The queen is baring her soul to me because she believes I'm her sister, and I hate myself a little for it. I hate that I can't ease her mind. I want to say I don't dread becoming fae, but I know dread is precisely what Jasalyn feels.

"I'm not as vulnerable as you think." It's the best I can offer, though I know it does nothing to ease the queen's heartache.

She sniffs and draws a kerchief from a pocket in her skirts. "You don't have to go with Misha. We'll find a way for you to stay here if that's what you really want. I just—"

"No," I blurt. I swallow, composing myself. I'm supposed to have a lover here—one I'm so distraught about leaving that I stole away for an extra night just to have more time with him—but I'm far too likely to be found out if I stay here. Let alone the fact that I need to be looking for a magical Hall of Doors in the Wild Fae Lands. "No, please. I've had time to think. And you're right."

"You're sure?" she asks.

I nod. "My friend . . . he wants me to go too. He said he saw bodies in a village north of here." I force myself to shiver, as if just remembering his description is upsetting. "He wants me safe."

Her lips curve, but the smile doesn't reach her eyes. "I like that he's looking out for you. Even if it hurts that you never told me about him."

I don't want to dig into that, so I stand. "I should pack," I say, heading toward the door.

"Do I get to meet him at least?" she asks my back. "Your baker's son?"

I stop and study the floor. "No."

I can't even see her face, but I can feel the energy in the room shift as her heart breaks at that answer. "Why not? Are you ashamed of me?"

"I broke it off." I squeeze my eyes shut. I need the queen and everyone else in this palace to forget about my fictional love interest. If I don't make them let it go, they'll try to find him, and nothing good will come of that. Because now that I'm here, now that I feel exactly what the queen feels for her sister, I know she would do it. She'd make any random male a prince if it would make Jas happy.

"You truly believe I wouldn't let you be with the male you love?"

"It's better this way," I say, clinging to the brief answers Jasalyn prefers. "For both of us."

When I turn to face the queen, she's standing again, arms wrapped around herself. "You're sure about that? It's important that you can have someone in your life who you—"

"I'm sure." I point over my shoulder. "I'm going to get some things packed and then get a bath and some sleep."

"Jasalyn, while you're gone . . ." She grimaces. "You need to address your weaknesses, seek out your powers and—"

"I have no powers." Jas told me they might press on this and that this is how I should respond.

"They're *there*, Jas," Abriella says. "Just like they were there for me even before I turned fae. The more we get you to tap into them before your eighteenth birthday, the better off you'll be when that day comes."

I set my mouth in a belligerent line. "What are you saying?"

"I'm saying I want you to work with Misha and find out what they are. Just like he can teach you to block, he knows how to help you dig deep and find the root of your magic."

My magic is not one the faeries of this realm know, but if he starts pulling at strings, trying to prove to Jas—to *me*—that there's magic inside, he's going to find he's right. Even if he doesn't understand what he's seeing. I can't have that.

"Why?" I ask. "What's the rush?"

"You're next in line to the throne, sister." Never was there a smile so sad when someone spoke of another inheriting such power. "Mordeus *will* come for me, and if he's successful, the people of this court will depend on *you*."

CHAPTER EIGHT

◇

JASALYN

THERE IS CERTAINLY NOTHING *VIRGINAL* about the outfit Skylar put together for me. Actually, *outfit* is too kind a term for this. This is more of a *costume.*

"You about done in there?" Skylar calls, pounding on the bathing room door.

"Almost!" I cringe at my reflection.

The sleeveless green top ties behind my neck and reveals every inch of my midriff down to the low-slung and very tight brown leather riding pants.

When I joked about my disguise being that of Skylar's twin, I was trying to irritate her. I should've kept my mouth shut.

I allow myself ten seconds of pure mortification before lifting my chin and opening the bathing room door for the group's appraisal.

Remme's at the counter washing up the dishes from breakfast and is the first to spot me. He coughs out a laugh. "Wow. Shadow princess *who*?"

Skylar spins around. Her eyes go wide—not surprised so much as . . . maybe impressed? "Why would you hide all that under stupid dresses and gowns?" She looks me over slowly, and I force myself to keep my hands at my sides when they want to wrap around my stomach to cover my scars. "Natan, when you glamour her, cover her with tattoos, and be sure you hide the scars—they'll make her stand out too much."

"Yeah. I can do that," Natan says. If he looks at me, I'm not sure what his reaction is because Kendrick's eyes are on me now, his gaze tripping over my bare midriff and down to the skintight leather pants. I'm no longer the scrawny, underfed little girl he protected in Mordeus's dungeons. My sister and I had been living on scraps for years, and I was so underweight and overworked that I rarely got my monthly cycle. It wasn't until after my sister became queen and I was living in Faerie that my body changed—went soft and full in places and stayed small in others. Warmth gathers in my stomach at the sensation of Kendrick's eyes roaming over me, and I realize just how much I want him to like what he sees.

He shoves the maps out of his way and crosses the room to me, eyes roaming *up and down, up and down.* "You didn't have these scars in the dungeons."

The heat in my core dissipates. He's not studying *me.* He's staring at the scars on my arms and belly. That isn't desire in his eyes but anger.

Dumb little girl.

He takes my wrist in one rough hand and turns my palm up, sweeping his thumb over the gnarled circular knot of tissue on my forearm.

Despite myself, I shiver at his touch.

"Who did this?" he growls. "Is this from what Queen Arya did when she was trying to reunite the courts?"

"No." I meet his gaze but can't bring myself to say his name.

"Her sister would've healed any wounds left by Queen Arya," Natan says for me, scanning the scars. "These are something else."

Kendrick just stares, jaw hard.

"What's going on, Kendrick?" Skylar asks. "The sight of a little skin making you lose your words?"

I tear my gaze from Kendrick's to look at Skylar and catch something unexpected on her face. Is that jealousy or . . . *hurt*?

When I look back to Kendrick, he's returned his attention to my wrist again. "Mordeus," he says. I don't know how he guessed when no one else did and when it makes no sense, but his tone is lethal. "*He* did this." His eyes track across the scars on my stomach. "All of it."

"He and his guards."

"You never had wounds."

"Never had scars either, until recently." I shrug, as if it doesn't matter, as if I don't hate that these ridges in my skin make him see me differently. "He always made sure to heal me after."

Remme mutters a curse.

"Natan," Kendrick says.

Natan's glasses slip down his nose as he nods. "I'm on it."

Kendrick carefully lowers my hand to my side, as if I'm something breakable he doesn't want to play with anymore. When he steps back, his face is twisted into an expression I don't recognize. He turns and storms outside, letting the door swing shut behind him.

Remme moves to follow him, but Natan puts a hand on his arm. "I'll go."

Skylar frowns at the door before turning to me. "You should tie your hair up," she says, as if none of that just happened. "It would be the perfect finishing touch."

"Then you could see the short parts in the back."

Her turned-up palms seem to say *and?* "I'll undercut it all evenly so it looks intentional. You'll look badass."

"Why *did* you take my hair?" I ask. "Did Felicity need it for some reason?"

"I needed it for my witch's brew," she says. "It calls for a handful of the hairs from a spoiled princess's head."

I shoot her a glare but don't bother pressing the issue. When goblins work for hair and nails, we all gather what we can for future payments.

She has me sit in one of the chairs by the fire and gets to work. After pulling all the hair on the crown of my head into a high ponytail, she trims the back and sides close to my scalp. I cringe with every snip of the scissors, but at least I can hide it when I wear my hair down. It's not like it wasn't a mess before from the chunks I've cut off for Gommid.

"We leave in ten minutes," Kendrick says when he and Natan push back into the cottage. "She needs to be glamoured before we go."

Natan hands me a small glass vial of light yellow liquid. "Drink this. It will make you appear fae and give you tattoos like Skylar described."

I bring it to my lips slowly but stop when Natan holds up a hand.

"You'll want to do it quickly. This isn't a treat."

"She's scared," Skylar says.

I know she's baiting me, but still I meet her eyes as I throw back the liquid. It falls in a glob onto my tongue. I swallow before I can let myself think about how repulsive the taste and texture are. By the time I gag, the potion's already hit my stomach.

"Easy," Remme says. "Breathe through your nose. You don't have to keep it down long, but you *do* have to keep it down until—"

"There it is." Natan smiles at me, then points to the bathing room. "Take a look."

When I see myself in the mirror, my breath catches.

The first thing I notice is what Skylar did to my hair. I kind of like it. This isn't the style of a timid little princess. It *is* badass. And I look nothing like myself. Not only am I wearing Skylar's ridiculously revealing outfit, Natan's potion covered my skin with tattoos and hid the appearance of my scars. It also gave me the inhuman glow and strangely pointed ears of the elven fae.

A shudder skitters up my spine. *This is who I'd be if I hadn't traded it away for the ring. This is what lurks in my veins.*

I leave the bathing room quickly, unwilling to look at myself as a faerie too long. When I return to the main room, the others have taken their potions as well, and now they also appear fae.

"Whaddya think?" Skylar asks, tossing a pack over her shoulder and throwing me another.

I catch it, grunting under its unexpected weight. "I look like a faerie."

"A *hot* faerie," Remme says.

Kendrick grabs the pack from my arms and slings it over his shoulder. "You can flirt on the road. We need to load up the horses."

He heads out the door, and Remme chuckles at his back. "I'm just saying what everyone else was thinking."

I follow them and frown as I watch the team pack up the horses. I've left the capital countless times over the last few months—sometimes by goblin travel, sometimes on my own two feet—but somehow going on a journey with this crew feels more permanent.

Because this is the first time in years that you've left your sister for more than a few hours.

There are only four horses, which makes sense, since there are only four of them, but when I suggest we acquire another, Kendrick looks me right in the eye and laughs. "Absolutely not."

Apparently, he thinks I'm liable to run from them if I have my own horse.

Not their captive, my backside.

"How long will it take to get to this Feegus Keep?" I ask.

"It's three-days' ride from here," Kendrick says, tightening the saddle on his mare.

Three days? I'm supposed to ride on horseback with Kendrick for *three days*? "Why don't we just travel by goblin?"

Natan shakes his head. "The goblins know too much. We don't need to give them more."

Remme nods.

I look back and forth between them. "What does that mean?"

"Wish we knew," Natan says, but he smiles. Despite myself, I like him. At least he doesn't try to piss me off at every turn like Skylar or poke fun at me like Remme.

"How are we going to travel for three days? Didn't you say you

95

didn't want to travel at night?"

Remme and Kendrick exchange a look, and Remme says, "Did she ever leave that palace?"

"As protective as her sister is, I'm guessing no," Kendrick says, but his tone is kind, like he isn't judging Brie for being protective of me, more like he understands. And I guess, of all people, he would.

He shifts his attention to me. "I know you haven't explored the court much, but it's not as uncivilized as you might think. There are inns along the way."

Skylar looks me over. "Have you done much riding? Three full days on horseback will make even an experienced rider sore."

I lift my chin. "I'll be fine."

Three days? I was sore after three *hours*. Eight hours in, my muscles burn. Even the fact that the weather is perfect for riding can't distract me from the horrendous ache in my thighs, hips, and back.

Remme and Skylar lead the group, with Natan taking up the rear as we ride quickly through the more rural areas and slower through the towns. We stopped for a break midmorning and then again to eat lunch, but getting back on the horse after the relief of being off is almost worse than the agony of the endless riding.

It's not like I haven't been on horseback before. After moving in with Brie, I began taking lessons as soon as I was healthy enough to do so. Back in Elora, only the most wealthy have horses, so Brie and I didn't have much experience, and my sister made sure to correct that immediately. Of course, she never had me climb in a saddle in front of a very strong man for whom I feel a complicated variety of emotions, nor did she make me stay in the saddle for hours at a time.

Kendrick's arms are looped around me, his hands on the reins. I sit as stiff and straight as possible to avoid any additional contact between our bodies, but it's no use. Every step forward, every shift of the horse's hips brings our bodies in contact.

"Princess," he says, his mouth against my ear, "if you don't relax, you aren't going to be able to get out of bed tomorrow."

"Oh good," I deadpan. "A day in bed sounds lovely."

He grumbles something unintelligible that I think might be "You have no idea" before pulling me against him and urging me to relax against his chest.

He's warm and solid at my back, a reminder of the feeling of safety he brought me during those darkest days in the dungeon. My muscles seem to sigh, going loose in relief, while other parts go tight.

"Better?" he murmurs in my ear.

The heat of his breath sends a pleasant shiver through me. "Yeah."

I swear I can feel his smile. "I'm not so bad, if you'll remember."

Even if I'd been older, I was far too deep in my trauma to think in terms of physical attraction during our days in the dungeons. But today? Three years removed from the darkest nights of my life, and with Kendrick at my back and his warm forearm against my bare stomach, his fingertips brushing my side? Today, *safe* is mixed up with a whole messy bunch of other emotions I'd rather not analyze too closely.

I'm saved from having to reply when Remme falls back to ride alongside us.

"We have a couple of options," he says. "There's a village ahead where we'll be able to find dinner and a couple of rooms for the night with no problem. Or we could keep riding and hit Elligold, probably right before sunset, barring any complications along the path."

"We should head on," Skylar calls without looking back. "Get as far on day one as we can."

"But I'm guessing there's a reason you think we should consider stopping sooner," Kendrick says to Remme.

Remme nods. "According to our sources, Elligold is a much smaller place. So there's a chance they won't have available lodging for us or, worse, that like a lot of these small rural towns, it was wiped out entirely during Mordeus's rule. We could camp if it comes to that, but since we're trying to operate with an abundance of caution . . ."

Kendrick considers this, but only briefly. "We stop early. It's been a long day already, and I don't want Jasalyn to be so sore that tomorrow is excruciating."

Remme rubs his shoulder like it's bothering him. "I'll ride ahead if that's okay. I'll scout the area and secure our lodging."

"I need a window in my quarters," I blurt.

"Her *quarters*?" Skylar snorts and tosses a derisive look over her shoulder. "Where does she think we're going? The palace? Princess, we all share, and as for your window?" She shrugs. "You get what you get."

"Do what you can," Kendrick tells Remme.

Remme spurs his horse into a gallop to ride ahead.

"Who are you?" I ask, craning my neck to try to see his face.

I feel his chuckle more than hear it. "What kind of question is that? You know who I am."

"No, I mean, who are you *to them*? They look to you for leadership. They let you order them around. They follow your orders even when they don't like it. Why?"

"Every group needs a leader, Slayer. Anything else breeds chaos."

"Yes, but why you?"

"Because I'm the only one they are all willing to listen to without someone getting a knife in their gut," he says.

It strikes me as an evasion, but I let the subject drop. We have days ahead of us, it seems, for me to figure out him and this group of his and what they mean to each other.

Days and *nights*.

"What kind of place do you think Remme will find for us?" I ask. I can be flexible with how we spend the day—whether I get my own horse, how much I push my sore muscles—but the night is something different.

Kendrick tightens his arm around my waist. "I won't leave you in the dark," he says in my ear. "I promise."

And with those words, my fears of a dark night in a strange place fizzle away.

CHAPTER NINE

❖

FELICITY

SHE HAS A FRIEND.

The nights are still too dark, and the conditions are still wretched. Everything hurts. Her bones and muscles from sleeping on this hard, cold floor, her stomach from too little food, her throat from too many tears. But they threw another girl into her cell—a human girl. Fair-haired and fine-featured, like an angel. Terrified, like her.

Jas watches her from the opposite corner of the cell, and for the first time since she was thrown into this place, she feels . . . better. Calmer. I'm not alone.

The girl wipes her eyes and squints at Jas. A tiny stream of light comes in the slit of a window in the corridor, and she can see wispy white hair, light blue eyes.

"What's your name?" she asks.

Jas blinks at her. She hasn't spoken in days, and her throat is still raw from all those hours of wasted tears.

"I'm Crissa," the girl says.

Jas swallows. "Jasalyn." The three syllables come out scratchy. She doesn't recognize her own voice.

"Who are you?" Crissa asks.

She frowns and repeats herself, trying to make her unused voice louder this time. "Jasalyn."

Crissa smiles. Her tear-filled eyes shine in the light. "Yes, you told me your name. I'm wondering who you are. Why are you in here?"

Jas shakes her head. "I don't know."

"Mordeus always has his reasons."

Jas stares at the window in the corridor. She's been here long enough to know the patterns. When the sun streams in like that, dusk comes soon after and then the darkness.

A baby cries in the next cell. There's a stone wall, so she can't see the woman, but she's heard her cooing to her child, heard her begging the guards for more food and water so her body can produce the milk her baby needs.

"I have friends who will come for me," Crissa whispers. "Will someone come for you?"

Her sister will. No one is braver than Brie. But why is it taking her so long?

Crissa crawls across the cell on her hands and knees and touches two fingers to the back of Jas's hand. Jas sags in relief. It feels like a lifetime since anyone touched her with kindness.

"You aren't hurt?" she asks, scanning her face.

Jas hesitates. There are no marks on her skin, no bruises on her face. Even the spot where the king sliced her hand open is completely healed. So completely that she's not sure if it really happened or if it was a dream. "No."

"You are very pretty," she says, stroking Jas's hair. "I'm sorry you're stuck here."

"My sister will find me. She'll find me and take me home."

She gives me a sad smile. "She will rescue you, but you'll have to find yourself."

Jas doesn't know what that means, and she's suddenly too tired to care. There are places so dark, you can never find your way back.

"Bakken, please take my sister to Castle Craige," the queen says. "We will send her things along after her."

The goblin arches an unruly brow at Abriella before turning and looking me over. The shadow queen's personal goblin knows that I am not the princess.

When transformed, I am an exact replica of my subject the moment they shed their hair—and that includes scent. No keen faerie nose will ever sniff out an Echo as an impostor. But goblins always know—which would've been fine if I could've called Jasalyn's goblin, who she's asked to answer to me, but the queen called hers.

"This girl here?" he asks the queen.

Abriella frowns. "Yes, Bakken. Misha is expecting her."

I do my best to silently plead with the drooling, bug-eyed creature. *Don't tell her. Let this be.*

"As you wish, Your Majesty." He offers me his hand and I take it, heart pounding wildly as I mentally give thanks to the bond whatever long-ago ancestors formed between Echoes and goblins.

In the next moment, we're nothing. Spinning and turning and frozen all at once. Until we're standing at the base of a set of polished wooden stairs in the most beautiful place I've ever been.

"Thank you, Bakken," a husky voice says behind me.

I spin around and find myself staring at a broad chest cloaked in a viridescent tunic. I crane my neck to see his face. "King Misha." I sound breathless. Maybe I *am*.

I've only seen the golden-skinned male in paintings and heard him described in stories, and yet in person he's even more stunning and handsome than I could've prepared myself for. He's not just tall and broad. He has a presence that seems to take up the whole room. His black hair is silky and long enough I can imagine running my fingers through it—the gods certainly know most of the marriageable females in this realm have been imagining just that since he and the Wild Fae queen dissolved their marriage last year.

"*King* Misha now, is it?" He turns his head side to side, inspecting me. The silver webbing on his forehead glows with the same intensity as his upturned russet eyes. They're certainly peering into me right now. I can feel his talons digging into my mind, trying to get inside as he examines every inch of my face. When his eyes meet mine, I hold his gaze as steadily as I hold my shields. When it comes to mental shielding, I have more experience than the princess. And more to lose if I fail.

I meet his scrutiny with a stubborn lift of my chin.

He gives me a tight smile and a sharp nod. "Welcome to Castle Craige, Princess."

"Jas," I correct, just as Jasalyn would. I don't know why she objects to her title or if she's even conscious of it, but she made it clear she prefers her given name or *Jas* for family and friends.

His jaw is tense, making me wonder how he really feels about having the Unseelie princess in his castle. "It's past time you visited my lands."

Bakken looks me over one last time, shakes his head, then disappears.

Misha waves a hand to indicate the space around us, which feels simultaneously like the hall of a grand palace and the center of the wilderness. A burbling brook runs through the center of the flagstone floor, and the stair rail is a formation of branches and bows that seem to have grown from the earth for that very purpose.

The evening sun plays off the colorful autumn leaves in the woodland canopy covering the open-air hall, casting dappled shade all around us.

"What happens when they shed their leaves for winter?" I ask without thinking.

"Just when the air cools enough to bite, the leaves make way for the sun to warm these halls," the king says, studying the canopy. "Mother Nature tends to us when we let Her."

He steps into a sunny spot, and his black hair gleams. When he meets my gaze, he arches a brow. *I'm staring.*

I drop my gaze to the floor and focus on making myself as small as possible.

"Shall I show you your quarters?" he asks, gesturing toward the stairs.

"Yes. Please. Thank you." I duck my head and lift my skirts, following him up the stairs.

The hall at the top is lined with doors on one side, but the other side is a railing that overlooks the passage below, where the creek cuts through the hall with a comforting burble.

He opens a door and gestures for me to lead the way inside.

The room is large and airy with high ceilings and big windows that overlook the wooded valley beyond the castle. A massive four-poster bed sits against one wall, and a bathing room is opposite the windows.

The king waves toward a work desk in the corner. "There's some muslin, various needles, and thread as well as bolts of half a dozen fabrics, though your handmaid can let my staff know if you need something specific."

Unfortunately, when I take the form of another, I don't get their skills along with their shape. I hope the king doesn't ask me to sew him something while I'm here. I can stitch a tear in a seam competently enough, but I wouldn't know the first thing about designing or sewing an entire gown. "I don't need anything more," I say. "I don't sew much these days."

"That's what your sister said." He studies me, worry creasing his brow. "Is there a reason for that?"

Because she's too busy fantasizing about murdering a resurrected evil king?

I shrug. "It no longer interests me."

Misha folds his arms and rocks back on his heels. "And what does interest you, Pri—Jasalyn?"

I shrug again, only because I believe Jas would do the same. "My sister said you have a lovely library."

"Indeed. You can find it if you continue down that hall and go up the flight of stairs at the end. It was one of her favorite places in the castle when she stayed here."

"Thank you."

"I'm headed to the village in a bit." He strolls toward the sewing table and examines its contents before glancing at me over a shoulder. "Could I convince you to join me? The ride is almost as lovely as the market itself. We could have dinner together at one of my favorite restaurants there."

That sounds amazing, and I'd love to see it. I grew up on horseback and miss being able to ride regularly. But I shake my head and glance toward the bed. "I'm feeling tired, and I'd like to retire for the evening."

"It's early yet."

"It's later in the Unseelie Court." I yawn to drive my point home.

That wrinkle reappears between his brows. "Perhaps the exercise would invigorate you. I always find—"

"Please? We all agree that this is the safest place for me, but I'm here now. I just need some time to settle."

His gaze bores into me, and I can practically feel the intensity of his displeasure. "I wish you'd let me into that head of yours." He drags a chair out from under the table, and it groans against the stone floor. He lowers himself onto it and braces his hands on his knees. "I don't know what your sister's told you, but I didn't bring you to Castle Craige to make you my wife." The corner of his mouth twitches upward. "When I marry again, it will be for love, and while I may suspect your sister is trying to play matchmaker, you and I both already know we're not compatible."

The shadow princess and the Wild Fae king? Maybe Hale was onto something with his whole seduction plan.

Misha clears his throat. "I'm trying to say that you don't need to worry about me coming between you and your baker—baker's *son*? You couldn't even find a male that does the baking himself?"

I shoot him a glare.

Misha laughs. The sound is deep and full, and does something funny to my stomach. "You're in my lands so that you'll be safe, not so I can bed and wed you."

Well, now I feel sorry for the princess. Misha isn't just a *king*. He's handsome and charming, and if today's introduction is any indication, he's also warm and kind and caring. If Jasalyn knew what was good for her, she'd find out what her sister has planned and make it happen.

But she wouldn't want that. She'd be horrified by the idea of marrying a faerie. *Almost as horrified as she is by the idea of becoming one.*

"I'm tired," I say, because Jasalyn wouldn't entertain this conversation.

He nods sharply. "Of course. Just let your handmaid know if you change your mind about dinner." He backs toward the door. "Rest well. You'll be joining me for training before breakfast."

"What?"

His grin is so deliciously cocky I'm not sure how he's not constantly being chased by females who want to kiss it off his face. "Training. You know, with swords and bows. I'll see you at sunrise."

I could've said yes to dinner. Maybe that would've been the wise thing to do, but my days at Castle Craige must be a careful balancing act. On the one hand, if I'm to somehow convince Misha to reveal the location of his sacred Hall of Doors, I need to get close to him. On the other hand, I can't be too available. Jas has spent the last three years hiding in her room and pushing away everyone who tries to get close to her. If I suddenly seem eager to make friends, Misha will be suspicious.

Hale's plan is the most obvious. Legend says, after all, that the queen learns the location of the Hall of Doors upon her coronation, and perhaps he'd be willing to share with a trusted lover if she had a compelling reason to need the information. However, I suspect it would take many months if not years to earn that level of trust. Since every day that I spend in this form is a day I could be exposed, I'll have to find another way to get Hale the information he needs.

I know what I need to do.

I run my fingertips over the threads of my goblin bracelet. It's not quite like the one I saw on Jasalyn's wrist, but it's similar enough in function. Like mine, hers is invisible to the naked eye. Only the owner of a goblin bracelet can see its delicate strands. With two exceptions: goblins and Echoes.

Long ago, Echoes came through the portal to save goblin-kind. If it hadn't been for my ancestors, goblins would've been lost as a casualty of one of the most brutal battles of the Great Fae War, but my kind did theirs a favor the goblins still believe is unpaid. To this day, each Echo is gifted with a goblin guardian at birth and a goblin bracelet on her seventh birthday, as well the rare ability to see what only goblins could see before. Unlike others, we know if someone we meet has a goblin working with them, and we get to use our bracelets without any expectation of payment.

I pluck a thread and Nigel appears in my chambers, grinning at the sight of me. His yellow, pointy teeth are covered with a greenish slime from a dinner of which I'd rather not know the details. "Felicity," he says. "Beautiful girl. It's been so long. What brings you to the Wild Fae territory?"

"One of your kin brought me—the shadow queen's goblin. He saw me for who I was, and I don't think he was pleased."

Nigel sniffs. "Of course he did. My kind do not have the easily fooled eyes of humans and fae."

I hold up my arms. "I am an Echo. I shouldn't have to worry that a goblin will betray me."

"Bakken is partial to his queen, but he won't betray your identity." He scans the room. "I see you've begun a new adventure."

"So it seems," I say with a sigh. "And if all goes well, I go home at the end of it all."

He cocks his head at me. "The child speaks of home as if she is grown and has built one of her own."

I glare at him. "I miss my mother."

"You miss your ignorance. You want to be fifteen again and believe you are just another adopted child taken in by a loving family. You don't want to face the truth."

I do miss those days—before Erith's men came for me and my adoptive father was killed trying to protect me, before my mother confessed the truth of my birth, before I went to the oracle and discovered the horrible choice I was faced with. "I saw my brother today." I sit on the floor, folding my legs under me.

"Your brother lives in the Eloran Palace and has servants hunting you in every realm."

I scowl. "Sharing a womb with someone does not make them your brother."

"You saw Kendrick the Chosen," he corrects me. "And now you feel happy and sad and guilty all over again?"

"Pretty much." Leave it to Nigel to summarize my emotions so succinctly. "I can't help but feel like everything is my fault."

"Fault is so sticky—" he says.

"When no action lives in isolation," I finish. He's been saying these words to me since I was a little girl trying to shirk responsibility for breaking my mother's favorite garden ornament during a fight with Hale. "I know. I know."

"Do you?" He picks something from his teeth.

I cringe and change the subject. "When Jasalyn was Mordeus's captive, Crissa was there."

"You knew he had captured her."

"Yes, but isn't it interesting that he had them put in the same cell?" I've been thinking about this since last night's dream, and I'm not sure what to make of it. "Mordeus had to have done that for a reason."

"But this is not the question you called me here for. Tell me, child. I don't have all night."

I sigh. He either doesn't know the reason behind Mordeus's choice or he isn't going to tell me. But he's right. I called him to answer a different question. "The Hall of Doors," I say. "Is it real?"

He chuckles. "Of course. The child only calls when she has too great a favor to ask."

"Well, I would hate to waste your time with tedious favors," I say, smiling at my old friend.

He rubs his belly, and I suspect he ate too much of that slimy-green-whatever before I called for him.

"Is it real?" I ask again.

"Yes," he says. "Very real, and very secret."

"Where can I find the Wild Fae Hall?"

"You know I can't tell you that. You'd be better off finding the Sword of Fire."

As if my brother hasn't been killing himself trying. I cock my head to the side. "You know if this all ends with Erith finding me, I will die."

"He won't find you. You're too smart for that." He clucks. "The Hall of Doors is a magical hallway, and nothing so completely made of magic needs a fixed location. In fact, it would be dangerous for the Wild Fae to keep it in one place. Too easy for one to stumble upon it or to share the secret."

"Yes," I agree. "So where is it *now*? Tell me where to look, Nigel."

"I can only tell you to follow your heart. You know King Misha is in want of a new wife."

Groaning, I fall onto my back and stare at the ceiling. "Not you too. We don't have time for that."

"You have your whole life to fall in love."

Sitting up, I fold my arms. "The Hall of Doors, Nigel. *Focus.*"

"You aren't looking for the hall full of portals, my dear. You're looking for the single door, the single portal that leads to the hall of portals."

I close my eyes and nod. That makes perfect sense. Why waste all the time and magic to continuously move the countless portals that are rumored to be in the Hall of Doors when they can place the Hall behind a single portal and move *that* portal at will?

"Okay," I say. "And where can I find—" But then I realize my goblin has already left—his favorite way to tell me he's not sharing any more information. "Good night, Nigel," I tell the air where he stood a moment ago. "It was good to see you."

CHAPTER TEN

◆

JASALYN

THE VILLAGE "UP AHEAD" is nearly another hour's ride, and by the time we stop to meet Remme, exhaustion has me on the brink of tears.

Kendrick swings off the horse first and then turns to help me as if he understands just how much I'm aching. It's probably written all over my face.

This is why everyone thinks I'm so fragile.

When he reaches for me, it's easy to imagine his hands on my hips and the slow slide of my body down his. It's also easy to imagine how weak that would make me look in front of his friends.

I pull my shoulders back. "I know how to dismount a horse, but thank you."

His brows shoot up, but he steps back. "As you wish, Princess."

I dismount and stumble forward a few steps when my legs buckle under me. Kendrick doesn't say a word, just leads the way.

Remme meets us at the door to our lodging, which seems to be a rowdy tavern on the ground floor with rooms on the floors above. "Two rooms," he says, holding up two keys on oversize rings. "Looks like we are living in luxury tonight."

"And who's paying for that?" Skylar asks.

"I have money," I say. "I can contribute." But what I'm really thinking is, *Only two rooms?* Will they stick me with Skylar for the night or keep me with Kendrick? I'm afraid Skylar and I might claw each other's eyes out before morning, but I'm afraid of staying with Kendrick too. For different reasons.

Reasons that probably never occurred to him.

"Oh?" Skylar says, propping a hand on her hip. "You have money? And where is this money of yours? You have the coin on you?"

"It's . . . I . . ." I've never actually had to carry coin since my sister brought me to live with her at the Midnight Palace. I'm sister to the shadow queen, and I can charge anything I want to the palace accounts.

"Trust me, Sky," Remme says, "we couldn't all fit into one of these rooms."

"It's fine." Kendrick snatches a key from Remme's hand. "We can afford it."

Skylar grabs the other key. "I'll bunk with the new girl."

"Literally," Remme says. "They're bunk rooms."

"Seriously?" she asks.

Natan scans the road and the thatched vendor stalls and nods. "My sources tell me that lots of soldiers came through here during the war and the lodgings haven't been converted yet."

"I call top bunk," Remme says.

"Because you're an idiot," Skylar says. She meets my eyes. "You're on top. I need my feet close to the ground."

"Fine," I mutter. I doubt I'll be able to sleep anyway. And if

Skylar finds out how I feel about the dark, she'll probably paint the windows black and snuff out all the candles just to amuse herself.

You have your ring. You'll be fine.

Remme, Skylar, and Natan grab their packs and head inside, but Kendrick brushes his knuckles against my shoulder, so I stay back.

He watches them and waits until they're inside before looking at me. "Are you going to be okay?"

"I don't know. What are the chances she'll kill me in my sleep?"

The corner of his mouth twitches. "Believe it or not, she doesn't have it out for you. She's just a little abrasive."

"That's like saying water is a little moist."

This time I get a full-on smile. If my legs were unsteady before, the sight of those dimples makes them downright unreliable.

"Hold up a minute, okay?" He pulls his pack from his shoulder and digs around inside before drawing out a glowstone the size of my palm. "Take this. It will last all night."

I stare at it. It's a faint yellow in the evening sun, but in the dark, it will let off a buttery glow. It's magic from Elora. From home. I swallow a lump of emotion in my throat. "Thank you."

"Tell me again about this special sword," I ask at dinner. The tavern is crowded tonight, and the five of us are crammed into a corner, bowls full of stew and hunks of bread in front of each of us.

Remme's blade sings as he draws it from his sheath. "You see this?" he asks, turning the blade this way and that. "This blade was forged by the hand of the last true king of Elora, blessed by the priestess of the Oracle of Light, and passed down through the generations to fighters deemed noble enough to fight for the good of the land. *This* is a *special sword*. The Sword of Fire is *the Sword*. It can open portals to anywhere, bring strength to anyone who wields it, and guarantee your opponent's defeat."

I glance around the group to see if anyone is laughing, but they're not. "There are so many things wrong with the nonsense you just spouted."

"*Nonsense?*" Remme sputters.

"Here we go," Natan says.

"Like what?" Remme says.

"The idea of you being *deemed noble* aside?" I say, "Elora has never had kings, so that sword couldn't have been forged by its first, last, middle, true, or false king. We have the Magical Seven of Elora, and before them we ran as independent villages ruled by our own lords, all more or less unaware of each other."

Skylar scoffs and glances toward Remme. "Sure, and *you're* the one spewing nonsense."

I press a palm to my chest. "Do you forget that I'm Eloran too?"

"I don't forget," Skylar says. "I just happen to know the history that the Elora Seven work so hard to keep hidden from the people of the realm."

I choke out a laugh. "Oh, so now you're going to tell me that the Magical Seven are the bad guys?"

Kendrick just watches me for a beat before nodding. "Yes," he says. "If you want to know the truth."

116

I shake my head at him. "The Magical Seven are the purest hearts in the land. They have to walk through the Fire Portal before they rise. Murderers don't survive that."

"It's true," Skylar says. "The Seven like to make a display of their holiness. That's why they save their murdering for *after* they've taken their spots among the most powerful in the realm."

The idea that the Magical Seven would kill anyone is ridiculous. "They are the only reason the fae didn't take total control of us when the gates opened. They are the only reason our realm was protected from these *monsters*."

"*Monsters*, huh?" Skylar says.

Kendrick's gaze sweeps over me, landing on my arm where my scars are hidden beneath my glamour. "And how well protected were you?"

My skin goes clammy at the reminder—of my past, of the dungeons, of how easy it was for Mordeus to have his goblin sweep in and take me from my home. "That was because of the contracts," I say, my voice weak.

"And if the Seven are so great, why are those unjust contracts so pervasive?" Kendrick asks.

"It's not their fault. The system is broken. The—"

"It wasn't before." Kendrick's eyes are kind, as if he understands that he's asking me to rethink everything I ever believed.

"And who would you have lead?" I ask. "This old monarchy Remme seems to revere?"

"For starters," Kendrick says, tearing off another piece of bread. "I would have someone lead who wants what is truly best for all in the realm and not just the strongest magic users among them. I would have someone lead who would listen to the voices of a representative from every territory in the realm—not just the wealthiest. I would have someone lead," he says, his voice even harder now, "who wasn't so preoccupied by *greed* that they let children be sold into servitude every day."

I hear what he's saying, and it's not that I disagree, but the Magical Seven keep the portals between Elora and Faerie closed. They're the reason the fae don't just go into Elora and snatch as many humans as they'd like. Just because our realm isn't perfect doesn't mean the leaders are to blame. "It could be worse."

"It could be *better*."

Something about his words niggles at me. Because even though this is the first I've heard about the Magical Seven hiding the true history of our realm, my sister has been railing for years against the evil of those contracts and the way Elora works only for the wealthy.

"Is there a washroom?" I ask, pushing away from the table.

Skylar chuckles and points to the other side of the tavern. "End of the hall. Might have to wait your turn. I think I saw an orc going in there."

I ignore her smirk and head that way. It's funny that she thinks I'm so pampered. While I have lived in comfort for my years in the palace, she has no idea what my life was like before that. My sister and I had to work our fingers to the bone to get by. We worked all day, cleaned our aunt's house all night, and for the few brief hours we got to rest, shared a bed in a tiny windowless room in my aunt's basement. *Because of the very contracts the Magical Seven allow to go unchecked.*

"Are you okay?"

I jump. I hadn't even noticed Kendrick was following me. "Everything I've ever known to be true was a lie—down to my own blood." I shake my head, trying to force my jumble of thoughts into place. My eyes burn. "Now I'm supposed to believe even the Magical Seven, the most powerful mages of the human realm, are behind the very practices that resulted in my sister and me spending our childhood in servitude to a greedy shrew?"

He lifts a hand, and I think he might touch me—think I might want him to—but then he drops it. "Their transition into power was horrendous. For the first couple of generations, people knew the truth, but the Seven destroyed all evidence of the true history of the land and executed anyone who dared speak of it. Two generations later, they'd rewritten history. Everything we're doing here is to change that."

I bow my head. "And this Erith you want me to kill?"

"He's their patriarch. He leads them, and losing his rule would weaken them, but the biggest blow would be that they'd lose their seventh. Their magic—their strength—is tied to that sacred number. That's why I want to do this now, while they have no trained apprentice in the wings. Once he dies, the Seven fall. Only then can we begin to right the wrongs they've done to the realm."

They want me to kill one of the Magical Seven. I guessed as much from the things they said at the table, but hearing him say it makes my stomach sour. "I need to think."

"I understand." He steps back, then looks me over one final time before returning to the table.

When I go to the washroom door, it's slightly ajar, and I hear a soft whimpering from the other side.

I knock and nudge it open. "Hello?" On the far wall, curled up on the floor between the sink and the toilet, is a delicate female with glowing eyes and pointed ears sticking out of her short violet hair. "Are you hurt?"

She spots me and jumps to her feet. "So sorry. I'll get out of your way."

"No, you're fine."

She has a split lip and is holding her arm tenderly against her body.

"What happened?"

"Oh. He's just in a mood." She smiles but it looks too painful to be real. "He'll sleep it off and be better tomorrow."

She looks too young to be married, but it's hard to tell with faeries. Once they hit puberty, they age so slowly. "Your . . . father?" I guess.

"Husband," she says in a hush. "My father married me off to him when I hit maturity."

"You were sold?" I thought that only happened to humans.

She nods. "It was a fair deal, and my father needed the money."

Sold. Just like when my aunt sold me to Mordeus. What is wrong with these people? "When was that?"

"Two years next month."

My nails bite into my palms at the sight of her injuries. I make myself count my breaths before I speak again. "Do you need me to find you a healer?"

She shakes her head. "No. He'll see. He'll know. And anyway." She swallows hard. "He'll be gone soon. His cronies have finally

120

arrived. It's strange to be so grateful for a movement that you also think is so ugly."

I frown. "What movement?"

Her face goes stony, and she looks me over. "I need to get back to work." She wipes her hands on her pants and her tears on her shoulders. "Thank you for caring. You didn't have to."

I see her again when I return to the others. She's wiping down tables and sweeping behind the bar, getting scolded by a tall, dark-haired fae male I might call attractive if it weren't for the sneer on his face and the way he speaks to his young wife. No, this male is ugly on the inside, and his insides are showing.

Skylar digs her elbow into my side. "Would you quit staring?"

I drop my gaze back to my dinner, but in my periphery I'm aware of the male and the group of a dozen faeries gathered at a long table closer to the bar. They're all dressed in the same uniform of brown pants and olive vest. Many have sideways crescent moons tattooed on their necks. The proprietor keeps circling back to their table and laughing with them.

"What do we know about that group?" I ask quietly. "The loud ones the proprietor seems partial to?"

"Enough to mind our own business," Skylar says, not looking up from her bowl.

Remme chuckles and nods in agreement.

Kendrick flicks his gaze to the group then to Natan.

"I know," Natan says. "I'm on it."

"What does that mean?"

"It means we like to keep an eye on the people around us who could be trouble," Remme says, his voice low, "but we're smart enough not to let them know we're doing it."

The proprietor alternates between scolding his wife behind the bar and returning to the table with the rowdy males, filling their glasses with fresh ale.

"Would you please not stare?" Skylar says, elbowing me again.

"Sorry." I drop my gaze to my stew, but I can't do anything to contain the hate rolling off me. When he bought his wife, she was likely younger than I was when I was sold to Mordeus. She should've been allowed to be a child. Her father should've protected her. The world shouldn't be such an ugly place that things like that happen at all—not to humans or faeries.

My ring feels warm against my breast, where I tucked it into my bustier before dinner. I feel it calling to me.

"You want to steer clear of the likes of them," Remme says. "Trouble, through and through. I might not care about Faerie politics, but even I think this godsforsaken realm is better off with your sister on that throne than it was without her."

"Careful," Kendrick murmurs.

I glare at Remme. "You *think*? Of course it's better." I force myself to keep my voice low.

"Not if you ask those folks back there," Skylar says, gesturing with her spoon toward the table of uniformed males.

Kendrick flinches and rubs his temples. "Thanks, Sky."

She shrugs. "It's just facts. I don't see what the problem is."

Remme takes a long pull from his dark glass of ale, then wipes his mouth with the back of his hand. "*Problem is* all that rage in her eyes," he says, nodding to me.

Skylar chuckles. "You really think she's gonna do something

about it? About *them*? I'd like to see her try."

Kendrick rubs his forehead. "Please stop."

She winks at him. "I thought you liked it when I brought out the fight in your little girlfriend."

I decide to ignore all three of them and turn to Natan. "Someone told me that group is leaving. Where would they be going?"

Natan looks to Kendrick.

"No," I snap. "Look at *me*. You don't need his permission. Tell me."

Kendrick's jaw ticks. "Go ahead."

"We don't know where they're headed," Natan says, his tone hushed. He pushes his glasses up his nose. "But I would guess they're traveling around the court to gather recruits. They aren't strong enough yet, but if they keep growing like they have, they'll make a charge to remove your sister from the throne sooner rather than later."

Anger and hatred burn in my blood. I knew there were pockets of Mordeus's followers throughout the court, but I didn't realize any of them planned to act. They are lucky to have my sister. They have no idea how much my family lost so that fate or destiny or Mab or whoever is in charge of this idiocy could get her there. That they not only don't appreciate it but want to take it from her makes me want to tear them apart with my bare hands. I don't even need the ring to feel my chest cooling and my heart frosting over.

"Easy, Slayer," Kendrick says. "We can't save the entire realm today. We have to start by finding the sword."

What he means is we have to start by murdering the leader

123

of the Magical Seven, and I still don't know how I feel about that.

I've eaten only a few bites of my stew, but I can't stomach any more. I push away from the table. "Excuse me. I think I'll retire early."

"You should eat," Kendrick says, worried eyes scanning my face.

I snatch my bread from my plate and nod to him. "I'll see you in the morning."

As I head for the stairs, I hear them murmuring behind me and shortly after, I sense someone following. A glance over my shoulder confirms Remme's a few steps behind. He gives me an apologetic wave, but I'm just glad it's not Skylar. I want a few minutes alone.

CHAPTER ELEVEN

◆

JASALYN

OUR BUNK ROOM IS TRULY that—a room with a sturdy, utilitarian metal bunk and enough space to walk along one side of it. There is a small window on the far wall. Whether that's luck or Remme watching out for me I can't be sure, but I'm grateful.

A candle flickers in the wall sconce, and shadows dance on the ceiling.

My mattress is hard as a rock. Not that it matters. I have other things to do tonight than enjoy a restful sleep.

"You're acting weird," Skylar says.

I'm lying on my back in the top bunk, waiting for her to get in bed before I slip on my ring and head downstairs to see what else I can learn about the rebel forces gathered in the dining room. I don't want to wait too long, since I'm not sure how late they'll stay, but I would prefer to keep it simple and wait until Skylar falls asleep. Not because she'd remember but because her fawning over the Enchanting Lady would be awkward in the morning. For me at least. "I'm just tired."

She grunts and the bunks sway as she throws herself onto her mattress. "Nah. That isn't tired. That's pissed."

"Why wouldn't I be? I'm trying to sleep and my roommate keeps talking."

"You sure it has nothing to do with those piece of shit faeries downstairs who want to destroy your pretty sister?"

I sigh. "Don't try to bait me, Skylar. I'm not in the mood."

"Fine." The bunks shift again, as if she's rolling to her side.

Her breathing turns softer, and I'm about to reach for my ring when she says, "He cares about you, but he can't have you."

I freeze. "What?"

"The world is full of shit people, but Hale Kendrick is one of the good ones. Don't make it hard for him when this is all over and he has to walk away from you."

"I . . . We aren't . . . He doesn't . . ." I don't know what to do about the nervous mass of butterflies staging a riot in my belly. "Did he say something to you?"

She snorts. Loudly. The guys can probably hear her in their room. "He doesn't need to."

I close my eyes. It's so tempting to lose myself in thoughts of crushes and could-be love. To lose myself in thoughts of a future with a guy who was once the only piece of light in a world full of dark. But I'm not here for that. "I'm sure you're mistaken," I whisper.

"Even you aren't that naïve," she says. "You should consider yourself lucky. Most of us don't get the attention of someone that good for even a moment. But I'm asking you to keep your distance. For his sake."

"What about you? I haven't missed the way you look at him."

She's quiet for a long time. "He's not for me any more than

he's for you. The difference between us is that I've made my peace with that."

I pull the ring from the pocket in my undergarments and roll it between my finger and thumb, losing myself in thoughts of Kendrick while I wait for her to fall asleep. She's wrong. Of course she's wrong. I have to believe it. Because it's not like Kendrick wanting me would change anything. I still can't have him. And even if I could, when this is all over, he'll have to go home. To Elora. And I'll be gone.

Only when I hear the buzz of Skylar's soft snore do I slip on my ring and climb down from the top bunk.

"Where are you going?" Skylar asks, immediately alert.

"Nowhere. I'm still in bed, sleeping. You're dreaming. Close your eyes."

She does as I command, and I grab my cloak off the back of the door and slip it over my sleeping gown before taking the key from the dresser and stepping out into the hall.

It's Natan who's standing outside our rooms, not Kendrick, and I shove down the tangle of emotion that tries to shove its way into my cold heart. I don't know if I'm disappointed or relieved, and I don't want to look at anything I'm feeling too closely. *Because it doesn't matter.*

Natan's eyes are bright as he looks me over. "I think I might love you," he whispers, pressing his palm to his chest.

I press my finger to my lips. "Shh. I have to go. You never saw me."

He nods. "Okay. May I come with you?" he asks, voice softer now.

"No. I need you to stay here and look out for your friends."

His eyes lose some of their luster, but he nods. He'd do anything for me. "If that's what you want."

"It is. I'll be back soon."

His gaze is fixed on my mouth. Sweet, studious Natan, fixated on the Enchanting Lady. "You promise?"

"I promise." I wink at him over my shoulder as I make my way to the stairs.

When I return to the tavern, it's empty. The rowdy group from earlier is gone. Their table is littered with dirty dishes and empty glasses, and the lanterns have been turned down low.

My stomach sinks.

I could go upstairs and search each room until I find the proprietor, maybe ask him some questions about their plans and where they're going, but I hoped to find out more tonight.

A clatter of dishes behind me pulls my attention away from the filthy table, and I follow the sound to the kitchen, where I see the proprietor's wife scrubbing floors on her hands and knees.

"Hello," I say sweetly.

"The kitchen is closed," she says. Her knuckles are raw from her work. My sister's hands used to look like that, and now they're soft and healthy. Maybe there's a better future for this female as well.

"Please look at me."

She obeys, sitting back on her heels and lifting her chin. The moment her eyes meet mine, she drops her rag and jumps to her feet. "I'm so sorry, milady. What can I do for you?"

"Your husband and his friends were eating in the dining room earlier. Have they retired for the evening?"

"No, ma'am. They continue their revelry at High Captain Vauril's manor house. They will sleep there tonight and be on their way in the morning."

I tilt my head to the side in question. "High captain?"

She blushes. "He was named high captain of Mordeus's personal guard before the king was slain. His friends still use his title."

My gut clenches painfully at the sound of the false king's name. "I'm surprised the queen allowed him to keep his lands after everything."

"The queen doesn't know he lives, milady. She believes the compound is owned by his son and told the boy she doesn't believe in punishing children for the crimes of their parents. She's a merciful queen, perhaps too merciful for these lands, if you ask me."

She's twisting her hands at her waist, and I brush my fingers over them. "You're hurting yourself," I whisper.

"Nervous habit, milady," she says, but she stops and tucks her hands into her pockets. "Please tell me what I can do for you. I am a talented cook. May I prepare you some food? Or perhaps you'd like a foot rub? Or a warm bath in our nicest room? I could have its occupant cleared out and have it cleaned for you within the hour."

"None of that will be necessary. Tell me, do you have somewhere to go? If something happened to your husband?"

She blinks. "My best friend is a widow. Her husband died in the war and left her and her children a house. She's invited me to live with her. I wish I could, but as long as my husband needs me, I cannot leave." She drops her voice to such a low whisper I can barely hear it. "Sometimes I wish he would die in his stupid crusade against the queen so I could be free of him and his anger."

"I want that for you."

Her eyes fill with tears. "I don't deserve even such a kind thought from someone so lovely as you."

Sometimes I hate the ring and how fake these exchanges are. This female deserves true love and affection, not some magical substitute that she won't even remember tomorrow. I don't like manipulating those who deserve honesty, but if I must, I want them to benefit from it. "You deserve more and better," I tell her, putting all my will into the words. "And you'll need to remember that if you wish to find it."

"As you wish, milady."

"Now, tell me where I can find this High Captain Vauril's manor house."

The night is dark with very little moon, and the only light cast onto the small village road comes from the few houses that still have lanterns burning on their front stoop. Even with the ring on, the darkness bothers me tonight. Maybe it's the talk of Mordeus or maybe it's just the long day catching up with me, but fear creeps through my veins where the Enchanting Lady's ice should be, and by the time I arrive at the high captain's manor house, I'm grateful for the torches he has lining his gate.

The house has the look of a property that was lush in the

recent past but has since been neglected. The gardens are over-grown and need tending. The gate is broken in several places, and the paint is chipping on the exterior.

Getting past the guards at the gate and the front door is as easy as expected. Even easier is finding the group from the tavern. They're gathered around a battered wooden table on the main floor, and the tavern's proprietor is standing on a chair.

"I remember a time when being Unseelie was a badge of honor," he shouts.

"Hear! Hear!" his comrades cheer, raising their glasses.

"We didn't ally with the Seelie Court," he continues, "we plotted their downfall!"

"Those were the days!" a horned female sings from the corner.

A fork-tongued orc grunts. "Some of us never stopped."

The proprietor grins down at his audience. "We should go to the palace tonight. Kill her in her sleep. Mordeus has risen. Why wait for a full army when the gods are on our side?"

"You're drunk!" the horned female says.

"That's a death wish," another shouts.

"You don't think I could do it? I could. I used to work for Mordeus. I know all the palace's secrets. I could get in there without anyone knowing and have her blood on my hands before she could cry for her trash human mother."

That gets a laugh, but I've heard enough and emerge from the shadows.

The first night I found my way among Mordeus's followers, I hated every second. I hated walking among them, breathing the same air as them. I hated listening to their carefree laughter

131

mixing with joyous, boisterous music. How *dare* they be so happy when their souls were so stained? How dare they have so much when they've stolen from those who have nothing?

But I quickly learned to relish it. Learned to associate stepping into their strongholds with the satisfying final gasp of death. Tonight, I don't even have to fake my smile. I don't have to fake the thrill in my eyes as I direct the full power of my attention right at the drunken fool who would love nothing more than to plunge an iron blade into my sister's heart.

He sees me and straightens. "Well, hello."

"Hello." I smile as his eyes go glossy.

His entire table leans longingly toward me, and the female from the corner moves in my direction, but I keep all my attention focused on their drunken, ranting, wife-beating leader.

"Would you take me upstairs? Somewhere quiet, perhaps?"

He hops down from his chair, stumbling over his own feet before righting himself, then comes toward me. "It would be my absolute honor, milady." His pretty words are punctuated with a hiccup.

One of his friends jumps up from his chair and grabs his arm. "You should stay here. You have a wife. I'll take the lovely lady wherever she wants."

The proprietor yanks free. "She asked for me." He turns to meet my eyes again.

I pretend not to notice that he's shaking with nerves and glee. When he offers me his arm, I take it, letting him lead me to the stairs.

The second floor is darker than the first, and again my old

fears clutch at my heart and drive me to check to make sure my ring is in place. I'll finish this quickly. I don't want to linger near this male with his evil plans and his stink of ale and hatred.

"Where would you like to go?" he asks at the top of the stairs. He reaches out and opens a bedroom door. "There's privacy here. Does this suit milady?"

"Indeed." I step inside, turning toward him when he's only just beyond the threshold. "Kiss me."

"Yes." He bends toward me and brushes his lips against my smile.

I don't bother catching his body as it falls to the floor or hiding the satisfaction I feel as I saunter out of the room. Perhaps I should feel remorse. Maybe once I would have. But I don't. My sister will be safe. The male's young wife will be safe. This realm is better without him.

I return to the hall and pull the hood of my cloak back on as I move toward the stairs.

Voices in a room beyond the stairs make me hesitate, and I step into the shadows to listen.

"Our king is weak," a deep voice says. "He needs time before he can address the crowds."

"No one will believe Mordeus lives without seeing his face."

My cold heart skips a beat. I don't want to believe it's true—or maybe I pray it is. I'm not sure how I feel, but the more people speak of it, the harder it is to deny.

"Then they aren't true followers. Did he not promise us a better future? Did he not promise us a world where we can use our power as we were born to?"

"Yes, but—"

"So they wait. He will see them when he's ready."

"Of course."

"In the meantime, sober up those fools. That is no army fit for a king."

"Agreed, my lord. Do we have any word from our people in the capital?"

"Not yet, but we will soon. The king belongs in the Midnight Palace, and I won't have that bitch in the way when my king is ready."

Protective rage washes over me. I could go out in that corridor and end them both now.

"Perhaps Winstom was right. Perhaps we should strike sooner rather than—"

"Patience. Our king will make it so in his time."

I've heard enough, but I've only taken a step toward the stairs when rough fingers drag me into a dark room, and I find myself wrapped against a warm, hard chest.

"What do you think you're doing?" an angry voice growls against my ear.

"Release me," I sing, letting the seductive power of the ring honey my tone.

"First you tell me what you're doing here."

Even if I could turn around, it's too dark in here to see his face, but I know Kendrick's husky voice better than I know most anything. I know it as the only part of those nights locked in the darkness worth remembering.

"Jasalyn, answer me."

I jerk around at the sound of my name, taking only a moment to confirm with a swipe of my thumb that my ring is in place.

The magic of the ring makes people obey me. Those around me are hypnotized by my presence.

He must not be able to see me. I tug, but his hold on me is too strong.

"Release me," I repeat.

"Gods, it really is you. You really are this foolish." Then the heat of him is gone, and he's swinging the door shut and leading me into an attached room, where candlelight flickers on the wall. For the first time, I can see his face, and more importantly, now he can see mine.

"Kendrick."

His gaze rakes over me and his nostrils flare. Does he see the mystical, seductive aura of the ring or does he see me? There's no sign of that magical awe in his eyes. But if he sees me, then *how*?

"What are you doing here in your gods-damned *nightgown*?"

I lift my chin. "I could ask you the same."

"I'm here because the faeries downstairs who fancy themselves rebels know more about the plans and locations of Mordeus's followers than we do, and we need that information if the sword isn't at Feegus Keep. But, unlike you, I was wise enough to wear gods-damned clothes."

"I didn't think I'd be leaving the tavern." I shrug. "My plans changed."

"Why aren't you in bed? How did you get past Skylar? And why the hell did Natan let you leave?"

"Maybe I'm stealthier than you realize."

"Do you know where you are?" He glances over his shoulder toward the door he closed behind us.

"Do I look stupid?" I ask.

His jaw hardens. "You ask me that when I find you lurking around a rebel hideout. The Unseelie princess in the home of the queen's greatest enemies. Given the context, I don't think you'd like my answer. I'll ask one more time. *Why* are you here?"

I shrug. "Revenge."

"Go home, Jasalyn."

"Home?" I cock my head to the side. "Where is that, exactly? The human realm of Elora where I was sent to recover from Mordeus's dungeons only to find myself ripped from bed in the middle of the night for a *different* evil fae's purposes? Or is home supposed to be that palace where my sister—my *faerie* sister—rules? The palace that serves as a daily reminder that I have the blood of those whom I hate most running through my veins? Or is home that tiny bunk bed in that moldy inn with your friends who would've left me chained in that cottage if they'd had a choice? Which *home* would you like me to go to?" I draw in a ragged breath. *Why* isn't my ring keeping me calm?

Kendrick doesn't look surprised by my outburst. He scans my face, and I wonder what he's searching for, wonder again why my ring isn't working.

"I'm sorry," he says softly. "About *all* of that. But you aren't safe here. The second someone recognizes you, they will take you, and they will use you to manipulate the queen. They will use you to bring down your sister. Is that what you want?"

"They won't recognize me. I'm spelled." I hold up the hand

with my ring, hoping it's still true even though the magic doesn't seem to be working on Kendrick.

"And if this spell fails?"

I try to bite my tongue but can't. "What do you see when you look at me?"

He shakes his head. "I see Jasalyn." He sweeps his gaze over me, assessing. "A more grown-up version of the girl who was kept in the cell across from mine in Mordeus's dungeons."

I bite my bottom lip. "But how?"

"Are you okay? I see you because you're standing in front of me."

Taking his hand, I lead him to the mirror that sits atop a dresser on the opposite side of the dimly lit room. "What do you see there?"

Sighing, he lifts his gaze to the mirror, then tenses. He turns to me before turning back to the mirror. "Who is that?"

The woman in the mirror has my long brown hair and my eyes. She's me but *not.*

Her hair is even darker. More sleek. Her cheekbones are sharper, and her lips are plump and a red that matches her dress. The woman in the mirror is sensuality and confidence personified. She has a knowing gleam in her eye that is the opposite of the scared little thing Kendrick found in Mordeus's dungeons. He gave me the nickname of Slayer because I *wasn't*, but she is.

"How did you do that?" He tears his gaze from the mirror to look at me. "Is this your magic? Some sort of mirror manipulation? Which one is the real you?"

"What you see in the mirror is what everyone else sees when

they look at me." I hold up my hand. "So long as I'm wearing this ring."

"Why is it different for me?"

"I don't know."

"Aren't you worried this magic will fail on someone else if it failed on me?"

"I'm not afraid."

"You should be."

I narrow my eyes. "How is it any safer for you to be around these people than it is for me?"

"I'm not the shadow princess, for one. They think I'm supporting their cause."

"And why shouldn't I believe that too?"

Something sharp flashes across his face—hurt? anger?—before he schools his features. He studies my face for a long time. I forgot how comforting it was to have those eyes on me. To have his sharp mind always looking out for me. "Because you know me," he finally says.

"It's been three years. People change. I've changed."

"You've hardened"—his knuckles sweep across my collarbone—"but that's just a protective shield." He presses his palm to my chest. "Your heart remains the same. As does mine."

I draw in a deep breath, sure he can feel the organ in question racing under his hand. "My heart does not rule me, and neither should yours."

The cacophony of the group downstairs pitches up as someone shouts. Chairs squeal, glass shatters, and there's a chorus of laughter and the pounding of several large males running up the stairs.

Then suddenly the door is pushed open and a stumbling male enters the room.

In a flash, Kendrick spins me around and presses me against the wall, hiding my body with his.

He bends and lowers his mouth to mine. Panicked, I push him away, but he won't be moved.

I slide my hand between our mouths at the last minute to keep his lips from touching mine.

"Sorryboutthat," a drunken male slurs, then the *thunk* of a door closing again is followed by Kendrick sagging against me and leaning his forehead against mine.

My stomach shimmies, then flips at the contact. He was my protector in the dungeons, but Skylar made it clear that anything romantic I feel for him can't be reciprocated. I won't make the mistake of thinking she could be wrong when I'm smart enough to know better.

"Promise me something," I say, slowly pulling my hand from his lips.

He swallows. "What's that?"

I close my eyes, trying to memorize the sound of his voice this close and the feel of his breath in my ear. "Promise me you won't kiss me." Maybe part of the ring's magic doesn't work on him, but I can't risk assuming that the rest doesn't. It's the second time I've warned him. I need to protect him when I'm wearing this ring, and I need to protect myself when I'm not. "Not ever."

He pulls back and straightens to his full height. "I—" He snaps his mouth shut and scrubs a hand over his face. "Yeah. Sorry. I was just trying to hide you."

"When I wear this ring, you don't need to hide me." I hope it's still true, but the fact that we're having this conversation is making me doubt the ring's magic more than even my fear of the dark did on the walk here.

"What is that ring? Why do you have it?"

"Like I said, revenge."

"You never told me how bad it was for you in there." Kendrick takes my hand—the one with the ring—and strokes his finger over the silver band before rubbing the moonstone under his thumb. "I wish you had. Promise me you'll never go out hunting like this again. I cannot stomach the possibility of you having to relive that hell."

I swallow. "That's a promise I can't make."

When he lifts his ice-blue eyes to mine, they're as hard as gemstones. "You *will*."

I lift my chin and glare up at him. "Don't treat me like a child."

"Then don't act like one. Stop with this recklessness."

"Not until Mordeus is dead again. Not until I've killed him myself."

He shakes his head. "We'll talk about this in the morning. Let's get out of here." He tugs me toward the back of the room. "There's a servants' entrance back here."

I let him lead me down the stairs and away from the manor, and when we return to the inn, Natan's still on watch outside our rooms.

"Look who I found at the high captain's house trying to get herself killed," Kendrick tells Natan.

"Oh no." Natan's eyes are wide with panic as he looks me over.

"Are you okay, Jasalyn? I hope you didn't get hurt."

"I'm fine," I assure him. "Kendrick is exaggerating."

"You want to tell me how she got past you?" Kendrick demands.

Natan frowns. "I don't . . . Did I do something wrong?"

Kendrick looks back and forth between us. I lift my hand and wiggle my fingers, reminding him of the ring. "We'll talk about this in the morning." He points to my door. "Sleep." He nudges Natan toward the other door. "You too. I'll take watch for a few hours."

Natan looks at me, waiting like a puppy hoping for some attention.

"I'll see you in the morning, Natan," I say, smiling. "Thank you for your help tonight."

His shoulders sag in relief. He pleased me, and that's all he wants.

We watch him slip into the room. When the door closes behind him, Kendrick frowns at me. "What did you do to my historian?"

"It's the ring. He'll be himself in the morning and won't remember any of this."

"Is that supposed to make me feel better?"

I shrug. "It's just information. It's up to you how you want to feel about it."

His gaze slips over me again. "You panicked when I almost kissed you. Is that about the ring too?"

I hesitate a beat. "Yeah."

"Care to explain?"

I hold his gaze. Can I explain that my magical ring gives me the kiss of death without sharing how I've been spending my nights for the last three months? "Ask me in the morning."

"Will *I* remember this in the morning?" he asks.

I turn the knob to my room, ready to step inside. "That's a good question. Only one way to find out."

CHAPTER TWELVE

◆

JASALYN

I TIGHTEN MY GRIP ON the Throne of Shadows and gaze out the windows and into the night beyond. The sky is dark and deep, stars glittering overhead, dancing around their crescent moon.

I should feel powerful. I should feel as mighty as the throne that rejects me. Mightier. But the crown isn't mine. I'm weak, and I cannot allow weakness.

"Does my king need anything else?" my servant asks, her dirty-blond hair falling forward and covering her human face as she bows her head. She's shaking. Shaking so intensely I feel myself smile.

I'm aware of the servants lining the opposite wall, aware that they watch my every move.

Fear. This is what I should inspire. Fear of mortals and fae alike. Because the throne should be mine. The crown should be mine.

"Indeed." I take her trembling hand and turn up her palm to study the soft, pink skin there. "You will bond yourself to me."

"I . . . I'm here to serve, my king." Her voice quavers. I relish the sound. The proof of my power. Relish the sight of her tears dripping onto the floor by her feet. "But, please, I do not wish to take the

bond. Let me serve you in another way."

She won't look at me, so she doesn't see it coming when I whip out my knife and plunge it through her hand.

Her scream echoes off the throne room walls, rattles the window.

I lift my gaze to the servants behind her. Men. Women. Some cowering, some watching me like the wildebeest watches the lion. I pull the blade from the girl's hand and blood gushes onto the floor. She clutches it to her chest and her light blue gown blooms with red.

"Anyone who denies me that which I ask will suffer."

I extend my blade again, but the girl scrambles away this time. Laughing, I hold her in place with my magic.

"Watch as I demonstrate what happens when you don't serve your king."

I slice the blade across her face, then plunge it into her eyes. I relish her howl of pain, the way her body surrenders, limp in the face of her powerlessness. I will take my time. I will show them all the consequences of denying me.

"Wake up, Princess. We need to get moving."

Gasping, I bolt upright in bed, breathing ragged, half expecting my sheets to be covered in the blood of the girl from my dreams.

Instead, I see Skylar, who's climbed halfway onto my bunk to shake me awake.

"Oh look, she lives." She drops to the floor and starts throwing things in her pack.

It was a nightmare. Just a nightmare.

I wrap my arms around myself and rub my clammy skin. I can still feel the knife in my hand, can still hear the girl's scream echoing in my ears, can still remember how much I loved her terror and her pain.

That's not you. It's just a nightmare.

I hate when I dream of Mordeus, but these dreams—when I *am* him, when I'm the one doling out the torture instead of the one receiving it—these are worse. *I liked it.*

I sometimes think it's a coping mechanism—that my mind is processing my trauma from another angle to make sense of it. But when I spoke with a healer at the Midnight Palace about the dreams, hoping she could make them stop, she suggested that these dreams were an early manifestation of my unique magic. I didn't ask again after that.

"Sorry to break it to you, Princess, but if you're waiting for me to serve you breakfast, you're going to be sorely disappointed," Skylar says.

A lantern flickers beside her, and my glowstone illuminates the space around my bed. I squint toward the tiny window at the end of my bed. "It's still dark outside."

She doesn't look away from her pack. "You're observant."

"Kendrick said we were leaving at first light."

"If we're going to leave at first light, we need to be ready *before* first light." She tosses a pile of clothes onto the bed. "For you."

I rub a hand over my face, trying to wake myself up. It feels like I just closed my eyes. I climbed into bed right after leaving Kendrick in the hall. That should've been enough sleep, but my eyes are fighting to stay closed. The only reason I can find the strength to stay awake is because I fear returning to that dream.

While Skylar has her back turned, I strip out of my sleep clothes and spot a new scar on my hip. It's thin and curved and plunges me into memories of silver eyes locked on mine, a blade piercing my skin. *Look at me, and I will take away the pain.*

I relish the sight of the scar, cling to the reminder that I was the victim, not the one inflicting the torture.

But you enjoy killing his followers. You relish the moment life leaves their eyes.

Bile surges in my throat, and I shove away the unwelcome train of thought as I pull on today's outfit. It's a near identical match to Skylar's long-sleeved crop top, but mine is golden to her black.

"Did you sneak out to see Kendrick last night?" she asks.

I freeze while folding my sleep clothes then clear my throat. "N-no. Why? Did he say something this morning?" Does he remember? I can't decide if I hope he does or doesn't. I need my ring to work, and if Kendrick is immune to its powers, who's to say others might not be? But maybe part of me doesn't want to carry the secret alone anymore.

"He didn't say a word," Skylar says. She turns to face me and shakes her head. "I don't know. I just feel like I was alone most of the night. It's an instinct."

"Nope. Slept right up here. You can ask Natan."

She furrows her brow, frowning as if she knows I dodged her question.

I'm climbing out of bed when a soft knock comes at the door.

Skylar cracks it open, and I know by her smile that Kendrick is waiting on the other side.

"Your princess wanted to sleep all day," she says.

I'd argue for the sake of my pride, but my yawn undercuts my retort before I can make it. I lean against the bedpost, letting it support my weight. Even my head feels too heavy this morning, and I just want to close my eyes for a few more minutes.

"Rough night?"

I force my eyes open and am treated to Kendrick's smiling face. He's so handsome with those clear blue eyes. And his smile makes warmth—

I straighten and clear my throat. "Just not feeling myself this morning." Instead, I'm feeling like a wicked king. I'm feeling like the male I'm determined to kill.

"She's used to the pampered life," Skylar says.

I don't bother arguing. Maybe she's right. Maybe I've gone soft in the last few years.

Kendrick is studying me, though, and there's nothing in his expression to indicate he agrees with her. I'm not sure I deserve the respect I see in his eyes. "Yesterday was a lot—physically and otherwise. You're okay?"

"I'll be fine. Just a slow start this morning." I bite back another yawn. "Any chance there's coffee?"

"There's no one working the kitchen downstairs this morning for some reason," he says. "We'll stop somewhere in a couple of hours."

Skylar grumbles something about the cruelty of waking before the sun and being deprived of coffee, and I can't disagree.

While Skylar heads into the hall to talk with Remme and Natan, I motion for Kendrick to stay back.

"Everything okay?" he asks.

I swallow. "About last night . . ."

He shakes his head. "Don't worry about it. I know seeing Mordeus's supporters is going to upset you, and I wasn't about to make you finish your dinner when you were uncomfortable. I just hope you're not too hungry this morning."

"That's not what I was talking about."

He folds his arms, frowning. "Is this about the Elora Seven?"

He doesn't remember. "No . . . I mean, I'm still thinking about all that."

He nods slowly. "Well, you're still here, so I'm taking that as a good sign." He grins. "Anyway, we have the oracle on our side."

"Yes, but . . ." Maybe I shouldn't push the issue, but he was so unaffected by the ring, I need to be sure. "Did you go somewhere last night?"

He waves this away. "I needed to see if I could get any decent intel from those guys we saw in the dining room, so I pretended I wanted to join their cause and followed them to a captain's manor down the road."

"Did you see anything interesting while you were there?"

He shrugs. "Just the usual rebel machismo."

My heart twists. It shouldn't matter. I should be glad my ring works, glad my secret is still a secret and the magic is still intact.

"Oh, before I forget." He pulls a vial from his pocket and tosses it toward me. "You'll need to re-up your glamour before you leave the room this morning."

Frowning, I glance toward the door. How is it that they all

already have their pointed ears and ethereal fae glow? "Did Skylar take hers while I was sleeping?"

"Nah, we've been at this for a while. We can handle bigger doses, so we don't need to take it as often."

"Oh." I fight my frown but can't help it.

He laughs. "What's that look for? Jealous that we get to chug *more* of that sludge than you?"

"It's not that." I shrug and study his ears, then his light blue eyes, which glow even in his human form but more so when he's glamoured. "I was just looking forward to seeing you as your human self each morning, I guess."

His face goes serious. "You really do hate the fae, don't you?"

"I feel like we've covered this."

"Time is running out for you to deal with it. You hit your eighteenth birthday without coming to terms with—"

"I should pack up." I shove him out of the room, close the door behind him, and sink to the floor. Exhausted on every level.

We weren't on the road by first light, and it was mostly my fault. It took me longer than I expected to load my pack, and by the time I reached the stables, the sun had already crested the horizon.

Now we're finally riding, but we don't make it past the high captain's manor house before Remme lifts a hand, indicating we should all slow down.

Then I see why. There are uniformed sentinels ahead, blocking the road. Beyond them, several children cling to their mothers' legs, crying.

"What's going on?" I ask, straightening in the saddle and trying to see what the guards are blocking.

Remme falls back, and Kendrick draws our mare beside his friend's while one sentinel breaks rank to approach us.

Kendrick flattens a rough hand against my bare stomach, and I suppress a shiver. "Let us do the talking, okay?" he murmurs in my ear. "Those are palace uniforms, and the last thing we need is them recognizing the princess's voice."

I nod. He doesn't move his hand. Instead, he pulls me closer, as if he's afraid this guard might try to snatch me away.

"Can't let anyone ride this way through the village," the guard says. "You'll have to go around."

"What seems to be the problem?" Kendrick asks. "You're a long way from the Midnight Palace."

"Her Majesty, Queen Abriella, has charged my squadron with investigating the mysterious deaths plaguing the court. This village is, sadly, the most recently afflicted."

"I'm sorry to hear that," Kendrick says solemnly.

"How can we trust her to find the cause when she may be behind this?" a horned male calls from behind the guards.

"She sent her guard," a tall female beside him says. "What else do you want?"

"She could be doing more!" the horned male protests. "How do we know the queen isn't using the faceless plague to kill off her enemies? It was no secret that my brother and sister were no fans of the queen, and now look at 'em."

The child clinging to his leg whimpers. "I want my daddy."

"How many are among the dead?" Skylar asks.

"I'm not at liberty to reveal details at this time, milady. If you're concerned for your family, I recommend you contact them personally to make sure they're safe. We're advising everyone stay in at night. The curfew is voluntary for now, but ignoring it is hardly worth the potential consequence."

"Thank you, sir," Skylar says.

He bows his head before returning to his post.

"It's getting worse," Natan says. "If the queen has this many of her own guard in this location, it *has* to be getting worse."

"All the more reason to move quickly," Skylar says.

Frowning, I look back and forth between Kendrick's friends. "Why do you all care about someone killing fae? And what do you know about it?"

"Not enough," Natan says, turning his horse around. He leads this time, and Kendrick and I follow with Remme and Skylar at our back.

"It's all connected," Kendrick says when we're moving again. "Whether we want to care or not, ties were made between this realm and our own ages ago. Our priority is Elora, but trying to correct the problems there without digging into what's happening here is like trying to tend to a sick child while continuing to give him rotten food."

"I hadn't thought of it like that," I say.

His arm tightens around my waist again, in a brief squeeze that feels equal parts comforting and protective. "That's because they don't want you to."

"My sister isn't behind these deaths," I say, my eyes straight ahead but looking at nothing. "If she was killing traitors, she would own up to it."

"I didn't think she was," Kendrick says, nudging our horse to pick up speed.

But why would that male even suspect my sister? "Stop." I

don't realize I'm speaking until the word's out of my mouth. A command even Natan hears. His eyes are wide as he looks toward us over his shoulder.

"We should get going," Kendrick says in my ear, his words only for me. "The last thing we need is palace guards looking too closely at you."

My sister has hundreds in her guard. None of those stationed inside the palace or assigned to my personal protection would ever be sent here. "Please?"

I twist in the saddle to get a look behind us just as a sentinel steps to the side to speak to another member of his team. My eyes land on the bodies beyond him and my stomach plummets. I recognize those clothes—the brown pants and olive vests, and the crescent moon tattoos. *The insurgents from the captain's house.*

I shake my head. "No." I took care of the proprietor and went back to the inn with Kendrick. I only killed the one, then I slept the rest of the night. *Only the one.*

And then dreamed of violence all night.

A guard notices us lingering, narrows his eyes, and steps forward. "Is there a problem?"

"Is it contagious?" Skylar asks, her tone so convincing I'm not sure if she's sincerely worried or just covering for me. "We ate dinner next to them last night."

I close my eyes and count my breaths the way one of my tutors at the Midnight Palace taught me. Their voices fade into the background as I breathe in for seven, hold for seven, exhale for seven. Breathe in for seven, hold for seven . . .

I don't open my eyes when we start riding or register the

conversation around me when I hear my travel companions discussing the route for the day. I just breathe with my eyes closed and clear my mind of everything else.

When I'm calm enough to look around again, we're riding right into the morning sun and Kendrick's arm is tight around my waist.

He loosens his grip at my deep breath. "Are you okay?"

"Yes. Sorry." *All those fae are dead. All those fae are dead, and there's no sign of blood or brutality. Just death. Just like when the Enchanting Lady visits. And I don't remember touching any of them.*

"I'll admit," Kendrick says, "it spooked me too—seeing death on their faces now when I was with them so few hours ago—but I'm fine. You don't need to worry about me."

I shake my head and try to focus on my surroundings—the low mountains in the distance, the trees on either side of this gravel road, the smell of crisp autumn leaves—pushing my mind to latch on to anything but the pale faces of those dead fae rebels.

"What do we know about this so-called plague?" I ask after we've ridden in silence for a long while.

"Not a lot," Kendrick says. "Enough to be cautious."

I squeeze my eyes shut and see that little girl clutching her uncle's leg. *I want my daddy.*

"I won't let anything happen to you, Slayer. The Mother has bigger plans for both of us."

I press my hand to my chest and feel the lump of the ring beneath my fingertips. "I'm not worried about that."

"Then what is it?"

"The ones we saw today were insurgents. Do we know if the others affected were too?"

"It's impossible to know. Unlike the idiots we encountered last night, most of Mordeus's loyal followers don't advertise their allegiance to a dead king."

I glance over my shoulder and meet Kendrick's eyes. "Dead? You don't believe the rumors, then?"

He grimaces. "I don't think it's impossible, just improbable. It's more likely that someone has something to gain from making Mordeus's followers believe he's been resurrected, and they started the rumor and are using it to their advantage."

"*You* have something to gain. That's how we're going to find this sword, right? Follow the path to Mordeus?"

"Indeed, but if I'm right and he's not really back, I suspect there's someone pretending to be him."

"Like a shifter?"

"A very good shifter," he says. "And, whoever he is, he'd be using his position to gather all of Mordeus's resources."

When I heard those males talking last night, I was sure Mordeus was back, but Kendrick's theory has me questioning again. Conflicting emotions twist inside me—relief that the male I fear most might still be dead, and regret that I won't get the only revenge that might heal this gaping hole in my chest.

Kendrick glances over his shoulder. "Natan! What can you tell us about the faceless plague?"

"What do you want to know?"

"Are Mordeus's followers falling more than others?" Kendrick asks.

Natan rubs the back of his neck. "I don't know, but I can find out for you. I'll ask Shae when we see him tonight. If he doesn't know, he'll know who to ask."

"Thank you," I say softly. I try to shift my thoughts to something else but can't. "I just don't understand it. They all seemed perfectly healthy last night."

"Are you so unhappy that their lives were cut short?" Kendrick asks.

"No, but . . ." I chew on my lip for a beat, trying to understand my own feelings on this. "The dungeons left me hard, taught me to hate like I never had before. In some ways, that makes me stronger, but I don't want to be someone who wishes death on swaths of my enemies." *I don't want to be someone who relishes torture and death and power. I don't want to be* him. "Perhaps the realm is better without them, and perhaps my sister's claim on the throne is more secure but . . ." *But I'm afraid of what their deaths might mean. I'm afraid of who I'm becoming with this ring and even more afraid of giving it up.*

"I won't judge you for having complicated feelings about it, Jas," Kendrick says, "if that's what you're worried about."

I bite the inside of my cheek until the pain makes the image of those bodies fade from my mind. "I don't know what I fear more. Being the naïve child I was before Mordeus destroyed that part of me or being so cold and callous that I never again see the humanity of my enemies."

Or maybe my fear is that I've already become the second— that I don't need the ring to be cold and callous, but that I already was. Mordeus changed something intrinsic in me during my

155

weeks in his dungeon, or I never would've sought out the ring to begin with.

"Humanity would imply they're human," Kendrick says softly.

"They had families. They had people who loved them. It's easy to forget that when they're drunkards raging against the queen."

"Maybe there's a little of both in all of us—naïve child and callous enemy," he says, fingers stroking along my bare side in comforting circles. "And maybe the key is in never losing sight of either. We can have mercy without being naïve, and we can be judicious while seeing our enemies as whole people."

I focus on the pleasant cadence of our horses' footfalls. "Do you ever worry that you tell yourself that you're those things—that you've struck the balance—but you're really fooling yourself? Do you ever worry that, at the end of the day, you're no better than them?"

"Yes," he rasps. He buries his nose in my hair and breathes in, as if my scent is the cleansing tonic he needs. "And I cling to that worry because it's exactly what separates us from them. The world isn't black and white, and when we fight evil, when we work for the common good, sometimes we find ourselves doing things that feel too much like the acts of our enemies. I wish it weren't so, but I find it's more often true than not."

"If we have to act like them, then how do we keep from becoming them?"

"We remember who we are and what we're fighting for. We put our cause before ourselves."

"Remind me what our cause is again?"

His chuckle is dry, as if he's not so much amused as trying to lift my spirits. "Elora. The future of Elora and the end of the ugliness and inequities there."

I nod, and for the first time, I realize maybe I need to care about this mission Kendrick's brought me on. Maybe the best thing I can do is make it my own, so I don't become like the faeries in Mordeus's dungeons. So I don't become the very thing I've traded my immortal life and every day after my eighteenth birthday for the chance to hunt.

CHAPTER THIRTEEN

◇—————◇

FELICITY

SHE JERKS AWAKE TO A bright light coming into her cell. A knife clatters to the floor between her and Crissa.

"Who will get it first?" the guard singsongs. "Who will survive?"

Crissa jumps to her feet and stares at the knife. Her gaze darts to meet Jasalyn's and then back to the floor.

"Maybe you want me to throw one of the other prisoners in there with you," he says. "See if they want my gift."

"No." Crissa moves so fast Jas barely sees her, but then Crissa's standing a foot away from the bars, glaring at the guard with the knife clutched in her hand. "I should use this to gut you," she says.

His chuckle is a raspy wheeze. "I'd like to see you try."

Her grip tightens on the handle of the knife, her knuckles going white. Jas tries to make out the guard, but the light behind him is blinding, casting his face in shadow.

"Ever cut into another human, little girl?" the guard asks her. "Ever watch the pain contort their face?"

"You are disgusting." Crissa charges at him, blade out, poised to slide it between the bars and meet his chest, but she freezes a second before it makes contact.

"Look what a fun little gift my king has given me to play with," he says.

Crissa turns toward Jas, her movements so jerky and harsh Jas knows Crissa's no longer in control of her own body. Step after step, she lurches toward Jas, that blade pointed out.

Jas curls into the corner, but there's no point. She's been here long enough to know there's no use fighting.

"Relax," the guard says, and he makes Crissa drop to her knees. Tears stream down her face. "All I want is for you to draw her a pretty picture."

There's so much terror in her eyes. So much fear.

"It's not your fault," Jas whispers. Then Jas can't say anything at all because she's frozen. Forced to watch as the guard guides the blade to pierce the flesh of her wrist.

"That's right," he says. "Make a pretty circle."

When I imagined living as a princess in the Wild Fae castle, I never thought that would include the king pounding on my door at dawn and dragging me out of bed before I'd wiped the sleep from my eyes.

Yet here we are.

As exhausted as I am, I'm not sorry to have been pulled from the dream that delivered Jas's memory. The horror of those moments hangs over me like a heavy blanket on this unseasonably hot morning.

The training yard at Castle Craige is positioned at the back of the castle, on a smooth stretch of rock that juts out from the mountain. It's sparse, the dusty earth clear but for a few piles of spears and training rods and a collection of neatly organized bows. We're alone here, and I wonder if Misha's sentinels train elsewhere or if he intentionally chose this hour to spare me from curious eyes.

Misha pulls his sword from his scabbard and tosses it to me. I catch it on instinct and then shoot him a glare.

He chuckles, and between the smile and the tight black shirt straining against his chest and biceps, his hair tied back, my mouth goes a little dry.

I'm staring again.

I make myself shift my attention to the sword, and the sight of the blade sends my mind back to Jas's memory. My stomach turns.

"You will never command a weapon you fear," Misha says, watching me.

"I'm not afraid of it," I say, and I push the dream to a locked corner of my mind so I can focus.

I haven't held a blade since I left home. Haven't wanted to, given the reason I ran in the first place. No doubt I should have. At twelve, I could spar with the best in my village, but right now my hands feel awkward even gripping the hilt. The fact that I'm in Jasalyn's form doesn't help. Her thin frame isn't built for sword-play, and her hands are small and delicate.

"Has your sister taught you *nothing*?" Misha asks as I fumble with my grip.

I narrow my eyes. "The queen is too kind to drag me out of bed before the sun."

"And what about all the other hours of the day?" he asks. "You act like you've never held a sword before."

"I train." I lift my chin. No wonder the princess has a chip on her shoulder. They all underestimate her. "I can defend myself."

"The weight of that sword could knock you over if a heavy breeze blew in. You should've been spending the last three years putting some muscle on that frame."

"I'm not in training beyond what is required of me." From everything I gathered during my short conversation with Jasalyn, she wasn't interested in anything but being left alone.

"Well, interested or not, you will train while you're here."

"Why?" I'm careful to keep my tone annoyed and aloof. Jasalyn isn't a whiny child. She's a wounded bird.

"Self-defense?"

"Isn't that why I have guards?"

"And what if your guards turn on you?" Misha steps closer. "What if they're enemies who've infiltrated the ranks of the palace guard to get to you?" He looks down his nose at me, and my heart beats faster. My breathing turns shallow. "Or what if your guards are killed? Or what if you're ambushed and they can't get to you?"

In one swift movement, he knocks the blade from my hand, spins me around, and traps me against him, my back to his chest, my arms pinned to my sides.

Ass.

"You are in such utter denial of your weaknesses," he says, "while simultaneously refusing to acknowledge that you become fae in nine short months."

"I get it," I say through gritted teeth, far too aware of the heat and solid strength of him against my back. I can't *think* when this male is close to me.

"Do you?" he asks, his breath hot in my ear. "I'm not convinced you grasp how serious this is."

"How serious *what* is? Hiding in your fancy castle?"

"You're *mortal*," he growls, tightening his hold on me.

I lodge an elbow into his rock-hard stomach, sidestep, and spin, but I know I only get out of his arms because he lets me. "Don't judge me based on how I grip a hilt intended for your meaty beast paws," I snap.

"These?" He scoffs and holds up a hand, splaying his fingers wide. "You have a problem with my hands? Funny. You'd be the first female who's complained."

Heat rushes to my cheeks. I've gotten this all wrong. I mentally curse myself for failing to use the gifts at my disposal.

Relationships have an energy, and Echoes are gifted to be in tune with it. While the gift often feels like an invasion of privacy, I'd be lost without it right now. Jas never would've been able to describe this side of Misha to me.

Misha isn't just a friend of the shadow queen who *knows* the princess. He cares for the princess. Deeply. Feels responsible for her, even.

Jasalyn didn't say anything about that when she told me about him, and I wonder what else she missed—if the way he's looking at me right now speaks to another kind of feelings entirely. Is he romantically interested in the princess?

Someone behind me clears his throat, and Misha retreats like he's been caught with his hand in the cookie jar.

I turn to see a dark-skinned male with short black dreadlocks and a curious cocked brow.

"Lucky for you, Tynan has agreed to help with your training," Misha says. "Tynan, you remember Jas."

Tynan gives me a polite smile and a nod. Like his king, he has silver webbing across his forehead, but unlike his king, he doesn't seem keen to run his mouth. How well do he and Jas know each other? He might remember her, but she didn't mention him to me, and none of the handful of Jas's memories I have include him.

"Tynan will show you some drills," Misha says.

"And what about you?" I ask before I can stop myself.

"Did you want me to stick around so you can insult my hands some more?" He winks, then nods to a pair of fae males emerging from the castle. "I have my own training to do, but I'll be close if you need me."

"Thanks," I say awkwardly, then tell myself I'm not allowed to watch as he walks away. But I've always been better at breaking rules than following them, and I struggle to believe even someone as stoic as Jasalyn could resist that sight.

Tynan clears his throat, and I pull my gaze off the retreating king.

He has me warm up with calisthenics, then shows me the proper way to hold a sword when—like with Misha's this morning—the hilt is too big. It comes back to me quickly, but I make sure to "forget" the footwork and hand positions a few times so it doesn't appear I'm learning too quickly or am too skilled for a princess who only did minimal training.

While we work, I'm vaguely aware of King Misha doing drills with the pair of sentinels on the other side of the courtyard. I like the way he laughs with them, like he's one of them. And when they speak—telling him of goings-on in the village—he listens, more like a friend than their superior.

As if sensing my thoughts and trying to test my determination to ignore my attraction to him, Misha has shed his shirt at some point, exposing a broad chest coated in a thin sheen of sweat. He's so tall and built that no one would mistake him for thin or lanky, but shirtless, his strength and muscle mass are all the more evident.

Crushing on the king will not help you find the Hall of Doors.

As soon as I think it, I hear Hale's voice in my mind, telling me that the best way to the Hall is through Misha's heart, but my crush hardly equates to him trusting me.

I need to focus on the matter at hand. I pull my attention back to Tynan.

He's watching with that curious cocked brow again.

"What?" I ask, but my cheeks are already on fire.

He shakes his head. "It's not my business."

"You can ask anyway." Because if I'm completely screwing this up, I should know now.

Tynan hands me a towel, his gaze jumping to me, then Misha. "I'm just wondering what's changed between you and Misha."

"Nothing's changed. What do you mean by that?"

He shakes his head again. "It's not my place."

I want to push more, but I bite my lip. Obviously, there's a tension between Misha and me that wasn't there between Misha and the real Jas. That never should've been an issue. I'm letting my personal attraction get in the way, and it could ruin everything.

"Drink lots of water today," Tynan is saying, "and make sure you eat a good breakfast. Once we get some meat on those bones, you'll take to the training much faster. You have a natural talent."

"I was thinking the same thing," Misha says, wandering over flanked by his training partners. He grabs a towel and wipes the sweat from his chest.

I drop my gaze to the ground.

"Speaking of which," Misha says. "Breakfast will be served in an hour on the dining terrace."

I don't lift my eyes from the dirt, too afraid I'll stare. "I'll take my breakfast in my room, thank you," I say. *Be Jas. Be distant.*

"Fine," he says, "Eat breakfast alone. But be ready to ride an hour after."

I snap my head up and find him staring at me, looking cocky as hell, like he just won this round of chess. "Why?"

"Your sister needs me to make a queen of you," Misha says. "And a queen doesn't hide in her rooms while her court is in peril. She goes out and finds answers." He flashes me a quick, completely fake smile and then strides from the training yard and back into the castle.

Two hours later, Misha bursts into my chambers without bothering to announce himself. "We have a change of plans and won't be leaving until after lunch."

I frown at him. "Please, come in. Make yourself at home."

He grins, those russet eyes full of wicked amusement. "I *am* home."

"I could have been undressed," I mutter.

"Disappointed by the missed opportunity?" he asks. I gape at him, and he grunts. "I saw your handmaid in the hall. She told me you were ready. Calm down."

"Next time just send the message with her."

"And miss these moments in your delightful company?"

Misha is just Misha, Jas said. *He's my sister's best friend,* she said. Nothing about this constant flirtation, playful irritation, whatever. How can Jasalyn speak of him as if he's just another member of the fae royalty whom she can't be bothered with? He's *magnetic.* Anytime he's near, I find myself staring or fighting or wanting him to tell me exactly what he's thinking.

I give him my back and fix my braid in the mirror.

"We'll have to travel by horseback," he says. "It's not an easy ride into the mountains, but the exercise and fresh air will be good for you."

"Where are we going, exactly?"

"I told you. We're looking for answers."

I finish tying off my braid and fold my arms. "Are your responses always so oblique?"

Misha mimics my pose, rocking back on his heels. "Don't you want to know if the rumors are true? If Mordeus lives?"

I draw in a ragged breath.

"That's what I thought."

"How . . ." I lick my lips, trying not to seem too eager. "Where will you get these answers?"

"Unlike your sister's court, mine hasn't been embroiled in wars for centuries, which means many of our wisest elders have

166

survived. Today, we see Gaelynn, Jewel of Peace."

"That's her name? Gaelynn, Jewel of Peace?"

His lips twitch. "Her name is Gaelynn. Her title is Jewel of Peace. You might understand the concept of titles if you attended to the duties of your position rather than just hiding in your rooms."

The criticism is a reminder of who I'm supposed to be, and I sigh heavily. "I still don't see why I have to go."

"I need you there," he says. He throws himself into an upholstered chair and taps out a beat on the arms. "You represent the Unseelie crown. I realize that might not matter to you now, but someday you *will* be expected to serve an active role as the shadow princess."

I drop my gaze to the floor. "My sister is the crown. I'm nothing more than a human girl who—"

"You won't be human for long, Jasalyn," he says softly. "And I know that's not what you want to hear, but it's past time that you prepare for that."

"Isn't that what we were doing this morning? With the training?"

"Training your physical body has nothing to do with your magic." He drums his fingers, as if it's difficult for him to be still. "I've asked Amira to meet with you tomorrow morning. Her gifts will help you access your powers—help bring out latent abilities."

"I don't have powers," I say tightly.

"That's my point. You *think* you don't, but there's no way you can be a child of Mab and be powerless—even in your human form. Work with Amira, see if she can draw it out of you."

That sounds dangerous. Pushing me to draw out my magic is only asking for trouble. If the former queen has a way of pulling out *my* true powers, I'll be exposed. "Leave it alone," I say. "*Please.*"

He shakes his head, but I can sense he's done pushing for now. "Eventually you're going to have to face the facts."

I swallow hard. I need to do whatever is necessary to keep Misha and his friends from poking around in my mind, and if that means exposing some of my own magic as if it's Princess Jasalyn's, then so be it. "There might be something."

Misha's head snaps toward me, eyes sharp. "What?"

"It's easier to show you than to describe." Jasalyn is going to have a lot of explaining to do when she can't duplicate this later, but I imagine this won't be the only thing she'll have to answer for.

The longer I'm here, the bigger mess she'll be left to clean up and the harder it will be for her to pretend she never left. If we're going to make it even a week in this ruse, I can't let that be my problem.

"Introduce me to someone you have any sort of connection with—anyone you know that I don't—and don't tell me who they are or how you know them."

He lifts his brows, curious, then walks to the door. My shoulders sag in relief until he turns back to me.

"Aren't you coming?"

"What—now?"

His lips twitch. "Now, Jasalyn."

Misha leads me up to the third floor to a gorgeous circular library. The walls are lined with books while the glass ceiling floods the space with natural light. Spaces for working and lounging are located throughout the massive room, and I can imagine spending days here curled up in a cozy chair and losing myself in book after book.

I don't get to spend much time taking in the space before Misha is ushering me over to a young, pale-skinned female who is slight of frame with one of those ever-present smiles.

"Good morning." She bows her head to her king and curtsies quickly, her cheeks turning pink.

I hold back a groan. If she has a crush on him, he's never going to believe this ability is magical, and his former queen will be rooting around in my head tomorrow. I imagine most of the females who spend any amount of time around their king have a crush on him at some level.

"Good morning," I say. "I'm Jasalyn."

"*Princess* Jasalyn," Misha corrects, and I shoot him a glare because the real princess would find the correction tiresome.

"What's your name?" I ask her.

"Blake, Your Highness."

"Blake, would you mind having a short conversation with King Misha—about something trivial, if possible." I step back, as if to make physical room for their conversation.

She wrinkles her brow. "Am I in trouble for something?"

"Not at all," Misha says. "The princess wants to show me a skill she has, and to illustrate it, she needs to see us speak with each other."

Blake's face lights up. "Oh. My aunt's new husband's grandson can predict future loyalty based on a short conversation between two people. Is it like that?"

"Nothing so useful, I'm afraid," I say, smiling. I like her. And I like what she feels for her king. *Not* a crush. Respect, honor, a pinch of friendship that she's a little unsure about. And Misha . . .

"Maybe you should just tell me what you have planned for the day," Misha suggests.

"My shift in the library ends in a few hours and then I'm going to enjoy the evening outside. The cold days are coming too soon."

"Unfortunately so," he says. "What do you like to do outside?"

He's grateful for her work—I can guess in his libraries from context. But there's something else there. A jealousy? No. Not jealousy.

"My husband, daughter, and I like to explore the forest behind our cottage. It's the same forest I grew up exploring, and I love that we can give her the same childhood." The pink in her cheeks deepens.

The tug is so hard and strong I feel it in my own gut. *Family.*

"There's no gift quite like the one the Mother gives us every day," she adds quietly.

"Agreed. And no forest in the realm as beautiful as those in our court," Misha says.

"I'll have to take your word for it," she says on a laugh. "I've never left these lands. I've never wanted to travel when the other courts seem to be steeped in so much turmoil."

"Can't blame you there," he says, chuckling.

"No offense, Your Highness," she says, ducking her head toward me.

I paste on a polite smile. "None taken."

"Do you need more?" Misha asks me. "For whatever it is you want to show me?"

I shake my head. "No, that will do."

"Thank you, Blake," he tells her. "I will see you soon."

"Don't be a stranger," she says. She nods at me, lowering her gaze. "Pleasure to meet you, Princess."

"You too," I say, and then Misha's leading me away from her and to a quiet corner of the library.

He gestures to an upholstered chair, and I take a seat, watching as he pours a cup of coffee. He hands the steaming cup to me without adding so much as a splash of cream or a teaspoon of sugar. "So?" he asks, lowering himself into the chair across from me.

I cradle the cup in my hands and silently curse Jasalyn for what she described as an unhealthy obsession with coffee. I hate the stuff, but obviously Misha's going to expect me to drink this. I take a sip, schooling my expression when the bitter liquid hits my tongue. "I'm surprised you allow coffee around all these books."

He arches a brow. "They're spelled. Protected from anything so trivial as a spill."

"Oh. How . . . convenient." I might have magic, but I spent the first sixteen years of my life in Elora where my kind of magic could've gotten me killed, so aside from shielding and learning how to use my skills as an Echo, I only used enough magic to make sure I knew how. The only place in Elora where magic is abundant enough to do things like spell a whole library is the Eloran Palace, and I've spent my entire life avoiding that place.

"You're stalling," Misha says, leaning back in his chair.

"Well, I'm not sure what I can share is helpful since anyone could see you two have a friendly relationship and respect each other."

"You're telling me you can pick up on the kind of relationship two people have?"

I set my cup down on the small glass side table. "I guess. If they're in the same room and interact in any way, I can sense how they feel for each other. I didn't think it was magic at first, just growing up and being more aware of the people around me."

Misha leans forward, hands on his knees. "But you think it's magic now. Otherwise you wouldn't have brought it up. You just don't *want* it to be magic."

I blow out a breath. I realized my gift wasn't just about observation the time a man came to my mother's house from the Eloran Palace and I knew she loathed him, despite the fact that everything she said and did was welcoming and kind. "Sometimes I feel like I know more than I should."

"Like an empath," he says.

I shake my head. "If I were an empath, wouldn't I know what you are feeling right now?"

"Not necessarily. Empathic gifts come in many forms."

He's right, and I know that, but Jasalyn wouldn't. Or if she did, she'd likely deny connecting her own gift to a known kind of magic. In truth, my gift is an empathic magic, but not one most are familiar with.

"Tell me what else you got out of that interaction with Blake. What else did you learn?"

"She respects you, as a king and a male." I clear my throat. "And sometimes she thinks you two might be friends, but she doesn't know what to do with that, given that she's just a scholar and you are her king."

"Fascinating." He props his ankle on the opposite knee. "What else? Give me something impressive, Jas."

I worry my lip between my teeth. "The worst thing about sensing the things I do is that it feels intrusive." The same is true for being an Echo in general. When I think of how the shadow queen would feel if she knew she'd spilled her fears and love to someone pretending to be her sister, my gut twists with guilt. "Those emotions aren't mine."

"But they can be helpful to know. And when they aren't, you can block them. I can teach you how."

I bite back a smile. Misha is incredibly skilled at mental magic and blocking, but my life has depended on my ability to block even the most gifted faerie from a young age. I could probably teach *him* a thing or two. "I suppose it can be helpful."

"Tell me what you just learned about me—what it is you feel guilty knowing."

I meet his eyes and hold his gaze. When he and the former queen first dissolved their marriage, the queen spoke freely about their decision, citing kings from Wild Fae history who had taken on second or even third wives when the first was unable to give them children. She was choosing to step down and make way for a new queen who might succeed in giving the king an heir. While the kings she spoke of had only dissolved their marriages once they found their new wife and Misha hasn't yet, the court seemed to accept this explanation. But now I wonder if it was truly about the child alone. Misha wants a family. He wants *love*.

It's a wonder to me that a male as good as Misha hasn't yet found romantic love. Even if it wasn't part of his marriage, I'm surprised he never found it with a lover outside the bounds of that political arrangement, surprised that he, like the kings before him, didn't have a lover waiting in the wings to step into the role of queen.

"What you feel when she speaks of her family—at first I thought it was jealousy," I say, "but it's not. You *envy* her. Her marriage, her child. You want a family, and while you think Blake deserves every moment with the family she built, she is a reminder of how much easier those things might've come to you without the burden of this crown—because no matter how much you try to hold hope for the future, no matter how brave you try to be, part of you will always remember the marriage your parents had and think that you are doomed to the same."

His face goes stoic and his throat bobs, but he holds my gaze. "You were in my mind? I didn't feel you . . ."

"No. Like I said—it becomes clear to me in the connection you have with someone else. I can't read thoughts."

"So even when someone is well shielded, you're saying that they can be exposed."

I've said too much. I've revealed too much. I shrug. "I don't know. Like I said, maybe it's not magic at all. Maybe it's just feeling out a room and using common sense."

"You don't believe that," he says softly. "You might wish you could, but you don't."

I tear my eyes from his and look at my hands.

"It's not so terrible," he says. "This life. Being fae and having magic. You haven't allowed yourself to see the good in it. I hope you'll allow me to show you."

In my periphery, I see him reach for me and drop his hand at the last second.

He stands, as if he is suddenly anxious to get away from me, from this conversation. "I'm sure Amira would still be happy to meet with you if you'd like. She'll be able to help you hone this gift."

"I'm not interested."

He's already walking away. "You might change your mind."

CHAPTER FOURTEEN

◊

FELICITY

THE RIDE THROUGH THE MOUNTAINS is incredible. I've lived in the shadow court since arriving in Faerie three years ago, and it is breathtaking, but the Wild Fae territory boasts a different kind of beauty. These people speak of nature as the Mother, speak of her as their deity, and it's as if nature blooms up around them to reward them for that devotion. Even as the leaves slip into their autumnal colors, the trees appear lush and full of life. Mums and late-blooming hydrangeas line the roadside as if every inch of the land here is groomed by an expert gardener.

Misha and I ride side by side, two of his sentinels following behind—not too close, but near enough to protect their king should someone use this as an opportunity to attack.

Misha's quiet on the ride. None of that flirtatious poking at me like he was doing before training or in my chambers this morning. I think I got to him when I revealed what I felt between him and Blake. I don't get the impression it's that he doesn't want me to know how he feels about the subject. Instead, I think it's those words he spoke later that have made him withdraw.

I hope you'll allow me to show you.

I could've written them off as the words of a male trying to help his best friend's sister. Or even as the courtesy of a kind host. But there was something about the way he reached for me after. Something about the way he retreated when he seemed to realize what he was doing.

I feel a pull toward Misha that I cannot deny—a pull I don't think has anything to do with the shadow princess. As much as I want to flatter myself by thinking he feels the same, any such whimsy must be tempered by reality. I am not Felicity right now. I am the king's best friend's little sister. I am the shadow princess. I am Jasalyn to him—both beautiful and an advantageous political match.

If Misha did happen to feel something for whatever bits of *me* have emerged in the last couple of days, there would be no way for him to disentangle those feelings from what he feels or felt for the real Jasalyn. And the truth is not something I have the luxury to share. It would ruin everything.

If the king does harbor feelings for me—for *her*—I need to use those feelings to my advantage. Hale's plan seemed ridiculous to me. Misha wouldn't share the location of the Hall of Doors with just any female he has feelings for . . . but perhaps if that female is the shadow queen's sister, perhaps if she's already so close to his inner circle, he might.

Now that I understand how much he longs for a partner—for someone he'd want to share the bond with—I hate the idea of manipulating that yearning for my own ends. Hate it so much that when he left me behind in the library, I asked Blake to point me toward references about portals and portal magic. One way or the other, I need to find the portal, but if I find it on my own, I might be able to live with myself when this is all over.

I might not have the kind of power to create a portal, but I know enough about them to understand that a portal leading to a series of other portals would have to affect the environment. By the time I'd gathered the books and dug into the first in the stack, my handmaid informed me that Misha was waiting at the stables.

"What are you thinking about so hard over there?" Misha asks.

I glance toward him and force a tentative smile. "I'm wondering who exactly lives out here?"

"Gaelynn, Jewel of Peace," he says, casting a glance my way. "Having issues with your memory today?"

"I mean how does she live out here when there's nothing else around? What does she eat? You said she's one of your elders, but does she still hunt for her own food? Who does she talk to? Does she do more than wait for someone to come seek her counsel? Does she guard the secrets of your court?"

According to the first book I found, very powerful portals can create a sort of magical vacuum, as happened in the Unseelie Court with a portal to the Underworld. In that case, the whole area became what is now known as the Silent Ridge, a mountainous area where the only magic that works is the portal itself. As a result, the fae avoid spending any significant amount of time in the area, and none live there.

The book said, however, that magical vacuums are rare, that often the most powerful portals simply give off an energy that dissuades people from lingering near them. These mountains are so remote that I can't help but wonder if we're coming onto something similar.

Misha chuckles. "So many questions."

I sigh. "Sorry. Never mind."

"No. It's good. Ask your questions." The incline turns steep, and Misha spurs his horse forward. "The Jewel has a group of priestesses who stay with her in her sanctuary. They provide her with anything she needs that magic can't supply."

I wait for him to answer the rest of my questions. Even if he denied the Jewel is guarding something, I would likely be able to detect the lie.

He flashes me a look over his shoulder. "Don't like being this far away from everything?"

I love it. I'm social by nature and prefer being around others, so I don't know that I'd want to be this isolated, but it might be worth it to see this kind of beauty every day. The leaves are changing, and every so often we reach a vista that allows us a view of the valley below—a stretch of green, yellow, russet, orange, and red dappled throughout the trees so they look like an artist's palette smudged together.

I hesitate before responding, measuring my words against what I think Jas would say. "Perhaps I envy her," I finally answer. "She doesn't have to worry about people bothering her when she just wants to be left alone."

He grunts. "Everyone has responsibilities, Princess. While they can seem heavy and burdensome, if you give it a try, you might find you're happier with the burden than without."

"Has anyone ever told you that it's egotistical to assume you know what's best for everyone?"

"No." He shifts to the side in his saddle, leaning toward me, and whispers, "They told me to be king."

I snort. "So pompous."

"Don't mistake wisdom for arrogance."

"And what makes you so wise?"

He laughs softly. "A very, *very* long life, for starters."

"In other words, you're old?"

He winks at me, then nods ahead. "There it is," he says, and I see it. Just barely peeking out of the trees ahead, a white stone steeple, softly glowing as if it might be made of clouds backlit by sunshine.

Misha spurs his horse on, as if anxious to get there now that we're close, and I hurry my horse to keep up, my breath catching as the full sanctuary comes into view. It's not overly large, but it is beautiful—all that glowing white stone, with the steeple in the center and two turrets on either side, the entire structure surrounded by fluffy white hydrangeas and fluttering butterflies.

A boy is waiting at the steps and when Misha dismounts, he hands the boy the reins to his horse before turning to me, arms lifted.

My heart races and feels too big for my chest at the thought of him helping me off my horse, so I ignore him as I imagine Jas might. I throw one leg over and lower myself down as gracefully as possible.

Misha scoffs behind me as my feet hit the ground. "Stubborn girl," he mutters, but I don't miss the note of pride in his voice.

I hand the reins to the boy, and I turn to Misha with a smirk.

"Not as helpless as you think."

"It's true you handled the ride better than I expected, though I imagine you'll be sore tomorrow."

I probably will. I'm more accustomed to time on horseback than the princess, but I imagine this body will feel that ride in the morning.

Misha extends a hand, indicating for me to lead the way up the steps. "I'm proud of you," he says, remaining by my side as we ascend. His voice is rough, as if these words are hard for him to say but they've been waiting in his throat the whole ride. "I'm not heartless. I want you to know that I am aware of what a mark Mordeus left on you, and under different circumstances, I would allow you to stay out of any information gathering regarding him."

I cut my gaze to him briefly before focusing on the steps again. He and Brie both say they know Mordeus made a mark on Jas, but from what I can tell, neither one of them has any idea how deep that mark goes, how dramatically her days in his dungeon made her lose faith in the world. In the fae. And worse, in herself.

We come upon the curved oak doorway, and I turn to him. "Different circumstances being what?" I ask.

"You've been hiding in your shell for too long, Jas." His eyes are full of sadness as they scan my face. "For a long time I wanted it for your sister—hoped you would wake up and break free of this darkness for her sake. Or for her court." He swallows hard. "But now I just want you to do it for yourself. To live again, for yourself."

My heart twists. I wish Jas were here to hear that. I don't think she realizes how much the people in her life care. I don't think she's wanted to realize. It was easier to hide if she believed they didn't understand, if she believed they didn't see her.

"Do you really think he's back?" I ask.

Misha tilts his head side to side thoughtfully. "If such a thing is possible, the Jewel would be able to explain how. Her time is precious, so I wouldn't be here if I didn't think there was a chance." He reaches around me and opens the door.

The sanctuary is made of quartz and glass. Every surface sparkles and shines, a visual match for the low, pleasant humming that fills my ears. The moment the door falls closed behind us, a quiet comes over me—not a comforting quiet, but something instinctive that tells me I need to be cautious here, something primal that reminds me of my vulnerabilities and makes the next world, whatever comes after this life, feel too close.

Misha turns to me, arching a brow, and I realize I've stopped moving. I've frozen in the foyer of this disturbingly beautiful sanctuary.

"It's okay," he says softly. "What you're feeling is normal. I imagine it's more intense for a human. Just keep your guard up."

Nodding, I follow him in and keep my body as near to him as I dare.

The deeper we get, the more the humming amplifies, and the space seems to grow around us—as if we're walking down the hall of a grand palace and not the entrance to a small sanctuary. A chill runs through me at the wrongness of it.

"That doorway," I whisper, still walking, still putting one foot in front of the other even as the hair on the back of my neck stands on end, even when my mind tells me we should've hit the rear of the small building by now.

"Don't speak of it here," he says, his voice just as low.

I grab on to Misha's hand, and he squeezes mine in return.

Deeper and deeper into the sanctuary we go, and at the back, sitting on the floor with her eyes closed and her legs crossed, waits a wizened ancient fae, the silver webbing on her forehead pulsing with light. Is she praying? Meditating?

Misha puts a hand in front of me, stopping my progress. He lowers to his knees and bows his head. I follow his lead, kneeling on the hard floor beside him. The humming, I realize, is coming from her. It vibrates the floors, and I feel it in my limbs.

"Thank you for seeing us, Gaelynn, Jewel of Peace," Misha says.

I feel his fear. He has never liked coming here, visiting her, has seen it as both a duty and an honor, but one he dreads all the same.

The female doesn't reply, but the humming continues, low and steady.

"We are here because we need to assess a threat. We need to know if someone has crossed from the other side and back into the world of the living."

The Jewel nods, the only sign that she is even listening. "Go on," she finally says. The words come out with the hum, a part of it.

"There are rumors that Mordeus, the false king of the Unseelie Court, has returned from the dead. We have no proof of this supposed resurrection but need to know if it's true."

The humming stops, and her eyes open—white and milky.

The silence that takes the place of that low hum feels deafening. "Why do you concern yourself with the affairs of other courts, Mishamon Nico Frendilla? You are Wild Fae. You are free of the petty clashes and treachery of the sun and moon courts. Do not entangle yourself with the likes of their politics."

Misha bows his head again. "You honor me with your wisdom, my Jewel. But I come here asking for the future of my court as much as any other. If Mordeus has returned, no court is safe."

She studies him for a long time with those milky eyes. "You are a good king, my child. Your court thrives under your leadership and will continue to thrive. But this girl beside you drives you to worry about matters that aren't yours. Do you deny it?"

Misha doesn't spare me a glance or even meet Gaelynn's eyes. "No, my Jewel. I deny none of your wisdom."

"Good. Then I will say this: When the gods brought Mab back from death, the world was altered, not only in this realm but beyond. Fates took turns that changed the course of millennia. They declared they would not do it again for even the greatest leader and certainly not for the likes of that wicked false king."

Misha exhales slowly. "Thank you for your wisdom, my Jewel. We will rest easier knowing he doesn't live again."

"I didn't say that, my child. I said the gods didn't bring him back."

Misha lifts his head, but I keep mine bowed. "Will you explain for me, my Jewel? Could such a thing be done without help from the gods?"

"Whether or not it was done, I cannot say. I have no connection to the Court of the Moon and their line of rulers. But I can say it is possible. Unlikely but possible. To bring he who has passed into the Twilight back to this world would require incomparable magic—both in the catalyst, which brings back the spirit, and in the physical realization, which brings back the body."

"Is there a body?"

"His most fervent supporters believe Mordeus's trusted advisors retrieved his body the day of his assassination and preserved it with magic, waiting for the day they had powerful enough magic to bring him back."

"Where would one get such magic? Fire gems? Bloodstones?"

"Not even the sacred stones could provide enough power to raise the dead."

"Then how?"

"There is no resurrection without great sacrifice. We all know death will come for us, but returning requires sacrifice the likes of which no true king would ever accept. For this reason, we will never see the best kings and queens return for their thrones. Only the worst."

"What kind of sacrifice?" Misha asks.

"There are legends of ancient spells that can take the living and use their magic to raise the dead." She shakes her head. "But it requires countless deaths of devoted followers, all for one resurrection."

I hear Misha swallow. "So for such a thing to happen, many would have to die."

"Where else would such great magic come from? Life is magic. Magic is life. The foresight required makes planning for such a thing nearly impossible. There are too many factors," she says.

185

"Thank the gods anyone worthy of such a thing wouldn't allow it and those unworthy rarely have the devoted followers to make it happen. Therein lies the beauty of it."

Misha blinks, and I wonder if he's thinking the same thing I am.

The faceless plague. All the dead fae. Are they connected to Mordeus? Is he somehow taking their life force to bring himself back?

"But what if one had the legions willing to give their lives?" Misha says. "Then it would be possible?"

The Jewel flashes her teeth in a haunting approximation of a smile. "Even after the sacrifice brought back the spirit, no resurrection is complete without the body, and bringing a body back from the grave would require great magic indeed."

"But it could be done?" Misha asks.

Gaelynn hums again, the sound filling the space that seemed so empty without it. "I would hate to meet the faerie who could command powers meant for the gods alone," she says. "My priestess will give you the name of a skilled witch who lives on the coast. Bring her an object that belonged to the false king, and she will be able to tell you if he lives."

Misha holds my hand all the way down the too-long hall and out of the Jewel's sanctuary.

When we come to the doors, a priestess is waiting. "For you," she says, handing Misha a rolled-up sheet of paper.

He tucks it into his vest. "Thank you, and all my thanks to the Jewel."

"Long may she live," the priestess murmurs.

When she opens the door for us, Misha's sentinels are waiting with our horses at the bottom of the steps.

We're still hand in hand as we descend the stairs.

"Have they been waiting here the whole time?" I ask.

Misha shakes his head, confirming my suspicions.

"How did they know we were coming?" I ask.

"Those who are closest to me allow me to speak into their minds." He shoots me a look. "That is, those who don't keep their minds locked down like a steel cage."

I shrug. "You're the one who taught me to guard my mind."

"If you trust me, you can guard it and still let me in," he says.

"Trust doesn't come that easily for me."

He squeezes my hand. "I'm realizing that."

We reach the bottom of the steps, and I allow him to help me onto my horse before I think better of it. He doesn't linger, though, and moments later he's mounted his and we've begun our trek back to the castle.

I glance over my shoulder for one last look at the sanctuary before focusing on the trail ahead of me. "Is that place a doorway to another realm?"

"The Jewel of Peace lives in a pocket realm. It's how she stays safe when many may try to find a way to steal the power she's gained through her years."

I shiver. "It felt . . . wrong to be in there."

"I never cared for it, either. I think it's a step closer to the Twilight and our bodies resist it for that reason." He turns to me, hands on the pommel of his saddle. "Are you okay?"

I swallow, trying to imagine how Jasalyn would feel about what we learned. She already believes Mordeus is alive and plans to kill him. That's the only reason why I'm here next to Misha and not her. "I'm okay," I say. "Did you have the same thought I did? About a connection between the faceless plague and Mordeus?"

"I did." His knuckles turn white as he tightens his grip on the pommel. "I'll get in touch with your sister. She needs to know."

"You think it's true, then? You think he's back?"

"Magic is life. Life is magic. Mordeus never hesitated to use others for his own means. If he found a way to extract the life force from those fae in order to feed his own, he would."

"But what about the second half—what kind of fae has the power to revive a body after death?" I ask.

He scrapes a hand over his face. "I don't know. None of the necromancers I've met could perform true resurrections. They could bring someone back for a moment or two if they got to them quickly enough after their death, but at the end of those moments, the dead remain dead. Their bodies are rotting even as they speak."

"While we figure out who could revive Mordeus's body, we need to stop the faceless plague. If people are still dying and there's a connection, it must mean the resurrection of his spirit isn't complete." I'm thinking out loud and shouldn't. Jas would keep her ideas to herself.

"My thoughts exactly, but that's why Abriella needs to know about the connection. If we can figure out the cause, then maybe we can stop it." He drags a hand through his hair. "And we need something that belonged to Mordeus."

"You still plan to see the witch? Even though you believe he's back?"

"Operating on assumptions—even strong ones—is foolish

when we have the tools we need to get the answers. I'm sure Finn can identify something in that palace that was important to his uncle."

"Probably." I should ask to go to the palace myself to retrieve it. That's what Jas would do, isn't it? But facing Abriella makes me nervous and—

"What we need," Misha says, "is Mordeus's seer. The Jewel kept talking about the foresight necessary to plan something like this, and I'd like to know just what he was told. That may be the only way to find his necromancer."

"Aren't seers notoriously vague and contradictory?"

"They are. Trust me, my niece has the sight, and if you aren't sure how to proceed on something before you speak with her, you'll be even more baffled after." He laughs to himself. "I'll ask Finn about that too."

"Good idea," I say, but I don't think Finn's going to be able to help him. If Mordeus knew he was going to die and had the foresight to plan for his own resurrection, I doubt a seer was behind it.

That sounds like the work of an oracle.

When we stop, we're not at Castle Craige but in the bustling little village in the foothills around the castle.

"What are we doing here?" I ask as Misha dismounts his horse.

He hands his reins to one of his sentinels and turns to me. "It was a hard ride today, and we learned some difficult information. You handled it beautifully. The least I can do in return is take you to a nice dinner."

I shift to dismount and cringe at the ache in my thighs.

"It's okay. I've got you." He waits beside my horse, and when I swing my leg over the saddle, he takes me by the hips and guides me down. I'm too warm, too tangled up inside as he pulls his hands away.

He leads me into a small thatched-roof cottage that I only realize is a restaurant once we step inside. We're met by a hunch-backed female with wings that are way too small for her body and elven ears that are too big for her head.

"My king," she says. She takes a bow that looks painful. "I am honored that you allow me to serve you tonight."

"Fancee, please stand. It is truly my pleasure to dine on the most delicious fare in my whole court."

"You flatter me, Your Grace, but surely you mean the whole realm."

He chuckles. "Indeed. My mistake."

She turns and, with a hurried limp, leads us through the cottage. We weave our way through tables and diners and onto a back patio framed by faerie lights above and candles along the ground.

Of the four tables, only the one in the center is set. It overflows with roses and candles and crystal goblets. Someone made sure no detail was overlooked for this special dinner for the king.

"It's lovely, Fancee," Misha says. "Thank you for the trouble."

"My king is courting again," Fancee says, nodding to me. "It is no trouble but an *honor* to help find our new queen."

"Oh no." My cheeks heat. "This isn't . . . I mean, I'm not—"

Misha squeezes my hand. "Thank you, Fancee. We appreciate it."

She winks at me and then scurries back into the cottage.

Misha pulls out my chair. "I apologize for this."

I sit and clear my throat as he takes his position across from me. "I had no idea you were planning such a romantic evening, my king. And *courting* me. That's such interesting news. Perhaps I can know in advance before our wedding?"

"I really wasn't . . . I'm sorry." His cheeks go slightly pink. "I knew it would likely be nearing sunset by the time we arrived, and given how you feel about the dark, I asked her to provide us with extra lights and candles. She must've gotten the wrong impression."

"Or perhaps she's growing impatient for a new queen."

His lips press into a thin line. "Perhaps. Everyone seems to be."

"Are you?" I ask, dragging a finger through the condensation on my water glass.

He's studying the lights around the patio as if they might show him the way to that queen everyone is waiting for. "Sorry— am I what?"

"Anxious for your new queen?" My stomach flips and tightens with the question. I'm both breathless and terrified to know his answer.

He blows out a breath. "I suppose that depends what you mean by anxious. My *advisors* are certainly anxious about it. They don't like that I don't have a queen and like even less that I don't have an heir, but my sister is well. She's next in line for the crown should something happen to me, and she has an heir if something happens to the both of us. So there's not the urgency that they like to pretend there is."

"And yet?" I say, propping my forearms on the table and leaning forward.

He lifts his eyes to mine. "And yet . . . when someone is given a second chance at finding love, he finds himself eager for it to fall into his lap." He swallows. "As you said this morning, I once thought that I would be stuck with no better than what my parents had. The truth is that my marriage with Amira may have been no more than a friendship, but it was a good one. As far as marriages go, it was better than my parents'. I valued it."

"You miss it?"

A brown, spotted hawk cries, flying over our heads and perching on a post on the corner of the patio. It's one of the largest birds I've ever seen this close, and Misha watches it while he answers. "Not really. Amira's done me the honor of remaining my friend, even though she owes me nothing."

"Perhaps she doesn't remain your friend out of a sense of obligation but because your friendship is reward enough in itself."

He huffs out a breath. "Now you sound like her."

"I don't get the impression that's a bad thing."

"No. Not at all." He traces an invisible pattern on the table-cloth. "If I marry again—*when* I marry again, as my advisors would prefer I say it—I certainly won't do it for what my parents had. I won't do it for an heir alone, and I won't do it for something less than what I had with Amira."

"Why weren't you two romantically . . ."

He lifts his head and arches a brow at me. "Your sister never talked to you about it?"

I tense. I have no idea. Would Brie have shared something like that with her younger sister? It seems probable, but that would've bordered on gossip, and the shadow queen doesn't seem the type.

Plus, Jas probably wouldn't have been interested. "I guess I never got the details," I finally say.

"Amira and I were a political match, but when we married, she was in love with someone else. I . . . I respected that."

"You're saying you never expected her to love you in return?" I ask, because it's clear the king harbored at least some feelings for his queen.

"I'm saying we approached our marriage in the best way we knew how, given our unique circumstances." He glances toward the cottage door as if he wants to make sure no one is listening. "I'm saying that we never had a reason to expect our union to give us an heir."

I clear my throat. "Oh. I see."

The old faerie scuttles out onto the patio again and sets bowls down in front of each of us and a covered basket in the center of the table. "Carrot ginger soup with curry and coconut crème and fresh-baked sourdough bread," she says. She pulls a bottle of wine from her apron and fills our glasses. "And a sparkling wine that will bring out all those autumnal flavors—a true faerie wine. It's our house specialty."

"Thank you," I say. "If this tastes half as good as it smells, I know I'm in for a treat."

The old faerie beams at me. "I like this one, Your Majesty."

Misha scans my face and nods. "As do I," he says without taking his gaze off me, and my stomach flip-flops.

She winks at him before trudging back into the cottage.

"Thank you," he says, expression softening.

"What? What did I do?"

"For being kind to Fancee. It's a small thing, but it means everything to her. And to me."

My cheeks heat, and I reach for my wine. "I was only being honest."

Misha puts his hand on top of my glass. "That's her *special* wine."

"Should I only drink after I try the soup?" I ask, confused.

"When someone says something is a true faerie wine, they mean it's going to loosen your inhibitions, make you lose track of time. Fancee is apparently set on making this a date to remember."

I release my glass. "Oh."

His grin goes wide and a little wicked. "I'm not saying you *can't* drink it. I just want you to know what you're getting into."

"I think I'll stick to water." My cheeks heat further, and I'm sure the redness is creeping up into my hairline at this point. The last thing I need to do is loosen my inhibitions around this male. I already seem to lose control of my tongue in his presence. I'd hate to see what would happen if we added faerie wine to the mix.

I pick up my spoon. "Is the soup safe?"

He chuckles. "Yes. The soup is safe. And I do trust her. She's not trying to trick us—just trying to help in her own way." He waves to our surroundings. "Just like the ambience."

"Well, I've never had a romantic dinner before," I say. "So I guess it's kind of nice."

"Not even with your baker's son?" he asks.

"I—" I duck my head. *Focus, Felicity.* "We had to be discreet." I hate the lie. I'm beginning to hate all the lies.

To distract myself, I bring a spoonful of soup to my lips. Misha

194

watches me. It's delicious, but it's hard to focus on anything but his eyes on my mouth as I swallow. "Is that your hawk?" I ask, nodding to the bird if only to get his eyes off me.

Misha glances toward the hawk for a moment before returning the full weight of his attention to me. "That's Storm, my familiar."

I arch a brow, waiting for an explanation.

"I can only be in one place at a time, so Storm helps me keep an eye on things in all the places I cannot be. Our minds are linked, so what he sees, I know."

I grin. "Your personal spy."

Misha grunts and picks up his spoon. "Does it bother you? Would you like me to ask him to leave?"

I shake my head. "I'm just surprised you have him here." I take another steaming spoonful from my bowl and barely stifle a moan as all the flavors explode on my tongue.

"He's done as I asked for the day, and he likes to be close to me when he can be."

"That's kind of sweet." I stir my soup. It's so delicious I want to make it last. "And who did he spy on for you today?"

"Truth be told, I have him watching a few different groups for me right now. We're hosting our yearly ball at the castle at the end of the week. It's always a security risk to invite so many outsiders into my court and into my home." He removes the napkin from the basket and hands me a piece of crusty bread. "Storm's skills are just one of the ways we take precautions against those who might have less than honorable intentions."

I tear off a hunk of my bread and dip it into my soup. "Will I be expected to attend this ball?"

"As the special guest of my court, you'll be invited to come, and as the princess of the shadow court, you'll be expected to make an appearance. But, Jasalyn"—I lift my head and meet his eyes, so lovely and so serious all of a sudden—"expectations and invitations aside, I hope you'll come because you choose to. I hope you'll come as my friend."

My name rests on the tip of my tongue. *Felicity. Call me Felicity.* But I swallow it back like the painful truth that it is.

CHAPTER FIFTEEN

———◇———

JASALYN

I DON'T KNOW IF IT'S the fresh air, the comforting closeness of Kendrick's body, or simple logic, but by the time the sun is sinking toward the horizon, my panic from the morning has dissipated. There's no way I killed all those rebels.

I remember my night very clearly. I went home with Kendrick and climbed in bed. The fact that those people are dead is nothing more than an unsettling coincidence.

It has to be. People have been dying all over the court. The deaths among this group are no different.

"Are we stopping soon?" I ask, only because my stomach is growling loud enough that even Remme can hear it from two horses ahead of us.

Skylar frowns into the distance. "Shae should've joined us by now."

"Don't jump to conclusions," Kendrick says. "Remme, what are our lodging options?"

"We passed the last good one about an hour back," he says.

I squeak. "What? Why?"

"Our friend was supposed to meet us on the road this

afternoon," Kendrick explains. "He was going to take us to a place to stay for the night."

"I don't like it," Skylar says, hand on her forehead shielding her eyes from the setting sun as she scans the horizon. "What if they—"

"Don't think like that," Remme says.

"We'll find a place to make camp here," Kendrick says. "Remme, if we haven't seen him by morning, I want you to ride ahead and see what you can find out."

"I could go now," Remme says.

"No. I don't want anyone out there alone after dark. Not with what's going on."

I glance up at the cloudy sky and a prickle of dread crawls across the back of my neck. I've never felt afraid of whatever's been killing the Unseelie, but I'm pretty sure none of the dead was scared either. "I thought you said it was too dangerous to camp."

"Tonight it's our best option," Kendrick says, frowning toward the trees. "I'd rather make camp now than ride another two hours to arrive in a strange town in the dark."

Half an hour later, we've made camp in a small clearing surrounded by trees and Kendrick has some sort of stew bubbling over the fire. I don't know what's in it, but it smells amazing. The others are in the forest gathering more supplies to feed the fire overnight, and I'm cutting apples to go with our meal.

"I am sorry, for what it's worth," he says. "Our friend was supposed to have a house for us to stay at tonight—one with soft beds and clean tubs. You deserved the reprieve."

"What about you?" I ask, glancing up at him.

"I can sleep anywhere, but I wanted to give you a night of comfort—and a safe place to stay before we reach the keep."

"I don't need anything that the others can do without."

He stirs the stew, quiet for so long I think the conversation must be over, but then he finally says, "Are you sure you want to go?" He draws in a ragged breath. "When I asked you to come, I hadn't seen your scars. He hurt you there—hurt you in a way I still don't fully understand. I don't want you to face that if it's not necessary."

My skin goes cold, and I drop my knife. "Are you talking about Mordeus's dungeons?"

"Yes. Feegus Keep." When I turn to meet his gaze, he frowns. "You didn't know."

I shake my head. "No. I wasn't sure where they were. For a long time, I assumed they were in the Midnight Palace."

"The palace dungeons there were too civilized for Mordeus's liking." He grabs a stick and nudges the logs beneath the pot of stew, adjusting the flames.

"I know that now." I turn back around and stare straight ahead so he can't see my eyes. "I lived at the Midnight Palace for over a year before I had the courage to walk down to the dungeons. I'd sit in my room at night, terrified of the dark hole beneath the place my sister claimed was our true home. I'd have nightmares of waking up in my old cell."

With a curse, Kendrick abandons our dinner and comes to stand in front of me. His blue eyes burn into mine as he takes my hand and threads our fingers together.

"Ultimately," I say, swallowing around an unexpected surge of emotion, "it was Misha who convinced my sister that I needed to walk the halls of the dungeons, needed to be on the other side of the bars to convince my mind that I was truly free."

"Not a bad plan," he says softly. "If you could handle it."

"I vomited three times that morning. I would've done anything not to go—anything *except* letting my sister know just how horribly broken and haunted I was from those weeks. So I went. I took her hand and let her lead me down into the bowels of the palace, where she informed me we had half a dozen insurgents imprisoned for plotting against the throne. She used her own shadow magic to shield us, so the prisoners could neither see nor hear us, but I knew the moment we reached the last few steps that those dungeons were not the ones from the worst nights of my life."

"What did she say? Did she try to find where you'd been kept?"

"I never told her. I let her guide me up and down the row of cells, pretending I was looking for something familiar, as if I could have forgotten. And when we were done, she told me she was proud of me." A shiver runs through me as I remember that day, how I'd smiled as if I were healed, as if I'd faced my monster and emerged triumphant. Why tell her I would've preferred that prison to the one I knew? Why tell her nothing she could do could fix me?

"She would be proud of you even if she knew the truth."

I shrug. There are too many truths I've kept from Abriella. Perhaps some would make her proud, but others?

I would hate to see the disappointment in her eyes if she knew all my secrets.

"I hate the idea of you returning to that keep without any weapons of your own," he says.

I lift my gaze and frown. "Then arm me. Give me a dagger or a sword."

He pulls a short blade from his scabbard and places it on the table. "There's a pocket on your hip where you can hold it."

I arch a brow. "You aren't afraid I'll turn on you while you sleep?"

His grunt implies that nothing about me scares him. "I trust you to keep any murderous tendencies to yourself, but I was initially referring to *magical* weapons." He searches my face for a long moment. "If there was a way to awaken your dormant fae magic, would you want to?"

I take the dagger and shove it into the sheath built into my leather pants, all the while avoiding his eyes. An image of Mordeus's face flashes in my mind. *Why did the gods see fit to grant such magic to a human girl?*

"What if I told you I rejected that part of myself long ago?"

"It's still there. It's just sleeping."

"What about teaching me *your* magic? You have more than any human I've ever met."

"We were trained since childhood—potions, spells, incantations. Our parents insisted that we be versed in every magic available to us."

Even when our mother told us fanciful stories about magical worlds every night, she never taught us how to use any. "Why?"

He puts two fingers beneath my chin to tilt my face up toward his. "Because we were the ones who were supposed to lead the revolution, and they knew we'd need it."

That almost makes me smile. I've never been part of something like this before. Never had a cause. I didn't realize how good it would feel. "Why did they choose you?"

His eyes turn sad before he answers. "The oracle predicted that I would overthrow the Elora Seven. And so, for every day I've hunted Erith, he's hunted me in return."

"Is that how you got tangled up with Mordeus—back when we were in his dungeons together? Was it about the revolution?"

He pulls away, turning back to the fire. "Everything was strategic with Mordeus. I was nothing more than a chess piece." He draws in a long breath and slowly exhales. "The Seven had a sort of alliance of convenience with Mordeus and tasked him with finding and ending me, but Mordeus was far too self-serving for that. He wanted me alive for leverage—so that they would have to answer to him. It's the same reason he kept the Sword of Fire. Because they needed it. Because they knew it was their greatest weakness."

"So the oracle predicted that I would kill Erith and you would overthrow the Magical Seven?"

"Dream team, aren't we?" he says, but the words sound too heavy.

When he stares over my shoulder, I realize Remme and Skylar have returned to camp.

"Is the perimeter secure?" Kendrick asks.

Remme sighs, and Skylar lifts her chin. "We have neighbors," she says. "A group of Unseelie rebels to the east. Closer than I'd like."

"Rebels?" I ask. "Mordeus followers?"

"Interestingly enough," Skylar says, "they were talking about their king when we were checking out their camp."

"Learn anything useful?" Kendrick says, rising to his full height and wiping his hands on his pants.

"More of the same," Remme says. "They think he's been resurrected and were talking about him touring the court and blessing his followers. Obviously, they hope he'll surprise them with a visit."

Kendrick's eyes flash to mine for a beat, and I have no doubt he sees the fear in my eyes before I can lock it down. "They're fighting a losing war and desperate for something to believe in," he says softly, and I know the words are for me.

I bow my head, not wanting him to know how complicated my feelings are regarding Mordeus's return.

"Are we close enough to them that we need to move again after dinner?" Kendrick asks.

"They won't bother us if we don't bother them," Remme says, "but we should take turns on watch tonight in case any of them decide to look for trouble."

"How did it work in Elora, before the Magical Seven?" I ask after dinner. We're all gathered around the fire, and no one seems in a rush to go to sleep. Judging by the way their gazes keep drifting back toward the road, I think they're still hoping to see their friend. I'm not complaining. The moment they all fall asleep, I'll be wide awake with nothing but the darkness for company. My body may be exhausted, but my mind never rests, and I'm not looking forward to another night of fighting it. "Who was the ruling family?"

"I see how it is," Remme says.

I glance his way. "See what?"

"I talk about a time before the Elora Seven and I'm full of it, but Perfect Kendrick tells you there was a matriarchy, and all your skepticism falls away."

"Aww, are you jealous?" I ask Remme.

"Maybe a little," he mutters.

Kendrick's chest shakes with silent laughter. He's mindlessly whittling a stick with his pocketknife and occasionally tossing the shavings into the fire.

"Given that you're full of shit eighty percent of the time, I don't think we can blame the girl," Skylar says.

"Natan," Kendrick says, "would you like to answer Jasalyn?"

Natan nods, taking my question as seriously as he does any. "I've visited three realms in my years and studied seven, but none has a royalty structure quite like historic Elora."

"Wait—what?" I shake my head. "You've visited *three* realms? So you've been to a realm other than Faerie and Elora?"

"Three in addition to Elora," he says.

I gape. Travel between Elora and Faerie is difficult, but common compared to how closely the other realms guard their portal gates. "How? You can't be older than, what, twenty?"

"*How* is a story for another time," Natan says. "Do you want to know about Elora's royalty or not?"

"Yes, please."

"Before the Elora Seven stepped in and abolished the political system, Elora was long led by a matriarchy. The queen presided over lands that were divided into territories, each ruled by lords and ladies."

"That doesn't sound so different than the typical monarchy," I say.

"It's not so much the power structure that makes it stand apart," Kendrick says beside me, "but the way power is passed after the queen's served her term."

Natan nods. "Crowns and thrones weren't passed through blood in Elora. Your mother could've been the queen, but you'd have no claim to the throne, and it would be unheard of for you to be chosen as her successor."

"So how was it decided?" I ask, rolling my shoulders and trying to stretch out the soreness in my back. "By vote of the lords?"

"The oracle would name a child at her birth as the next queen, and she and her family would be moved into the palace and protected until her time to rule."

"The oracle? They let magic decide it?"

"I suppose you could say that," Natan says.

"But what about free will? What if the child made choices or led a life that made her unfit to lead? What if the child didn't *want* to lead? Or what if the oracle was corrupted—if someone was able to manipulate the prophecies and rig the future of the crown?"

"If that ever happened, it never made it to the history books," Natan says.

I grunt. "Well, that doesn't mean much, since this matriarchy you describe never made it to the history books either."

"It did, though. The Elora Seven just destroyed them."

"How do you know this? There's been a Magical Seven ruling Elora for almost five hundred years. How could you possibly know about what was written in books that were destroyed so long ago?"

Kendrick glances toward Natan before looking at me. "Natan's family did everything they could to preserve the true history and pass it down. He was very young when his parents were killed for it—the Elora Seven found the books they'd painstakingly preserved and destroyed them, and then executed them in front of the whole town."

My chest feels too tight. "Natan, I'm so sorry. That's awful."

Natan's staring ahead and doesn't spare me a glance. His jaw is hard, his usual softness nowhere to be found. "It was."

"It's difficult to explain," Kendrick says, "the extent of their evil. Do you see why I want you to have every possible advantage when you go after Erith?"

"I'm not exaggerating when I say I haven't had any signs of magical powers. I don't think they're there." Though Mordeus believed they were, and that was before anyone knew I was a descendant of Mab. If he was right, I never felt even a flicker of that power. Though maybe I lost it when I traded my fae life for my ring.

"Natan has worked with magic users who are blocked and helped unblock them," Kendrick says. "I think he could do that for you."

I frown. "Why would you think I'm *blocked*?"

"Because, like you keep saying, you have no magic. Only that doesn't make sense. You're the descendant of one of the most powerful faeries to ever walk this realm. Her blood runs in your veins. The magic *must* be there. So I think we should have Natan help you find it."

"What if I'm not interested in finding it?" I ask.

Kendrick puts down his knife and studies me. "I know what the oracle showed me, Jasalyn. I had a vision of you killing Erith, but I won't send you into that fight if I think your only advantage is prophecy. Fate isn't static, and Erith is too dangerous."

"So you're worried the oracle lied to you?"

He shakes his head. "Oracles don't lie, but the future isn't set in stone. We make choices, and our paths change. The oracle can't show us everything, so we must prepare ourselves as best we can."

I consider this. "You said she gave you a *vision* of me killing Erith. As in, she never said my name."

"That's right," Kendrick says.

"Then how do you know it will be me and not Felicity while she's in my form?"

Skylar chuckles. "This one's smarter than Felicity."

"Felicity believes what she needs to," Kendrick says, frowning at his whittled stick.

"It doesn't matter." This comes from Remme. "Whether it's you or Felicity in your skin, we're doing everything in our power to move toward that end. It's time for the Seven to fall—and bringing down Erith is step one."

"May I ask what's so awful about having magic?" Skylar asks. She walks around the fire and lowers herself onto the ground beside me, folding her legs under her. "Do you fear the responsibility of having that kind of power or do you truly hate the fae so much that you cannot stomach the idea of being one of them?"

I'm quiet for a long time, and I consider refusing to answer at all, but there's a patience in her silence—in all their silences—that soothes me and makes me feel . . . understood? *Accepted.*

They *want* to understand and will accept my answer, whatever it is.

"I don't fear power, but I don't know what to do with it either," I finally say. "My sister was the one who dreamed of being powerful, who would imagine herself saving the less fortunate and punishing the cruel."

"You didn't want that?" Skylar asks, cocking her head to the side.

"I wanted it, but I never saw myself leading the charge."

"Maybe because you were always in her shadow, you never bothered to notice that you had your own light to give the world," Remme says, and it's such a tender and thoughtful sentiment coming from him that I feel my throat go thick with emotion.

"Maybe," I whisper.

"And what about the other part?" Skylar asks.

"I don't hate the fae."

He and Skylar exchange a look.

"What's that about? I don't. I have met many faeries who have earned my hatred, but I'm not so blindly prejudiced that I believe all their kind are evil. My own sister is fae."

Natan's eyes soften with his kind smile. "You see your sister as the exception." His words are gentle but firm. "Prejudice prevails beyond exceptions. Has for millennia."

I open my mouth and then close it again before dropping my gaze to my hands. "My sister's inner circle is respectable as well,

208

but I will admit that faeries have to prove themselves to me. I can't trust them easily. And if I had to choose . . . yes, I wish my sister and I had never been thrust into this world and into these roles. I want our lives back as they were in Elora—without all this magic and . . ." *Fear.* I was never so afraid in Elora, but I don't say that out loud. I don't like to admit the weakness.

When I lift my head, Kendrick's watching me, his beautiful blue eyes sad.

"Why are you looking at me like that?"

"Maybe because *you* are fae," Skylar says. "And it is tragic to see someone so riddled with self-loathing."

"I didn't ask for some ancient faerie queen's blood," I snap. "I do not wish to be fae, and I despise everyone treating me like I am so gods-damned lucky to have never been given a choice in the matter."

"Oh, you poor little—"

"Let it go, Skylar," Kendrick says.

She holds his gaze for a long time. Tension fills the air before suddenly falling away, as if it were never there. "No problem." She hops to her feet and brushes the dirt off her pants. "Remme, why don't you come check the perimeter with me while these two dig around in her head?"

Remme stands and awkwardly surveys the group before following her. "Let us know how it goes."

I bow my head, listening to the crunch of his boots in the leaves as he walks away.

"Don't think of it as faerie or human," Kendrick says beside me. "Think of this as a weapon—something to wield when you find yourself facing your enemies."

But what if I use it and realize I'm no better than them? What if this drive for revenge isn't just about justice but something dark inside me—the part of me that relishes others' pain in my dreams, the part of me that wants Mordeus to live for no reason other than how desperately I want to be the one to kill him for good?

Kendrick reaches for my hand and squeezes. "I'll be right here the whole time. Okay?"

I nod. Because he's right. I should know what I'm capable of. When they caught me and took my cloak, I had no defenses against them—and they only have human magic. If I'm captured again without my ring and by someone who truly wants to hurt me, I need as much power as I can get.

Natan moves to sit at my side but turns his body to face me. He taps my knee with his fingers. "Turn this way?"

Taking a breath, I swallow down my fear and do as he asks.

"This is your magic." Natan's brown eyes meet mine and there's so much kindness there, I feel myself relax. "You don't need to fear it. It answers to you. You are its master."

"Okay," I whisper. *It's like the ring. I decide when I use it. I decide how.*

"Close your eyes."

I obey and feel his hands settle on my knees.

"Now I want you to lower your mental shields. You're safe here. It's just me and Kendrick, and you can bring your shields back up at any time."

When Misha taught me to shield, I imagined mine built from the same cinder blocks that made the walls of our tiny basement bedroom at my aunt's house. It's thick and heavy, and I imagine taking it down block by block to clear a path in for Natan.

"Good," he says. "That's enough. Now I want you to remember a time when you were happy and safe. What do you see? How do you feel?"

I don't answer his questions out loud, but I'm there. In that stupid little basement room that was never intended to be a bedroom, that was never intended to be a home for anyone. It was cold and dark and far too small for two growing girls. Brie hated it. She hated it more than she hated Madame Vivias, I think, but I didn't. It wasn't much, but it was our space, and when we were there, the rest of the world went away.

There were no windows, but I was never afraid of the dark when we were in that room. Because I'd never known the horrors I'd face in Faerie. And because Brie was with me.

I let myself imagine lying on the bed, sleepiness making my lids heavy as Brie dresses for the day. She's telling me a story about our spoiled cousins—the girls who live upstairs who we're forced to serve and clean up after when we're not at our other jobs. They're brash and dreadfully cruel and treat us like we should thank them for the opportunity to wash their clothes, but I don't care about any of that because I'm with my sister and in this moment she's not so stressed. In this moment, she doesn't feel the weight of our debts weighing so heavily on her. She's happy, so I'm happy.

"Good job, Jas," Natan says. "You're doing great. Now I need you to imagine something that scares you."

My hands clench at my sides, nails biting into my palms.

"Shh. It's okay. You're safe. You're just picturing this fear, nothing more. Take a breath, Jas. Breathe and imagine a moment you were terrified. It doesn't have to be your worst memory. Just pick a moment of true fear."

My lungs burn when I finally force myself to draw in air. Then my hot tears are rolling down my cheeks.

"Aren't you a pretty thing?"

His hand is around my neck, and he isn't squeezing, but I know he could. He wants me to know he has the strength and the power to end me in a second.

A sob tears out of me, shaking my chest.

"Oh, come now, why are you crying? Surely I'm not that repulsive?"

His orcs laugh like this is a spectacular joke.

"They tell me you're not eating, little human, and that you're refusing to drink the water they put in your cell," Mordeus says.

I look to the male behind him—the one who's been spitting in my water—before dropping my eyes back to the ground.

He lifts my chin, but I keep my eyes cast down. "Look at me!"

I won't, but then—then I do. My body isn't my own. My eyes connect with his, and no matter how hard I try to point them elsewhere, they won't go.

"You see this? This is how it will be. You are mine. *You cannot refuse me."*

"That's enough!"

The sound of Kendrick's voice snaps me out of the memory and back to the present. I'm still by the fire, sitting cross-legged in front of Natan, but my body's shaking and my face is wet with tears, just like it was that day—that first time my body wasn't my own to control.

Natan is pale-faced in front of me, his eyes red, like he's been awake too long and forced to keep his eyes open.

"So?" I sniff back more tears. I'm unsteady and need to get my footing in the present, but it's hard. When I think about Mordeus, I feel like he's close. Like I carry him around with me. That's why I need to see him dead myself.

Natan's looking at Kendrick. "Nothing," he murmurs. "I went as deep as I could, and I couldn't find anything."

My chest squeezes.

"You're sure?" Kendrick asks.

"Nothing at all."

I drag in a breath, drinking in the night air, the campfire smoke, the lingering smell of dinner—anything to remind myself I'm *here* and not *then*. "So maybe I'm not fae after all." But I know it's not true.

I stand because I need to prove to myself I can.

This is my body.

I am in control.

"I need a minute." I spin to the woods and take two steps before I stop cold, staring into the darkness. Fear claws at my chest until suddenly Kendrick's hand is gripping mine and all the terror falls away.

He gives my hand a squeeze, then nods toward the trees, and I let him lead me into the darkness of the forest, where the leaves crunch under our boots and the drone of the insects grows louder.

"I'm sorry," he says.

"About what?"

"I pushed you to go there with Natan, pushed you to remember something terrible and . . ."

And it was all for nothing. Because I have no power at all. I squandered it to feed my darkest desires. Squandered it for a ring when I could've been part of something good for once.

"I'm sorry," he says again.

"Maybe I'm sorry too."

"For what?"

I shake my head. "I don't know. For everything—for being a scared girl, for not having any magic, for jumping at the sight of my own shadow." *For trading everything for revenge.*

"I think you're pretty damn brave."

I scoff. "Obviously you're not paying attention."

He stops walking and turns toward me. "There's nothing braver than doing the things that scare you."

I pull back so I can meet his eyes, search his face, study his soft mouth.

His gaze mimics mine, snagging on my mouth. His tongue darts out to wet his lips.

Then he backs away. One step. Two. And disappointment leaves me hollow.

A twig snaps, and Kendrick darts to put himself in front of me. *Protecting me. Always protecting me.*

"Skylar," Kendrick says on an exhale. "What's going on?"

"Sorry," Remme says, and I glance their way in time to see him tugging Skylar back toward camp. "We didn't mean to interrupt. It can wait."

"Say what you came to say," Kendrick says.

"We've been listening in on our neighbors," Skylar says. "Since it sounds like they're headed to the same place we are, we figured we could gather intel."

"And?" Kendrick says.

Remme looks at me and grimaces. "Whether they're right about their king or not, it sounds like Feegus Keep redoubled their security detail. Something's got them spooked."

Remme and Skylar exchange a look, then Remme bows his head.

"We heard Natan say he couldn't find any power inside her," Skylar says, waving in my direction. "We're thinking that if we want to adjust our plans for how we'll approach the keep, we should decide now and find a place for her to stay until we can get what we need."

Kendrick stiffens.

"No," I blurt, my hand instinctively pressing the ring hidden inside my cloak. "I don't want to wait anywhere. I want to go with you."

Kendrick winces. "We need to be smart about this, Slayer. You could be hurt. Or captured."

"I have a goblin bracelet." I shove out my hand and brush my fingers across the invisible threads on my wrist. "I snap a thread, and my goblin comes right away."

"But if you're truly in peril, he can't come," Skylar says.

"What? That can't be right."

Kendrick frowns at my wrist. "Didn't he tell you when he gave you that bracelet?"

I vaguely remember there being an explanation of rules when Abriella introduced me to my goblin. But everything was so foggy

215

back then—the world muffled under the heavy blanket of my memories. It was hard to listen for details when I was focusing on taking my next breath.

"Why not?" I ask.

"The goblins' code forbids them from interfering with fate. So when you snap a thread on your bracelet and you're captured without a path of escape . . ." Remme says.

Skylar nods. "If death is imminent, they can't interfere."

"But Brie's goblin—Bakken?—he saved her once." I look at each of their faces, desperately wanting them to be wrong about this, and not just because I want to go with them to have my chance at finding Mordeus. This bracelet has given me a certain sense of security for years, and if they're right, I never should've trusted it to get me out of a mess. "She'd stolen something from a Seelie castle, and the guards were coming for her. She snapped a thread on her bracelet, and Bakken came and got her."

"And this Bakken is still around?" Skylar asks, brows high.

"He's her goblin to this day."

Remme shakes his head. "Then either those guards would never have laid a finger on her or she somehow proved that she could handle them herself."

I smile. I might not love faeries or magic, but I always enjoy stories of my sister being a badass. "She threw a blanket of shadow on all of them before Bakken would take her."

"Then he didn't break any rules," Kendrick says, his words so measured I know doesn't like having to break this to me. "The only way goblins can work around the rule is if the person they come for has a clear path for escape—or if they call for the goblin

216

before death is reaching for their hand."

"What keeps the goblins from breaking the code?" I ask.

"They have free will, just like we do," Remme says, "but they can't break the code without consequence."

I frown down at my bracelet. My goblin can be a know-it-all jerk, but I thought he cared about me. It hurts to think he'd leave me at the will of my enemies because of some code. "What's the consequence?"

"They cease to be," Kendrick says. "Their lives are ended."

Remme holds Kendrick's gaze, and his voice is soft as he says, "We need to find somewhere for her to stay while we evaluate the situation at Feegus Keep. We can't risk losing her on a simple perimeter breach when we need her for Erith."

"I can help," I say. I sound like I'm begging, but if they've increased security at the keep, I wonder if it's because Mordeus is there. "I can get us in."

Remme frowns. "Say that again."

"This is a big compound, right? Like if we can get past the guards at the gates and maybe put on the appropriate uniforms, no one will know we shouldn't be there once we're inside?"

"It's not that easy," Skylar says. "These aren't some easily distracted boys sitting at the gates. They're sentinels that are trained to kill first and ask questions later."

I swallow. When she puts it that way, it sounds terrifying, but it's no different than any other time I've put on the ring. "I can do it. I can get us in."

"You're going to have to give us more than that, Slayer," Kendrick says.

217

If I don't tell them now, I could miss my chance to get to Mordeus. "I have a magic ring. I got it from a witch in Elora. I wanted to be able to come and go from the Midnight Palace as I pleased, and I needed to be safe doing so—for people to do as I said and not remember that I'd been with them."

Kendrick studies me. "What happens when you put it on?"

"People do as I say."

"Bullshit," Remme mutters.

"Not likely," Skylar adds. "No offense. I'm sure it *feels* like it's working. But magic that powerful isn't that simple."

I sigh. "Fine," I say, pulling it from my cloak. "I'll show you."

CHAPTER SIXTEEN

❖

JASALYN

WHEN I TAKE THE RING off again, I'm wearing a satisfied smirk. And a few other things as well.

"Are you going to show us?" Skylar asks.

"I already did."

"But you didn't *do* anything," Skylar says.

I arch a brow and wave her earrings in the air. On my wrists, I'm wearing Remme's beloved leather cuffs, and I have Natan's glasses perched on my head. "Didn't I?"

Her jaw goes slack. "What kind of witchery is this?" She spins on Kendrick. "She *does* have magic."

"I don't." My gods. I'm smiling. I don't remember the last time I gave an honest smile that didn't belong to the Enchanting Lady.

Kendrick doesn't look at her—doesn't take his eyes off *me*. "Tell me how it works."

"I put the ring on, and people do as I ask." Do they really need to know the rest? Would they believe me if I told them about the kiss of death? "Just like I said."

"And they remember *nothing*," Remme says. He extends a hand. "Give me my shit back."

I unsnap his leather cuffs and return them and then return the others' things as well.

"You didn't take anything from Kendrick?" Skylar asks.

"No."

"Favoritism," Remme grumbles.

"Why not?" Skylar asks.

I flick my gaze to Kendrick, then shrug. "He doesn't follow my orders when I'm wearing the ring, and I didn't feel like wasting time talking him into it."

Skylar throws up her hands. "Wait, if it doesn't work on everyone, why are we even considering this?"

Kendrick drags a hand over his face. "Because I don't remember anything either. So even if I don't hand over my riches, she can walk away anytime she wants or get the rest of you to turn on me. I'll never remember a thing."

"And he's the only one it's ever not worked on," I admit. Though I still wonder about the night I saw my sister while wearing the ring. Misha and Finn were tripping over themselves like idiots, but not Brie. "It's . . . odd."

"Just how many people have you used this ring on?" Remme asks.

I give him a hard look. "Enough."

Natan drags a hand through his hair. "What kind of witch did you get this from?"

I shoot him a look. "The magical kind?" I snap before looking back to Kendrick. "I can demonstrate again, but no matter how many times I do it, you won't remember what happened or how I did it. That's how the ring works."

"It's not that we don't believe you," Kendrick says, exchanging a look with Natan. "But that's some serious magic."

I straighten. "You're questioning my ring when you throw around magic all the time." I wave a hand over myself and point to my elven ears. "Look at me. Look at you."

"Not the same," Natan says. He shakes his head. I've rarely seen this guy look even a little riled up, but right now he looks truly shaken. "My potions . . . those are surface. Even your sister's magic over darkness and shadow is limited. But the kind of magic in this ring is affecting the subconscious of everyone you come into contact with." He ticks his concerns off on his fingers. "Their free will, their future, their memory. The complexity of a magic like that is baffling."

"It's messed up," Remme says. "You're sure it's not faerie magic?"

"I don't know—are there faerie witches selling magical rings in Elora?"

"What did she want for it?" Kendrick asks.

I tear my gaze from his—as if he can see the answer in my eyes. I gave too much for this ring. Some of it was mine to give, and some of it wasn't. I'm not proud of any of it.

"I don't like this," Natan says. "Whatever this is, it's going to bite us in the ass. Mark my words."

"We don't know that," Remme says. "And it would be stupid not to use the tools we have in the meantime. She can get all of us in those gates, just like that." He snaps his fingers. "Let's do it and fix whatever mess she got herself into later."

"At what cost?" Natan asks.

"I agree with Remme," Skylar says. "Let's get in there, find the sword, and worry about the fallout later. She already has the damn thing. What's done is done."

I lift my gaze and find Kendrick's eyes still on me. I don't think he's stopped staring since I took off the ring and was wearing their things. "What?" I ask.

"What did you give for that ring?" he asks. It's the first time he's sounded angry with me.

I hold his gaze and say nothing.

"She's gonna freeze you out, brother," Remme says, nudging him. "Maybe take this for the gift that it is."

When Natan turns back to me, his brow is furrowed and he's staring as if I'm a puzzle and an unexpected piece just appeared in front of him. "Let me see it." He holds out his hand, and I withdraw, pressing my hand to my chest where I've tucked the ring away.

"Slayer," Kendrick says, his voice cautious, "if we're going to trust this ring to get us into enemy territory, I need my historian to examine it first. I promise he'll give it right back."

He's right. They have no reason to trust it and every reason to want more information. Even so, my hands shake as I pass it over.

"Thank you," Kendrick whispers.

Skylar murmurs a few words I can't make out and casts a stream of light toward the ring. The moonstone glints in the light.

Natan holds it up and turns it this way and that. "I've never seen anything like it."

I cringe. "Please be careful."

"What do you think is going to happen to it?" Skylar asks.

"That he's going to drop it in his mouth and accidentally swallow it?"

Remme peers at my ring from over Natan's shoulder and frowns. "Those etchings on the inside—those aren't from the old Eloran alphabet. What are they?"

"Good question," Natan says. He tilts the ring left and right. "I'd need my books to confirm, but I think they're ancient Elvish."

"Elvish?" I ask. "You mean Fae?"

Natan spares me a glance before returning his attention to the ring. "I mean Elvish."

"I've never heard anyone call the old fae tongue Elvish." I ball my hands into fists at my sides, itching to snatch the ring back from him.

"That's because you were lied to your whole life in Elora," Remme says.

Kendrick nudges his friend. "What Remme is so clumsily trying to say," he says, "is that here the elven fae are just *fae*, because this is an entire realm of fae. But in a realm that has both magical and nonmagical beings—say elves and humans, but no other fae to speak of—the elves are simply *elves*."

"So what realm has *elves* and humans?" I ask.

"Elves have lived in many realms, including Elora," Natan says.

"You're trying to tell me that the elves are an ancient Eloran race," I say, propping my hands on my hips. "And the magical words written on my ring are in their alphabet."

"Sure seems like it," Natan says, lowering the ring and handing it back to me. He turns to Kendrick and holds his gaze for so long I wonder if they're having a silent conversation.

Kendrick blows out a breath. "Everyone needs to get some sleep. I'll take first watch. We leave at first light."

"But I get to go, right?" My voice is lined with a panic I can't hide. I look to Kendrick. "Don't leave me behind."

"I never would've left you behind," he says softly.

Everyone heads to the tree line, presumably to take care of their needs before turning in for the night. I move to follow, but Kendrick steps in front of me. His eyes are luminous in the light of the nearby fire.

"Why are you looking at me like that?" I ask.

Kendrick coughs out a laugh. "Why am I looking at you like you've been keeping secrets?" He taps his index finger to his lips. "Maybe because you have?"

"If I'd told you about the ring from the start, you might've taken it away from me. I couldn't risk that."

He glances over his shoulder toward where his friends have already disappeared into the trees. "I need you to tell me the rest. You don't have to tell the others, but I need to know."

"What else is there to tell?"

"Everything. Where in Elora did you get it?"

I shrug. "Fairscape—that's where Brie and I grew up." I glance up toward the dark sky, thinking of the tangle of fear and loathing that led me to that day. "I visited for my seventeenth birthday, and . . . I bought myself a ring."

"From *whom*?"

"She was a witch." I'll never forget the old hag who called me into her cottage. Lured me in with promises of the wrongs she could right. "She terrified me, but she promised me a ring that would make my fear go away, and she delivered on that promise."

He takes my wrist loosely in his big hand, running his thumb back and forth across the pulse point. "But you carry so much fear."

"Not when I wear the ring." I swallow the lump in my throat. I love him being so close, and I don't know what to do with that feeling. "Or, at least, that was true at first. Now it seems like it's sneaking back."

"The magic is fading?"

I bite my bottom lip and shake my head. "I think so, but I'm not sure? Maybe not fading but changing?"

"I won't depend on this ring to keep you safe if its magic isn't reliable."

"Let me worry about that."

His expression is grim enough that I know it's not that simple for him. "What other powers does it give you?"

I step closer and lift my fingers to his lips. His breath catches. I let them drop. "A deadly kiss."

His gaze dips to my mouth and locks there. "And have you used this deadly kiss on anyone?"

I study his mouth and imagine how his lips would feel against mine, how he'd taste. "Yes. That's why I wanted it. I wanted to be rid of every person who hurt me in that dungeon."

His gaze locks on my mouth. "So you've kissed your enemies, but you won't kiss me."

"Seemed like a dangerous habit, considering."

His throat bobs. "I can see that."

Do you want me to kiss you? Is that a question I can ask?

He's still frowning. "There are very few in Elora who have the kind of magic necessary to create a ring with that kind of power. And among those who do, all have an agenda." He sweeps my hair behind my ear, then lets his fingers trace the sensitive shell and lobe. I shiver. "Very little scares me, Jas, but I am terrified to think of what she may have required of you in exchange for that ring."

"She didn't ask for anything I wasn't happy to give," I say softly.

"Tell me."

"I can't."

"Can't or won't?"

"What's the difference?"

With the hand that holds mine, he brushes his thumb across my knuckles and sighs. "Sometimes it is that which we readily sacrifice at our lowest that we most ardently desire when we emerge from the darkness."

That wisdom hits too close to the truth, and I cover the ache of the blow with a forced laugh. "Oh, and I suppose you have all this wisdom because you're *so old*?" His expression seems so somber by the light of the fire, his lips so close.

"I'm older than you," he says.

"How old?"

"Twenty-one in a few months. But I've been told I'm very wise for my age." His gaze lingers on my mouth for one more beat before moving back to my eyes. "What did the witch require as her payment?"

I can't make myself answer. Shame traps the words in my throat. *My life. Every minute after my eighteenth birthday. Every day that I was to spend as fae.*

I never wanted that part of my life. If anything, I felt like she was doing me a favor. The months seemed to stretch out too long. I was too numb, too terrified of the monster in my memories to be scared of meeting my end on my eighteenth birthday. But now I wonder what she gained from my sacrifice, wonder if there's a way to take it back.

Kendrick's still staring. Still waiting for the answer I won't give. "I need to know if there's a problem so I know if I need to fix it," he says.

"You can't fix it."

"In a world full of magic, there isn't much that cannot be fixed."

I hold his gaze and cut myself open, just a little, because he deserves to see how broken I am. "I would've given anything for just one hour—one *moment*—without the fear."

Closing his eyes, he tips his head down. I think he might kiss me. I want to feel a kiss that gives life instead of takes it. I want to feel a kiss that's wrapped in tenderness and affection and not vengeance and hate. But he simply touches his forehead to mine and whispers, "I know," before pulling away.

"Why do you do that?" The words are out before I can stop them.

"Do what?"

I'm an idiot. "Nothing." I turn away, but he grabs my hand before I can go far. I stop but don't face him.

"Why do I do *what*, Slayer?"

"Sometimes the way you look at me is confusing. I don't understand what you want." I stare at the glint of firelight on my

227

boots. "Forget I said anything."

Slowly, he turns me to him, then studies my face. "I'm trying to follow your rules." He's doing it again—looking at my mouth like he can't stop thinking about it.

The ache of longing unravels something low in my gut. "What rules?"

"On the day you agreed to help us with Erith, you very specifically told me not to kiss you."

I blink. "That was before you knew about the ring."

"I need you to be very clear right now, Princess." His gaze dips to my mouth and holds there. "Are you saying your rules have changed?"

My belly is riot of butterflies. *Yes. No.* What if I kiss him and the reality of what I've lost—what I've given away—is worse than ever? What if these nine months pass and I never know his kiss?

"You wonder what I *want*?" He dips his head, the bridge of his nose skating over mine. His breath dances across my lips, and I arch into him. "You say your kiss is deadly, but every hour that passes, I feel more and more like I might die without it." His lips ghost across my mouth. "Tell me the rules have changed."

I draw in a long breath, gathering my courage. "Those rules only apply when I'm wearing the ring." I meet his gaze, watching the reflection of the fire's flames flicker in his eyes. "I don't even know what a kiss *should* feel like."

He cups my face in both hands, his eyes shifting back and forth between mine. "Like this." So slowly, so painfully slowly, he lowers his mouth to mine.

I didn't realize until this moment how much I needed this.

How much my heart ached for it. This warmth. This tentative sweep of lips. Every kiss I've had before this moment has ended in death. Every time I've pressed my lips to another's, I've felt the life drain from them. Every kiss before this has been for the darkest, most broken parts of me, every kiss a reminder of how much of myself I lost during those weeks in captivity. But when Kendrick's mouth latches on mine, there's nothing *but* life. His tongue flicks over my bottom lip, and I open instinctively. He tastes like mulled cider and warmth. Like safety.

Like home.

I suck his bottom lip between my teeth because I want more of him. More of his taste. More of his warmth. He grunts against my mouth, and I fist my hand in his hair.

When he parts his lips over mine, I follow his lead, angling my head and touching my tongue to his.

I tilt my head, desperate for more of his kiss. *Deeper.*

His hands roam up my sides and back down, sweeping the underside of my breasts with his thumbs before he tears his mouth from mine and slowly pulls away.

It's all I can do to keep myself from yanking him back. I never dreamed of his kiss when I was locked in that cell, but I did in the years after. And since seeing him again? It's been hard not to imagine it every time I look at him.

His chest is heaving. His lips are swollen.

I wonder if that's how I look. Mussed and unaware of the world around me. I want him pressed against me again, and this time I don't want him to stop.

He traces my bottom lip with his thumb. "You are so beautiful," he murmurs. "It's no wonder that ring of yours doesn't work on me. I'm already bewitched every time I look at you." His nostrils flare, and he glances to the woods. "The others will be back soon. You should get ready for bed."

"Okay." I wrap my arms around myself and nod, not wanting to seem too pathetic or desperate by asking for him to kiss me again.

Just beyond the tree line, I spot two figures deeper in the woods—males from the look of their silhouettes. From the flickering lantern at their feet, I can make out one lounging against a tree and the other leaning over him, one hand braced against the bark while the other caresses his partner's face.

If they saw me, I could slip my ring on and get away, but I keep my steps soft because I don't want to interrupt the moment. Then my breath catches as the light reflects off a pair of glasses and I realize who I'm looking at.

It's Natan and Remme.

My chest squeezes at the sight of such tender affection, but any momentary warmth that brings is chased away by the realization that I don't really know these people. I've begun to trust them, to think they're my friends, but these two are obviously in love and have been hiding it from me.

What else have they been hiding?

As soon as I doze off, I wake up again. Over and over again—a tug-of-war between my body and my mind.

I hear the low murmur of voices just beyond the fire and roll over to see Kendrick and Natan are still up, sitting fireside and talking.

"But you're sure you went deep enough?" Kendrick asks, poking at the fire with a long stick.

Natan tilts his head back and stares up at the stars. "I'm sure." He plunges his hands in his hair, elbows pointed to the sky. "I don't understand. I could feel her power. It's smoldering there, but it's like a blank slate."

"How can it be both?"

"I can't answer that," he growls. "That's why I kept looking. Otherwise, I would've thought maybe she was right—that maybe she didn't get her ancestors' magic."

"What do you think it means?"

"I don't know, but I can't help wondering if the blood magic's to blame."

"I wondered that too." Kendrick mutters a low curse. "But *no sign* of power when she's a child of Mab? I've never heard of blood magic allowing anyone to take so much."

"I've never seen it used so extensively on one person either," Natan says.

"True," Kendrick says. "And then there's the ring."

"Do you believe her when she says it doesn't work on you? It must, to some degree. You don't remember anything after she put it on. We're just taking her word for it that you don't follow her orders like everyone else when she's wearing it."

"Why would she lie about that?"

Natan shakes his head. "I don't think she would. I'm just pointing out that we don't know for sure." He chuckles under his breath. "Interesting."

"What?"

"Remember the old legends of sirens?"

"She's no siren."

"I'm not saying she is, but the power she wields while wearing the ring isn't so different than that of a siren, and in the stories, who were the only men who were immune to the song of the siren?"

"No one was immune. Women, men, fae—it didn't matter. Those creatures wrecked anyone they wanted to."

"Remember the tale of Fienna?"

"I suppose I do." Kendrick's quiet for a long time. "You think that's why?"

Natan low chuckle fills the air again. "So you don't deny it?"

He scrubs a hand down his face. "You know it's irrelevant."

"I want better for you than that."

"Better is coming for Elora," Kendrick says. "That's what matters."

I've dozed off again when I hear a scuffle of feet a few yards from my bedroll.

Skylar and Kendrick face each other a few feet away, arms crossed as if they're both angry.

"What if she's still alive? What if we find her? Are you losing hope? Because may the gods help us if *you*, Kendrick the Chosen, have lost faith. Why are we even bothering with any of this?"

"We don't know anything right now."

"Your *destiny* awaits, and you—"

"You know I will do my duty when and if the time comes. I've never chosen anything over duty."

"And you're sure it's so smart to make the girl love you. Is that

232

supposed to make it easier *when* the time comes?"

"I'm not talking about this with you. The winds are changing, and our fates with them."

"Perhaps," Skylar says, "but don't confuse lust for fate."

"So long as you don't confuse my friendship for deference. Remember your place."

CHAPTER SEVENTEEN

◇

FELICITY

"You will eat," Mordeus roars, and Jas's body slams down into the chair, her jaw snapping with the impact.

The food should smell delicious. If he had brought her to this room on her first day here, her mouth would've watered with the aromas filling the air. She's been a captive for less than a month, but it's been years since she's eaten well, and a meal like this is something she dreams about on nights when she goes to bed with an empty belly. But today, the sight and smell of the aromatic fare make her gag. She's too far past hungry, and her days in his dungeons, suffering the games of his guards, broke anything resembling appetite.

"I'm not hungry," she rasps through parched lips.

He narrows those unnatural silver eyes. "I didn't ask if you were hungry. I said you will eat."

Her hand reaches for the fork and jabs a piece of meat. It isn't her own. She has no control of her mouth as she opens her jaw and chews.

She gags as she swallows, but the magic is too strong and the food goes down, scraping like crushed glass with every inch.

Bite after bite, these hands that don't feel like her own feed *her and put water to her lips.*

The king never takes his eyes off her.

It's a violation she never could've imagined. If someone had told her the horrors of finding yourself taken by a faerie who forced you to eat delicious food, she would've laughed and asked if she could volunteer, but every bite is a betrayal by her body. Every morsel of food that makes its way to her stomach is an unwelcome intrusion into this last remaining piece of herself. Even her body is no longer her own.

When the plate is empty and her face is smeared with sauce, her shirt wet with water, her stomach convulses—too full after too many days of being so empty—but when she thinks she'll vomit, magic sweeps over her again and it settles.

He doesn't let her leave even then. Doesn't let her have control of her limbs. She's locked in that chair while he stares, like she's a puzzle he's trying to figure out.

"Refusing food and water is senseless," he finally says. "I control your fate. Your future is mine to rule. You understand now?"

She understands nothing, but it doesn't matter. She can't answer anyway. Her lips won't move. But even if she could, she wouldn't have anything to say to him. There's no point in begging. No point in asking why he's doing any of this. He's evil, and all she wants is to be free.

I bolt awake and dry heave at the side of my bed, the sensation of food and water being forced down my throat—*Jas's* throat—still too fresh.

"Princess," my handmaid says, rushing to my side.

The sound of her coming into the room must've pulled me

from that horrible dream. *Memory.*

"Are you okay? Should I cancel with the king this morning?"

I sit up in bed and try to get my bearings. "Cancel what?"

"Your training."

I squeeze my eyes shut and will my queasy stomach to settle. *It was just a dream.* Only it wasn't for Jas. For her, it was very real.

"I'm fine. Just had a bad dream."

I climb out of bed and dress in the leather pants and cotton top the maid laid out for me, but I can't stop thinking about the memory. The horror of it. The violation.

No wonder she wants to kill him.

Misha is already in the training yard when I arrive for our session. The sight of him in his tight black shirt as he looks off into the distance pulls my mind from the dream for the first time since I crawled out of bed.

His muscles bunch and flex under his shirt as he spins a spear in his hands, fingers dancing deftly on the staff.

"Are you going to teach me how to do that?" I ask.

He tosses it in a pile with the others before spinning to look me over. "I wasn't sure you'd be able to move this morning. How are you feeling?" His voice is low and husky, as if he just crawled out of bed himself, but his eyes are as sharp and keen as always— those russet owl eyes, always on the lookout.

"Not horrible," I say. "I got a tonic from my handmaid before bed." I would've preferred to make it myself. I could tell from the taste that it had lavender instead of willowroot, which I've found to be twice as effective at reducing muscle soreness.

"Good. Then you'll be ready for more training."

He moves closer, and the scent of him hits me. Like pine, rosewood, and something distinctly *male*. I want to lean into him, close my eyes, and breathe deeply until the horror of that memory clears my system.

"You still look like you're half asleep." He sweeps a rogue lock of hair behind my ear and his gaze snags on my lips for a beat before he pulls away. "Getting your blood flowing should wake you up." He steps back as if maybe he likes touching me too much.

Me or Jas? I need to stop trying to figure that out. At the end of the day, it won't matter.

I glance around the barren yard. "Where is my trainer this morning, anyway?"

"You're looking at him. We're working on hand-to-hand combat today."

I gape. I am far too unsteady to spend my morning not just close to Misha but *training-close*. "What—why you?"

"Tynan's unavailable. He's leading my other sentinels in a daylong training exercise at one of our outposts."

"Oh."

He laughs, his eyes lighting up. "Sorry to disappoint you."

"I'm not *disappointed*. I just didn't expect to be training with you."

He looks me over, slower this time. "Is that going to be a problem?"

"That depends. Do you have a healer handy? I know you're *very old*, and I wouldn't want to hurt you."

He chuckles. "I think I can handle it." He crooks a finger at me. "Come on, try to take me down."

I glance at the body I'm in and then at him. "You're twice my size."

"All the more reason I'm a good partner to train with. Do you think your enemies are only going to send small females after you?" He crooks a finger at me again. "Just give it a try."

My mind is racing in two directions at once. On one side everything I've ever learned about taking down an opponent that's bigger than me, and on the other side trying to imagine what Jas knows about all this. I know her sister made her learn self-defense, so I can probably get away with *most* maneuvers, but—

"If you think that long in the middle of a fight, you're going to end up dead," Misha says. He lunges forward and in one swift motion grabs me, spins me so my back is to him, and loops his arms around my neck. "Or worse—find yourself at someone's mercy."

I immediately flash back to the dream and the feeling of having someone else control my limbs and force me to eat. Being trapped like this would make the princess lose her mind, so I flail and use all my strength to push out with my arms. He doesn't budge.

"Stop trying to muscle it," he says in my ear. "You're too small. You're not going to be able to overpower your enemies. Work *smart*. Get free. You keep telling me you're not helpless. Now prove it."

Fine. I grab his arms and turn my head to the side, yanking on his wrist and bending my knees to drop my body weight down.

"Good," he murmurs, but I'm experienced enough to know he's not even trying to fight me.

I throw one leg back, seeking the leverage I need—just enough to get my center of gravity behind him. Then I drop down farther, and he releases me. I throw my leg up to pull his legs out from under him. He hits the ground with an *oomph* as his breath rushes out of him.

"I'm *not helpless*," I say.

I pull back, but he grabs me behind the neck before I can get far, hooking his leg around my waist and rolling our bodies until he's on top of me.

"I never said you were," he says. "But you don't stop fighting until it's *over*."

I cough and pull in air. "Noted," I croak.

Cursing, he lifts himself onto his elbows. "Are you okay? Did I hurt you?"

"I'm fine. Didn't need my pride anyway."

He grins, brushing the hair from my face. "You're different," he says, still breathing hard.

Those words should panic me, but I can't think straight when the weight of his body still rests between my thighs and his lips are so close to mine. He has the most perfect mouth. Bow shaped and soft. A little too wide for his face. Hungry looking, like his eyes.

"Different?" It's hard to push out the word, hard to do anything when it's taking all my energy to keep my hands from plunging into his hair and pulling his mouth to mine.

Kissing him is a bad idea. It's a terrible idea to follow this gut-level attraction with this male, with this *king* who thinks I'm someone else.

"I can't put my finger on it," he says, eyes scanning my face.

"You look no different. You . . ." His tongue skims the ridge of his teeth, and I want to do the same. What would those teeth feel like on my lips? On my neck? "Ever since you arrived in my court. Maybe that was what it took to make me *see* you."

I shift beneath him, pulling up one leg and giving his powerful thighs more room between my smaller ones. His body sinks *closer*.

He closes his eyes and mutters a curse. "What are you doing to me?"

"I don't know," I whisper. "I've never felt this. I . . ." I'm entranced by the sight of his throat as he swallows. I want to taste that too.

"It's not your scent. It's not the way you look or even your voice." His fingers skim across my cheek again, as if to tuck my hair back, but there's none left to tuck, no excuse left. He's just touching now. Memorizing. Cataloging. "Is it the fae in your blood? Is it because you'll turn so soon, and now . . ." He shakes his head. "Even that doesn't make sense to me." When he meets my eyes, his look is almost nervous. "Do you feel this too?"

I can't deny it. I won't. *I should.* "Yes."

"But your baker's son back home. Your—"

I shake my head. "I let him go." *What am I doing?*

"And do you miss him? Do you think about him?"

I can't think about anyone else when I'm around you. I can't remember who I am or why I'm here. But I only say, "It was best for both of us to move on."

His hand cups the side of my face, and his gaze locks on to my mouth. Then just as suddenly as we found ourselves on

240

the ground, he's rolling off me and hopping to his feet in a fluid motion. He wipes his hands on his pants, then helps me to my feet. But his gaze shifts from me to someone behind me.

"I didn't mean to interrupt," a female says, her voice delicate. "I wondered if you still wanted me to meet with the princess this morning."

I turn and blink at the former Wild Fae queen. She's tall—nearly as tall as Misha—with ebony skin, dark brown eyes, and hair that is cut close to her scalp. I know she's an empath just by the sense of peace I feel looking at her. At this moment, she's trying to ease my mind about what she just walked in on.

"Another time, of course," she says. "I didn't realize you'd be training with the king this morning."

Misha clears his throat and looks back and forth between us. "I think we'll end our session early this morning, Jasalyn," he says, glancing toward me without meeting my eyes. "I'd like to speak with Amira."

I swallow hard, feeling awkward and scandalized and rejected all at once. "Of course." I duck my head, not wanting to see the regret in his eyes. He almost kissed me, and he knows it was a mistake. *Noted.*

I should feel the same. It just might take me a few minutes longer to get there.

Spying on the king and his former wife is unforgivable.

Yet I find myself taking the form of a servant just so I can sneak into the king's quarters. Just so I can see them together.

Echoes aren't like shifters, and taking the form of another

241

requires sleep—dreaming—so it can't be done on a whim. Here? Where I'm expected to be Jasalyn and where her absence will be noted? Being anyone else is practically reckless, but when I found out the king and former queen were planning to take lunch together in the king's quarters, I couldn't resist.

I need to know what he thinks about what happened this morning. It's one thing for him to declare that I seem different in the heat of the moment, but if he's had more time to contemplate those feelings and he's grown suspicious, I need to know.

I left the training yard and found a member of the kitchen staff to send on an errand in the village, then retired to my chambers for a quick nap, a piece of her hair wrapped around my fingers and pressed to my chest. When I returned to the kitchen, the other staff members were surprised to see her back so soon but happy to let her take lunch to the king so they could get ahead on dinner preparations.

Misha's quarters are larger than mine, as I would've expected, but they aren't opulent by any means. They're comfortable. The kind of place you'd want to escape to after busy days of too much responsibility. As I prepare their plates in the small dining area, he sits in a wingback chair, eyes on the book in his lap. The midday sun accentuates the sharp angles of his cheekbones and the dark fringe of his lashes. From her chair beside him, Amira pours herself a cup of tea.

She smiles when she notices me, then cocks her head to the side. "Are you okay today, Welsey?"

Of course she would know even the names of all the staff members. I smile and train my thoughts on calming memories—riding through the fields as a child, baking with my mother, anything but how reckless it is to be here right now. It's one thing to shield my thoughts from Misha. It's quite another to shield my emotions from his empath wife. "I'm fine."

She frowns but doesn't push. I'm sure she has a lifetime of experiences with people denying their emotions. "You tell me if you need anything," she says. These two are so kind. It's no wonder they're beloved by their people.

I busy myself plating lunch for the two. I'm not sure what I thought they'd talk about, but so far their visit has been a quiet one. Like old friends who don't need to talk to enjoy each other's company.

Just when I think my efforts have been wasted, Misha closes his book with a huff and tosses it onto the table. "Go ahead and say it."

Amira meets his eyes. "Say what?" she asks innocently.

"I made a mistake today. You caught me in a weak moment, and I deserve to hear whatever it is you have to say about it."

She hums quietly.

Misha tilts his head back and stares at the ceiling. "I don't know what I was thinking."

"Perhaps that she's beautiful and kind. Perhaps that she looks at you like you're a god walking among us."

He frowns out the windows. "But isn't that strange?"

Amira coughs out a laugh. "Really, Misha, it's not like you to be so modest."

He grunts. "I mean she's different. Since coming here. Before this visit, I never—" He shakes his head. "It was inappropriate."

243

Amira turns in her seat and gives him a sad smile. "No one can fault you for your attraction. And it makes sense that it's new, that you're seeing her in a different light now that she's become a woman."

He scrubs a hand over his jaw. "If I lay a finger on Jasalyn without wedding bells in mind, Abriella will have my head." He pushes out of his chair and paces in front of the windows. "Brie wanted me to bring Jas out of her shell, but I don't think an affair is what she intended."

Amira sets down her tea. "Maybe it doesn't have to be an affair. Maybe matching you with the shadow princess is exactly what our realm needs."

Misha stops pacing and turns to his former wife. "If we were to truly pursue that which is best for the realm, we'd marry the shadow princess to the golden king."

She tilts her head to the side. "Neither would want that. He still carries a torch for her sister."

"Are we talking love or duty?"

"I'm suggesting maybe you have an option here that could allow you to be true to both," she says, her tone infused with patience.

There's a hollow ache in my chest at the idea of Misha marrying Jas. Which is ridiculous, since he thinks I'm her. Ridiculous, since she'd have none of it.

"Be honest," Amira says. "Are you resisting out of a sense of honor or because you're still waiting for the female in your dreams?"

Another tug in my chest—now jealousy over a *dream*? I'm

ridiculous. But his eyes are haunted when he looks at Amira. "Surely they mean something."

"They haven't lessened since the princess arrived?"

He shakes his head, then bows it. "If anything, they've redoubled. I spend my nights longing for a female I've never met and my days wondering at this pull to another."

"You could wait on a dream forever, and I would support that. But if you're feeling these things for a *real* woman. One who's under your roof and who seems to feel them for you too—"

"She can't be queen of an entire court when she doesn't even want to be fae."

Amira's quiet for a beat, then adds, "You deserve love. A true romantic partner."

I watch him from the corner of my eye as he drags his hands through the waves of his silky black hair.

"You'd have me give your throne and your crown to a young human?"

"She'll not be human for much longer."

Misha turns sad eyes on his former wife. It's hard not to stare when I want to analyze every emotion flitting across his beautiful face. He strolls slowly toward her. "What about you?"

She laughs lightly. "What about me?"

"You are the Wild Fae queen."

"Not anymore."

"You're beloved by your people. And I wouldn't have allowed you to release me from this marriage if I hadn't believed you were looking to pursue your own great love."

She strokes his cheek, and I drag my gaze away, imagining the feel of rough whiskers and soft skin. It makes no sense to be jealous of her. Not when their marriage was no marriage at all. But it doesn't matter that there's no romance between them. Misha may call Abriella his best friend, but it's Amira who knows him better than anyone.

"I had my own great love for a time," she says.

"But perhaps you could have her again," Misha says.

"She's never forgiven me for choosing duty over love. I won't ask her to do so after all these years." Her gaze flicks to where I'm standing—staring—at their plated meals, ready on the table. "That will be all, Welsey. If you need nothing from us, you can come gather the dishes later."

I shake my head before rushing from the room. I wait in the hallway until they call for me.

CHAPTER EIGHTEEN

◇

JASALYN

"My blood is yours to wield. Your blood is mine to preserve," the young fae warrior before me pledges, his dark head lowered in deference. "Blood for blood, magic for magic, life for life, I declare myself your servant." He slices into his palm, watching the blood well up there before making a fist and directing it to flow into the goblet between us. With a brief swirl to mix the contents, he lifts the goblet to his lips and takes a drink.

They line up for their chance to bow to me, for their opportunity to bend a knee to the king they deserve, the king who would never abandon them for the sake of a lowly human. It is I who will protect their rights as magical beings. It is I who recognize their birthright as members of the fae elite.

"You honor me," I say, accepting the goblet from him. I take a drink of our combined blood and close my eyes as I feel his power—his magic, his life force—attach to mine. "Now your death shall never be in vain, and through me, you too shall reign forever."

The hands are everywhere, holding me down while his magic cuts into my skin like a hot knife sliding through butter. He always makes me meet his eyes. "Look at me, little human. Why are you so scared? Together we can rule the world."

"Look at me, Jasalyn." *Hands on my shoulders, rough fingers on my chin.* "Look at me. Come back to me."

The voice cuts through the fog of my nightmare, but the memory pins me down like those too-strong hands. *"Wake up, little human."*

"Please, Jas. Look at me."

I blink and focus on the blue eyes in front of me. *Blue. Not silver. Not Mordeus.* "Kendrick," I whisper, and I lean forward to kiss him—to touch those lips to mine. Because I need to. It's what I want, and something nameless drives me to *take*. The comfort of his mouth, the warmth of his embrace.

He pulls back. Keeps me at a distance with stiff arms, hands on my shoulders. "No."

"No?"

"Jas. The ring."

"The ring?" I glance down to my hand, remembering—the ring, the magic, the *kiss*—and see where we are. My whole body goes cold.

We're in the forest, and the midmorning light sifts through the trees, casting dappled shade on Kendrick's worry-stricken face.

How did I get here? Did I black out?

A spike of panic has me scanning the trees, and I catch sight of Gommid a few feet away. His lips purse into a frown before he disappears.

"What happened?" I look side to side, searching for an explanation. Several yards behind Kendrick, standing with two horses by the trees, Remme and Skylar stare with adoring eyes that tell me my ring has them in its grip.

The last thing I remember is listening to Kendrick and Skylar argue. When did I put on the ring? Did I have Gommid take me somewhere?

"Jas." He cups my face, eyes scanning every inch and strokes my jaw with his thumb. "Where did you go?"

"I don't . . ." Dizziness crashes over me, and I close my eyes. *I reached for him. I almost kissed him.*

"Jas, look at me. You need to take off your ring."

The ring. That's why I feel this way. The ring is meant for the darkness.

But I'm shaking too hard, and Kendrick has to slide it from my finger.

We take two steps toward our friends before my head spins. The world tilts on its side, and I collapse.

"She must've snuck away while we were sleeping."

"We need to know where she went. If she told someone about our plans—"

"We can trust her."

"I want to believe that as much as you do, but the fact is she used the ring to sneak away in the middle of the night. We need to know why."

Their voices seem distant, but I know they're not far. I'm somewhere safe. Soft. Warm. A bed.

"Answers can wait. She's halfway to death."

"And is that the cost of the ring's magic?"

"Do you think she was telling the truth? About it giving her the kiss of death?"

"I'll go to the archives today and find what I can."

They need to know I blacked out. I want to tell them I don't remember sneaking away. I should call for my goblin. Gommid could tell us where I was. But I can't find the strength to open my eyes.

"I'm sure she had a reason for leaving and for going wherever she went. We'll get our answers soon enough."

"You're assuming she wakes up."

"She's going to wake up."

The last comes from Kendrick, and even though the rest of their conversation has my mind spinning and clawing to avoid sleep, those words soothe me. *She's going to wake up.*

CHAPTER NINETEEN

◆

FELICITY

"*THERE IT IS.*" *MORDEUS'S SILVER eyes drag over her, assessing and bright. Satisfied. "There's the power I was promised. It blazes bright inside you."*

She wants to spit at him but, again, has no control over her body. These visits are worse than the cell. Worse than the torture by the guards and the bugs crawling over her food. This paralysis is everything her sister was talking about when she warned her against the fae. And I didn't listen.

The cry that rips from her lips is the only way she knows she has control of her vocal cords again. She tries to wiggle her fingers, to squirm from her chair, but nothing happens. Speaking is all she can do.

Tears stream down her cheeks. "I don't know what you're talking about."

"You have a gift. I see it behind your fear." He cocks his head to the side. "Why did the gods see fit to grant such magic to a human girl?"

He's mad. A mad faerie king raving nonsense at a human girl he stole in order to play some mad faerie game. She has no power, and if she did, she would never use it on his behalf. Never.

"I have no power." She's sobbing and hates him for it. Hates herself for it. She's so sick of being powerless, so sick of being weak and letting these horrible creatures know it.

Then the darkness grabs ahold of her—biting, clawing, pulling her in all directions, threatening to tear her apart. Her sobs turn to keening cries for help. She cries for her sister, who hasn't come, for her mother, who left them long ago, for the gods, who left them to be preyed on by the fae.

The pain is there. It is one with the darkness. And then, in a flash of flames, it's gone. The room reappears—the table before them with its flickering candles.

She flies to her feet and falls to the floor just as quickly, unprepared to have control of her limbs again. The pain is gone, but she can feel its echo in her bones. She curls into herself because moving is too terrifying.

Mordeus kneels in front of her. "The pain makes you stronger, little human. Endure."

His face is blurry through her tears. Nothing he's saying makes sense. The only thing she understands is her hatred. It boils and rages, a tempest inside.

If she ever has any power, she will use it to end him.

"Do you believe in destiny?" Maybe it's a strange question to ask a goblin, but I trust Nigel more than I trust almost anyone, and I know that with the collective knowledge of the goblins, he understands this world better than I ever will.

"There are certain inevitabilities," he says. He's playing

solitaire on the floor in front of my bed while I sit curled up in a chair by the window.

It's a cold afternoon in the Wild Fae territory, winter threatening to blow in early, and though the castle remains warm, I always feel cold weather in my bones.

"Inevitabilities?" I ask. "Sounds like another word for destiny."

"You can call them destiny if you like." He flips over a card and cackles in triumph. He loves solitaire. I gifted him with his own deck of cards years ago, and he asked me to keep them for him—said he doesn't like to play alone. He didn't see the irony.

"So there's no free will?" I ask.

He looks up from his spread of cards. "My child, for every vision that oracle had of you plunging the blade into your father's heart, she had another of him cutting your throat while your first cries still filled the halls of his palace. Both cannot be true, so there is most certainly free will."

I draw my knees to my chest and wrap my arms around my legs. "So you don't think I'm being selfish for refusing to assassinate my father?"

He shakes his head but keeps his eyes on his cards as he shuffles one pile to the next. "My girl has never been selfish, though I might call her foolhardy."

I scoff. "Foolhardy? How can you say that?"

"She who tries to manipulate the fates falls right into their trap."

I shake my head. "I can't do it. I won't sacrifice Hale if there's a chance we can bring Erith down another way."

He flips over a card and smacks it. "Drat." He sweeps the lot

253

into a pile before looking at me again. "Are you asking about destiny because you're curious about who you kill or because you're hurt that the male you're falling for has been avoiding you?"

I frown. Misha *is* avoiding me. He wasn't in the training yard when I arrived there at sunrise today, even though I hadn't spoken with him since we tussled there yesterday. Tynan ran me through my exercises. When I asked if Misha would be meeting me for breakfast, I was told the king had left the castle on court business and I could take my meal wherever I pleased.

I shouldn't have spied on Misha and Amira. I was nervous that he was onto me, but afterward I realized that may have been nothing more than an excuse. I wanted to know what Misha was feeling, but hearing him contemplate a relationship with Jasalyn only left me morose.

I hate that yesterday's fleeting moment together—whatever it was—scared him away. I've been telling myself it's because my research on portals isn't getting me anywhere and I may truly need him in order to locate the Hall of Doors. But the truth may be less devious than that. I enjoy being around the Wild Fae king, and even though it's only been a day, I miss his company.

I'm ashamed to contemplate how much of the day I wasted stewing and pining when I needed to be researching. I skimmed through a book that discussed the merits of placing portals in the mountains, where their power would echo along the nearby cliffs and circle back rather than dissipate along an open horizon. That, however, does me little good when the Wild Fae territory has more mountains than plains.

"That's what I thought," Nigel says.

I make a face. "I am not falling for anyone, so stop it."

His big eyes bulge. "She lies! I swore my allegiance to the child during her days in swaddling clothes, and now she lies to me about her heart."

I look out the window and toward the valley in the distance. "I don't know what you're talking about."

"You're finally in love, and you plan to hide it from *me*?"

"Don't be ridiculous. This is not love."

He chuckles again and waddles toward me. "Silly girl. You forget how long I've lived. I know the smell of early love. It's too stinky to miss—earthy and ripe, and laced with hope."

I chew on the inside of my cheek. "He thinks I'm Jasalyn."

He bops the tip of my nose with his knobby finger. "Ah, but he wishes you were not."

I give him a quick smile. "Thanks, I guess?" Nigel always delivers words of comfort that don't feel very comforting at all. "Is my mother okay?"

"Your mother was killed by your father the day he found out she hid you from him."

I cringe. *So literal.* "No, I'm asking about Hale's mom—the woman who *raised me*."

"Oh. Her. She's not dead."

Ask stupid questions, get stupid answers. "Emotionally speaking, Nigel. How is she getting along?"

"Fine. Strong-willed, that one." He shrugs. "She rarely calls for her goblin."

I nod. She's always been more interested in doing for others than in letting them do for her.

255

"What else is troubling you tonight, my child?"

"I keep thinking about the resurrection of the wicked king." I can't stop thinking about last night's dream. The pain. Mordeus and his insistence that Jas has a magical gift shown to him by the oracle. Why would the oracle show Mordeus Jasalyn's magic? And what kind of powers might she have for him to believe he needed them? Is she the necromancer he would need to make his resurrection complete? Is it possible that she would be more powerful than any necromancer Mordeus ever met? Even if she is, how would he convince her to use such powerful magic to bring him back when she would do anything to destroy him for good?

As much as I want answers, I have to be careful what and how I ask Nigel. I trust him with my life, but I can't trust all goblins. Anything I tell Nigel becomes part of the greater goblin consciousness, whether Nigel wishes it to or not. Sometimes the wrong people make payment to the right goblin and ask the right question, and information you shared when trying to help your cause suddenly works against you. "How would something like that even work if the gods weren't behind it?"

"Sacrifice, my child." His head snaps to the closed door on the opposite side of my chambers. "You have a visitor," he says. Then he disappears.

After two brief knocks, the door swings open and Misha strolls in wearing riding leathers, a bandolier of knives strapped to his waist, and his sword on his back. "Good afternoon, Princess. I see you've returned to your old habits of wasting away the day."

I barely refrain from springing out of my chair. Instead, I

calmly unfold myself and settle my hands on my knees as I lean toward him. "Are you serious?"

He frowns at the strap of my chemise that's fallen off my shoulder. "Are you denying you've been reading in your room since breakfast?" He shoves his hands into his pockets. "Hurry and dress. We should leave."

"You blow me off last night, then for training and breakfast this morning, and now you show up in my chambers and have the nerve to *criticize me* for how I spend my time?"

His lips twitch. "You missed me."

"Look who's full of himself."

"No." He leans against my armoire and folds his arms, studying me. "Simply observant."

"I was led to believe we'd be training together," I say. His gaze is too knowing, so I study my book, tracing the letters on the cover. "I was worried."

"I needed to run an errand." He strolls toward me and pulls a silver necklace from his pocket. The chain is thick and holds an ebony crescent moon charm. The moon is upended, like a cup set to catch rainwater. "To retrieve this from the Midnight Palace."

My breath catches. "That belonged to Mordeus?"

"Yes." He tucks it back into his pocket. "Now, get ready. We're going to see Gaelynn's witch and confirm what we already know to be true."

I lift my gaze to his. "Why didn't you tell me where you were going?"

With a grimace, he narrows his eyes at the view outside my window. "In truth, I was afraid you'd want to go with me, and

I thought that if you did, you might want to stay." He clears his throat. "Since your sister seems incapable of telling you no, I didn't want to put her in that position."

I bite back a smile. "Oh. You did it for Brie."

"She is my friend, Jasalyn."

"You didn't do it for any other reason?" I ask, setting my blanket to the side. "Like maybe you'd miss me if I were gone?"

"Look who's full of herself now."

"No," I say, pushing out of my chair and standing toe to toe with him. "Just observant."

This witch's cottage is worse than Gaelynn's sanctuary. While the sanctuary itself left me unsettled, it's this witch whose presence my instincts tell me to escape as soon as possible.

After I dressed, Misha's goblin took us to the coast, where a mountain bluff holds a tiny hut that looks like it should've been blown away ages ago.

"And this necklace belonged to him?" the witch asks when Misha explains why we're there. She walks around with a cane and looks every bit as rickety as the old house. Her appearance says she could break if you breathe wrong. Her energy says she could break *you* if you breathe wrong.

"Indeed. His nephew said it was one of Mordeus's favorites."

"Do you need it back?"

"Do whatever you need to do. I just need to know if he lives."

She spins and drops the necklace into a steaming pot, where it hisses and moans. "He lives," she says, watching the steam rise. "He lives, but he dies."

"What does that mean?" I ask. It takes all my courage to stand *beside* Misha instead of cowering behind him.

"He's fighting for his life—floating between life and death. He has a body, but it stinks of death and rot. It cannot hold. He's conscious but is not fully of this world. His magic is weak." The steam dissolves in the air, and she shrugs. "That's all I can tell you."

"That's all we need to know," Misha says. "He's been—is *being*—resurrected."

"No. Resurrection is a gift given by the gods alone." She touches her fingers to her forehead and bows her head, murmuring something, as if saying a prayer of apology to those gods for Misha's very suggestion.

When she looks up, she braces her hands on the counter. "Is that all?"

Misha glances at me, then back to the witch. "I have one more question."

"Then ask it. I do not grow younger."

"The princess has these scars. They have been appearing out of nowhere, a new one every week or so for the last few months. Do you have any idea why?"

I spin on him. "What? What are you doing?"

"Show me," the witch snaps.

"Please," he whispers.

There's a vise around my chest. I *don't* want this female examining me. I don't want her anywhere near me even in my true form, but in *this* form, I'm practically shaking as I pull up my sleeve and reveal my forearm.

The witch pulls out a magnifying glass and holds it over the circular knot of scars above my wrist. "Out of nowhere, you say?"

"Yes. She goes to bed without them, and sometimes a new one will be there when she wakes."

I wish he'd told me he'd planned to do this. I would've found a way to get out of it. For one, Jas has lied to her sister and friends if they think these scars are coming from nowhere. Never mind that if the scars have been appearing weekly for the last three months, it's going to seem terribly suspicious that no new scars appear while I'm at Castle Craige. And no new scars will—even if Jasalyn's getting new scars daily, I won't. I'll only match the scars she had when she cut the hair I'm using to take her form.

"Every week?" the witch asks.

Misha looks to me, and I shake my head. I have no idea, but the more inconsistent this can seem, the better off I am. "At random intervals."

"Scars tell a story," the witch says, running her fingers over the mark again and again. "An adventure, a betrayal, an injury, a trauma." She presses her palm against the scar and closes her eyes. Her brow wrinkles and she presses harder.

"That *hurts*," I say through gritted teeth.

She opens her eyes to slits. "Oh. I'm sorry. Did the girl want me to solve this mystery without any discomfort?"

"The *girl* isn't worried about this mystery," I mutter. It's true. I've dreamed one of Jas's memories of waking up with a new scar, and she was oddly ambivalent about it. She knew where it came from but didn't know why it was showing so belatedly. She was unconcerned about the effect on her appearance, and any memories the marks triggered, she pushed down deep.

"Sit," the witch snaps. "You're blocked. We need to open you up."

I look to Misha, wide-eyed. "I don't want to do this."

He pulls out the green velvet chair at the witch's small table. "You can trust her. We need answers."

I lower myself into it while quietly fortifying every single one of my mental shields.

The witch opens a cabinet and retrieves vials and bottles filled with liquids and powders of various colors. "There are parts of Elora," she says as she begins mixing them, "that dabble in blood magic. Ever heard of it?"

I have, though I'm sure Jas hasn't. It's one of those pieces of Eloran history that was lost—or, rather, *buried*—when the Elora Seven came into power. Now the magic is something that only they know and only they use. Magic is more powerful when fewer people have access to it, and the Elora Seven care about nothing more than power.

Misha folds his arms across his chest. "Blood magic? This is something Eloran mages practice?"

"Mages? Those spell-muttering humans?" she scoffs. "No, no. Blood magic is ancient. It's from a time before the gates between our realms were ever opened, and it was outlawed across their lands, but that didn't stop some from using it anyway."

"If mages aren't using it, then who?"

She stills with a vial ready to pour into another and turns narrowed eyes on the king. "Have you never been told the true history of the Eloran realm? From the days before the portals were open?"

He rocks back on his heels. "I haven't spent much time worrying myself over the history of other realms."

"Perhaps you should. Especially when you see evidence of blood magic used on a Faerie princess."

"What does it do?" Misha asks.

She taps some powder into her glass of various liquids, and it fizzes. "Blood magic has many purposes—from borrowing someone's magic to connecting your life force to theirs for extra strength in battle—but it's these scars that make me suspicious." She takes the seat across from me and meets Misha's gaze. "I've never seen blood magic scars myself, but my mother told me of them when she trained me. When the flesh is cut for a blood magic ritual, no mark is left behind. The magic heals it. It is only when that magic is called upon later that the scar appears."

Misha sinks into the chair next to mine and studies me. "Could these scars be tied to something that happened to you in Mordeus's dungeons?" He fists his hands on his thighs, as if bracing himself. Assuming I won't answer? Or preparing himself for the anger he might feel when faced with the truth?

Jas probably wouldn't answer, and I hate that responding differently feels like a betrayal to Jas, but I don't have a choice. Continued stubborn silence will only make him push harder. That's something I can't risk.

"I don't know if he was doing blood magic," I say, "but these scars?" I swallow and nod. "It's as if they are scars from what happened in his dungeon."

"And how many are there?" the witch asks. "More than this one?"

I watch Misha as I nod. "Quite a few more."

Misha pales, then squeezes his eyes shut. I know what he's

262

thinking because I have thought the same. *No wonder she hates the fae. No wonder she's so broken.*

"What did he want with a human girl?" the witch whispers, swirling the potion in the glass. "And why are the markings coming to bear only now?" She takes my wrist again and lifts the glass, her hand shaking. "This will only sting for a minute."

With a turn of her wrist, she dumps the steaming liquid directly onto the gnarled scar, and I scream. It's as if the flesh is being ripped from my bones. As if she has inserted hundreds of tiny red-hot knives directly into the scar. As if she's twisting them and digging them deeper.

When the pain subsides enough for me to open my eyes, the room is filled with steam, and I can't see Misha or the witch.

A chair squeaks, and the steam clears enough for me to see her stand. A glass slips from her fingers and smashes on the floor.

"Get out."

"What's wrong?" Misha asks.

"Get out of my house!" The witch points at me. "She is not a human girl, and those scars are not right."

I back toward the door, hands shaking as my gaze bounces between the witch and Misha. *I'm caught. This is over.*

"Tell me what you saw," Misha says. He's so calm. So unbothered by what she said.

"Nothing," she screeches. "I saw nothing, and that is not possible." She backs into the counter behind her, knocking a vial over. It rolls to the ground and shatters, sending a puff of red vapor into the air. "Leave this house and do not come back with your lies. You are *fae* hiding in human skin."

"She has fae blood," Misha says, standing and offering his hand to calm the witch. "She is a child of Mab."

She dodges his hand. "Perhaps, but those scars have no story, no pain, no feeling in them. There are lies and trickery behind what we see there. You be careful, my king."

Misha's quiet for a long time as we walk away from the old witch's house. I try not to stare, but I'm desperate to know what's going on in his mind. The witch told him my scars are a lie. She told him this is trickery.

But he stays at my side as if we're old friends and not as if he's about to throw me in his dungeons. And I think that might be worse. The guilt I feel over this trust might be worse.

"How many more scars?" he asks. "I've seen the ones on your arms, but how many . . ." His feet scuff in the gravel as he stops and turns to me, eyes haunted.

"I haven't counted." I place my hand on my stomach. "Many here. More on my back. Some on my ankles."

"He did this to you." It's not a question. He's saying it for himself, as if he's trying to wrap his mind around it. "You were trying to protect Brie. That's why you wouldn't tell her—you knew where they were from, but you didn't want her to know what he did to you."

Swallowing, I bow my head. "What good would it do?" How many times has Jas thought the same thing?

He pulls me into his arms, one hand behind my back and another in my hair, and tucks my head under his chin.

I stiffen, at first because I'm so surprised at the gesture and then because I remember that I'm supposed to—that Jas doesn't like to be touched.

Misha releases me and steps back. "I'm so sorry," he says, retreating another step and shoving his hands into his pockets. "I wish you'd never had to endure that, and if I could go back—"

"You can't. We can't."

He nods, but his gaze is on my stomach, as if he can see the patchwork of scars through my clothes. "He was a special kind of evil. I knew it even then."

I glance over my shoulder toward the howling sea wind and the cottage, now hidden behind the thatch of trees. "What do you make of what she said? About my scars being lies?" I swallow hard. "Do you think that could be part of the blood magic? The absence of the scar's memory?"

Misha looks toward the cottage as well. "That's what I'm guessing. She said herself that she's never encountered this type of scarring before. I don't think we should make too much of her panic. Remember she also told us resurrection isn't possible without the gods right after telling us Mordeus lives."

"And what about what she said about me not being human?"

Some of the thoughtful calculation falls off his expression. "I'm sorry, Jasalyn. I think that's just a fact. You are fae. You just haven't fully transformed yet."

I hang my head to hide my relief. He's not concerned at all. Not even a little suspicious—though he should be.

If he ever figures this out, this will be one of those moments he hates himself for. Hates *me* for. I've done my job too well, and his affection for me has clouded his judgment.

"I'm sorry," he says again. "Maybe the more time you spend around us, the sooner you'll see that we're not like him. Some are, and I make it my business to give them what they have coming to them, but the majority of us are mostly good and want to make this whole realm a better place."

"I know," I whisper. But I don't think Jas knows that at all. I draw in a ragged breath. "Is it possible that this blood magic the witch talked about is responsible for Mordeus's resurrection?"

"Even if your power comes to rival the Great Queen Mab's, that wouldn't be enough to bring a king back from the dead. But if you weren't the only one he used this blood magic on. If he was calling upon the magic from others as well . . ." He shrugs. "It's all so unprecedented. I'm not sure I can say what is or isn't possible."

"She spoke of him being alive but dying. His body is dying. I wonder if that means he hasn't found his necromancer yet." I'm thinking out loud again. I really need to stop that.

"I should hope not," Misha says. "I shudder to think of anyone with that kind of power. Even if we're right about the faceless plague making him stronger, true resurrection should be a power only the gods can wield."

"The Jewel spoke of foresight—of everything that would have to be put in place, and Mordeus . . ." I press a hand to my chest, trying to calm my racing heart. What would Jas do if she knew Mordeus was drawing strength from her? If she knew she was even a small part of the reason he was able to return? Nothing good. "When I tried to stop eating and drinking in the dungeons, Mordeus forced me to. He said he needed me to live, and in the next breath, he'd torture me. He said the pain would make me stronger. I think he knew he would need to draw on my power before anyone else even knew I had power to draw on."

When I lift my gaze to Misha's, his expression is bleak, and I realize too late what I revealed: that Jas stopped eating and drinking. That her time in the dungeons was so horrible she wanted to let death come. "We all underestimated how bad those weeks were for you," he says, his voice hoarse. "And you let us. You let us think you were being stubborn and narrow-minded rather than let your sister know the truth."

I don't know what to say and won't let myself reveal more, so I don't say anything at all.

"I'm sorry I didn't see it before," he says, swallowing.

I hate the regret I see in his eyes, the way he's blaming himself for not knowing the truth when Jas did everything she could to keep it a secret. "I didn't want you to."

"We need more answers," he says. "But I won't make you be part of finding them."

"No," I blurt. I take a deep breath. "Maybe this is good for me. I think . . . I think I need to be a part of it."

"If you're sure," he says softly.

I give a jerky nod, but guilt and worry claw at my chest. Misha's right. We don't know enough yet. If we truly want to stop Mordeus, we need Jas to tell us everything she knows: about what happened in the dungeons and what's changed in the last three months since the scars began to emerge. She could help us figure out how Mordeus is calling on the blood magic. I'm beginning to think she's the only one who has the answers we need.

Hale should be sending someone to check in with me

sometime this week. I know he has spies in the castle, but he won't trust just anyone to take a full report from me. For that, he'll send one of his most trusted.

I just hope it's sooner than later. They need to know what we've learned before Mordeus finds his necromancer.

CHAPTER TWENTY

— ◇ —

JASALYN

When I wake again, I'm in a small bedroom, and the sun outside the window is low in the sky. I don't know how long I slept, and I'm too disoriented to tell if it's rising or setting.

I sit up and stretch, letting my sheets pool at my waist.

"Thank the gods," Kendrick whispers behind me, and I turn to see him sitting in a lounge chair on the opposite side of the bed. His throat bobs as he swallows. He looks me over. "How do you feel?"

I push out of bed and walk around to his side. I'm stiff and sore, but I don't feel any of that weakness I had when I heard them talking and couldn't get my eyes to open. "I'm fine."

He leans forward to adjust the bedside lantern. The room is flooded with light. When he lifts his gaze to mine again, the color drains from his face. "What happened?"

"What do you mean? What's wrong?"

"What did that bastard do to you?" He unfolds from the chair and cups my face in both of his hands, sweeping one thumb from the middle of my cheek and up around the outside of my eye, his eyes wide.

"I don't know what you're talking about." I place my hand atop his. "I'm fine. Don't look so panicked."

His throat bobs. "It's a new scar."

Maybe I'll just cut these pretty eyes out. Then you'll have to look at me.

I step back and rush across the room to the small mirror that sits over the dresser. My hand shakes as I lift it to the ragged, puffy scar extending from the center of my cheek and hooking up around my eye.

I've never been particularly vain—at least not since living in Faerie. I never cared that these scars from years-old wounds were appearing from nowhere. It didn't matter. I didn't care about this body that has fae blood. I didn't care about this life trapped in a realm I hate or the fate I never asked for.

But that was before I knew what it felt like to want something other than numbness and revenge. *That was before Kendrick.*

My eyes burn with the tears of the weak girl I won't let myself be, and I squeeze them shut so I don't have to see. I grip the edge of the dresser and hang my head.

It doesn't matter. It's just another scar. In nine months, none of this will matter anyway.

I'm so lost in my self-pity that I don't realize Kendrick is behind me until he wraps his arms around me, pulls my back against his front.

I lift my head to meet his gaze in the mirror. "Everyone will see," I whisper, and I didn't realize until now that it bothered me so much. "Everyone will know I was a victim."

His eyes meet mine in the mirror as he traces along the edge of my jaw. "Everyone will know you are a survivor."

I swallow the lump of emotion threatening to choke me.

"I wish I could go back and make myself think twice about everything," he says, his breath feathering my hair. "I wouldn't assume that I knew what was happening. I wouldn't assume that your only wounds were the ones I could see." He buries his face in my neck, and his words become a prayer whispered into my skin. "Every time they brought you back, you were fine, and I didn't . . ." The band of his arms tightens, like he's trying to will us back in time so he can change things. "Of course he was healing you. Every time. Healing you so I wouldn't know how bad it was. Why didn't you tell me what was happening?"

I swallow. He's holding me almost too tightly, but I hope he never stops. "I would pass out, and when I'd wake up, the blood would be gone, and the pain was just a memory." I turn in his arms and look up into his searching eyes. "I didn't know if it was real or all a nightmare."

He bends his lips to the scar, like it's a fresh wound he's trying to kiss better. When he brings his mouth to my ear, his voice is deadly quiet. "I will kill him myself when we find him."

I close my eyes. It feels good, I realize, having someone share my rage. I've carried it alone for so long.

And maybe . . . maybe that's where I went wrong. Maybe holding it inside, hiding all the twisted, broken pieces—maybe these old wounds festered in the dark.

"I want to ask you what happened before I collapsed, but . . ." I look to him, hopeful.

"You don't remember either?" he asks.

"I was having terrible nightmares. Nightmares about . . ." Nightmares where I was Mordeus. Nightmares where I could feel what it was like to have his kind of power and to be willing to destroy everything to keep it. Except they didn't scare me. No, the nights when my mind imagines what it would be like to be him—those are some of the most restful nights I have. It feels *good*, and I don't like to think too much on what that says about me.

"You had nightmares about your time in the dungeons," Kendrick says.

It's not a question, and I don't want to correct him. I stare down at my hands. The hands of a girl who was once tortured by a monster have now become the hands of the monster. "I went to sleep and was dreaming, and the next thing I remember was you bringing me to consciousness in the forest."

"You don't remember leaving?" he asks. I shake my head, and he draws in a ragged breath. "We all woke up after the sun. You must've put on the ring and told Skylar to go to sleep before you left camp, because you were there when she started her shift and the next thing she remembers she was waking up on her bedroll.

"When we realized you weren't there, we searched for you. The camp, the woods, calling your name."

"And then I reappeared with my goblin."

He turns me to face him and shakes his head. "I don't know. The next thing I remember is pulling the ring off you."

Panic seizes my chest in a sweaty fist. "Where is it? The ring?"

"Natan has it. He's researching."

I swallow down my panic at being separated from the only real power I have.

Kendrick reaches for my hand and toys with my fingers. "Do you know where you might've gone?"

I shake my head. But then remember the rebel camp nearby, and my mind flashes with images of the dead bodies lined up outside of the captain's manor. What if I blacked out that night too? What if . . .

"Have you blacked out like this before?" Kendrick asks.

"I was at Captain Vauril's the night they all died—*before* they all died."

There's a long beat of silence. "You were?"

"Wearing my ring. I was following the proprietor. I wanted to . . ." I swallow. "I hated the way he treated his wife, and I needed to make sure he didn't hurt my sister. I only remember killing him. I left the rest. But then the next morning . . ."

"That's why you were so shaken when they were all dead? You suspected you were responsible."

"Yes." I stare at my hands. "But I didn't know. I only ever killed one at a time—or so I thought. But . . ." I snap my head up. "The rebels camping near us. What if I went there? What if I—"

"You didn't. We searched the camp when we were looking for you." He pulls me into a hug and lets me rest my cheek against his chest. "The rebels were alive and well. Wherever you went, it wasn't there."

"I need to call my goblin. I saw him after I came to. If I had him take me somewhere, he can tell us."

Kendrick grimaces. "As much as I'd like to know what he could tell us, we can't ask."

"Why not?"

"Goblins' loyalties are too divided. We can't risk the information about this place getting back to the Elora Seven."

"So we just have to be okay with not knowing?"

He nods. "For now."

Swallowing, I glance around the room. "And where are we?" I can make out voices beneath us and the sound of flatware on dishes.

"Ironmoore. It's an Eloran settlement. It's the safest place we could find for you while we figure some things out."

"Elorans? In Faerie?"

A ghost of a smile passes across his face as he tucks a lock of hair behind my ear. "Why's that so hard to believe? *We're* all here."

"Yes, but you're just . . ." I wave my hand in the air as if to indicate him and the friends I can hear below us. "There are only a few of you."

"Many Elorans have been displaced under the rule of the Seven," he says. "More than you can imagine. Believe it or not, Faerie is a good option as far as temporary homes go."

I don't argue for fear of him pointing out the hypocrisy in my feelings toward the shadow fae. Maybe his friends are right. Maybe what I feel is nothing but prejudice.

"Let's get you some dinner," Kendrick finally says.

"I still want to go with you," I blurt, registering the rest of what he said. *The safest place for me.* Are they planning to leave me here? I lift my chin. I won't lose my chance to end Mordeus. "I want to be there when you go to Feegus Keep."

Kendrick huffs out a breath and shakes his head. "What happened to that timid little girl from the dungeons?"

I know he means to be flippant, but I hold his gaze as I answer, "She didn't make it."

Remme and Skylar are sitting at a small table in the home's main floor kitchen, steam rolling off bowls of stew in front of them.

"Going before the ball still feels risky," Remme is saying. "The king's sentinels will be watching for anything suspicious."

"That's why we're sending Shae and not you," Skylar says. "*He* isn't suspicious."

"You found your friend?" I ask, and their eyes turn to me.

Skylar's face splits into a grin as she looks me over with an arched brow. "Sick scar. How are you feeling, Slayer?"

I pull back, surprised. She's never used that nickname before. "Better. Where's Natan?"

"He's doing some research," Remme says. "He'll be back soon."

I frown. "About the ring?"

Remme nods. "We don't make a habit of engaging with magic we don't understand. And after what happened yesterday . . ." He shrugs.

I frown. *Yesterday.* "How long was I sleeping?"

"A day and a half," Kendrick says, and there's a tenderness in his eyes that makes me want to prove I'm not helpless or weak.

But is that even true without the ring?

"Do you always get that sick after using it?" Remme asks.

I shake my head. "No. It's using it during the daylight that comes with complications."

"What kind of complications?" Kendrick asks.

"Nausea, lethargy, a little weakness."

275

"You collapsed and slept for thirty-four hours," Skylar says. "That's more than *a little weakness*."

"Death's kiss and now this?" Remme asks.

I look to Kendrick, who shrugs. "They needed to know," he says.

"Any other details you'd like to share with the class, Princess?" Remme asks.

"Just that one. It's a tool meant for the dark." I glance around the small kitchen, desperate to change the subject. "Is there coffee?"

"On the counter," Skylar says, but Kendrick is already heading that way.

He fills a mug and hands it to me. "You need food too." He nods to a chair—the only available one at the table. "Sit and I'll get it for you."

"Aren't you going to eat?" I ask, lowering myself into it.

"Already did," he says.

"Never once has he brought me my dinner," Remme says.

"He doesn't look at you like that either," Skylar mutters.

I squirm and reach for a change of subject. "Where's Shae going, then?"

"To the Wild Fae Lands," Remme says. "To check in with Felicity."

"Have you heard anything?" I ask. "About how Felicity's faring at Castle Craige?"

Remme shrugs. "Seems like it's going great."

"Misha isn't suspicious at all? Or is she just keeping to herself like I told her?"

Kendrick slides a fresh bowl of stew in front of me, and I flash him a grateful smile.

"Relax," Skylar says, poking at her dinner. "She's fine. She's been winning the king over just like we need her to."

I straighten. "Excuse me—what? I told her to stay in her chambers. If she spends too much time with him, he'll figure it out, and if Misha figures it out, he *will* tell my sister."

Remme and Skylar exchange a look, and he sighs. "Listen, I appreciate where you're coming from," he says, "but Felicity is good at what she does. You saw her yourself."

"And *Misha* is really good at what *he* does. He *reads minds.* Don't you get that?"

Skylar folds her arms. "He doesn't read yours."

"Well, yeah, because he trained me how to block against him."

"Then he can't be all that skilled with it," she says.

My fist tightens around my spoon. "Brie says she's watched him break people."

Remme sighs. "But he hasn't broken you because he respects you. He trained you how to shield your mind, and he respects that shield—and he'll respect Felicity's shield because he believes she is you. You have *nothing* to worry about."

I stir my stew, shaking my head. "Why does she need to get close to him? That seems like an unnecessary risk. No one told me this was part of the plan."

"We need to get into the Eloran Palace," Kendrick says, leaning against the wall behind Skylar. "There are only two ways to do that: with the Sword of Fire, which we may or may not be able to acquire, and through a Hall of Doors, which holds portals to many places in many realms. The location in each court is a closely held secret."

I shake my head. "If each court has a Hall, why not use the one in the shadow court?"

"Because the Halls are hidden," Skylar says, "and the location passed along from one ruler to the next. But Mordeus didn't exactly leave notes for your sister."

Remme nods and scrapes the last of his stew from his bowl. "If we can't find the sword, we'll need a portal."

"If there's another way to get to Erith," I ask, "why have you been looking for the sword for so long?"

"The sword doesn't just open portals," Remme says, putting down his bowl and leaning back in his chair. "It's the almighty weapon. Having the sword would guarantee Erith's defeat. He has no defense against it."

My gaze flicks to Kendrick, who's watching me. "So if you find the sword, you don't need me." I don't know why that revelation makes me feel so sad. I didn't come along because I wanted to kill some Eloran supermage. I came to find Mordeus. But now I want to be part of their mission.

"If we find the sword, then we find the sword," Kendrick says slowly. "But who's to say what will happen between finding it and getting to Erith? There are too many variables, and like I've said before, if I can choose, I'm going to go with the oracle every time. If we can go to Erith with you, one fated to bring him down, or with the sword he can't defend himself against, I'd rather have"—he grins, dimples popping—"well, *both*."

"We still need Felicity to search for the Hall," Skylar says, "because our time is running out. We don't know when they'll tap the next novitiate for the Seven, and taking them down when they don't have a seventh will be much easier."

Kendrick points to my bowl. "Eat."

I scoop up a bite. "Yes, sir." My stomach is still unsettled, and I'm not sure about eating, but the stew is rich and flavorful and seems to warm me from the inside out. I scoop up another bite right away. "So if only Wild Fae royals know how to get to this Hall, why would Misha share the location with Felicity?"

Remme chuckles, and Skylar grins. "Males will share most anything with a good lover," she says.

"A *lover*?" I sputter. "But he thinks Felicity is *me*!"

"If I had to guess, he's been carrying a torch for you for a while," Remme says.

I gape. "Then you'd guess *wrong*."

Remme shrugs. "Either way, the king is falling fast."

"But when this is all over—when I go back . . . do you expect me to keep this secret?" I shake my head. "No. No one told me she was planning to seduce Misha in my form. This isn't okay."

Remme shoves his bowl to the side and leans forward, elbows on the table. "Once you kill Erith for us and Felicity is out of that castle, you can tell Misha and your sister and whomever else whatever you want about all this."

And then they'll all know I was part of this. Did I think I'd never have to face the consequences of my choices? Did I think no one would ever find out?

Will it even matter by then? Will we finish our mission before my time runs out?

"Don't pout," Skylar says. "That king is *delicious*. Tall, dark, and powerful? Consider it a favor and just pick up where Felicity leaves off."

I draw back. "You're disgusting."

"No. *You* are unimaginative. Word has it your sister fancies marrying you off to him. Embrace it. You could be a *queen*."

"Hard pass." I glance toward Kendrick. Surely he'll have something to say about her outrageous ideas, but he's turned toward the window and is frowning out into the setting sun.

"At least as the Wild Fae queen, you'd be safe," he says, not looking at me.

My heart sinks. When we kissed, I thought there was something between us—something more than the one-sided feelings I've been wrestling with since seeing him again—but he hasn't touched me since I woke up. Not in that way, at least.

Kendrick pulls a vial from his pocket and puts it on the table in front of me. "Natan left a potion for your glamour if you want it."

I flick my eyes up to meet his and glance to his elven ears. The rest of them are glamoured, why wouldn't I want to be?

"It's probably a good idea that you continue with the disguise," Skylar explains. "Humans are safe here, but there are too many people to guarantee they're all trustworthy. Only a select few here know about our mission, and it would be better if the whole village didn't realize we're traveling with the shadow princess."

"Finish your dinner," Kendrick says. "I'll meet you all outside after." He strides out of the kitchen and disappears down the hall.

"Way to go, Skylar," Remme mutters, elbowing her before

standing and taking his bowl to the sink.

"I didn't mean to strike a nerve." She glances toward the stairs and grimaces. "Think I should let him be or go talk to him?"

Remme frowns. "Let him be. He's struggling."

"With what?" I ask before I can stop myself.

Skylar exchanges a look with Remme before leaving the table and taking her dishes to the sink. "Hale is a good person," she says. "You won't find better. He'll figure it out."

She didn't answer my question, but I don't push.

Remme studies me. "I'm glad you're okay, kiddo," he says softly. "You really worried us."

My vision goes blurry, and I have to look down at my bowl to hide the tears burning my eyes. I never expected these people to care about me. I never expected their opinion of me to mean so much. "I'm fine," I whisper.

"You are most definitely not *fine*," Skylar says, "but you're still with us, so we'll figure out the rest as we go." She squeezes my shoulder. "Sorry for being an ass about the sexy king thing. I forget not everyone can joke about stuff like that. I'm just jealous."

"Finish eating, and we'll show you around," Remme says. "We have an old friend who's eager to meet you."

CHAPTER TWENTY-ONE

— ◇ —

JASALYN

THE ELORAN SETTLEMENT IS MASSIVE. I expected maybe half a dozen tents around a fire, maybe a few more secure structures, but this place isn't anything nearly so temporary. Small A-frame homes with grass roofs line the streets, and the town center has a gathering area, a pavilion, and an altar.

A quarter hour passed before Kendrick joined us outside. He's been quieter than normal, and I can't stop looking at him. He's usually covered in the belts and straps of various weapons. Even in Mordeus's dungeons, Kendrick was in riding leathers. I'm not sure I've ever seen him in something so casual as the cotton tunic and trousers he's wearing today.

He's even more handsome like this somehow, and my heart tugs hard at the truth. I like seeing him like this because I won't get much of it. Every day is a reminder that my time with him is limited. He's working to go back to Elora, and once I help him get there, I'll be back at the palace, and then I'll be . . . then I'll be nothing at all.

"Did you get enough to eat?" he asks as we start down the street toward the village center.

I wrap my arms around myself. I haven't even been awake for two hours, and I already feel like I could crawl back into bed and sleep. "You don't need to coddle me."

In front of us, Remme and Skylar are arguing under their breath.

Kendrick tucks his hands into his pockets. "I'm not coddling. You were ill, and I want to make sure you fully recover."

I bow my head. "Well, thank you, but you needn't worry. I'm fine."

His brow pinches as he studies my face, and I can tell by his expression that he can see my exhaustion.

"Does my sister know about this place?" I ask, more to change the subject than anything else.

"I would imagine so," Kendrick says, "though I can't say she's aware there are more Elorans here than anywhere else in her court."

"How did that come to be? Did the fae welcome them?"

"This village was ransacked by Mordeus five years ago," Skylar says, glancing at me over her shoulder. "He looted the homes and businesses, then burned it to the ground when he heard a rumor they'd hosted his nephew, who, of course was the one who should've taken the throne when Oberon died."

My stomach pitches. "That's horrible." I've always known Mordeus was cruel—never had a reason to doubt it—and yet I've never given my sister enough credit for the good she did when she took the throne. Maybe I didn't want to understand.

"This village was only one of many he destroyed," Kendrick says.

"So Mordeus didn't notice when Elorans moved in and took over?"

"We were more strategic than that," Remme says. He turns toward me and walks backward so he can look at me as he talks. "We didn't really start rebuilding the town until your sister took the throne, and at that point many fae were coming out of hiding and rebuilding areas that had been destroyed by Mordeus—either directly or by his oppressive laws."

"Jenkish," Kendrick calls, waving over a brown-skinned older man with white shoulder-length hair. He's not glamoured, I realize, and I wonder if it's because humans feel safe to appear as they are while they're in this settlement.

"Hale," he says, smiling broadly and nodding at me. "I'm glad to see your friend recovered."

Kendrick turns and extends a hand toward me. "Jas, this is Lons Jenkish, my father's oldest friend. Lons, allow me to introduce you to Princess Jasalyn, child of Mab."

I frown at Kendrick. Surely this old friend of his father's doesn't care that I'm not just a human glamoured to look fae—that fae lurks in my blood. I hate the idea of meeting these Elorans and having them see me as something they're taught to fear. "Just Jas is fine. I had nothing to do with my ancestry."

Lons's eyes go bright, and he laughs. "This one's sharp, isn't she?" His eyes sparkle when they land on me. "Even if you didn't have such a unique bloodline, you would be special to me. Any friend of Hale's is a friend of mine."

"Same," I say softly.

Remme grunts behind me. "You never extended that courtesy

to me. I had to *work* to win your heart."

I glance toward him. "But you did, so why are you fussing about it now?"

"All those lost days, Princess," Remme says, winking.

Lons turns to Kendrick. "It was lucky Felicity was available to stand in for the princess. Do you know—is that going well?"

As if sensing my tension at this question, Kendrick takes my hand and gives it a hard squeeze. "Better than expected."

Lons's shoulders drop. "Good. The last thing we need is an angry shadow queen tearing apart our camp looking for her sister."

My heart twists at the thought. She would. If my sister realized Felicity was an impostor, Brie would tear apart her whole court to find me, and she'd make an example of anyone who stood in her way.

"You will be our guests of honor tomorrow night," Lons says.

I glance toward Kendrick. I assumed we'd be leaving in the morning. "What's tomorrow?"

"The people of Ironmoore want to host a celebration to wish us luck on our journey," Kendrick says.

I wonder if he even knows he's still holding my hand, or if he realizes how much the tiny gesture means to me in this place where they all seem to know each other but I'm the stranger.

"It's the least we can do," Lons says, but then his gaze catches on our joined hands, and his expression turns stern for a beat before he pastes on a smile.

I take my hand from Kendrick's to press it against my stomach. Happy and full of fluttering butterflies moments before, now it's sinking. I didn't imagine the disapproval in his eyes. Is it because he sees me as fae or something else?

"Thank you for everything, Lons," Kendrick says.

"Son, it is we who are thanking you. We owe the future of Elora to you."

"We haven't done anything yet. Let's not get ahead of ourselves."

Lons claps Kendrick on the back. "I have full faith in you." He turns to me and gives a courteous nod. Am I imagining it, or are his eyes a little less bright than they were when we were introduced? "I'll let you alone to your evening. We look forward to celebrating tomorrow."

We wander the streets for a while longer, Kendrick pointing out where they have school for the children and the grassy village square that will host the celebration tomorrow night. He doesn't take my hand again, and I try not to think about it.

I can't tell how he feels about our kiss. It seems so long ago now, but I can't *stop* thinking about it. Does he think it was a mistake? And if he does, does the reason have anything to do with the way Lons looked at our joined hands?

I'm so tangled in my spinning thoughts that I barely notice the sun is setting until Remme says he's going to the archives to check on Natan, and Kendrick says we should go back inside.

Skylar excuses herself, and Kendrick walks me back up to my room, closing the door softly behind us.

The space suddenly seems too big and too small all at once. It's impossible to be this close and not want him closer, but I have no excuse to press my body into him the way I long to.

I clear my throat and blurt out the first thought that comes to mind. "So, Natan and Remme? They're . . . lovers?"

Kendrick stiffens and glances over my shoulder, as if checking to make sure the door is closed. "Don't say that."

I frown. "Because it's a secret?"

He steps closer. "You were young the last time you lived in Elora," he says, his voice low, "but did you know any men who loved each other?"

"No, though we didn't really know many people at all. Brie and I were busy trying to make the payments on our contract."

He draws in a long, ragged breath. "A contract you signed when you were children? The contract that allowed your aunt to sell you to Mordeus?"

I can't hide my flinch at his name.

"We're going to make those contracts a thing of the past. *That* will be a day to celebrate."

"So, Remme and Natan?" I prod.

"I ask you not to say it because if it becomes a habit, you might say it somewhere that could get them killed. The rulers of Elora do not allow men to love other men. It is a crime punishable by death."

My heart twists with the unnecessary cruelty of it. "That's . . . It's senseless. There are children starving, and they are busy persecuting people for who they love?"

"One of the countless reasons it's past time for change."

I think of the tenderness I witnessed in the forest. Why would anyone want to have *less* of that in the world? "I will help you, Kendrick. Whatever I have to do. I knew my life was hard at home,

287

but I don't think I understood the extent of . . . I didn't know."

He's quiet for a long time, and he spends the silence searching my face. "You couldn't have."

"I can be trusted with a secret, but between you and me, I am sorry I can't tease Remme just a little. Natan is *way* out of his league."

I see his laughter in the shaking of his chest more than I hear it. He takes another step closer, and I have to crane my neck to look up at him.

"They are more than lovers," he says. "They are a bonded pair."

"Elorans can't bond."

"Can't they?"

"Well, they can bond to fae, but not to each other."

He lifts his hand to my face and sweeps his knuckles across my cheek. Everything in my chest feels like it turns inside out. "Keep an open mind. You've been made to think so little is possible because it keeps you weak. You'll be amazed when you see just how much magic rumbles beneath the streets of Elora."

"Magic strong enough to make my ring," I say softly.

He scans my face. "You're tired. There's a handmaid coming around soon. She'll draw you a bath and get you anything else you need, but I want you to relax tonight and tomorrow. You're still recovering."

"And where will you be?" I won't be so pathetic as to ask him to stay with me.

"Right next door if you need me."

I study his face—those ice-blue eyes, and his strong jaw, his full lips. I want to curl up against his chest, want to trail my thumb along his jaw and over his rough stubble. "You haven't kissed me again."

His gaze dips down to my mouth then my breasts, before sweeping back up. Straightening, he meets my eyes. "Jas, after I return to Elora, our lives will be complicated. You're the shadow princess, and I—"

I press my fingers to his lips and shake my head. "Don't. I don't want to be her. Not tonight. Not tomorrow. Let's not do that."

He gently pulls my hand away. "It matters. You deserve to know what I can and can't offer before anything else happens between us."

"I'm not asking for anything." Panic climbs up my throat. Before Kendrick was back in my life, the future was something I wanted to dodge because the days and hours stretched ahead of me like a prison of their own. Now I don't want to talk about it because I've already ruined it.

I don't want to talk about it because the regret might destroy me. I can't let myself waste the days I have left.

"You should," he says. "You should ask for *everything* because that's what you deserve. I'm being selfish by even being here now. By standing this close. By looking at you. By wanting you. I've been selfish this whole time."

"Your future is in Elora. I know that." I lift onto my toes and sweep my lips against his, too eager to touch him again, too desperate to feel the bloom of heat in my chest.

I want to wash away the chill I used to relish, want to banish the ring's numbness from my heart.

His big hands rest on my hips, and I lean into every point

where the soft curves of my body connect with the hard planes of his. He closes his eyes. "You'll be the death of me."

My stomach shimmies, and I smile. "Time your kisses right, and I think you'll be okay." I shift against him, and he curses. I might not have any experience with men or this kind of physical connection, but I know enough to know he wants me—or at least his body does.

He cups my jaw and skims his thumb over my bottom lip. "I'm trying so hard to behave myself, but it turns out my will is not as strong as I once believed." He leans forward, mouth ghosting across mine. "Why can't our fates align? Why did the Mother put you in my path if I'm going to have to let you go?"

How do you know you have to let me go? But I don't ask. He's human, and he thinks I will be fae in a few short months. And what I will be instead . . . Well, perhaps that's even worse.

I don't want to think about any of that, so I slide my hand into his hair and pull his mouth down to meet mine. When our lips touch, he sighs against me.

In nine months' time, he will be back in Elora, and I will be gone. I can pull my hair and gnash my teeth over the foolishness of my mistakes, or I can enjoy the final days we have together. I would have willed myself dead in Mordeus's cell if Kendrick's voice and stories and calming words hadn't found me in the darkness.

I only have this moment because of him, so I will revel in it with him.

He trails his hand down my hip and along the outside of my thigh before grabbing my leg behind the knee, pulling it up to hook over his hip. At the first press of his body, I nearly melt, but he's there, holding me up, his mouth exploring mine.

His hand tangles in my hair, tugging my head to the side as he trails kisses down my neck. Shivers explode along my spine.

Kendrick glances toward the door, then rests his forehead to mine. "Your handmaid will be here soon." His fingers deftly fasten the top few buttons of my blouse.

"When did those come undone?" I ask, watching his strong hands and wishing we hadn't been interrupted.

The corner of his mouth twitches up in a lopsided grin. "Let's just say it's a good thing I can't stay."

"Hmm. We might have different definitions of *good*."

He groans. "Don't tempt me, Princess. I'm already struggling with restraint when it comes to you." He fastens the final button, then presses a hot, open-mouthed kiss to my clavicle just above his fingers. He sucks lightly before pulling away, and my whole body goes tight and hot, but then his mouth is gone and he's backing toward the door. "Enjoy your bath. I'll see you in the morning."

CHAPTER TWENTY-TWO

❖

FELICITY

HER FRIEND HAS MAGIC.

Not like these wicked fae, and not like the mages back home in Elora. Crissa knows the words to murmur when the pain and the darkness and the panic are too much and Jasalyn can't stop shaking. She knows how to make the panic stop, how to protect Jasalyn from her own thoughts.

Her whispered incantations calm Jas. They bring sleep when the terror threatens to destroy her from the inside.

But they leave her friend weak. Make her sleep for hours.

Her friend says magic is life, says she knows how to channel her energy into healing, says it's okay, she doesn't mind, says she needs Jas to hold on.

Can you do that for me? Can you hold on?

Her friend says the sleeping is normal. She says it's because she's a human using fae magic. She says help is coming. She says Jas needs to have faith in the life waiting for her beyond their cell walls. She says Jas will get to go home soon.

But her friend's been sleeping for two days now, and Jas is afraid she won't wake up.

* * *

Another day without the Wild Fae king in residence, another day wondering what exactly I think I'm doing.

I can't deny it anymore. I have *feelings*. Big, complicated, inconvenient *feelings*.

And to top it all off, the ball is tomorrow night and chatter around the castle is that dozens of the guests are eligible females who would be ideal as the new queen. As someone who's expected to be in attendance and cannot be Misha's queen for dozens of obvious and less obvious reasons, I'm dreading the spectacle of watching females throw themselves at him.

I'm so desperate for some time alone with him before the big night that I find myself breaking early from my research and wandering the castle looking for a sign he's returned from whatever important, kingly errand he's been on today.

I'm headed out to the training yard for the second time since lunch when I run into Tynan.

"Still looking for the king?" he asks.

My cheeks heat. "I'm not trying to bother you. I didn't have anything better to do, so I thought I'd check out here."

I should return to my books, should get back to scouring the Wild Fae maps for remote mountain ranges where the portal could be. But instead, I'm chasing after a male I can't have.

Tynan smiles at me. "You miss him."

I drop my gaze to the floor, worried he can read too much there. "I wondered if he wanted to have dinner with me. It's not a big deal."

"He was called out to another realm unexpectedly this morning."

293

My head snaps up. *Another realm?* "Where? Elora?"

"The Wild Fae have close ties with Summerbend, it's another faerie realm." He cocks his head to the side. "I promise you, he's perfectly safe there. He might be more respected in that realm than he is in his own."

"Did he go by goblin?"

"No. Goblins travel between Faerie and Elora because the realms are so closely tied, but even they aren't powerful enough to travel between here and Summerbend."

Which means he traveled through a portal.

"Ah, and there he is now," Tynan says. "See? I told you there was nothing to worry about."

"Who was worried?"

I spin at the sound of Misha's voice. Tynan was right. I did miss him, and I can't deny the feeling of relief that falls over me at the sight of him. His olive skin looks darker this afternoon, like he spent his day out in the sun, and I can't resist skimming my gaze over him, as if I need to make sure he came back unharmed. I find no wounds. Only his broad chest in his lightweight tunic and his muscular thighs visible through his fitted leather riding pants.

"The princess wondered where you'd gone. When I told her you were in another realm, I think she was worried you were in Elora and might find trouble there."

"Is that true?" He steps closer, then seems to remember himself and stops in the middle of the corridor, tucking his hands into his pockets.

Blushing, I meet his gaze. "You didn't tell me you had to go away today."

Tynan clears his throat and steps back. "If you'll excuse me, my king, I need to check on something in the stables."

Misha nods at Tynan before turning his attention back to me. "I was called out at the last minute. I didn't realize you would be looking for me."

"Misha!" a young girl calls, rushing past me and into his arms. She looks to be eight or nine years old and has the same dark hair as Misha, though hers falls in long waves down to the middle of her back.

He picks her up under her arms and spins her around, making her laugh. "I can't believe you know who I am," he says. "It's been so long, I thought you would forget me."

"Never!" she says, laughing.

He turns her toward me and smiles. "Lark, do you remember Princess Jasalyn from Abriella's court?"

"Hi, Lark." I force my hands to relax at my sides. "It's good to see you again."

Misha returns her to the ground, and she purses her lips and cocks her head to the side as if she's trying to figure me out. "Soon you will take your true form."

My heart trips, and I glance to Misha.

He meets my gaze with a haughty arch of a brow. "Less than nine months now. Sooner than ever."

Oh. I clear my throat. "My . . . You mean on my birthday?" I ask the little girl.

"Lark is a seer," Misha says, and I am a ball of panic, desperately searching for something to say that can keep her from talking, but all words evade me.

Lark frowns. "No. Not in nine months. *Much* sooner." She reaches for my hand, and it's all I can do to keep myself from snatching it back. Her silver eyes go unfocused and a little distant. "Why are you so afraid? You know this isn't who you really are. Why don't you want—"

"That's enough." Misha pulls her hand off mine. "I'm sorry."

She frowns up at her uncle. "You'll break her heart," she whispers. "Be gentle. She's scared, and she wouldn't do this if she had a choice."

Misha drops to his haunches and gives an indulgent smile to his niece. "I know she's scared. That's why I think you should be gentle about the way you're delivering your information. Remember how we talked about this?" He looks up at me. "Lark's gifts are complicated. She often sees things that don't make sense."

She narrows her eyes at her uncle. "Mother says my gifts are among the most valuable in the entire realm." She turns back to me. "You already know your destiny. Don't fight it. You cannot keep everyone you love safe without sacrificing everything they deem sacred."

My eyes burn and I squeeze them shut. Is that what I've done by refusing to murder Erith the way the oracle showed me I would? Have I been trying to keep Hale safe at the cost of what he holds dear?

Misha clears his throat. "That's enough out of you," he says, but his tone is gentle. "Now, go find your mother and tell her I'll join you in a few minutes. We have a surprise planned for you in town tonight."

She grins. "Okay!" Her dress shoes click against the stone floors as she disappears down the hall.

As he watches her go, I catch sight of something red in his hair.

I step closer and pull it out. "What's this?" It's fluffy, almost like the head of a white dandelion, but it's a vibrant red and not nearly as delicate as it appears. "I've never seen anything like it."

Misha drags a hand through his hair, ruffling it. "The hiluca tree likes to leave its autumn blossoms on anyone who passes."

"Hiluca tree? I've never heard of such a thing." I let the blossom roll in my palm. It's almost sticky.

"That's because it's unique to my territory. There are no hilucas in the other courts, which is why my ancestors declared it our land's sacred tree."

"Why have I never seen one?"

"They only grow in the northern mountains, where the wild horses roam." His smile is tender. "I should take you to see them before winter comes. They are breathtaking this time of year. Especially at sunset."

"I would love that."

He takes the blossom from my hand and tucks it behind my ear. "It suits you," he says, stepping back, as if he can't trust himself to stand so close. "I've promised to spend the evening in the village with my sister and niece, but if you need anything or were looking for company at dinner, I'm sure Tynan can help you."

I bow my head to hide any hurt I feel at not being invited.

With two fingers beneath my chin, Misha tilts my face up until I meet his eyes. "Unless you want to come with us?"

It's better this way. Pretha knows Jasalyn better than Misha does and spending too much time with her is inviting trouble.

"No. Thank you," I say. "You should catch up with your family without me."

He drops his hand with a curt nod, then turns to the stairwell door.

"Misha?" I call when he reaches for the knob. He stops and turns back to me. Regret is a sharp knife in my lungs. I wanted to do this myself, to find the portal myself so he might hate me a little less when this is all over, but if he takes me to the trees he walked among today, I'll know where to find the portal. I can't pass up this opportunity. "I would truly like to see the hilucas. I hope you'll find the time to take me."

He searches my face for so long I wonder if he can see the traitor beneath this skin. "Perhaps after the ball."

My stomach knots. The ball where he hopes to find his bride. And what if he does? What if he becomes mad for some female who's the perfect candidate to be his queen and he has no time to bother with me anymore? What if this female from his dreams appears?

Then you will have to find the Hall of Doors without him.

But the twisting ache in my chest has nothing to do with fears of failing in my mission and everything to do with my renegade heart.

Heartsick and homesick, I wander the castle gardens alone after dinner rather than facing the quiet solitude of my chambers.

The stars are bright tonight and feel close enough to touch. I wish I could reach up and rearrange them. Would I give myself a different fate? If the oracle had never foretold the twin daughter who would end Erith, would I have grown up like my twin brother? Would I be training to become one of the Seven? Or maybe even be one of them by now? Would I have never known the woman who I'll always see as my mother?

"I thought I might find you out here," someone says behind me. "My niece has a way of making people contemplate their stars."

Warmth and pleasure spread through me as I turn to Misha. He strolls toward me, his hands in his pockets. His hair is tied back, and he's dressed in all black. He's so beautiful, and my heart aches at the sight of him. "Maybe I was overdue for a little contemplation," I say as he comes to stand by my side.

"It's interesting, though, isn't it? What Lark had to say to you?"

My skin goes clammy. "I haven't really thought about it." Such a lie. I've thought about little else since I saw them this afternoon. That child wasn't prophesying for Jas, she was doing it for me. *You already know your destiny.*

But how can I accept something when I've seen the awful outcome?

"I wish you didn't dread it so much," Misha says, misreading the sadness on my face. "But I can't help but wonder at what she said about the timing—about it happening before your birthday." When he cuts his gaze to me, worry is etched all over his face. "Perhaps it's time to take you home to see your priestess. Maybe she'll know—"

"No."

His brows shoot up. "No? You don't want to go home?"

"I don't want to be that close to Mordeus. I . . ." I don't have to

299

fake the tremble in my voice. The idea of leaving this castle one moment before I have to *hurts*. I know the end of my time with Misha is coming, and I need to accept that, but seeing an Unseelie priestess would be even worse. I can't risk her looking too deeply at my blood.

He nods and drops his gaze to his hands. "I'll admit that I'm shaken by what Lark said."

"About you breaking my heart?" I ask. I meant it as a joke, but there's no humor in my voice.

He blows out a breath. "Maybe that too, but mostly I'm shaken by the idea of you turning before your birthday."

"But didn't you say the future is constantly shifting, so not all her visions come to light?"

"Yes, but—"

"Then try not to worry about it."

"How could I possibly do that?"

Because I'm not Jas. Because it's a waste of your worry and a waste of your energy.

"I do worry," he says. He looks so wrecked, as if he's been turning this over and over in his head all evening and it's left him ravaged. He turns to study a late-blooming mum as he speaks. "I worry because Mab herself said you'd become fae on your eighteenth birthday, and the only reason I can imagine it happening sooner is if you took the Potion of Life. Given how you feel about becoming fae, there's only one circumstance in which I can imagine you taking that potion."

"And what's that?"

When he looks up, his eyes are bleak. "If you were dying,

Jasalyn. I can only imagine you taking the Potion of Life rather than waiting to turn fae on your eighteenth birthday if you were dying and that was the only way to save you."

I thought he was pushing me away this afternoon, but he spent his whole evening worrying about the possibility of me coming close to death. Worrying about the possibility of losing me.

No. *Losing Jas.*

My breath catches. I'm so twisted up inside, and I have no one to blame but myself.

Misha takes me by the hips and turns me to face him. I crane my neck to look up at him, and we stay like that, only inches apart, staring into each other's eyes.

He doesn't move his hands, just keeps them on my hips and studies my face. "There's only one good thing that would come of that."

"What's that?"

"It would mean you would finally choose becoming fae over death."

I didn't tell him, did I? I revealed how bad it was when Jas was a prisoner, but that she wished for death even after? That wasn't my secret to tell.

"You haven't done a very good job of hiding it." He brushes my hair back from my face but then leaves his hand cupping my jaw, thumb stroking. "But I was hoping you'd started to feel differently since coming here."

"I feel so many things, and none of them are simple."

"I can relate to that," he says softly.

He touches his lips to mine in what must be the world's most tentative first kiss. He's asking permission. He's preparing to end the kiss before it's truly begun, and I might weep if he does.

I tilt my head ever so slightly.

His long fingers slide into my hair. Our lips part.

He tastes like wine. Did he have some at dinner? Was it faerie wine? Is it loosening his inhibitions?

When I think he's going to angle his mouth over mine and deepen the kiss, he pulls his mouth away and sighs.

Forehead to forehead, we catch our breath. I try to remember who I am and what I can and can't have, but I still can't think. Not with him this close. Not with the taste of him on my lips.

His thumb strokes across my cheek. "I never expected this."

"Me neither," I say. Gods, I want to curl into him. I want him to hold me all night long and keep these thoughts away.

He tilts my face up to his. "Will you come with me? I want to show you my favorite place."

I nod, trying not to appear too eager. He could take me any-where. I just don't want to be away from him yet.

"It is so dark down here," I say, clinging to Misha's side.

He's brought me to the cavern deep under Castle Craige, and I can't see a thing in front of me, but I can feel his heat against my side and hear water in the distance.

I may not fear the dark like Jasalyn does, but I don't mind the excuse to stay close to Misha.

"I could cast light on our path," he says, "but then you'd miss—" Suddenly stalactites above our heads cast a dim glow on the underground path. "That."

"Wow. What is that?"

"Cave pixies live in the dew on the stalactites. If we bring too much light with us, they won't glow."

"So this wasn't all a ruse to keep me glued to your side?"

He chuckles and pulls me even closer. "I didn't say that."

I tilt my face up. "They're beautiful."

"Agreed. Pixies are earth fae, and while many spend their days aboveground, they thrive down here." The sound of running water grows louder. "It's right around this corner," he says.

We walk another minute, and the curved path leads to a smaller cavern at the back of the large one.

With a wave of his hand, Misha fills the space with a soft light, revealing a pool of crystal-clear water fed by a trickling waterfall.

"Our ancestors are said to have blessed the water for the strength and good health of their rulers," he says, "but the darkness and solitude always seem to do more for my mind than my body."

"Isn't it cold?" I ask. It's colder beneath the earth than it was in the garden, and I'm nearly shivering.

"It's a natural hot spring." He nods toward the water flowing into it. "Touch it."

I wave my hand under the flow and nearly moan with the warmth. "It's like the perfect bath."

"And it never goes cold," he says. He's quiet a moment, as if he's nervous and trying to make a decision. "Do you want to soak with me?"

"Oh . . ." My cheeks heat. "I . . ." I can't bring myself to decline. I want to stay here. I want to experience this amazing place. I want to be with him. "Turn around?" I ask.

He obeys and the light he cast on the space slowly dims. He's trying to give me privacy without leaving me in the dark, I realize.

I unfasten my dress, stripping down to my shift before I pull off my boots and stockings. His back is still turned to me as I step into the hot water and lower myself onto the stone bench.

"How's it feel?" he asks without turning.

"I'm never leaving."

He chuckles. "Well, would you mind some company? Not forever but for the first hour or so of your lifetime in my hot spring?"

"I suppose that would be okay." I bow my head, trying not to stare but aware of every move he makes as he removes his tunic and drops his bandolier of blades onto the cold limestone ground.

When he peels off his boots and pants and is left in nothing but a pair of tight undershorts, he steps into the water, keeping his eyes averted. "Would you prefer more or less light?" he asks.

In truth, I want no light. I want to be with him and not have to think about him spending this time with me while looking at another female's body. I don't let myself think on that too long. "It's fine like this."

He's on the side of the pool opposite me, and I wonder if that's what he intended—if he really planned to bring me down here and not kiss me again.

My gut clenches painfully at the thought. Tomorrow is the ball, and the next day I need to go out in search of the hiluca blossoms and the Hall of Doors. If I can't be the one to kill Erith and bring down the Elora Seven, then I need to do everything I can to help my brother do it.

Before I can let myself think about it, I move across the pool to sit beside him.

His gaze tracks every move, then skims over my bare shoulders before going back to my mouth. "I can't stop thinking about kissing you." He says it like a confession, as if I won't want to hear it. Then he closes his eyes, as if he's still fighting it.

"I was hoping you wouldn't."

"If you don't want me to, tell me because—"

I put a finger to his lips. I don't want him to say any more. I don't want him to talk himself out of kissing me. I don't want him to talk me out of letting him. I shouldn't, but I need tonight. Once I find the portal, I'll leave Castle Craige and never have a reason to return. If Jasalyn is successful, I'll leave Faerie as well.

"I was hoping you wouldn't stop thinking about it. Because I can think of nothing else," I say. "And I was thinking about it a long time before you kissed me tonight."

He slowly takes my hand and threads our fingers together before tugging me through the water toward him. "She said I'm going to break your heart."

"Probably," I whisper. I straddle his waist and loop my arms behind his neck.

"I don't want to hurt you at all." His lips part and he scans my face over and over. "We haven't talked about what happens when you go back to the shadow court."

"I know."

His hands slide through the water and find my hips, gripping, his thumbs stroking across my stomach through the wet fabric of my shift. "And you're going to let me kiss you anyway?"

"No." I sweep my mouth over his, lips still not touching but barely a breath away. "I'm going to kiss you."

Then I do. Selfishly, I kiss the Wild Fae king. His mouth is soft under mine, and when I suck his bottom lip between my teeth, his grip tightens on my hips and he pulls my body flush with his.

He angles his mouth, opening. I exhale a groan of pleasure.

I want him so acutely that need tightens in my core.

His hands fist into the wet fabric of my shift, shoving it up until it's bunched around my ribs and his hands are at my waist, his thumbs stroking the sensitive skin above each hipbone. Pleasure and hunger tangle together and pool low in my belly.

He pulls his mouth from mine and presses a finger to my lips, looking toward the long, dark path that leads to the stairs. Then I hear it too. *Someone's coming.*

My eyes go wide, and I bite back a giggle, like a schoolgirl caught doing something mischievous. Misha's hand is still on my waist, and I can taste him on my tongue. I'm delirious. Drunk on him.

"What do we do?" I ask. "Should we . . . hide?"

Two voices. I can hear them more distinctly now. They're close.

He eases me off him with low groan, but his hands linger at my hips until the last minute, as if he's reluctant to release me. "Grab your clothes."

He wants me to dress?

But then he steps out of the hot spring and scoops his clothes to his chest. Then, before I can react, he grabs mine and offers a hand to help me out.

I take it, and he grins as he draws me against his chest. "Hold on," he whispers.

In my next breath, we're in my chambers, four stories above the hot springs.

He drops our clothes on the floor and pulls me back to him.

"How?" I ask against his mouth.

"Magic." He's smiling, his hands roaming over my wet shift—down my back, up my sides, sliding over my breasts.

I gasp. "That's . . . impressive."

He kisses his way down my neck and scrapes his teeth over my bare shoulder. "I know. I was showing off."

I laugh and then shiver. The air is so much colder than the water in the hot spring was, and my wet shift clings to me as goose bumps race down my arms.

"You're cold," he says, pulling back.

I shake my head. "I'm okay." But then a shiver racks my frame again, belying my words.

Someone knocks on the door. Once. Twice. "Princess, I'm here to draw your bath."

My eyes go wide. "My maid!"

Misha takes my chin in his hand and presses a hard kiss to my lips. "Take a hot bath and warm up. I'll see you tomorrow."

"You're *leaving*?"

He closes his eyes and takes a deep breath before nodding. "Yes. I don't want to. *At all*." His eyes search mine before studying my lips and burning cheeks. "And that's exactly why I need to."

He disappears just as the maid enters with a fresh sleeping gown for after my bath.

I spot his clothes—left behind in a pile on the floor—and kick them under the bed.

"Oh, my!" my handmaid says. "Princess, you're soaked. Did you get caught in the rain?"

I hadn't even noticed it started to rain. It was a cloudless night earlier. But sure enough, there's a steady thrum on my windowpane now.

Misha, I realize, and bite back a smile. Showing off more or covering for me? Maybe both. "I guess so."

"I'll go get some hot water," she says.

When she closes the door behind her, a low whistle comes from my bathing room.

I spin toward the sound and see Shae strolling out, his dark braid swaying, his green eyes piercing. He leans against my dresser, and I press my hand to my chest. "Gods above and below, Shae. You scared me." But we both know there's another reason my heart is racing. One that has everything to do with the night I came home from the oracle and he begged me to follow my fate despite what I'd seen.

He almost kissed me that night, lips hovering over mine as he begged with a whisper, "Don't make me choose him over you."

"I'm sorry to interrupt your evening," he says now. He looks me over, and his cold eyes go dark with something I'm afraid might be lust. Too much of me—of this body—is visible through the wet shift.

It's like a knife in the gut. He never looked at me like that when I was in my own form. With tenderness and affection, yes, but never bald lust. I only wanted him to.

I lift my chin, daring him to make me feel guilty over what he just witnessed. "I wasn't sure I'd ever see you again," I say, but I wonder if he hears what I mean. *Did you ever look for me? Did you miss me at all? Did you mean it when you said you couldn't stomach letting Erith live if it meant I might be in danger?*

He only showed any interest that one night—because he'd been hiding it before or because he was trying to manipulate me into action?

I never dared to suspect anything then, but it's been three years. Three years of running and hiding. I had to grow up fast, and I'm not nearly so naïve now.

"Did you want me to stand idle while your father hunted you?" he asks.

My gut twists. "I don't want to have this argument again."

He searches my face, but his expression's too guarded to read. "I was told to come check in on you," he says, voice cooler now. "What's the update?"

I expected Remme or Skylar, maybe Natan. But the sight of Shae sends a cluster of emotions surging to the surface. Adolescent angst, longing, and rejection all tangle with the loneliness I've carried with me for so long.

Until Misha, some quiet voice in my mind whispers. *You never feel lonely with Misha.*

I release a breath, determined to get through this. For Hale. "We think Mordeus used blood magic to set everything in place for his own resurrection."

His eyes go wide. "You know this from a dream?"

I shake my head, though I suppose my dreams contribute to

it. "Misha and I have been investigating. I need you to tell Kendrick that Jasalyn's scars are from blood magic. Somehow, Mordeus came back, and now he's using the princess to get stronger. Every time a new scar appears, it's the magic being called upon. But from what we've been told, the resurrection isn't complete. He'll need a necromancer to revive his physical body. We need to make sure that doesn't happen."

Shae folds his arms. "And the portal?"

"I'm close, but this is important. Hale needs to find out everything he can from Jas so we can figure out how to stop the blood magic. Maybe she knows something about Mordeus that I haven't learned yet—something that will help us stop him."

"Fine. I get it. I'll tell Hale that his girlfriend is a wizard who can resurrect a faerie king."

His flippancy is a punch to the gut. "You know that's not what I'm saying."

"We need that portal, Felicity. Time is running out." He crosses to me and cocks his head. "Are you even trying?"

"Of course I'm trying. I know where to look—the northern mountains where the hiluca trees grow. I'm going after the ball."

"Can I trust you? You and the king seemed mighty cozy tonight." He glances toward the bed and arches a brow. "What would've happened if that maid hadn't come? Do you think you can just pretend to be the princess forever? That you and the king can live happily ever after and he'll never notice that you aren't who you say you are?"

"Are you jealous?" I ask, and at the same moment, I realize I don't want him to be.

"Would it make a difference if I were?"

Three years ago, my blood would've hummed at Shae feeling territorial over me. Now the idea is simply exhausting. At some point in the last three years, I let go of whatever it was I felt for Shae. Maybe it was because he never came for me—never offered company when I was forced to run from Elora. Or maybe it's because after what I've begun to feel for Misha, I can see that none of my feelings for Shae ever ran that deep. "I laid my heart out for you, and you walked away. Did you expect me to wait?"

"I walked away because someone needed to save Elora if you were too scared to do it."

I set my jaw and scowl up at him. "You *know* why I won't do it. I won't be the reason Hale doesn't survive to see the new Elora."

"Has it ever occurred to you that maybe that's what the *Chosen One* means? Maybe it's his noble sacrifice that will make this all happen?"

I shake my head violently. "Elora needs Hale. Our queen needs him."

"Then you better hurry and find that portal."

I narrow my eyes. "When did you become so cold?"

"Around the same time you chose cowardice over destiny." He lifts his fist, and I realize too late that he's holding my collection of the princess's hair. "They gave you too much time, and it's given you a false sense of security. Maybe all you need is"—he pulls a tiny swath of hairs from the bundle—"a dozen? That should motivate you to get this done." He shakes his head and takes away half again of what's left. "Nah, if you already know where it is, you don't need more than a few of these, right?"

311

My stomach knots. "You're going to get me killed."

Shae's eyes flash with anger. "How many people have you gotten killed by refusing your destiny?" He drops the handful of Jasalyn's hair into the trash can and, with a flick of his fingers, lights it on fire.

CHAPTER TWENTY-THREE

JASALYN

DESPITE MY CONCERNS ABOUT SPENDING the night alone in a strange room, I sleep hard and deep, and by the time I wake up, I can hear the others downstairs cleaning up from breakfast.

I slip out of the thin white shift my handmaid gave me after my bath and find fresh linen pants and a matching top waiting on my dresser. Beside them is another one of the vials I recognize as the potion for my elven glamour. I don't have to look in a mirror to know yesterday's has already worn off. I'm painfully aware of my scars as I dress, and I avoid the mirror above the dresser until I've swallowed the vial's contents.

When I head downstairs, I struggle to shake my dreary mood. I dreamed of Crissa as she was before they pulled her from my cell, unconscious and limp, but in this dream, she lay on a pile of white linens, and I wasn't myself. I was someone else, watching with satisfaction as she struggled to pull in breath.

A fae male stood beside me, sneering down at her. His eyes were a mossy green, his dark hair was shaved on the sides, exposing two white slashes of scars above his left ear. The length on top was pulled into a tight braid that began at the crown of his head and fell to the middle of his back. "And you're sure she's the best vessel?"

"There is no other." I nodded toward the body at his feet, *my* body, curled unconscious, chestnut hair in tangled knots around my head. "The oracle speaks the truth. I see the power within her."

The green-eyed man knelt beside the girl—beside me—and sliced into my stomach, dipping his fingers into the bloody flesh before drawing them out and pressing them to his nose. "We'll win her trust," the male said with satisfaction in his eyes. "And when the time is right, we'll bring her to you and, like a phoenix, you will rise again."

"Good." I heard myself chuckle and woke up with the sound in my head—Mordeus's deep rattle that haunts me and reminds me of those sadistic silver eyes peering into my soul.

Last night's dream felt so real that I woke feeling sick. What if these dreams are more than dreams? What if they're memories? What if—

I slam a door on my thoughts before they can pull me too deep and head to the kitchen.

Natan, Remme, Kendrick, and Skylar are gathered at the table. Natan's rolling my ring between his forefinger and thumb.

I stomp down the instinctive urge to snatch it from his hands.

Kendrick rises as soon as he sees me. "How did you sleep?" he asks, looking me over.

"Better than I expected," I admit. I nod to Natan and the ring. "Did you find anything from your research?"

Natan and Kendrick exchange a look.

Natan clears his throat. "Your ring has markings similar to those rumored to be on a pair of ancient Eloran rings. It might even be an exact match—it's hard to know, as drawing its likeness was forbidden."

"Why?" I ask.

"Because these rings were for royalty. In Eloran tradition, the king's chosen to protect the queen. He commits his life to it and uses every tool at his disposal to fulfill his purpose."

"How does the ring help him?"

"These ancient rings allowed him to pull strength from a devoted servant, one who would wear the ring's twin. The ring makes the king more powerful."

"So you think my ring might be part of a pair and I'm drawing power from someone when I wear it?" I ask.

Again, Natan looks to Kendrick before speaking. He draws in a breath. "Perhaps."

I can almost hear the words they're not saying. *Or someone is drawing power from me.*

Kendrick's jaw ticks as he stares at the ring. "Are you sure the witch who gave you this didn't say anything about another? Did she ask you to recite any words—to pledge yourself to something or someone?"

Frowning, I shake my head. "Nothing like that. She said it would give me the kiss of death and chase the fear from my heart. She didn't say anything about a second ring."

Natan studies me, brow furrowed. "I contacted a friend who studies Eloran artifacts and, with his help, created an echo of the ring's magic. Like calls to like. If the ring has a match, the echo

315

should point us to it." He hesitates before offering the ring to me. "In the meantime, I suppose you want this back."

"Yes." I take it and quickly tuck it into a pocket. "Thank you."

"I can't believe you still want that thing," Kendrick says, arms folded. "Please just tell me you don't plan to use it without me there to keep an eye on you."

I shrug. "I don't plan to use it, but I don't like being caught without it. As you keep pointing out, I don't have any other magic to protect me."

Kendrick grunts. "I don't like it."

"You just don't like that you can't remember anything that happens when she's wearing it," Remme says.

"Among other things," Kendrick mutters.

I can't resist looking up and find him watching my mouth.

He winks, and my stomach somersaults.

Among other things.

I haven't worn a dress since I left the Midnight Palace, and while I didn't much miss all the fussing over clothes and hair, I'm loving it tonight. I suspect I could walk outside in a pair of Kendrick's riding breeches and a torn-up tunic, and he'd still have that look in his eyes that makes me feel like the most beautiful thing he's ever seen, but I want one night where I have a chance to put myself together for him.

Before my bath last night, my handmaid took my measurements, and when I woke up this morning, she had a dress waiting for me. "For tonight," she told me.

It was perfectly fine—serviceable—and I felt a tinge guilty for wanting something lovelier, but I decided tonight was worth a little selfishness.

I requested scissors, a needle and thread, and while Kendrick and the others were off reuniting with old friends, I spent the day reworking the plain frock into something that my cousins would've fought over when I was a seamstress in Elora. I cut out the back to nearly my waist and made a slit up the side, the way Brie prefers her dresses—so she can move freely, she says, and it's true, but I know she also loves that Finn can't take his eyes off her. I altered the bodice into a deep V-neckline and added a strap behind my neck to secure it.

When the maid helps me dress, she smiles. "I like what you've done with it."

"Sewing used to be my favorite hobby." I take a seat in front of the mirror. I don't even mind seeing myself with the fae ears tonight. I want the glamour to let me pretend that I'm someone else. Someone who isn't broken. Someone who didn't trade everything for a ring.

I close my eyes and shove down my unwelcome thoughts. My handmaid sweeps my hair off my neck and into a twist she holds in place with pins. "If you could take that needle of yours to my wardrobe," she says, "perhaps I'd be able to find myself a husband."

I laugh and meet her gaze in the mirror. She's my size, but without quite as much fullness in the bust and hips. She's fair, with auburn hair and sparkling hazel eyes. "You're beautiful. Surely a daring wardrobe wouldn't make the difference."

She casts her gaze downward. "That's sweet of you to say. In truth, I'm standing in my own way. I hoped I'd be home before starting a family. My mother likes to point out that it can take decades to be blessed with a babe, and that is if the gods are even kind enough to give me one."

I frown at her in the mirror. *Decades?* What a strange way to say it. I suppose there are couples who try for a family for ten or fifteen years before accepting that it's not to be, but *decades*? Only fae, who live hundreds of years and have a notoriously difficult time conceiving, would speak of fertility in terms of decades.

"I noticed that not all the humans in this village wear a glamour," I say carefully, studying her elven ears.

Her brow wrinkles with her frown. "What kind of glamour would you have them wear?"

"I thought they might be glamoured to appear fae," I say. "As I am. For protection."

She lifts her chin in understanding. "Perhaps before your sister took the crown and ended the golden queen's curse, but not since. There are enough humans in Faerie—brought in as changelings or during the years of the curse—that the humans from home don't concern themselves with being noticed."

Strange that Kendrick and the others still believe it's safer to travel as fae. That we might be targeted if we traveled as humans. "How old are you?"

She blushes. "Only five and thirty years. Young for my kind, it's true."

"So you truly are fae? This isn't a glamour?"

She laughs softly. "No glamour. I would give myself some curves like yours if I were to bother with a glamour."

My shoulders loosen as some of the tension drains out of me.

I was worried that maybe I was being lied to, so her sincerity is a relief. Still, I have questions. "And you were born in Elora?"

She meets my gaze. "Yes, milady. My family didn't flee to Faerie until I was a girl. Easier to hide in plain sight here than to hide entirely there. And being able to use my gods-given magic instead of passing everything off as mage magic—well, it's a relief."

I shake my head. It doesn't make any sense. I spent the first fourteen years of my life in Elora—how could there have been fae around me without me ever knowing?

"About ready?" a deep voice asks from the door.

I turn to see Kendrick, hair tied back, resplendent in crisp dark brown breeches and a sable tunic with dark embroidery. Knowing I'm going to spend the evening on his arm sends a riot of anxious butterflies through my belly and up into my chest.

"Just finishing," my handmaid says, sliding a final pin into my hair. "I hope you have an amazing night. Perhaps I'll see you at the celebration."

I stare at myself in the mirror—my faerie self with the ears and bright eyes and glowing skin—and feel a hard tug of regret that I'll never know the female I could become if I hadn't traded my immortality for a magical ring. I still don't know what that life would look like, but maybe I should've had the courage to find out.

I close my eyes and bow my head. *Now is not the time for this.*

Callused fingers gently scrape up my exposed spine. I draw in a ragged breath and meet Kendrick's gaze in the mirror.

"Let me look at you," he says, voice as rough as those fingertips.

Swallowing back a sudden rush of nerves, I stand and smooth

down my dress as I turn to him.

Kendrick's eyes darken and his nostrils flare as he looks me over. He scrubs a hand over his face, but when his gaze returns to the smooth, pale flesh of my exposed thigh, he bites a knuckle. "If you're trying to slowly kill me, this is the perfect way to do it."

"You're saying this is torture?" I tease, glancing down at my dress. "But I worked so hard on it."

His hands flex at his sides, opening and curling into fists, as if he's trying to control himself. "Every second I'm not touching you is torture."

"Oh. Then in that sense perhaps I *am* trying to torture you." My nerves fizzle away, replaced with a kind of confident self-awareness I've only known as the Enchanting Lady. But I'm not her tonight. I'm Jas, and Kendrick doesn't want me because of some great and powerful magic. He wants me because I'm *me*.

He steps forward but keeps his hands at his sides as he lowers his mouth to my ear. "The only thing better than seeing you in that dress is knowing how easy it will be to take it off."

His fingertips sweep against the small of my back, sending a shiver racing up my spine. I lean into him.

When I turn my head, he cups my jaw in both hands and angles his mouth over mine. He tastes like whiskey and warms my blood the same.

I grip his shirt, needing him closer, and one of his hands drops from my face to my rib cage, his thumb stroking the underside of my breast.

The door behind him swings open, and I'm vaguely aware of someone saying something behind him.

But I can't be expected to make out words when my mind is so full of *him*.

"Out," Kendrick growls without looking.

There's a soft chuckle. "Sorry to interrupt," Remme says, "but they're asking for you outside."

Kendrick tears his mouth from mine and nods, his chest heaving with his ragged breaths. "In a minute," he says, his gaze still on me.

"I'll let them know you're on your way." Remme looks me over and cocks a brow. "Looking good, Princess." He clicks the door shut behind him as he leaves, and I step out of Kendrick's arms.

"Are you okay?" he asks.

Nodding, I turn toward the window that overlooks the village. The bonfire for tonight's celebration blazes in the distance. "I know we need to go, but I just want to stay here."

Kendrick steps up behind me, slides his arms around my waist, and nuzzles his face into the side of my neck. "I wish we could." His lips are warm. I want to close my eyes and sink into the pleasure of it, but he straightens before I have the chance.

My neck feels too cold where his mouth used to be.

Sighing, I survey the people in the distance and remember my conversation with my handmaid.

"How many of the fae I meet tonight will be actual fae?"

"What do you mean?"

"I know they aren't all humans that have been glamoured. My handmaid is fae, and you said that there were fae long ago in Elora who called themselves elves. How many of the Elorans that I will meet tonight will be in their true form?"

He studies me for a long time. "As far as I know, everyone you meet tonight will be in their true form. It is in Elora that they must hide who they are. They come here to be free."

"And the humans? Did the people of Elora know that fae—elves—lived among them?"

"Once, it was no secret, and there was no animosity between the two races. That came later."

"With the Magical Seven," I say, connecting the dots.

"Right. It served them to turn the humans against the fae and against faerie magic, and they used fear and misinformation against the native Eloran fae until they could no longer live openly in their own realm."

I study the people milling around the bonfire in the distance with a new kind of sympathy. I know what it's like to long for home but know you'll be unwelcome there. "So they hid?"

"Some left, seeking out a realm where they wouldn't have to disguise what they were. But others stayed and lived disguised as humans."

"But why? Why would they do that?"

"Why does anyone hide part of who they are? To escape persecution and protect their families. To live in peace." He draws in a ragged breath. "To avoid the prejudice of those around them."

I sink into a chair, trying to sort it all out. "Why did the Seven hate the fae so much?"

"Because only the fae could expose them for what they were."

I shake my head. "I don't understand. You mean the fae could prove they were evil?"

Kendrick doesn't answer but keeps his gaze leveled on me.

The Magical Seven. The most powerful magic users in the entire human realm. The collective that rules from afar to keep the fae from our lands, to keep the portals closed—or at least more difficult to use—and to make sure magic isn't misused. "No," I whisper. "Surely they aren't . . ." He doesn't look away. "They're fae? This Erith I'm meant to kill is *fae*? How could that be? How could they have tricked us for so long? How . . ." But the *how* is so obvious. Magic and lots of it. More than any mage could ever wield. "Why?"

"Power. Greed. Unfortunately, it's almost always as simple as that."

"Why didn't you tell me Erith was fae from the start, knowing how I feel about their kind?"

He's quiet for a long time, doing nothing but studying my expression. "I didn't want that to be your reason for agreeing."

I understand that, and I'm glad I didn't get on board for that reason alone. "You want fae and humans to live peacefully together again in Elora—the way you said it used to be."

"Yes. I know many who want to go home as badly as you do."

I drop my gaze to my hands. "There's little I want more."

He tucks a lock of hair behind my ear. It must've come loose when we kissed. "Sometimes I think you don't remember what it was really like in Elora because you romanticize those years with your sister. You want to believe life was better before she took the throne, so you remember the good parts, probably the parts with you and her, and you let yourself forget just how bad the rest was."

"Is it really so terrible that I wish I could go back? That, in my heart, Elora will always be home?"

"It's not terrible," he says, pulling me to stand, "but I'm not convinced it's true."

So you don't want me to come with you? But I don't ask. I bow my head because I already promised I wouldn't ask for his tomorrows. It's not fair to break that promise when I have nothing to offer.

"Jas . . ." His hand skims down my neck and between my breasts, and he presses his palm against my steadily beating heart. "Maybe this homesickness isn't about missing Elora. Maybe it wouldn't go away if you got to go back. I think you miss your sister—missed her even while you lived in that palace with her—but you love her too much to let her see how deep these scars really run. I think this ache you feel has nothing to do with the realm we're trying to save and everything to do with you spending the last three years shutting out the one person who's always been home to you."

His words hit me so hard, I squeeze my eyes closed, and when grief and regret threaten to drown me, I step into his arms and hold on. I've been walking through life in a trance, choosing numbness over pain and vengeance over fear. I've been so shut down. For years I was going through the motions of life, too scared to let myself feel anything, and then, more recently, numb from the ring. Finally, I'm remembering how it feels to be alive, remembering the flip side of the pain and fear.

It's as if Kendrick's waking me up. And it's both wonderful and horrible—to realize I still can feel the good, to find myself wishing for the future for the first time in a long time, and to know I traded so much possibility for revenge.

"Promise me something," he says into my hair. His palm's still pressed against my chest, trapped between our bodies. "After all this is over and you return to the Midnight Palace, tell your sister about what happened in the dungeons. Tell her what Mordeus did to you."

I couldn't. It would destroy her, but still I hear myself ask, "Why?"

He draws in a ragged breath. "Because you'll never believe she loves you as you are if you keep hiding the truth."

"I'm fine. I don't need anyone's love."

He gives me a sad smile and strokes along my cheek and around my eye, caressing my scar through the glamour. "I've never met someone who needed it more."

"It would break her," I confess. "The truth. She'd believe she failed me. At least this way only one of us is broken."

"Hale! People are waiting!" Remme calls from downstairs.

He ignores him. "You think you're broken?"

I scoff and pull away. "Obviously." I try to cap my retort with a grin, but his expression is too severe, and I can't hold it. "Let's go. You're late."

"Jas—"

"It's not a big deal," I say, swallowing back the emotions that are threatening to choke me. "We're all a little broken."

I try to step out of his arms, but he holds me fast.

"Most of us, sure." He scans my face over and over. "And no one could've blamed you if you'd fallen to pieces, but you didn't. You have all these scars to prove it—and everywhere there's a scar, you're a little bit stronger."

"Don't." My eyes burn. I don't want to do this. Not when it's such a lie. "I don't need you to feed me a bunch of motivational nonsense. I'm fine."

"You're *not* fine, but you're not broken either." He holds my face in both hands and presses a hard kiss to my mouth. "Fear isn't a measure of cowardice, and pain isn't a measure of weakness. You are brave and strong and anything but broken."

Remme calls for him again, and I wipe at my cheeks. "I can't go out there yet."

"Take all the time you need." Kendrick backs out of the room, eyes lingering on me until he turns to the stairs.

"Hope you weren't counting on seeing much of Hale tonight," Skylar says as she leads me to the village center a quarter hour later. "Everyone will be wanting more of him than there is to go around."

The celebration is crowded with fae and humans alike, and I weave through the crowd, watching people enjoy food from the long tables overflowing with fruit and bread and pastries and pour themselves glass after glass of a sparkling pink wine.

Luckily, I had a few minutes to pull myself together before Skylar showed up in my room wanting to know why I didn't go down to the party with Kendrick.

I spot him chatting with Lons, the man who seemed so unhappy about us holding hands yesterday. They're laughing, and another man seems to be waiting his turn to greet Kendrick. I can't blame them for wanting him to themselves. I feel the same. But I don't understand it. "Who is he to them?" I ask, rubbing my arms. The night is too cool for the way I cut this dress, and I'm already regretting that bit of vanity if Kendrick won't even be around to enjoy it. I wish we could be closer to the fire and the comforting snap of the flames.

Skylar grabs a bottle of wine and fills two glasses. "Hale is magnetic. He has the charisma necessary to change the world, and that's because he believes in what he's fighting for. He believes in it with every bit of himself. But what people don't understand— what *you* don't understand—is that his fight, his cause, will always come first. It's how he was made, and it's commendable and admirable, and you can't help but adore him for it." She hands a glass to me. "That is until you need him to pick you over his cause and he can't."

"I would never ask him to pick me."

Her smile is sad. The pitying curve of lips that comes from a person who thinks you're walking the path they once walked. "That's what we all think."

"You still didn't answer my question," I say. "Who is he—other than another crusader? You all look to him, and everyone here is celebrating just seeing his face, so don't pretend he's just like you."

"I shouldn't be the one telling you any of this," she says.

"But you're the one I'm asking."

She sighs. "He's Kendrick the Chosen." The look on her face is a mix of admiration and sadness. "He's the one the oracle believed would overthrow the Elora Seven."

I nod. "He told me that."

She holds my gaze for a beat before adding, "And if he's successful, he will be our new king."

Why can't our fates align? Why did the Mother put you in my path if I'm going to have to let you go?

His objections to being with me suddenly make sense in a totally different way.

Skylar tried to warn me, didn't she? *He's not for me any more than he's for you. The difference between us is that I've made my peace with that.*

I swallow back hurt. "And who's his queen? She'll be chosen by the oracle, right?"

"She was already chosen." Her eyes go steely as she scans the crowd. "And we lost her. Mordeus captured her only weeks before he was killed. Kendrick bartered for her release, but she disappeared. Some are beginning to lose hope that she'll ever be found, but until the oracle names a new queen, we must believe she lives."

That's why Skylar's always been so disapproving of anything between me and Kendrick. She wants him to keep his distance from me because she believes his queen is out there somewhere. Waiting for him.

"Does he . . ." I swallow hard. "Does he love her?"

Skylar's lips press into a tight line. "He loves Elora. That's all that matters."

I watch the bubbles in my wineglass fizzle and pop, and bite back every objection that wants to launch itself off my tongue. What I have with Kendrick feels special—fated even, if I believed in such a thing—but Skylar's been trying to tell me all along that everyone has this pull toward Kendrick.

Their future king.

"I'm sorry," Skylar says. "For what it's worth, I didn't want you to get hurt."

Am I really no different than anyone else? Just another person charmed by the goodness in his heart? Have I been fooling myself to think that my cursed stars might be changing? That maybe what I feel for him he feels for me in return? Did the way he showed up in the dungeons just when I needed him most mean nothing? And the fact that the ring doesn't quite work the same on him? Does that mean nothing?

"I should go," Skylar says, glancing around awkwardly. "I don't do this painful shit well."

"Skylar, wait." I search my memory for the name Kendrick and Natan discussed the night after I first showed them the ring. "Have you ever heard of the legend of Fienna?" It was the legend Natan pointed to as an explanation of why the ring didn't work on Kendrick.

She lifts a brow. "Wow. That's random. Um, yeah. I don't remember all the details, but she's the siren, right?"

I shake my head. "I've never heard it. Could you tell me?"

She gulps her wine, looking up at the stars thoughtfully. "From what I remember, she was a siren who left her island for one reason or another. She met this sailor and they fell in love, but of course he didn't know she was a siren. Eventually she had to return to her family. Years later, the same man was sailing by. It was her day to sing on the rocks, but the sailor didn't crash. Her song didn't work on him because he was already in love with her."

Remme appears, stepping up beside Skylar and nodding knowingly. "True love is more powerful than the imitation the siren's song creates," he says, smiling into his own glass of wine. "I always loved that story."

Skylar scoffs. "Yeah, until the chick's mom sends her sisters out to sing for his return journey, and Fienna has to watch as they make the man she loves crash into the deadly rocks and die."

"Okay, so *parts* of the story are nice," Remme says.

Skylar rolls her eyes. "I'm going to grab some food. Find me if you need me."

Remme watches as she strolls away, then turns to me. "Sorry about interrupting earlier." He clears his throat and cringes. "*Again.*"

I smile, despite myself. "You do have horrible timing."

He glances over his shoulder to where Skylar disappeared into the crowd. "The Fienna thing—is that your hypothesis on why the ring doesn't work the same on Hale?"

I avert my gaze to the fire before the concern in his eyes can pull more tears from me. I've had enough of that tonight. "I heard Natan mention it."

"Well, Natan is by far the smartest person I've ever met. He's probably onto something." Remme's eyes are bright as he nudges me. "I like you for Hale, Jasalyn. I sure hope you don't go anywhere."

The smile falls from my face. I've never had as much trouble keeping myself held together emotionally as I have in the last two days. This is the cost of waking up—the cost of the joy and yearning and passion. It's thrown open the doors to everything I so carefully had caged up inside.

Remme frowns. "Did I say something?"

I shake my head. "No. I'm just tired."

"Bullshit." Somehow the word is soft and filled with compassion.

"It's just that Kendrick's queen is out there waiting for him, so none of that matters anyway, right?"

Remme grimaces. "Skylar told you?"

I set my jaw and nod. Didn't Kendrick try to warn me? And I told him I didn't care about the future. It's not fair to change the rules now.

I need to get out of here.

"Hey." Remme takes me by the wrist before I can turn away. "We have oracles and prophecies, but they all change constantly. They're misinterpreted and misconstrued, bent by misconceptions and ultimately trumped by our free will. I'll never give up on someone I love for what others claim is fate. No matter how bleak it all looks, there's a path in your stars worth fighting for."

"And what if you find yourself living beneath nothing but cursed stars?"

Remme hunches over so we're eye to eye, and there's only tenderness and understanding in his eyes when he says, "Then you go find yourself a world with a whole new night sky." He slides his hand down to mine and gives it a firm squeeze. "And some friends who will show you how to get there."

CHAPTER TWENTY-FOUR

◊

JASALYN

"There you are," Kendrick says, wrapping his arms around me from behind.

I stiffen—not for the reason I've recoiled from touch for three years, but because this man holds my heart in his hands. I put it there despite all Skylar's warnings. All *his* warnings. And I can't even ask him not to break it. It turns out neither of us has a future of our own to promise.

"Are you okay?" he asks.

"Yeah." I scan his face, dodging those beautiful ice-blue eyes. He's promised to another, and I'm being chased by the ticking clock that's counting down to my eighteenth birthday.

He spins me around to face him and rubs his hands up and down my bare arms. "You sure?"

"Just a little cold and tired."

"I need to stay here for a couple more hours, but you can go back to the house if you want."

I search his face as if it might explain why he never told me he was promised to another. *He tried to tell you.* "I don't want you to keep things from me. No matter how much they might hurt.

If you really think I'm so strong, prove it by telling me the hard things."

The space he puts between us is fractional, but it might as well be miles. "I was trying to protect you from it. Until I see Mordeus for myself, I—"

"What?" At the back of my mind, Kendrick's words from yesterday click into place. *I'll kill him myself when we find him.* When *we find him.* I lift my head and hold his gaze. "You believe Mordeus is back."

His expression goes blank. "What were *you* talking about?"

"Who you are to them." I shake my head. *Mordeus is back.* I've suspected all this time, but to understand that Kendrick believes it makes it too real. "How long have you known the Mordeus rumors are true?"

He searches my face for a long time, and the silence stretches taut between us, threatening to snap. "I suspected when I saw your scars and you said they were from Mordeus. Only scars from blood magic are delayed like that."

Blood magic. They also talked about that the night at the campsite. He and Natan discussed it as if it might be the reason Natan couldn't find my powers. I'd meant to ask about it, but then I blacked out and I was too busy recovering to think of it.

Kendrick takes my hand and skims his thumb over the knot of scar tissue on my wrist. "Blood magic was forbidden long ago, but some still use it." He swallows hard. "When I saw your scars and you confirmed they were from your time in Mordeus's captivity, I suspected the rumors about his resurrection were true—or perhaps he was never dead at all. When wounds don't leave marks

333

until much later, when scars suddenly appear like yours did, it's a sign that the magic is being called upon."

I shiver. "What does that mean—*called upon*?"

"Blood magic allows the caster to draw power from their subject. It's not unlike the tethering Mab's line was blessed with, where one faerie can use the power of another. Except blood magic doesn't require a gift from the gods, only pain and suffering, and in some cases fear. Each wound inflicted as part of the spell becomes a small deposit of magical power that can be accessed by the caster at a later date. I knew he was alive because one cannot call on blood magic from the grave."

"No." I shake my head. "I would know if he was pulling from me." *Wouldn't I?*

"I don't think it works like that. The only way of knowing is by seeing the scars appear."

"So *you* knew." I pull my wrist from his grasp and retreat a step. "That was days ago."

"I know."

My stomach roils. "We discussed his resurrection after you saw my scars, you said it was unlikely. You told me you thought someone was pretending to be him."

He sets his jaw. "I told you what you needed to hear."

"You lied to me." It's easier to focus on this than try to grapple with what it all means. Easier to latch on to the omissions of the man in front of me than to contemplate that my existence might somehow be *helping—strengthening*—a monster. "So is that how he did it? Am I responsible for his resurrection?"

"No. Nothing like that. If he's back, there's another explanation.

Blood magic is powerful, but it can't bring someone back from the grave."

"You still should've told me. *You* are supposed to be the one I can trust."

"I didn't want to say anything until I had solid evidence."

"And would you have told me then? Once you had your *evidence*?"

He closes his eyes, exhaling slowly. "I don't know."

I recoil. Three words never hurt so much. "I thought we were a *team*, but you're keeping things from me. I thought I was part of your mission, but maybe I'm nothing more than a tool."

His voice drops to a low rumble. "You know that's not true."

"Do I? You know what a mark Mordeus left on me. You know how much he haunts me. And you kept this horrible truth a secret."

He closes his eyes, and when he opens them again, the careful blankness of before is gone and his expression twists with raw emotion. "I've had informants in the Midnight Palace for *months,* Jasalyn. They tell me you've been a shell of a person since moving there. They tell me your sister had your maid search your chambers for knives because she believed you might hurt yourself—or worse. So, no. I didn't want to tell you. I was afraid of what you might do if you knew that Mordeus was not only back but that he was using all that pain he once caused you to become stronger. Can you blame me?"

Can I blame him? He's right. The idea that Mordeus is somehow drawing power from me makes me want to crawl out of my own skin. Three short months ago, when I hadn't heard a single rumor of Mordeus's return and when I had no idea he was drawing power from me, I traded my *life* for a mere taste of vengeance.

"What else are you keeping from me?" I snap, ignoring my internal alarm that warns how hypocritical I'm being. Kendrick isn't the only one keeping secrets.

"Hale!" Remme calls, jogging to reach us. He's flushed and out of breath. Natan follows shortly behind.

Kendrick's brow wrinkles as he turns his attention to his friend. "What's wrong? Did something happen?"

"Isaak of Lune has returned."

Kendrick straightens. "I was convinced he'd met his end."

"We all were," Remme says. His eyes are bright, but he gives me a strange look—as if he doesn't want me to overhear this. "He was captured and being held at the Wasted Burrows, but now he's back and he's not alone."

"She's alive, Hale," Natan says softly. "Crissa's alive and has been returned to us."

"Crissa?" I say the name aloud before I can stop myself. There's no way it can be the same person. What are the chances that these humans would be looking for the same human girl I've been wishing I could save?

"She's from Elora," Remme says, gaze drifting my way before quickly darting away. "She's important to us."

Kendrick's face has gone pale, and when he looks at me, there's something like pity in his eyes. "We thought she was dead." He says it like an apology, and I don't understand.

Skylar joins us next, chest rising and falling quickly as if she ran here. "Did you hear?"

"Mordeus put a girl named Crissa in my cell," I say quickly. I have to know. "She was my age, and she had this silky white hair. She always believed she'd be rescued. She said she had people coming for her." I bite my bottom lip. "She knew these incantations that would help me calm myself when I started to panic."

Skylar releases a puff of laughter. "That's our Crissa."

"We're sure it's her?" Kendrick asks.

"Yes," Natan says. "Isaak had a vision and went out to find her. He was captured trying to get to her, but then he found a way out. *With Crissa*."

Skylar beams. "Isaak's back, and Crissa's alive." She claps her hands. "What a day."

"Where are they?" Kendrick asks.

"They've been taken to the infirmary," Natan says. "Isaak is in such rough shape I don't know how he made it here, and Crissa's unconscious. Our healers are tending to them both."

"They're expecting you," Skylar says. "I'll stay with your slayer here."

I fold my arms. "No. I'm going." Everyone stares at me like this is a terrible idea. "Before Kendrick was thrown into the cell across from mine, Crissa was my only friend in those dungeons. She made herself weak to the point of unconsciousness trying to help me through. I want to see her."

Skylar cringes. "I don't think—"

"She can come," Kendrick says, and everyone stares at him as if he just suggested I could fly.

"Thank you," Kendrick says when we've cleared everyone out of the infirmary. Their friend Isaak was beat up pretty badly, limping and bruised but healing. He's already been sent home to rest.

I look at Crissa, her small body laid out on the bed, the blankets wrapped around her. She's so small. There's a tug-of-war in my chest. Relief and guilt and gratitude and fear. "Will she be okay?" I ask. "She was unconscious in the dungeons when they took her away. But I thought . . ." I thought that once she stopped draining herself trying to protect me, she'd recover. Or I hoped.

"We came for her," Kendrick says. "Just like she knew we would. She was okay last I saw her. Weak but conscious."

I lift my gaze to his, eyes wide. "That's why you were in there right after she left. You traded yourself for her?" Of course. Of course he would. Of course he did.

His jaw ticks. "I made a deal with Mordeus to get her out of there."

"Kendrick—"

"Don't. Don't look at me like I'm a hero." He looks away. "I did what I thought was right that day. But then she was lost again, and I was left wondering if it was all for nothing."

"And why do you question it now?" I catch sight of something sharp and shiny from the corner of my eye, but when I look, it's only Crissa's hand curling into a fist on top of the blanket. "Who is she?" I know who Crissa is to me, but she's obviously important to them as well.

His chest expands as he turns to me. "I truly believed we'd lost her for good this time." He searches my eyes, then his hungry gaze lands on my mouth. His nostrils flare, and his pupils dilate. "I've never wanted to be selfish so badly in my life."

I back away and my thighs hit the bed. Because I know. I think

I knew the moment his friends surrounded him with the news of her return, but seeing the agony in his eyes drives it home. "She's your queen." My voice is dull. Empty. "That's why she knew so much magic despite being mortal. She's the one the oracle said would be queen." I swallow. "And you bargained for her freedom because, as her future king, your job is to protect her."

The ache in my heart is reflected in his eyes as he speaks. "I've never turned away from my duty to the rightful kingdom of Elora—to the *people* of Elora. I don't have the privilege of choosing with my heart. I need you to understand—" Kendrick takes a breath, then his eyes go wide. "Jasalyn, run."

I spin around and immediately back into Kendrick's chest. A scaly, winged beast unfurls from the mattress where Crissa lay just moments before.

Kendrick grabs my hand and drags me out of the infirmary and into the street. "Wyvern!" he screams. "Remme! Skylar!"

A horrible, beastly cry comes from inside the infirmary, and in the next breath, the building is ablaze, flames licking the sky, and the wyvern is tearing out through the roof, angry wings beating.

"Shelter!" Kendrick shouts to the crowd. "Get to the underground shelter. Now!"

I tear my gaze from the beast and find chaos. People around us run in every direction. I can taste their panic in the air.

The wyvern swoops toward us and opens its mouth with an angry cry. Kendrick throws his hands out, and the fire that rolls from the beast's mouth is deflected—blunted as if hitting an invisible wall.

"Jas, get to the storm shelter on the other side of the town square. If you see Remme or Skylar, tell them to meet me on the roof of the apothecary."

The wyvern screeches again and then a trail of fire pours from its mouth and onto a row of cottages. *Those were people's homes.*

"You'll be an easy target on the roof!"

He glares at me. "You're not moving fast enough."

I stare at him for a long, painful beat of my heart. I don't want to leave him, but if I stay, I will only be a distraction. I wish I had magic. I wish I had something other than this stupid ring. "I will never forgive you if you die," I shout.

"Then get in the shelter so I don't have to worry about you."

With one last look in his direction, I enter the chaos and run toward the opposite side of the square.

The wyvern screeches again, and this time when it unleashes its fire on the village, screams of pain tear into my eardrums and the stench of burning flesh fills the air.

Behind me, fire races across the dry grass, licking at my heels. I don't dare turn to look.

I run as hard as I can, never allowing myself to glance back but thinking of Kendrick and my friends with every step. *Please be okay. Please don't die.*

Behind me, I hear the shouts of people preparing for battle.

The door to the storm shelter is already open, and people are running down the stairs, but several yards away, two girls are kneeling on a patch of scorched earth and clinging to a blistered form.

I cut in their direction and grab their arms, pulling them toward the shelter.

"Mama!" the girls scream, yanking out of my grasp and

dropping back to the ground.

Their mother is long gone—nothing but carnage from the wyvern's attack.

"You have to come with me," I shout. "You need to get to shelter."

The girls link their hands together and squeeze. "Families stay together," the oldest says.

They're so young and so desperate—not so different than Brie and I were when our mother left us. We would've done anything to have her back. My chest aches for them.

Arrows fly through the air, and the wyvern dodges, then screeches again before raining more fire onto the village.

"Your mom would want you to go to shelter," I say. I don't touch them again. My strength is nothing against the adrenaline of trauma and desperation. "Please come with me. She would want you to live."

The fire behind me is reflected in the eyes of the youngest as she screams at me. "No!" Her chest shakes with her sobs.

I glance over my shoulder where people are still streaming into the underground shelter. I need to get these girls down there before it fills.

I remove my ring from the bodice of my dress and take a deep breath before sliding it on.

"Please come with me," I say before she can look away. "I want you to come with me into the shelter."

Her expression changes immediately and her body relaxes. "Can I stay next to you?" she asks, already standing. "I would feel less scared if I were by your side."

Her sister turns around, and I see the moment my magic locks onto her. "Can I come too?" she asks.

"Please." I wave my hand for her to follow. "Let's go now."

We climb down into the cellar, and I urge the girls to take a seat on the floor. It's crowded, and there's barely enough room for the three of us. *We made it.*

"Here." An old man stands on shaky legs when I reach the bottom of the stairs. "Take my seat."

"I'm fine," I tell him. "You sit, please."

Everyone's staring at me, so I go to remove my ring.

Only it doesn't move.

I try again.

It's stuck.

CHAPTER TWENTY-FIVE

◆

FELICITY

OUTSIDE MY WINDOW, THE LIGHT show of the evening sun competes with the vibrant colors of the trees for the most beautiful sight. I want to ignore the soft knock at my door and sit here all night. If I could, I'd hide from the guests who've filled the castle for tonight's ball. Hide from the responsibilities of Jasalyn, Unseelie princess, and sit here and relive every moment of last night with Misha.

But I don't have the luxury of time. Shae made sure of that when he left me with only a few hairs. I have tonight. Tomorrow morning, I'll leave to find the portal.

"Come in," I call, not bothering to move from the window.

My handmaids warned me they'd be here to help me dress early this evening so I could be announced at the ball at the beginning of the night. "As a queen should be," one said, winking at me like she was in on some big secret.

The thought is so laughable. I am no queen. I am the daughter of a horribly evil man, a girl who was raised in the rural farmlands of Elora and has been in hiding her whole life. I grew up running around the farm barefoot with scuffed knees and elbows. The only reason I learned anything about court etiquette was because Hale's mother knew I might need to use my skills to take the form of a royal one day, though in truth she hoped I'd never have to leave the safety of the farm at all.

I hoped the same, but fate had other plans.

"Good evening," someone says behind me.

I turn and straighten at the sight of the former Wild Fae queen. "Queen Amira." I pull my robe together as best I can and dip into a curtsy. "My apologies, Your Grace, I expected my handmaids."

"Please, it's just Amira," she says, gliding into the room. She's so graceful—her movements a perfect match to her peace-evoking presence. She clasps her hands in front of her and gives me a small smile. "I hoped we could speak for a moment before the ball."

Why, yes, I am in love with your former husband, the king, and yes, I am deceiving him every day, and when he discovers I'm not who I claimed to be, he will hate me forever without ever knowing my face. Nice chat. Bye!

I return her smile. "Of course!"

She turns to the wardrobe where my gown for tonight hangs on a hook outside the door. The gown is lovely. A burnt-orange, off-the-shoulder wrap dress that accentuates all of Jasalyn's best attributes—her coloring as well as her petite hourglass figure.

It's not the first time I've wished I didn't have to be here stuck in this form, but I dread the fuss over the dress and makeup and hair for tonight. I have no doubt that by the time I step into the ballroom, I will look beautiful. Because *Jas* is beautiful.

And when Misha looks at me and his eyes go dark, when he tucks his hands in his pockets as if he's struggling to keep them to himself, I already know it will hurt a little, and I will have no one to blame for that hurt but myself.

I've let this go on too long.

When Amira turns her gaze from the dress to me, her brow is wrinkled. "You don't like it?"

I wince. As an empath, she must find my conflicting emotions confusing, given how beautiful the dress is. "I do." Emotion clogs my throat. "I think it might be the loveliest dress I've ever worn."

She cocks her head to the side, studying me. "But you aren't sure what Misha will think." She sighs and glances toward the bed. "May I sit?"

"Um . . . yes, if you please."

She smooths her skirts and takes a seat on the edge of the neatly made bed. "Misha isn't simply my king and my former husband," she says. "He is my dearest friend."

I clasp my hands in front of me. "Of course. He's told me as much. I admire the relationship you two have."

Her eyes are bright with sincerity. "When he brought you to Castle Craige, he never intended for anything . . ." She clears her throat and drops her gaze to her lap. This is not a female who meddles. She's here because she loves Misha—no other reason—but this is awkward for her. "Well, I don't want you to think this was all some grand scheme to win your hand. He brought you here as a favor to Abriella, and I believe the change that's arisen between you two has been a surprise to you both."

I grip one hand in the other so tightly I'm likely to bruise. "What are you trying to say?"

When she lifts her gaze to meet mine, her eyes are brimming

with tears. "All I want is for him to find the love he couldn't have with me. And while I know it's not my place to be here or to say anything to you at all, I know him well enough to know how he's come to feel for you. My gifts being what they are, I know you"—she blows out a breath—"I know you are not the same scared little girl that I met last time I visited the shadow court, but I also know what you feel for Misha terrifies you. I feel it every time I see you look at him. I don't know if it's because he's fae or because he's king or because anyone with any sense of self-preservation feels at least a little scared of love so big, but I'm asking you . . ." She looks away, as if she can't bring herself to finish that sentence.

"What?" I ask.

"I want to ask you to give him a chance." She sniffs and wipes the tears from under her eyes. "But that's not fair, given all you've been through and been asked to do. So instead, I'll just say please don't hurt him."

The ache in my chest is too big. "I don't intend to," I say softly.

She holds my gaze for a long moment before giving a curt nod. "Thank you. I will see you at the ball."

When I look in the mirror, I'm both awed and saddened by the image I see there. My handmaiden dabbed a pink gloss on my lips and lined my eyes with kohl before setting my hair into curls she let cascade down my back.

Misha's gaze will no doubt linger on me tonight, and each longing glance will be a turn of the knife I've put in my own chest.

What would I see in his eyes if he ever looked upon the real me? Maybe it's better that I don't know. Maybe that would earn me nothing but pain.

"It's time, milady," my handmaid says.

I smooth out my dress and follow her into the hall, where a sentry greets me. He offers me his arm and escorts me down the stairs and along the winding creek through the castle to the ball-room doors.

"Wait here until they announce you," he says, and moments later the doors are thrown open to reveal a grand stone staircase that descends into the courtyard. The space has been transformed into a ballroom for the occasion, lit by twinkling orbs that float over the dance floor with the moon and stars above.

A booming voice says, "Jasalyn Kincaid, princess of the Court of the Moon, sister to the Unseelie queen, child of Mab."

Then all eyes are on me. Music plays, and one of Misha's military officers takes my hand and leads me down the stairs and onto the cobblestones that will be tonight's dance floor.

I spot Misha at the other side of the courtyard. He's surrounded by people vying for his attention, but his eyes are on me—slowly sweeping over every inch of me in this dress.

My body goes hot, and my stomach twists with anxiety. *He's looking at Jas, not you.*

"May I have this dance?" someone asks behind me, taking my elbow in his hand. Before I realize what's happening, the orchestra has transitioned to a soft tune and the handsome white-haired male has swept me into the throng of dancers.

"Good evening," I say awkwardly. I look up into his sea-green eyes and nearly stumble at the sight of the male looking back at me. The Seelie king. I'm *dancing* with *King Ronan*.

"You made quite the entrance," he says. "Every pair of eyes will be on you for the rest of the night."

My cheeks heat. "I don't know about that."

"I do. Half the females here are trying to win Misha's hand, and now they've seen the way he looks at you. You have a target on your back whether you like it or not."

"That wasn't my intention."

"I wasn't trying to imply that it was." He smiles, and his eyes crinkle in the corners. "It's good to see you, Jas. I've missed you."

Oh no. They're friends? "It's probably my fault," I say, dodging his gaze. "I admit I've not been good about keeping the company of others in the last few years."

His expression softens. "I don't blame you. If anything, I should've done more to find time." He lowers his head so his mouth is by my ear when he says, "I am still your friend, just as I was in Elora, and I am here for anything you need. Please know that."

I swallow hard, unsure what to make of that and positive a response is more dangerous than my silence.

The song ends, and King Ronan steps back, squeezing both of my hands. "I have no doubt you will be kept busier than you're prepared for tonight, so I will say now that I hope you come visit me at the Golden Palace. You are welcome anytime. It would do my heart good to have an old friend walking the halls."

I squeeze his hands in return. "I appreciate the offer, and I'll consider it."

He glances over my shoulder and nods toward the opposite

side of the courtyard. "Now, make your way toward Misha before he explodes from jealousy."

He winks, and I take two steps away before I spot Misha. He's speaking with a beautiful fair-skinned female with silky dark hair. Their bodies are angled toward each other as if they're in the middle of a private conversation. He's laughing.

He deserves to be happy.

"Look at you," someone says, touching my shoulder.

I spin and my eyes go wide. *The queen*. "Abriella!" I squeak.

"Surprise!" She leans forward to press a kiss to my cheek.

"Why didn't you tell me you'd be coming tonight?" I'm not sure what I would've done if I'd known. Likely I would've feigned sickness and stayed in my room.

No. I would've risked saying the wrong thing to the princess's sister. I would've risked exposure. Just for this last night with Misha.

"Honestly, I wasn't sure we were going to be able to make it and didn't want to risk disappointing you." Abriella glances over her shoulder, where Finn stands. He surveys me with silver eyes that—

My stomach clenches at the sight of those silver eyes. Just like his uncle's. I'll never be able to see eyes like that without remembering the horrors Mordeus made Jas endure. Did she think of Mordeus every time Finn looked at her?

Brie exchanges a look with Finn, and when she turns back to me, she lowers her voice. "We were helping Sebastian with a problem in the Court of the Sun. It seems there's a sector of his population demanding he take a wife."

I paste on a smile, though I have no idea who *Sebastian* is. "Does he have any prospects?" I ask.

"His advisors made a suggestion, but I'm not sure I like it."

"What's that?" I ask.

"I'm not sure you would like it either." She cocks her head to the side, studying me. "Especially if what I hear about you and Misha is true?" My cheeks heat, and all my worries about not knowing any Sebastian skitter away. A grin splits across the queen's face. "I'll admit I always hoped you two might truly see each other."

I bow my head. "I don't know what you're talking about."

She wraps an arm around my shoulders and leads me to a less crowded corner. "You don't need to be ashamed, Jas. Tell me everything."

I shake my head. "There's nothing to tell."

"The red in your cheeks says otherwise." She glances over her shoulder, and I follow her gaze to the male in question. I realize he's watching me—*no*, watching *Jas*. "The way he looks at you says otherwise."

"It's nothing. We've become friends."

"He's searching for a wife, and he's spending all his time with you instead of the females he should be courting. *That* means something."

"Well, you did ask him to, did you not? Spend time with me? Get me out of my room and away from my books?"

She waves this away. "I need to know what you think about this. I know you didn't want to leave the shadow court, but you look so good and seem to be settling in beautifully here. If Misha is interested in pursuing something *more*, would you be interested?"

My heart aches. Misha is caring and thoughtful, and he deserves better than the games I'm playing. I don't know if he and the real Jasalyn would make a good couple or not, but I hate that I'm interfering with his future like this. Worse is that, deep down, I know that I would stay longer if I could. I would give myself more time with Misha. Even if none of this is real. Even knowing it would hurt that much more when the time to leave comes.

Tomorrow. This will be over tomorrow.

I stare at my shoes. "I don't think so."

I can feel the shadow queen's disappointment, but I don't look up.

"I won't push you," she finally says, "and I will always fight for you to have full agency over your future. I don't want you to be a political pawn, but, Jas"—she waits until I meet her gaze—"you need to know that as long as you're single, advisors of every court will attempt to use you that way. If you have a chance to pursue a relationship that is truly based in love, *that* is what I want for you."

I nod but avoid her eyes. "Thank you."

With a sigh, she squeezes my shoulders. "We need to make our rounds. Unfortunately, Finn and I can't stay long tonight, but we are planning to return next week for a proper visit."

"I'm glad you got to come."

She pulls me into a hug and whispers in my ear. "You deserve all the happiness. If you catch even a glimpse, run after it and grab it with both hands."

Her words remind me so much of something my mother would say that my eyes burn, and my throat feels thick with tears. I want to tell her that she never failed Jas, that the princess is lucky to have a sister like her, that any secrets Jas has were secrets kept in an effort to protect Brie. But I can't, so I only nod.

"I will see you soon." She peers over my shoulder, toward Misha. "Think about what I said."

CHAPTER TWENTY-SIX

◇

FELICITY

THERE IS NO SHORTAGE OF balconies with beautiful views at Castle Craige, and the grand balcony jutting out over the mountain just off the courtyard is no exception. Only it's lousy with partygoers with their faerie wine and fake smiles.

My head is spinning, and I need a bit of privacy, so I slip away from the ball through the servants' hall back into the castle. I weave through the kitchen where the staff is preparing trays of sparkling wine and desserts. On the other side, I find a narrow staircase and take it up two flights. I don't know where I'm going, and I'm not sure I care. I just need to be alone. I need to be away from that crowd and the idea that somewhere among those females might be the one Misha will love. *One who deserves his love.*

Off the stairwell and down a long hall that takes me away from the cacophony of the ball, I find Misha's favorite dining terrace—empty tonight but for the breeze and the starlight. I take in several shaky breaths of night air before finally feeling my muscles relax.

I feel like I just walked away from a gift, but what could I do?

Tell the shadow queen that, yes, I want to be with Misha? Stay here and allow him to think he's courting Jasalyn only to drop the real princess in the middle of this once Erith is dead and I can go home? Or worse? Allow Misha to get close to me simply because I can't resist and have him realize the truth before I'm safely back home?

The wind picks up and lifts my hair off my shoulders. I lean my forearms on the carved wooden rail and close my eyes, letting the breeze dance across my skin.

"How did I know you'd find a reason to sneak away from the party?" Misha's deep voice asks behind me.

Turning, I give him a gentle smile. I can't help but be glad he's here. Can't help that my heart unclenches and my blood hums in the warmth of his presence. "How did you find me?"

A caw echoes through the sky, and his hawk lands on the opposite railing.

"Good evening, Storm," I say to the bird before turning back to Misha. "I forget you have eyes everywhere."

"Not quite everywhere," he says, looking me over slowly. "I haven't had the opportunity to tell you how lovely you look in that dress."

My cheeks heat, which is ridiculous. He probably wouldn't find the real me attractive at all. Plump figure, white hair, blue eyes—Jasalyn's opposite in nearly every way. Not that I have the right to feel bitter about such things. "Thank you."

"I'll admit, I was surprised when you didn't want to make it yourself. I always loved your work. I know your sister's favorite items in her wardrobe are the ones you created as well."

I shrug. "Just a little burnt out on it."

He nods and steps up to the rail. The sun has long since set, but the moon is bright and the streetlamps in the valley beyond make for a lovely view.

I shift to stand by his side. I feel natural here. *Safe.*

"Brie said she talked to you about what's happening in the Seelie Court. The pressure their king is under."

Does that have anything to do with the Sebastian she mentioned? "Briefly," I say, hoping we can move on before I say something damning.

"I think the advisors are grasping at straws. Marrying you off to the golden king won't appease anyone, but your sister is in an awkward position, given her history. If she shoots it down, it will look like she still harbors feelings for him."

Does Abriella call the golden king Sebastian? "Wait—shoots what down?"

"She didn't tell you that part." He flinches. "There are advisors in this realm who think all political woes can be solved by a wedding. Some of my advisors default to the same problem-solving, but personally, I don't agree. Those in Ronan's court who are questioning his legitimacy as king are the same ones who would balk at an Unseelie princess as their queen."

I cut my eyes to him. "Then why push the idea at all?"

"Because they're fools. Devious fools." Misha shakes his head. "I can't decide what's worse, that his advisors may really be so foolish as to believe a marriage to you would quell any unrest or the more likely reality."

"Which is what?" I ask.

He swallows. "That they know very well that it wouldn't work, but they prefer to have *you* be the object of any political ire rather than their king." He slaps the rail. "Lunacy either way."

"Do you think King Ronan *wants* to marry me?" I ask in a squeak.

Misha cocks a brow at me. "King Ronan, huh? Are you practicing for your day at court now?" He huffs out a breath. "In truth, I think he's still in love with your sister."

"But she's bonded to Finnian."

"Of course, and we all know that's never going to change so long as they both live, but what he felt for your sister? That kind of love doesn't fade so easily."

I'm reeling. If Hale knew the depth of the connection between the courts' rulers, he would've found a way to send me to the Court of the Sun instead of the Wild Fae Lands. I have no doubt the queen would've allowed her sister to spend this time there instead, had she—had *I*—asked. I'm glad that I'm standing here instead.

"Would you . . ." He turns and studies my face, as if he's trying to memorize every inch. "Politics aside, would you want that? A marriage to the Seelie king? A life as queen to the Court of the Sun?"

It's always dangerous territory when I have to answer questions of the heart as if I'm Jasalyn, but Misha isn't asking what Princess Jas, the girl he knew before, thinks of this. He's asking about *me*. Maybe I'm fooling myself to believe there's a difference. Maybe my deception is all the worse for it, but I dismiss any thought of how Jas would answer and answer for myself. "No. I wouldn't want that."

Misha looks down at our hands next to each other on the railing and moves his pinkie finger to rub against mine. "Am I selfish to want to keep you here?"

"Am I selfish to want to stay?" I ask, and my breath catches on the swell of emotions in my throat. I wish I could hide away here forever. I wish I didn't have to face the horrors that await me in Elora. I miss my family, but so long as Erith lives, I will never be able to return to my life as I knew it.

Misha's face falls, and he pulls me into his arms. I don't try to stop him. I curl into his chest and breathe him in. He smells like clean pine and a new day, and with his warmth against my cheek, I don't feel so scared of what the future brings.

He rests his chin on my head and toys with the baby hairs on the back of my neck. "You can stay as long as you want. As long as this kingdom is mine, you'll always have a place here."

I close my eyes and flatten my palm against his chest. "Your new wife may feel differently."

He grunts. "I'm in no rush to find a new wife, Jas."

At the sound of that name and the reminder of what I'm doing here, I push away and straighten. "You need an heir, and you're not getting any younger."

He smirks. "Well, I am very old."

Laughing, I look up at him through my lashes.

His expression goes serious as he studies my face. "I can't decide if I love or hate that you won't let me into your mind."

My smile falls away. "Misha . . ."

"I understand," he says, settling a hand over mine on the railing. "And I respect it. But since I can't poke around and figure it out for myself, tell me what you think about tonight—about the ball. About the pomp and circumstance of it all."

I arch a brow. "*That's* what you'd want to know if you could get in my mind?"

"Not really." His gaze dips to my mouth and holds for long enough that I feel breathless. "If I could choose, I'd want to know if you thought about me after I left your chambers last night, and what, exactly, those thoughts entailed." The corner of his mouth lifts into a roguish smile. "But I'm trying to be a gentleman."

My cheeks are burning now, and I want him to kiss me so much that my heart aches. Want it so much that my lips tingle. I have to focus on taking my next breath. "The ball is beautiful." I give a coy smile. "As are all your guests."

He gives a grunt that is half laugh, half begrudging agreement. "It's a spectacle. My court isn't as regimented as the Court of the Sun and the Court of the Moon, but the people want to see that I'm at least looking for a queen."

"Perhaps you should be in there, letting them see you look," I say, finding my gaze on his mouth this time.

He notices, and the air between us goes taut. "Perhaps I should."

When he lowers his mouth to mine, every thought leaves my head and every word leaves my lips. I know nothing but how much I want to feel his kiss again.

His big hands sweep up my sides, cupping my breasts through my dress. I want it gone. I crave the contact of last night—with nothing but the thin, wet shift between his hands and my skin.

I grab fistfuls of Misha's hair, and he deepens the kiss. Our lips and tongues speak a language of their own, a call and response that feels like part sacred ritual and part forbidden pleasure.

He drags his mouth down the side of my neck, then lower, and I hear my own gasp. His hands are everywhere—behind my neck, sweeping over the exposed skin of my back, dipping to grip my rear. When he scrapes his teeth over the swell of my breasts—hot and wet and promising so much more—my body shudders.

I might be whimpering when he straightens again, pulling my body flush with his and bringing his mouth to my ear. I'm definitely trembling.

"I know," he murmurs. One of his hands is in my hair, and I can feel the artfully pinned curls falling. I don't care. "Gods, I know." He's clinging to me like he might fall off the world if he lets go. I'm clinging to him the same way. "I don't want to go back to the courtyard and dance and play nice. I want to take you to my chambers and get you out of this dress."

I curl into his chest. *Yes. Please. That.* "But you have to go," I say.

"You told your sister you weren't interested in pursuing a romantic relationship with me," he says. "And then you say you want to stay, and you kiss me like that, and . . ." He retreats a step and scrapes a hand over his face. "I don't know what to think."

I see the hurt in his russet eyes. I didn't expect that information to make it to Misha—at least not so quickly.

"Is it because of your baker's son or because I'm fae or—"

"No." My sinuses burn with the tears I won't let free. "None of that."

"I know what Lark said, but she's not always right. I promise you she's wrong about this. I won't break your heart. Not when it's so precious to me." He clasps my hand in his and brings it to his chest. "I'm not just a king looking for a queen. I'm a male who's found himself falling for the last person he expected. I know it's scary. If I'm terrified, I can't imagine how you must feel but . . . Give me a chance. Jasalyn, give this a chance."

Jasalyn.

Her name is the hammer that breaks my heart. Lark *was* wrong. Misha didn't break it. *I* did. And I have to leave. Not just because I'm running out of time, but because I couldn't live with myself if I hurt him.

"Go back to the ball." I touch my falling curls. "I'm going to go to my chambers and put myself back together."

"Is that a yes?" he asks, searching my face.

I press my hand against my chest as if I can hold my heart together with pressure alone. "If you still want me after tonight, then perhaps . . ." I know I can't hold a smile, so I let it shake, let my fear shine through. "Then perhaps tomorrow I will try to convince myself a male like you could truly want a girl like me."

"You have no idea how much." He skims trembling fingertips down the side of my neck, then tucks his hands into his pockets and turns back toward the castle and the party.

Goodbye, Misha. I'll miss you.

I don't dare say the words out loud, but he turns toward me, a question on his face as if maybe the thought found its way to him.

Then don't make me wait long, Princess.

The words are as clear as day—as if he spoke them aloud—but I know he spoke them into my mind. My heart races as I watch him heading back to his party, back to his guests.

How did that happen? Why did it feel so *right*? And how do I make sure it never happens again?

I push my worries aside and rush back to my chambers. Leaning against my door, I press a palm to my chest, where it feels like a demon is trying to claw its way out.

How did I let this happen? How did I fall for a male who doesn't even know who I am? How did I let him fall for a lie?

I don't have much experience in the ways of romance, but I'm not so naïve that I don't understand what's going to happen between me and Misha tonight if I go back to that party. I'll end the night in his room, or he in mine, and having to walk away after that might break me forever.

But even if I could handle it? I can't risk spending the night with him—or even a single dance—if he's suddenly hearing my thoughts. If my shields no longer work on him and he sees the web of deceit I've drawn him into, I won't have the chance to wait until tomorrow to search for the portal.

I need to end this all now. Tonight.

CHAPTER TWENTY-SEVEN

———◇———

JASALYN

TIME DRAGS IN THE SHELTER. My mind won't stop spinning, won't stop imagining what could be happening to my friends. To Kendrick. But when the wyvern's screeching finally ceases and someone throws open the shelter doors, less than an hour has passed.

"Jasalyn," Kendrick calls.

I run up the stairs behind a few others and throw myself into his arms. *He's here. He's alive. He's okay.*

He hugs me tightly for two beats before releasing me. His face is haggard, eyes red, but he's whole. "I was afraid you were hit. I thought . . ."

"The others?" I ask. Then I realize there are dead bodies all around me, and I need to be more specific. "Remme, Skylar, Natan?"

"They're okay," he says. His eyes grow haunted. "I wish I could say as much for all Lons's fighters. These people lost more than their homes today."

I squeeze my eyes shut. "I wish I could've helped."

I try to take in my surroundings, but everywhere I look is

another horror. Half the village is in ashes.

"That wasn't Crissa," I say.

Kendrick's jaw twitches. "No. That was a trap, and we fell right into it."

"The Magical Seven?"

"I think so." He drags a hand over his face. "They have to know we're close to something. They've never bothered us outside of Elora. I didn't think they'd know where to find us, but it was a targeted attack. It's hard to imagine anyone else was responsible."

"What about Isaak? Did he know he was bringing a wyvern into his home?"

Kendrick closes his eyes for a beat. "If he did, then he got his just end." There's no satisfaction in his words.

"He didn't make it."

He swallows hard, then shakes his head. "He was at home—where we sent him—and his was one of the first houses the wyvern hit."

People slowly emerge from the cellar and look around wide-eyed.

"Find Lons in the square," Kendrick announces as people pour onto the street from the cellar below. "He's assigning temporary housing to everyone who lost their homes."

He frowns, then seems to realize that people are staring at me, entranced when they should be looking to reunite with their loved ones. "You're wearing the ring?"

I give a shaky nod. "I needed it. To help." Then, with the most convincing smile I can muster, I say, "Go find your families and meet Lons in the square."

He frowns. "Are you going to take it off?"

"It's stuck," I say. I tug again, testing it, but it still doesn't move. Not even a little.

"What do you mean *stuck*?"

My gut knots. I haven't let myself think about it. I can't.

"Come on. I'll help."

He leads me back to our house and into the kitchen. My hand trembles as Kendrick wets it with soapy water, but dread is icing over my heart. I spent the entire wait in that cellar trying to get the ring off my finger, and I know there's nothing Kendrick can do.

When he takes hold of my shaking hands, his are steady. It's a comfort—those rough fingers on my slippery ones—but I already know.

"How . . . ?" He holds my hand up to the lantern, turning it this way and that, rubbing the edge of the ring. "It's like it's not a ring at all. It's as if it's *part* of you."

We're sitting in the kitchen when Natan, Remme, and Skylar return.

"We have a problem," Kendrick says. He squeezes my hand as their eyes glaze over, one by one.

"Jasalyn," Remme says, standing and stepping toward us.

Skylar jumps in front of him, eyes glued to me.

"How can I serve you, Princess?" Natan asks.

"Avert your damn eyes," Kendrick commands, but they ignore him.

Kendrick's authority means nothing so long as I'm wearing the ring.

I smile. "Please turn your attention to that wall," I say softly.

"We need to speak with you while you aren't looking at me—so you can focus."

Once their backs are to us, their shoulders drop, my spell loosening its grip on them.

"Jasalyn used the ring to help during the chaos of the attack," Kendrick says, "and now it won't come off."

Natan turns toward us.

"The wall," I remind him sweetly, and he fixes his face toward the wall again, hands clenched at his sides.

"What do you mean, *won't come off*?" he asks. "Have you tried getting it wet?"

"It's as if it's part of her," Kendrick says. "The ring has become one with Jas, and she can't rid herself of it."

Skylar presses her palm against the wall and squeezes her eyes shut. "Which means I'm going to feel like this every time she's around?" she asks.

Kendrick glances at me, then back to his friends. "Probably."

"I just want to *look*. I want to *please her*," Remme says, shaking his head. "I promise I will be so good."

"The longer you look away, the easier it gets," Natan says, his fists uncurling.

"Why can Hale look at her?" Skylar asks.

I hold his gaze for a beat. "That's a good question."

"I don't know," he says softly, but something in his eyes tells me he's lying or at least that he has his suspicions. *Fienna*.

Skylar's shoulders rise and fall with a deep breath. "Okay. I think I'm better now. So we can't look at her, and you're unaffected by looking at her, but what do we do about the memory part?"

Kendrick squeezes my hand again. "As long as the magic doesn't think we've parted ways, I don't think I'll lose my memories. And I'll keep my journal updated for if we have to be apart."

"And how are you going to make the magic *think* anything?" I ask.

He holds my gaze. "We stay tethered at all times. Especially when sleeping."

Sleeping. Tethered to Kendrick. My stomach shimmies, then goes into a free fall of dread when I realize what will come in the morning. "What do we do about the daylight?" I ask.

"Right." Kendrick flinches. "You'll be weak all day. Will your strength come back at night?"

"I don't know. I've never kept the ring on that long."

"Lovely," Skylar says.

Remme mutters a curse.

"We're sure it will act the same when it's permanently attached?" Natan asks.

"We'll have to wait and see, I suppose," Kendrick says. "If the daytime weakness holds true, we'll figure out something to combat it."

"We need to get that ring off," Natan says.

"Agreed," Kendrick says. "If it makes her that ill after a few hours of wearing it during the day, we don't know what it's going to do to her long term, but it can't be good."

"If it makes her too sick, we may need to cut off the finger," Skylar says.

I flinch. Remme and Natan gasp in unison.

"To *protect her*," Skylar growls.

"Let's save drastic measures until we know they're necessary," Kendrick says.

"We'll take her home and find a mage who can destroy it." Natan's words are so matter-of-fact. *Destroy the ring.* I wait for the kicked-in-the-chest feeling, but it doesn't come. I want to be free of this ring—the good and the bad.

"The sooner the better," Skylar says. "I've been hot for chicks before, but this feeling is what the straight folks call a *girl crush,* and that makes me want to punch myself in the face."

"Don't do that," I say.

"I won't. I promise I won't do anything that displeases you," she says, eyes big and voice placating. Then she growls. *"Make it stop."*

"Sleep first," Kendrick says. "We'll figure out the rest tomorrow."

The room Kendrick and I planned to sleep in together has very different energy when we enter it this time, the ring on my finger, tomorrow so unsure.

"I would give you some privacy to change, but—"

"No, right. I know." I look around the room. If I were Skylar, I'd probably just strip down to my undergarments in front of him. "Maybe just turn around?"

He faces the wall without another word, but my hands still shake as I change out of tonight's dress and into the soft cotton sleeping shift. It's off-white and sleeveless and hits me just above the knee. There's nothing sexy about it.

"Okay," I say, "I'm decent." I busy myself folding my dress so

I won't have to meet his eyes.

I hear the soft clank of knives and shucking of fabric behind me, but don't dare look. I wonder how he sleeps—on his side or his back? On one side of the bed or in the center? Will he sleep differently tonight for my sake?

I sense him approach behind me before feeling him sweep my hair over one shoulder. He trails his fingers over the sensitive skin at the nape of my neck. "What are you doing?"

"Trying to see if there's anywhere that sonofabitch didn't cut you."

I squeeze my eyes shut. This morning's glamour faded while we were in the kitchen waiting for our friends to return. "If you think these are ugly, you should see what he left in my head."

He turns me slowly. His broad, strong chest is bare, and I can't help but notice the tattooed line of characters over his heart. He tilts my chin up until I meet his eyes. "There's nothing hideous about you. Inside and out, you are beautiful."

I lick my lips. "That's just the ring playing its tricks on you."

"I don't think so. You were the most beautiful creature I've ever met long before I saw you with the ring."

"Creature?" I try to make the word sound like a joke but fail. *Creature. Not human.*

"Person. Human who will soon be fae."

I hold his gaze. "Does that scare you?"

"Not as much as it scares you."

I open my mouth to say more—to explain why it scares me, to tell him that if I could choose, I'd be human like him. But there's nothing more to be said to that end until I'm ready to reveal what

I traded for this ring. And I won't make this day harder for him by sharing that now.

"I'm sorry I didn't tell you about Mordeus. About the blood magic." He steps toward me, closing the little distance left between us. "I couldn't share my suspicions because I couldn't risk losing you."

"Because you need me to kill Erith."

He opens his mouth and then closes it again before sweeping his knuckles over my cheek. "My reasons for wanting you alive and well have never been that singular."

I can't muster any of the anger I felt earlier. Maybe I should, but when I reach for it, it's gone. I could've lost him tonight.

I glance toward the bed. It's big enough for us both, but not by a lot. And just like that, the nervous butterflies are back.

He follows my gaze. "This isn't how I imagined our first night together."

I blink up at him and feel a smile tugging at my lips. "You imagined this?"

His eyes are dark and serious as they roam my face. "Thousands of times in the last week alone."

My face is hot. "How was it different when you imagined it?"

"I could kiss you, for starters." He flashes me a sad sort of smile, then grabs a towel from a small pile by the wash bin. Before I realize what he means to do, he's torn it into three strips and is tying them together. "Wrist okay?" he asks, holding out his hand for mine.

I nod and watch as he ties us together, his movements gentle and almost ceremonial. It reminds me of a ritual from home, and

I look away halfway through to keep the lump in my throat from surging into tears.

"Is it too tight?"

I shake my head. "It's fine."

He studies me for another beat, then nods. I walk around with him as he snuffs out the lanterns on the far side of the room, but when he reaches the one by the bed, he only lowers the flame.

"You don't have to do that for me. I'm okay." I'm supposed to be okay when I'm wearing the ring, but here I am fighting tears over some ripped fabric on my wrist. Turns out I'm not very numb at all.

"I don't mind." He nods to the bed, motioning for me to climb in first.

I do, positioning my free arm under my head, and he follows right after, letting our tethered hands rest between our bodies.

Our eyes meet in the low light from the lantern.

"Tell me what's going on in that head of yours," he says.

I drop my gaze to the soft linens. "I was just reminded of something from my old life, and I guess it made me homesick." I flick my gaze up to his, then back down. "Brie and I didn't have a lot of close friends in Elora, but the few we made were very good, and once this couple we were close to invited us to their hand-fasting ceremony. And I remember . . ." My eyes burn again. "It's so stupid. It doesn't even mean that much to me. I just remember thinking that someday I'd like to celebrate finding my match with that kind of ceremony. I hadn't thought about it in years, and then suddenly . . ."

He threads his fingers with mine.

"So much for this stupid ring numbing my heart," I say, sniffing. "I think its magic might be dying."

"I'm glad for that. I like your heart."

I drop my gaze to our hands. To the ring. To the fabric tethering us together.

"That's an old tradition," he says softly. "Handfasting used to be the mainstream ritual observed in marriage ceremonies in Elora, but it fell out of favor. I like hearing that there are people who still observe the tradition."

"Was that something else that changed with the Magical Seven? Did they forbid it?"

"It wasn't so much that," he says, gaze still fixed on our bound hands. "It was that they came in and convinced the realm they needed to be saved from the fae, and the more the fae were demonized, the more their rituals were demonized."

I prop myself up on my elbow. "Handfasting is a faerie ritual?"

He nods. "Elven, yes. Originally."

"I didn't know." But it makes sense. It seems fitting.

He brings our bound hands to his lips and kisses my knuckles. When he lowers our hands back to the bed, his gaze is on my mouth.

"What are *you* thinking?" I ask.

He cups my jaw and presses his thumb to my bottom lip. "I'm thinking"—leaning forward, he skims the bridge of his nose over mine, his lips hovering so close I ache to taste him—"that these lips might be worth dying for."

"You don't mean that."

"It's painful how close to the truth it is," he says, his breath feathering over my mouth. He shifts, trailing his lips down the side of my neck before bringing them to my ear. "I've never craved anything in my life as much as I crave your mouth."

"It's the ring," I say, but I want to believe it's not. "The magic draws you to me."

"Then why did I want you like this before tonight?" He sucks my earlobe between his teeth, and pleasure shimmies down my spine. "The ring doesn't make me blindly devoted to you. It doesn't make me lose my thoughts and beg to do your bidding. And I don't believe for a second it has anything to do with why I'm drawn to you." His fingers trace up my back, grazing over each vertebra like he's scanning for a secret message. "Maybe the rest of the magic wouldn't work either. Maybe I could kiss you and survive."

I squeeze my eyes shut hard—at the things his touch is doing to me, and at how much I want what he's describing to be true. "Maybe it's the forbidden that really appeals to you."

"There have been countless pleasures forbidden to me in my life, but I never cared until you." He inhales deeply, as if he's trying to fill himself with me. "I felt such *relief* tonight. Such relief when I realized my queen hadn't been found after all."

"Kendrick . . ." But I don't know what to say. That he should want Crissa to be found? That he should stop wanting me? I can't. Not when I feel like my next breath hinges on his touch. Not when the idea of letting him go hurts so much.

"I'm not proud, but it's true. I've been looking for her for three years, and tonight when I thought she'd been found, I felt nothing but dread. I *need you*, Jasalyn. And I don't believe for a second the Mother would let me feel this way if I'm supposed to be with another."

I slide my free hand behind his neck and lean my head against his chest, my breathing uneven.

As his fingers reach my waist, they slow their tour of my spine. He traces a line around to follow the curve of my hip. Burying his nose in my hair, he breathes in deeply. "Your scent haunts me. But not at much as your kiss does." He inches up the thin fabric and slips his hand beneath it, gently tracing up my side with rough fingertips.

I shudder softly and let my fingers tangle in his hair. I bury my face in his neck and breathe him in, too afraid that if I meet his eyes and see the longing there, we might both lose the tentative grip we have on our self-control.

He sweeps my hair to the side and trails hot, open-mouthed kisses down my neck. I tilt my head to give him better access, and he follows the path to my shoulder, slipping the strap of my sleeping gown down my arms to expose more skin to his mouth.

Lips and teeth and lust.

I can't think. Can't remember what I'm supposed to be doing and why I'm supposed to pull away. I don't care that he's been promised to another. I don't care about anything but promising myself to him.

Kendrick pulls back and follows the hot path left by his mouth with his hand. His gaze darkens, locked on his fingers on my skin. When his rough fingers brush the swell of my breast, I gasp— from the heat that floods my belly and the matching heat I see in his eyes.

His gaze holds mine as he continues his journey down the front of my body. He searches my face as he slides his hand between my legs.

All the heat in my belly seems to follow him there. I gasp—because he's barely moving his hand, but it's so good, and I never thought to imagine anything like this.

His eyes go dark, but they stay locked on mine as he touches me, rough hands moving with more tenderness than I would've thought possible.

When my back arches and my body winds too tight, his breath hitches, and he shifts his body closer. "So beautiful," he murmurs, and for a moment the whole world seems to fall away. There is no queen. There is no ring. There are no scars. There is no carelessly sacrificed future. There is nothing but Kendrick and me and this moment.

I catch my breath, clinging to his arm, pulling as close as I can. "Is that what you imagined?"

"A very small preview." He sweeps his lips along my neck again. "Sleep, Princess. The sun will rise again tomorrow."

I close my eyes and think of Fienna's sailor. I think of how good this moment is—despite everything—and how I don't want it to end. And I think of how badly I wish I'd never gotten this ring, never traded my future for something I didn't understand.

CHAPTER TWENTY-EIGHT

⬥

FELICITY

"And why, when the moon is this high in the sky, does my child want to be taken to the northern mountains where the wild horses roam?" Nigel asks.

I fake my smile, even knowing I'm not fooling Nigel. "It's time. I can't wait any longer."

"I would like my child to stay here in the pretty castle where she is treated like the princess she should be. Where she is *safe*," he says, wringing his hands.

I step toward him. "My mind is made up."

He grumbles something about foolish little girls, but he takes my hand, and moments later we're flying and spinning and folding into nothingness, and as always, just a moment before I feel panic starting to rise, just a moment before I feel *this time* it's taken too long, my feet are on solid ground.

I scan the moonlit, rocky mountainside and shiver. It's cold, and I'm glad I dressed in my fleece-lined leathers, but there's something else that sends a shiver through my blood. Something primal warning of the danger lurking in these mountains.

"Perhaps my child would like to return to the castle now?"

Yes. Please. Please take me back. But what's waiting for me there? Heartache. Discovery. Worse? "Not just yet, though you can wait here if you wish."

Nigel reaches behind his back and produces a fist-size gem from thin air. "Take this," he says, and as I take it, it glows to life, casting light in a ten-foot radius around me.

"An illumination gem." My heart tugs. I was going to use my own magic, but since I have so little practice with anything other than taking another form, I'm not a strong enough magic user to reliably conjure light. He knows that. "Thank you, Nigel."

My boots scuff on the rocky ground as I turn toward the north. I spot the fluffy red flower of the hiluca tree ahead, and my heart stumbles over itself. *This is it.* This is the area Misha came to before he visited the other faerie realm, which means the portal to the Hall of Doors is hidden somewhere on this mountain.

I roll my shoulders and begin my hike.

Behind me, Nigel mutters incomprehensibly. When I look back, he's gone.

I draw in a jagged breath. *If I were hiding the court's most important portal on this mountain, where would I put it?*

I follow the trail for hours—until my thighs are burning from the incline and the skin that felt so chilled when I first arrived is covered in a sheen of sweat. I'm not getting anywhere and have no way of knowing if I'm any closer than I was when I started.

I could have Nigel come back for me now, but I can't return to Castle Craige. Not now that Misha's been in my mind.

If I can't find the portal, I'll have to go somewhere else. Start over like I did when I first came to Faerie. The thought makes me feel lonelier than I have in a very long time.

I sink onto a fallen log to catch my breath and drink from my canteen. When Misha returned from using the portal, he had the hiluca's blossom tangled in his hair, meaning he'd been off the path. If I had to, I'd guess I'm looking for an underground burrow or a cave.

I wipe my mouth with the back of my hand and stand up with renewed determination. I'll search every cave on this mountainside if that's what it takes.

I hike for another hour before I see it—a fresh trail in the leaves on the forest floor and boot prints. *Boot prints.*

I follow them around a thick patch of underbrush before I lose them again and have to search the area blind. The illumination gem is starting to lose its light. I'll need to call for Nigel soon—I won't die out here. But I'm *so close.*

So I search. And I search, and even when I feel like I've strayed too far from those prints, and I've turned myself around too many times to know which way to go to get back to the main path, I search.

The gem gives out right as I find the mouth of a cave.

It's low to the ground, covered by brush and trees, and would be the perfect place to hide a portal. *All I need to do is see it.* If I know it's there and pay close attention to how I return to the main trail, I can bring Hale back here.

I lower myself onto my belly to enter the cave, but the opening is even smaller than I thought, and I find myself wriggling through mud before the mouth of the cave finally opens and I can climb to my knees and then, finally, my feet.

I need light to find my way any farther, so I take a deep breath and focus my energy on the palm of my hand, willing it to glow.

When the cavern lights up, the light bouncing off the crystalline wings of the tiny pixies sleeping in the stalactites, I mutter a quick thanks to the Mother and push forward.

A small tributary flows across the cavern floor, draining out the mouth where I entered. It's mostly dry now but explains the mud. Ahead, the cavern forks. A glance to the right reveals a wide path toward the forest—probably the easier way to get into this cave than the way I entered. I make a mental note to exit that way. To the left, the cavern continues to wind deeper into the mountain.

As I advance, I watch my steps to dodge the stalagmites. I don't bother avoiding the water. My boots are as filthy as I am. If the portal is here, Misha must've used magic to clean himself off before returning to Castle Craige—or used it to shield his clothes as he moved through the cavern.

The tunnel narrows as it turns and twists deeper into the mountain. I have to walk sideways through the narrowest part, but a full-grown male would have to worm through the wider section at my feet.

Up ahead, on the other side of this narrow tunnel, something red glows.

The portal.

I need to get closer. To know for sure. Not all portals look the same. Some look like doorways and some look like tunnels, but when they're active, most glow, too full of magic to contain their light.

I shove through the last few feet of narrow tunnel and spill out into a slippery bowl. My feet shoot out from under me and my teeth snap together as I fall to my rear and slide all the way to the bottom of the muddy basin.

The red glowing portal is opposite the tunnel and stretches from floor to the cavern ceiling nearly ten feet above my head. It's the shape of a cat's pupil. All I have to do is climb up the other side.

My boots squish in the mud as I fight my way across. The glowing cat eye ripples.

I freeze and look again, watching something move on the other side. Is that a face? Is someone about to come—

The portal rips open.

No. *Not a portal.*

A bat as tall as this cavern. A cave demon.

The red-eyed beast spots me, and his angry cry echoes off the walls. His wings—bloodred and as glowing and translucent as a magical portal—extend at least twelve feet, nearly hitting the walls on each side.

His eyes meet mine, and I'm frozen. Frozen as my mind shows me images of my body rotting in this festering mud. He will tear me apart. And I will deserve it for waking him up.

I'm dead. I already know I'm dead. *I'm sorry, Misha.*

The demon scoops his wings back and lunges at me, his serrated teeth snapping only feet in front of my face.

RUN!

The word is a command, shouted in my brain. It doesn't come from me, but I don't question it. I conjure a fistful of fire and hurl it right into the demon's blazing eyes, then turn, fighting against the pull of the mud as I will my legs back to the tunnel.

Behind me, the demon roars. His pained cries threaten to tear apart my eardrums. With every step I take, I slide half a step back down toward the center of the basin, but I keep climbing, keep fighting my way toward that tunnel.

I grab for the ledge, and as my fingers close around it, a massive squelching sounds behind me. *He's coming.*

I take hold with the other hand and pull myself up, my hands aching, arms shaking. Up, up—if I can just get my knee on the ledge.

Something wraps around my ankle and in the next breath, I'm yanked back and my jaw slams into the ledge. I taste copper on my tongue. The cave demon has my leg, but I flail and kick until my foot comes free of my boot. I make it back to the ledge, but he's right there, only a step behind me.

Get out of there!

I pull my blade from between my shoulders. The demon's big hand swipes at me, long nails cutting deep trenches through my clothes and into my flank. With a scream, I plunge the blade right between his eyes.

He falls, taking my sword with him, and I run to the tunnel, pushing my way through as fast as I can with one boot and gaping wounds in my side.

When the tunnel opens again, I collapse to my hands and knees. All my strength is leaving with the blood seeping out my side. I can't bring myself to stand again, so I crawl, dragging myself around the turns.

Just as the cavern widens, I drop to the ground, my cheek lying in the mud. My eyes won't stay open. I'm so *tired*.

"Jasalyn, are you okay?"

This time it seems like Misha's voice is here and not just in my mind. I try to open my eyes to see if I'm hallucinating, but they won't obey. I'll just take a little nap. Just a few minutes and then I'll get out of this cave and figure out why I'm hearing the voice of the male I've betrayed.

"We have to go." Misha again. If I have to sleep in this awful place, at least I can sleep while hearing his voice. "You need a healer." The panic in those words has me fighting sleep again.

The cave demon screeches in the distance, and I'm scooped up into a pair of strong arms.

Misha's clean pine and rosewood scent fills my nose. I want to breathe it in, but don't have the energy for that.

Another angry shriek of the beast, and the whole cave shakes around us, as if threatening to fall apart.

"She won't make it if you don't get her an antitoxin immediately," a familiar goblin's voice says. "Take my hand." *Nigel.* Is he talking to me?

I want to tell him I'm fine. I'm just tired. If they let me rest for a minute, I'll be okay. But I can't find the strength.

"But you can't—"

"You can't outrun him," Nigel says. "And if you stay to fight, it'll be too late for her. I will return you both to Castle Craige. Now." Why does he sound so sad. So resigned?

I open my eyes and see the demon from the cave with his red eyes, wings tucked back as he dives toward us. There's a reason

Shae wanted me to be cornered into a search before Hale could find the sword.

"He wanted me to die." It's the last thing I say before we disappear into nothing.

When the world reappears around us, I'm barely clinging to consciousness, and when Misha lowers me into the soft embrace of a down mattress, I loosen my grip on this world. All I want is to let sleep take me.

"It'd be best to stay awake, my child," Nigel says, his voice weak. "Nothing good would come of dreaming now."

My eyes fly open.

Nigel.

He was at the cave with Misha. Did he bring him there? Then the demon was back, and Nigel . . .

"You saved me," I whisper, blinking my eyes and bringing him into focus. *He broke the code.*

He gives a sharp nod, but I see the fear in his eyes. Fear for me, for these injuries. And behind it, resignation for his own fate. Goblins aren't allowed to interfere in moments of mortal peril. The only time I've ever known them to make an exception is when their ward is in danger, but that doesn't free them of the consequences.

Tears burn my eyes, and I feel them streaking through the dried mud on my face. "Why?"

"You know why."

Misha looks back and forth between us, confusion wrinkling his brow. "You know this goblin, Jas?"

"I've known him longer than anyone," I whisper, even though I know it won't make any sense to Misha. I reach out a hand, take Nigel's, and squeeze.

"The girl needs antitoxin and a healer," Nigel tells Misha.

"They can't punish you," I whisper, "if you let me die."

"Not so long as I breathe," Nigel says.

But I hear the sound of feet running in my direction. Misha's healer is coming. They'll save me, and then Nigel . . .

"This is my fault." I squeeze my eyes shut and hold on tight.

"Fault is so sticky," he says. *When no action lives in isolation.* The last words are only in my head, and when I open my eyes, Nigel is gone, and I know I'll never see him again.

Where his fingers were clutched in mine, there's only a single strand of hair I already know belonged to Jasalyn. He saved my life, and now he's giving me another day. One more day before my secrets are revealed. One more day to save myself.

I twine the hair around my fingers and clutch my fist to my chest. "Let me sleep," I tell Misha around a sob.

"The healer is here," he says, even as I feel a needle sliding into my side. *Antitoxin.* "She'll help with the pain."

But she can't. Not with this pain.

CHAPTER TWENTY-NINE

◇

FELICITY

"Tell me what it is you most desire, child."

"I don't want to be afraid anymore."

The lady cocks her head to the side and looks Jas over. "So that's all you want? Fearlessness?"

No. I want more. I want them dead. I want every one of Mordeus's cruel and mocking guards gone from this world.

She doesn't say the words, but the smile that curves the witch's lips says enough. Somehow, through Jas's mind—through the shields that she's worked so hard to build—the witch heard.

"I can give you everything you want," she says, "but this is strong magic you request. Stronger than anything the average witch could provide for you."

Jas hugs herself and rubs her bare arms. It's so cold in here. So cold and so dark. She hates the dark. "I can pay anything. Whatever it takes, I'll get the money. Just tell me the price."

"I don't need more money. I need better tools." She pauses, eyes assessing even in the darkness. "I need the Grimoricon."

Jas shakes her head. "I don't know what that is."

"Your sister tells you nothing? It's a large book of spells and

enchantments sacred to the Faerie realm. The book itself is magical and holds the key to truly powerful magic. I cannot give you what you ask without it."

A book. Just a book to be free of this suffocating fear. "Where can I find it?"

"It's in the palace," she says. "For too long it was hidden in the Serenity Palace in the Court of the Sun, but your sister returned it to the shadow court as part of her deal with Mordeus when you were captured."

Yes, Brie said something about retrieving a book. A book that became a serpent and a little boy. A book that injured her.

It's been so long since Brie talked to Jas about the trials she endured during those weeks. She thinks Jas will break if she reminds her they're not in Elora anymore—as if it's not apparent every waking moment of every day.

"Bring it to me, and we will begin," the voice in the darkness says.

"That's it? Just the book?"

"The Grimoricon will have the information I need, but it won't be enough. I need a catalyst as well. I need the fae power that lives inside you. I need the magic that is lying dormant, the magic that is waiting for your eighteenth birthday. Bring me the book and surrender your power, your fae life, and I will make you a ring that numbs your heart. A ring that gives you death's kiss."

I wake in my bed at Castle Craige. The room is dark, but I know from the sliver of light coming from between the curtains that it's the middle of the day.

I try to roll to my side, and pain lances through me—bringing last night back to me in a rush. The cave, the demon, Misha carrying me out.

And Nigel.

I drag in a ragged breath as a sob breaks free. *Nigel is gone.*

"You're awake." The voice is deep and soft, and so soothing it can only belong to Misha.

I move tenderly as I roll to face him.

He's sitting at my bedside, leaning forward with his elbows on his knees.

As my eyes adjust to the dark, I make out his features—the worry twisting his mouth, the exhaustion around his eyes.

"You were in my head," I say. "How?"

He swallows. "It sometimes happens unintentionally when I form a connection with someone."

"But from so far away?" How did he know I was in danger? What else does he know?

"Who are you?" His words are so gentle that, at first, I almost don't understand what he's asking. There's a delay before my brain sends the bolt of panic through my blood.

"What?"

He leans farther forward and tilts his head to the side. Flames of rage dance in his eyes. "Who. Are. You."

I sit up in bed, and my entire body cries out with agony from the movement. I don't have to pretend to be afraid. I am. Misha may be kind, but he can also be hard and cruel. As king of his court, he has to be.

And while he may never be cruel to Jasalyn, there's nothing keeping him from exerting the full extent of his wrath on a girl pretending to be her.

"Misha, you're scaring me." Because I'm supposed to be Jas and Jas wouldn't run, I merely curl into myself. My body hurts so much, I couldn't run if I tried.

I came a breath away from death last night, but Nigel—

Misha pushes out of his chair. "Where's the princess?"

"I don't know what you're talking about. I'm the princess. *I am Jasalyn*. You know me."

"Jasalyn would have never entered a dark cave alone. *Jasalyn* wouldn't ask my scholars for books on portal magic. *She* doesn't need my Hall of Doors." His fists ball at his sides. "I've been such a fool. How many signs were there? From the moment you arrived in my court and looked at me like . . ." He swallows. "I knew something was off, but I let you fool me despite all the warnings along the way—the witch on the coast, Lark's words about you not being in your true form. I twisted everything I heard into what I *wanted*. I let myself believe what I wanted to believe when the truth was right in front of me."

"Look at me. You *know* me." Terror racks my bones and makes my voice shake. Terror and something more . . . something like a cracking in the center of my chest.

I can't think about my heart right now. I need to focus on escape.

I should have insisted that we put safeguards in place, should have insisted the princess give me something to tell the king in the event that I was found out. He'll never believe she sent me in her stead. He'll never believe she wants me here. And now I'm as good as dead.

"Who. Are. You."

"Jas," I try once last time, but it's too late now.

"Liar! Tell me why I shouldn't kill you this very moment." Vines erupt from the floor, wrapping around my legs and pinning me to the bed, thorns biting into my skin. A flash of lightning illuminates the window and thunder rumbles low and angry in the distance.

"Please," I gasp. Tears well in my eyes and roll down my cheeks. "Please let me go."

"You're lucky I don't end you now," he growls. Stepping back, he scrapes his gaze over me in disgust. "You almost had me. I don't know how you did it, but you almost let me believe . . ." His eyes meet mine. The flames of anger have burned to embers, revealing the scars of betrayal. *Heartache.* I hurt him. Just like I never wanted to.

"Misha," I whisper.

"I am *king,* and you will address me as such."

His anger leaves me hollow. There's nothing but an echoing cave where my heart should be.

I'm falling for you too, I'm hurting too, I want to say, but my confession would make this worse.

The heavy steps sound on the stairs, and armored sentinels stalk into my bedchambers. He must've mentally called on them.

"You can spend your last days in my dungeon while I wait for the shadow queen to arrive. She'll have the opportunity to question you before we arrange for your execution."

"Please, don't." I close my eyes, trying to slow my spinning thoughts, trying to make a plan.

Misha's vines release me so suddenly I sag to the floor, only to be scooped up by the guards—one under each arm.

"Let me explain. I'll tell you everything."

He drags his gaze over me, lips twisted in obvious disgust. "No. I think I'll let you rot in my dungeon for a few days before I listen to more of your lies. We'll see what you have to say for yourself after sleeping with the rats."

The guards drag me to the stairs, my toes barely brushing the floor.

"Jasalyn's in trouble!" I shout.

The guards don't pause, and every step brings me closer to the dungeon and further from my opportunity to explain.

"She traded her immortal life for the kiss of death."

The guards freeze and turn me to face their king.

Misha scowls down at me from the top of the stairs. "Are you accusing the Unseelie princess of murder?"

"I'm saying she's in trouble."

"Says the creature who's been living in her skin."

"At her request!"

"More lies!"

"I'll open my mind to you—just look and see that I speak the truth."

"You must think I'm truly a fool if you expect me to trust anything I might see there now, after all your convincing lies and scheming." I can't name all the emotions I see flit across his face, but I know the final one when it tightens his jaw. Steely determination. "Take her away."

CHAPTER THIRTY

◆

JASALYN

I SCOWL AT THE FAERIE who fancies himself the next Eloran king. "You're here for the child queen? The one the Seven fear so much?"

His eyes flash, and the intricate lines tattooed across his forehead, marking him as the Chosen One, glow, giving me my answer.

"My friends among the Seven wanted me to dispose of her." My smile stretches across my face. "Just like they want you dead."

He only lifts his chin a notch higher.

"They underestimate me, though. There's something I need more than your queen. Are you prepared to bargain?"

His nostrils flare. The cockiness in his eyes makes me want to slowly slice him to bits just to prove who's in charge, but the little Kincaid girl wasting away in my dungeons is more important to me than my pride.

My seer tells me that this male, this Eloran faerie with his arrogance and ice-blue eyes, has the power to make her want to live.

"I'll make a deal with you," I say. "I'll release your queen in exchange for you. You will take her place in my dungeons and befriend the Eloran girl I'm holding there."

"Why?"

I cock my head to the side. "Do you truly care? Kendrick the Chosen, who will sacrifice anything for the future of his realm. Would you not do this small thing? You want your queen released, and I need my girl to live. Now and after I'm gone."

"What do you have in mind?"

"She isn't taking well to being a prisoner. She needs . . . a friend. What better friend for her than a charming young man from Elora?"

Kendrick arches a brow. "A man?"

"I can't send you in there as a faerie, certainly not when she's so afraid of our kind. I need you to go in there as the human version of yourself. You're to give her hope. Courage. You're to be the reason she wants to wake up tomorrow. And after. You'll watch over her, and I will hand you the Magical Seven on a platter."

"You free my queen today, and I'm at your service."

My eyes fly open. Rage, as black as night and twice as fearsome, pumps through my blood. The room tilts sideways, and my stomach lurches.

Kendrick sits up beside me. "Are you okay?"

Not at all.

"What's wrong?" He brushes my hair back from my face. "Talk to me."

I lock my gaze on his fae ears. His glamour is still in place, but his forehead is unmarked where he wore a tattoo in my dreams. To reassure myself, I reach up with my unbound hand and skim a finger from temple to temple.

He shivers and his eyes drift closed for a beat. "Jasalyn."

"It was just a nightmare," I say—to him? To myself?

This is Kendrick. This is the man who is rallying against the evil fae who have destroyed his realm—*my* realm.

You'll watch over her, and I will hand you the Magical Seven on a platter.

No. It was just a dream. A nightmare. An elaborate concoction of my broken psyche.

"You would never hurt me," I whisper.

His blue eyes look haunted as he brings our bound hands to his lips, brushing a kiss across my knuckles. "I'd rather die."

The curtains are thrown open, and light pours into the room. "Get up, Hale," Remme grumbles. "We're heading to—Oh. Shit. I'm sorry. I'll just—"

"Wait, Remme," Kendrick says, adjusting the sheet over me with his free hand.

I shift under the covers and study his face. "Did it work?" I ask. "Do you remember?"

He nods, but there's something sad on his face I don't quite understand. "It worked."

"You two spent the night together, and you thought he might forget?" Remme asks. He frowns. "How could he forget a night with you?"

"Hey, Remme?" Skylar calls from the hall. "Have you seen Hale? Shae's back and needs to talk to him, but he's not—" She appears in the door and freezes when she spots us in Kendrick's bed together. "Oh. Jasalyn. How did you sleep?"

Kendrick sits up, chest bare. "Good morning, Skylar. Good morning, Remme. We saw you both last night and explained that

392

Jasalyn's ring won't come off, but you don't remember because, obviously, she was wearing the ring, just like you won't remember this, but please get the fuck out anyway." He adds a smile to soften the command.

Remme's brows creep up his forehead as he looks back and forth between us. "I knew it was a matter of time."

I lift up our bound hands. "Nothing happened. We slept next to each other so Kendrick would stay connected to me and wouldn't forget. Now please go?"

He nods. "As you wish, Princess."

"Do you need anything, Jasalyn?" Skylar asks. "I could run you a warm bath?"

I bite back a smile. This is going to get old fast, but right now it's still amusing.

"I'm good," I tell her. "Why don't you get yourself some breakfast, and we'll meet you downstairs."

"Oh. Okay. Thank you. That's so kind of you. I'm so lucky to know you."

We wait while they back out of the room and close the door behind them.

"Wow," Kendrick says, dropping back onto his pillow. "If she was able to remember that, she would absolutely hate it."

"I'm sure."

He rolls to his side to look at me, and my dream flashes to the forefront of my mind. Kendrick talking to Mordeus. Kendrick, as fae, promising to keep me from destroying myself so Mordeus could use me.

He cups my face in his big hand and rubs his thumb across my bottom lip. I attempt a smile, but I can't shake the dream. It's making me question this man who's saved me again and again.

"How are you feeling this morning?" he asks.

My dreams were nothing more than the ring messing with my mind, just like it distorts the perceptions of those around me when I'm wearing it. Or maybe it's the blood magic—maybe Mordeus is able to plant things in my mind as he draws power from me.

Whatever the reason, I'm sure there's an explanation. Kendrick was helping me plot my escape from the dungeons. He wouldn't have done that if he'd been working with Mordeus.

I shove down the surge of unfair doubts and suspicions. Kendrick deserves better.

"So far, so good," I whisper. The truth is, I already feel tired in a way that has nothing to do with the number of hours we slept. This ring isn't meant for the daylight, and every survival instinct tells me to stay in bed. Another kind of instinct is telling me to keep Kendrick here with me.

"Maybe the magic changes when you merge with the ring," he says.

"Maybe." His body is so warm next to mine under these blankets, and I focus on that instead of how real the dream seemed.

"So *nothing happened* last night, huh? Is that how you remember it?"

My cheeks heat. "Well, it's certainly nothing I'm going to talk to Remme about."

His eyes go dark as he skims his gaze down the front of me. "We need to get that ring off so I can kiss you again." Sitting up, he unravels the towel connecting our hands.

"What are you doing?" I'm so weak. How will I fake enough strength to get through the day?

"You don't feel well." He flicks his gaze to mine before focusing on our bindings again. "So we're going to have breakfast and then figure out how to get rid of this ring. Natan should hear back from his source this morning. I need you to tell him everything you can about the ring so we can figure out how to destroy it."

"Okay," I whisper. Could destroying the ring give me back all I traded for it?

The thing clutching me by the chest feels a little like hope with claws. It hurts to want something with this kind of intensity. And I'm a fool to have ever given so much away.

I let myself imagine days at Kendrick's side learning to stop judging myself for the fear. I let myself imagine how good it would feel to face my demons without this horrific crutch.

We're quiet when we climb out of bed. Kendrick turns away while I put on my riding pants and another one of Skylar's tops. He scribbles in his journal while I brush my hair into a high ponytail, but he watches me while I buckle into my boots.

I catch his gaze and wonder if he'll ever understand what he's done for me in our short time together. How hard it was for me to have someone so much as touch my arm before he came back into my life. How it's only because of him and his friends that I would even wish for a different set of stars instead of none at all.

How could I doubt him after all that?

The knock on the door pulls me from my thoughts.

"Hale, I need to speak with you." It's Natan, and he sounds unsettled. "It's about the ring."

Kendrick opens the door for him, and Natan comes into the room but slows when his eyes meet mine. "Jasalyn, how are you?"

I swallow hard. "I'm okay. Have you figured out a way to destroy the ring?"

He gives a jerky shake of his head. "Is that what you would like? I can go work on that right now."

"We need to know what you found out," Kendrick says, an impatient growl rumbling beneath his words.

Natan ignores him, his full attention on me.

"Look at Kendrick and tell him what you know about my ring," I instruct him gently.

Natan pulls in a deep breath before nodding and turning to Kendrick. "We used the ring's echo to track its match, and traced it to the Eloran Palace."

"Who's wearing the other one?" Kendrick asks.

"I don't have that answer, but I have my suspicions." Natan toys with the braided leather on his wrist, his hesitation like a piercing wail in the silence. "Princess, when did those scars of yours start appearing?"

I frown. "A few months ago, maybe? Did you find out more about the blood magic?"

"Did the scars appear before or after you got that ring?" Natan asks.

"They . . ." I search my mind to recall the first one. I was so exhausted because I'd stayed up late using the ring, and when I saw that first mark across my stomach, I felt nothing. No vanity, no surprise, no curiosity, nothing. It seemed fitting that the mark Mordeus had left in my mind was finally showing on my skin. "It was after." My words are too quiet. Suddenly, I want to end this conversation before he can say any more.

"Do you ever find yourself in two places at once?" Natan asks me. "Seeing through your eyes and another's at once? Do you find yourself knowing things—things you shouldn't know?"

My pulse skips a beat. Then two. I feel frozen and as helpless as I was at Mordeus's table, a prisoner in my own body as he used his magic to feed me.

Could Natan be referring to something like my dreams?

Kendrick's blue eyes are alight with fury. "Mordeus is pulling power from her, isn't he? He's using the ring to amplify the blood magic. That's why he needed her alive."

Natan gives a pained nod. "I don't have all the answers. This kind of magic is different than anything I've seen, but it seems the false king knew. Somehow he knew he needed Jasalyn—knew that there would come a point that she would be his only way to return to this world. Every bit of torture she endured in his dungeons was done to make her fear him and every faerie in that place. He needed her fear to be so great that when the time came and this witch found her, she would be desperate for a way to escape it."

"What are you trying to say?" Kendrick asks. "How could Jasalyn's fear and pain benefit Mordeus? What's the connection between the torture and his resurrection?"

"Her magic alone wouldn't be enough to resurrect him," Natan says. "But if she began taking lives that were pledged to Mordeus—either directly or through a proxy . . ."

My mind flashes with the image of a room full of tattooed insurgents falling to the floor. The pallor of death sweeping over their faces. "No," I breathe. Like the memory of a dream, the vision is there, then gone, slipping away like so many grains of sand.

Natan drags a hand through his hair. "We received word this morning about Mordeus's legion stationed at Feegus Keep."

The tremor that starts in my gut radiates out and down my arms until my hands are trembling. "They're dead," I say. "The night I went missing—that's when they died, isn't it?"

"We don't know for sure that you were responsible," Natan says, but I can tell he believes I was, even under the ring's enchantment.

"The bastard knew she was going to go after his people," Kendrick says, his jaw ticking. "He knew she'd use all the fear and hate and turn it on his guards, guards who tortured her on *his* orders."

There's a buzzing in my ears growing louder and louder. *Magic is life. Life is magic.* Isn't that the number one rule of this cursed realm?

I felt that magic. Every time I used the deadly power of the ring, I felt my victim's power funnel through me. The room spins, and I grip the foot of the bed so I don't fall down.

In my quest for vengeance, I brought Mordeus back.

I killed all those people.

I am the faceless plague.

I stumble back until I'm leaning against the wall. My head's spinning. This is all my fault. The deaths. Mordeus. The horror sweeping through my sister's court.

I'm responsible for all of it.

None of this would've happened if I hadn't bought this ring.

None of this would've happened if I hadn't so readily forfeited *everything* for revenge.

Bile surges in my throat, and I struggle to speak around it. "You're saying Mordeus isn't only pulling strength from me. He's *alive* because of me, *because of what I've done.*"

"That's not possible," Kendrick says. "To be the catalyst for his resurrection, she would've had to offer . . ." I feel the weight that falls over him the moment the answer clicks into place. When I meet his eyes again, there's nothing but devastation in those icy-blue depths. "What did you trade for that ring, Jasalyn?"

I want to crawl out of my skin. To escape the rot of my mistakes. To undo all the horrors I've wrought upon this world.

"Jas, what did you promise that witch?" Kendrick rasps.

Tears burn my eyes and the room swims. "It was nothing to forfeit a life I never wanted," I whisper. The whole point of the ring was to free me from my fear, and now there's nothing I fear more than what I've done because of it.

The irony cuts me off at the knees, and I sink to the floor.

"This wasn't you." Kendrick drops to his haunches before me. "If anything, it was that ring. But that's *not you.* You could never become like the monsters who gave you those scars."

No. Because I don't leave scars, only dead bodies.

"Jasalyn," Kendrick whispers. "This wasn't you."

But he doesn't understand. I wanted this ring because I wanted the power to be able to do just this. I traded *everything* for this *curse.* I *wanted* them dead. And now they are, and so many more.

"Mordeus is in the Eloran Palace?" I ask Natan.

"That is what I believe, yes." He shifts worried eyes between me and Kendrick. "The Seven must be protecting him while he gains strength."

"Why would they protect him?"

He sighs heavily. "The same reason they did anything for him before, even when he held what they needed most over his head. They stand to gain something."

I look to Kendrick. I have years of experience locking away my feelings, and I call on that now as I push to my feet. "And the sword—the one at Feegus Keep—that can get us to the palace?"

Kendrick's expression is bleak. He searches my face as he rasps, "Yes."

"And this sword—it can kill anyone? Even a resurrected king?"

He looks pained. "Yes, but so long as you're wearing that ring, the daylight will make you weak and—"

"We go today." I fight the panic and terror rising up in me with everything that I have and lift my chin. "I'm the reason he's back. I won't be the reason he gets stronger."

CHAPTER THIRTY-ONE

◇

FELICITY

IF I WEREN'T STILL FIGHTING the cave demon's toxin, I might've been able to keep myself from sleeping for a day, maybe two. But my body is too brutalized and battered, even after the healer, and I can't use any of my old tricks.

Pacing my cell wears me out in minutes instead of hours and makes me more exhausted instead of keeping me alert. The dungeon's too dark, and flooding my cell with light to keep myself awake uses more magic than I can spare so soon after my brush with death. Talking to myself gets old after an hour or two.

I doubt I lasted a whole day before my dreams dragged me under.

When I wake up, I'm in my own skin for the first time in three years, and it's such a relief. Like taking off a pair of boots that are a little too tight. I'd revel in it, stretch like a cat, if the consequences weren't so terrifying.

I'm dead.

I wonder how well guarded this dungeon is. Erith will come for me now—will know where I am now that I'm in my body again—and being down here might be the only way I survive. If

Misha doesn't kill me first.

I know I'm not alone before I even open my eyes. I feel him.

Misha is in the cell with me. It's dark, but I can make out the long lines of his silhouette as he lounges against the opposite wall, sitting with legs wide, knees bent. I don't dare move toward him. He could crush me with his magic. I see the rage in his eyes when they meet mine, and I realize he might.

With a snap of his fingers, fire ignites from his fingertips, and the flickering flames cast shadows that accentuate his angular features. "Is this supposed to be some sort of joke?" he asks, waving his free hand up and down to indicate my form. My *true* form.

I flinch. I suppose it might feel that way to him. I'm nothing like Jasalyn. Not nearly as appealing by traditional standards. Though I've not been in this body for three years, I don't need a mirror to know it's not changed much from how I looked at sixteen.

A joke. I wish he had kicked me instead.

"What do you want with my court and our Hall of Doors?" Misha asks.

I bow my head and don't respond.

"I'll admit I'm impressed," he says. "I've never met a shifter with such impeccable abilities nor one with the ability to alter her scent so *precisely*. You fooled even Finn's wolves. Perhaps I've underestimated shifters."

"I'm not a shifter," I whisper.

He scoffs. "Well, you are certainly *something*, and it's not Jasalyn. I wouldn't have thought it was possible. I welcomed you into my castle, let you live under my roof." He narrows his eyes, and I sense what he's not saying. It's worse than me living here. Worse than me fooling him for all these days. He had feelings for me. Believed he might have a future with Jasalyn. And not just any future but the kind he craves. I made him believe he had a chance at love and family. For that he may never forgive me.

"I'm sorry," I whisper, and I've never meant an apology so sincerely.

"I suppose you want me to believe that." He scoffs. "I know who you are, Felicity, daughter of Erith, Patriarch of the Seven."

A chill runs down my spine at the sound of my name on his lips. *He knows. He knows everything.* "You broke into my head." My chest aches. He never would've done that if he still had any respect for me.

"You broke into my castle," he growls. "I'd heard of you. I know the oracle told your father that his wife would give him twins. A boy and a girl. She told him the daughter would end his life. I know that your mother paid her midwife to hide you when you were born and to present your brother to her husband as a solo babe. I know that midwife ran to the other side of Elora to give you to another family, the Kendricks, who raised you and kept you safe—until Mordeus told your father of your mother's deception, and Erith put together a team to find you."

I squeeze my eyes shut. He knows more about me than I knew about myself until I was sixteen years old. The day Erith's soldiers showed up at our home was the beginning of the end of a life I cherished. Dad died trying to give Mom the time she needed to hide me, and when the soldiers left, Mom had no choice but to tell me the truth about my birth, about my father, and about my destiny. She sent me to the oracle then, hoping I might be shown a path to safety. Instead, I was shown an image of my birth father for the first time. After watching myself plunge a blade into Erith's heart, I was shown Hale's death, and found myself in a deadlock with fate.

If I killed Erith, I would lose my brother. And if I didn't, it wasn't a matter of *if* Erith found me. It was a matter of *when*.

My only option was to leave the only place I'd ever called home. As long as I never killed Erith, I wouldn't have to watch Hale die too. As long as I never took my own form, as long as I never lived in my own skin, Erith couldn't track me.

And for three years, I haven't. Until now.

"Tell me," Misha says, his voice louder than before, "what do you want with my court and Hall of Doors? What are you after, *Felicity*?"

Every day with him, I craved the sound of my name from his lips, and it hurts to hear him say it with such disgust. "I was never going to bring any harm to your court. My friends are looking for a way into the Eloran Palace. They want to bring down the Seven and restore Elora to her rightful queen. *That's* why I wanted to find your Hall of Doors."

"Try again."

"That's the truth."

"My Hall has no portal to the Eloran Palace. It never has. The Magical Seven have never allowed anyone from my court to portal in."

"But we were told—" I draw in a breath. That intelligence came from Shae. Shae, who's been so cruel. Shae, who wanted me to rush into my search for a portal guarded by a deadly cave demon.

"I opened up to you," Misha says, "and it was all a lie. Why? What is it that you're after?"

I squeeze my eyes shut and feel the hot tears roll down my cheeks. Nothing about what I felt for him was a lie, but he'll never believe that now.

"What did you do with the princess? What do you want with her? What do you want with my court?"

"I told you, I didn't hurt her. She wanted me here to cover for her." He doesn't believe a word I'm saying, so I'm not sure why I'm wasting my breath, but I keep going. "She has a magic ring that gives her the kiss of death. I think it's all connected with the face-less plague and the resurrection of Mordeus."

Heavy footfalls sound in the corridor beyond, and I turn to see Finnian, the Unseelie king consort, standing in front of my cell, his silver eyes glowing. Behind him, his queen glares at me, rage burning in her eyes. At any moment those shadows of hers will rise up from the ground and tear me to pieces.

"This is treason," she says, pacing the corridor in front of my cell as Finn falls back.

She stops and grips the cell bars, leaning forward—all menace. Wisps of shadow curl like fond cats around her wrists. "Where is my sister?"

"I told Mish—*the king*. I told the king I don't know. She asked me to come here in her place. I think she's still in the Unseelie Court. Everything I know . . ." I bow my head. I've spent my life hiding the full truth of what it means to be an Echo. The gift is sacred and not to be shared unless it's a matter of life and death. *And this is.* I swallow. "Everything I know comes from the memories I've gained when shifting into her form. And lately I've seen a couple of things that seem . . . more recent. About her buying a magical ring."

The queen spins to face Misha, who's still sitting on the opposite side of my cell, as if he doesn't trust me to be alone in here. "What is she talking about? Memories from shifting? Have you heard anything of the sort?"

Misha eyes me cautiously. "I've heard rumors but . . ." He shakes his head. "Felicity claims she's not a common shifter."

"Prove it," Brie says. "Tell me something no one but Jasalyn would know."

I grasp for something special. Something other than the scars and the horrors of Mordeus's dungeons. "Your mother told you stories at bedtime. Tales of this land. Jasalyn was small, but you'd hold her hand and giggle together about what it might be like to visit Faerie."

She folds her arms, expression harder now. "That could be any two human girls. Try again."

I meet her angry gaze and hold it. "I don't know everything about your sister, but I know enough—from meeting her and from what I've seen—to understand that she doesn't want you to know what she endured in the dungeons. She doesn't want you to know the truth about her scars."

The queen flinches. "We don't know where those are coming from. They've just been appearing."

"But *she* knows. They're scars from what Mordeus and his

guards did to her in the dungeons, but she didn't know that they were from blood magic—that they are signs that he's calling on that connection he made between them in the dungeons. That he's using her to come back."

Abriella looks to Misha. "She's just twisting what you learned from that witch."

He stares at me. "I don't know anything about a ring," he says. "Or the details of what happened in the dungeons."

"Tell us," Abriella says.

"Why should I?" I ask. "Why should I reveal her secrets when you've already decided I'm a liar?"

"Why?" the queen asks, brow raised. "Because otherwise you're *dead* before sunset."

I'm dead anyway.

"I'm waiting," the queen snaps.

"Do you even want to hear it?" I ask, voice hushed with the shame of sharing what Jas has spent three years trying to hide. "How scared she was to be in this realm? How she hated having to pretend she was okay each day but dreaded the nights even more? Do you really want to know that she hated being touched so much that even you—even her sister whom she loves more than anything—couldn't touch her without her wanting to crawl out of her skin?"

The queen's face crumbles, and tears leak from the corners of her eyes. "That's enough."

I lift my chin. "That's what I thought. I guess Jasalyn was right to believe you couldn't handle the truth."

A ball of shadow lunges forward, fists in my hair, and yanks my head back until I'm meeting the queen's gaze again. "What did they do to her?"

My eyes water from the pain but I don't care. "They hurt her. They made her bleed—for the magic but also . . ." I shake my head. "I don't know. Mordeus never explains it in her memories. He spoke like he knew she had magic and was going to be important to him—but I think he did everything he did to make her fear him, fear those dungeons, and fear everything about this court. I think he knew her fear and hatred would bring him back."

The shadow queen grips the bars, her knuckles turning white. "This story feels too convenient. You haven't told me anything to prove you haven't killed my sister and hidden her body with plans to take over her life."

Misha snaps his head to the side to stare at the queen. "Brie," he says, his voice simultaneously censorious and soothing.

"My queen has a point," Finn says, leaning back against the cell on the opposite side of the corridor and folding his arms. "We need more details. If you can't lead us to the princess, then at least give us something more. Something you'd have no way of knowing."

I throw up my hands. "How would I know *any* of this without her memories?"

"Perhaps you're from the old race that ate the hearts of their victims to steal their magic," Finn says.

I draw back in horror. "The princess was alive last I saw her. I don't *eat hearts.*"

"So this magical ring my sister is supposedly using," the queen says, "where did it come from?"

"She got it from a witch in Elora in exchange for her immortal life." I look to Misha. "What if he could take over her life somehow? What if Mordeus is planning to come back through Jasalyn?"

"You've gone too far," the queen spits.

"The witch made the princess get her a book—the Grimoricon—she said she needed it to create the ring."

"That's enough." Abriella spins, and her cloak flares behind her as she storms away, her king consort right behind.

"I speak the truth," I call to her back, determined. "There's something about your sister that Mordeus knew he would need—something about her unique gifts that will allow him to do what only Mab has done before."

Misha scoffs and pushes to his feet. "The Grimoricon doesn't leave the Midnight Palace. Even the shadow princess couldn't have gotten it out of there."

I blink and he's on the other side of the cell bars, staring at me with folded arms.

I jump to my feet and run to the bars. "My father will be coming for me. He's wanted to kill me since before I was born."

"Then I guess he'll save me the trouble." There's anger in his eyes but hurt too, and the sight of it makes everything feel too heavy. He keeps looking me over, like he doesn't understand me in my true form. At last, he leans closer—close enough to touch. "You better hope we find her fast. You better pray to whatever gods haven't forsaken you that her deepest wish is for us to spare your life."

I wrap my hands around the bars, framing his face. "I never meant to hurt you."

His eyes flash, going hard in an instant. "I never meant to let you."

CHAPTER THIRTY-TWO

◇

JASALYN

KENDRICK AND I WALK SIDE by side down the stairs. He's careful to stay close, to keep the ring's magic from making him forget anything.

I can't think straight. I'm already so tired, my limbs so heavy—from the ring, from the truth. I don't think I'll have much time before fatigue turns to weakness, but I'm determined to make it to Feegus Keep today, even if I have to crawl.

At the threshold to the kitchen, Kendrick stops in his tracks and grabs my hand. "We shouldn't travel today. We can wait until tonight. We can wait until we figure out how to destroy the—"

"What if I black out again? What if I kill another dozen of Mordeus's pledges?" The horror of it surges, and I slam it down. I don't have time to wallow. "I want to do this now. I made this mess, and I need to fix it."

When I turn into the kitchen, I freeze at the sight of a new face at the table. A face I recognize from my dreams. His braid sways as he laughs at something Remme said, and just before his green eyes meet mine, I catch sight of the two scars slicing across the left side of his head.

And when the time is right, we'll bring her to you, and, like a phoenix, you will rise again.

"What's wrong?" Kendrick asks.

"Who's that?" I rasp.

"That's Shae. He's part of my team. He'll help us when we reach Feegus Keep."

"I dreamed him. I dreamed that he—" He cut into me. Just like the others. He was working with Mordeus. Planning something with him.

We'll bring her to you.

I spin on Kendrick—stare at his unmarked forehead.

The dream couldn't have been real. Why would the Seven be protecting Mordeus if he betrayed them to Kendrick? Or did Mordeus never have the chance to betray them before Abriella killed him?

My gaze drifts back to the kitchen, back to the stranger with the familiar braid and scars, and my stomach sinks.

"Drop your glamour."

He pulls back. "Jasalyn—"

That's why he needed her alive. That's what Kendrick said to Natan upon learning Mordeus might be wearing the match to my ring. Why would he have said that if Mordeus had never made that deal from my dream? Why would he have said that if he wasn't working with the evil king?

"Drop. Your. Glamour. Now."

His throat bobs and then he shifts before my eyes, his ears rounding, that fae glow fading. "Is this better?"

"You lie." The words come out as a sob, everything slamming

411

into me at once. He didn't want me to know Mordeus was alive, and now this. "Don't lie to me."

He flinches. "I didn't want—"

"Let me see you as you are. No magic. *No lies.*"

With an exhale, he shifts. The changes are so small, and part of me wants them to be meaningless. But he's as he appeared in my nightmare. Fae. With softly glowing skin and elven ears.

With the lines of a delicately woven crown tattooed across his forehead.

I feel like he just tore my heart from my chest. "You made me think you were human."

"Jas . . ."

"And you did it because Mordeus told you to. Because you'd do anything to bring down the Seven."

His jaw ticks as he holds my gaze. "I had no idea what he was doing to you when he'd take you out of that cell. I had no idea how bad it had been before I got there. There were no markings, no bruises—"

"You made a deal with him. You'd keep me from destroying myself in exchange for your queen's release." My insides are folding in on each other, threatening to make me collapse. "You were working for him. You *still* are."

He looks away. His throat bobs. "Keep you alive, give you a reason to hold on, and in return, he'd let Crissa go. How can you fault me for that?"

I feel so cold, so hollow, that I'm surprised when I feel the tears sliding down my cheeks. "This whole time, I thought you saved me in those dungeons. But you held me there. And you did it for him. You helped me plot my escape—was any of that real? Were you really helping me get out of there or just giving me a reason to think it was possible?"

He bows his head. "I believed you were safe so long as you were with me."

"*Don't.* You knew I wasn't safe. You knew how scared I was. You *knew* I was a means to an end for him, and you *helped him.*" My voice breaks on the last words.

And now I'm a monster.

He lifts his gaze to mine. "You have no idea how sorry I am."

"Me too." A tear drops onto the stone floor, and I stare at it for a beat before blinking my attention back to Kendrick. It hurts worse than looking at Mordeus. That hurt was fear. This hurt is betrayal. "I have to go." My voice cracks.

"Jas, don't."

He won't remember any of this. Won't remember that I know how he betrayed me. Won't remember the way we touched last night. Won't remember how he found my deepest scars and ripped me apart.

"Once I met you, I would've protected you no matter what," he says. "Mordeus is irrelevant."

"But he's not." I lunge for the door, pushing outside.

"What are you doing?" he calls.

With the last of my energy, I sprint around the corner and squat behind the charred remains of a horse stall.

When I look back, Kendrick's standing on the steps, looking out toward the street and scraping a hand over his face, confusion knitting his brow.

413

He turns into the house. "Have any of you seen Jasalyn today?"

I know what I need to do. I've known since Natan told us about Mordeus wearing the match to my ring. But now I know I have to do it alone.

CHAPTER THIRTY-THREE

———◇———

MISHA

THE FAE GODDESS IN MY dungeon is straight from my dreams. I don't know what makes me more angry—how satisfying it was to see even an impersonation of her in the flesh after over three years of nightly visions or knowing that Felicity was manipulating me again. That she must've somehow gotten in my head and chosen the one face I'd be weak to.

I shouldn't be surprised. She's gotten in my head since the moment she arrived in my court. My gut told me something was radically different about her. Something big felt *off*. But I didn't trust that instinct. I let this unexpected attraction override my good sense. I let it scare me into ignoring all the signs when the truth should've been so obvious.

Once I opened my eyes, my mind was flooded with reasons I knew the woman staying with me couldn't be Jasalyn. The way she laughs too easily. The way she flips her hair. *The way she looks at me.*

"Misha," Abriella says, pulling me into my meeting room by my tunic. Her shadows slam the door shut behind me.

Across the room, Finn stares out at the dark night, stewing.

"I'm sorry." I shove my hands into my pockets. "I don't know how I let this happen."

"We have to find her," she says. The anxiety rolling off her is palpable.

"I promise we will turn the realm inside out looking, but I don't want you to get your hopes up. We have—"

"Misha." She's breathless, her eyes wild. "Listen to me. I've told no one that the Grimoricon was missing."

I freeze. "It's *missing*?"

Her expression is bleak. "Yes. It disappeared three months ago."

My stomach plummets. Felicity's story could be true. Jasalyn could've been the one who took it. "Would that be possible? How would Jas have been able to take it from the palace?"

Her throat bobs. "It was spelled so that it couldn't be moved by anyone who didn't have Mab's blood."

"Abriella." I drag a hand over my face. "It never *occurred to you* that your sister might have been the one to take it?"

"Misha, back off," Finn says. "It wouldn't have occurred to you either. You've seen what Jas has been like."

"Jas didn't even know about it," Brie says, "not beyond the tale of what I did to rescue her. She didn't know where I kept it or how we used it. She didn't care about things like that. And I hadn't—" She looks up to the ceiling, eyes still wet with tears. "I hadn't *made* her learn the things she needed to because I was so worried about her *healing*."

"You can't blame yourself for this," Finn says, placing a hand on her shoulder. "You were doing what you thought was right."

"I wanted to protect her from all the bad parts of this realm and pretend that everything was good, that everything was fine. And in doing so, I failed her."

I squeeze the back of my neck. "We'll get everyone looking, and we'll find her in no time."

"No," Brie says. "We must keep this quiet. If word spreads and people know my sister is out there on her own, she'll be in more danger. Never mind the kind of chaos it would cause in my court in the midst of the faceless plague and Mordeus's resurrection." She takes a breath and meets my eyes. "In fact, we need your shifter friend to help us find Jasalyn."

"No." I shake my head. "Absolutely not. Even if we *could* trust her, she's not going to want to do me any favors at this point."

"Then we bargain," Brie says. "There has to be something she wants."

She stares at me so long I know she's not going to let it go. Brie wants my prisoner to help her, and I'm not stupid enough to stand between the shadow queen and her sister.

I sigh, resigned. "She was trying to find the Wild Fae Hall of Doors."

"Why?"

"She said they were trying to get to the Eloran Palace, but our Hall doesn't have a portal to the palace. They never allowed it."

Brie and Finn exchange a look.

"The Court of the Moon does," Brie says. "It became part of the Hall back when Mordeus stole the throne."

"He was real friendly with the Magical Seven of Elora," Finn says. "At least when it served him."

"We can't simply let her use your portal," I say. "We don't even know what she plans to do with it."

Abriella sneers. "That realm is so broken and backward, she can blow up the whole Eloran Palace for all I care. I want my sister back."

"My king."

We all turn to see Tynan standing in the door to my meeting room, chest heaving as if he's rushed here.

"What is it?" I ask.

"The guard from the dungeons called for backup."

I give Brie my best *told you so* face. As if being right about some petty shit can make up for the fact that there's a gaping hole in my chest. "What did she do?"

"Nothing," Tynan says. "That's just it. She was sitting in her cell one minute, and the next she was begging the guard to help her, she said they were coming for her."

"That's impossible. The whole dungeon is warded against magic and goblin travel. There's no way out of that cell. It's a trick."

Tynan swallows. "Misha, it's no trick. She's gone."

I set my jaw. "Search the castle and the grounds," I tell Tynan. I wait until he's gone before turning to Abriella. "Why Jas? Why use her to come back? What necromancer could be strong enough for true resurrection?"

Finn and Brie exchange a look that tells me they have a very good idea why but haven't decided if they can share with me.

"Brie, if I'm going to help, I need to know."

"We've been so focused on *how* one might resurrect Morde-us's body that we never stopped to consider if his original body was ever part of the plan," Finn says softly. "There are no necromancers who can fully restore a life with both body and spirit, so Mordeus found the next best thing."

Abriella's composure cracks, and she spins to Finn. "Oh, gods, Finn, if she really traded her immortality, we don't have much time."

Horror rocks through me. Felicity's deceit cost us precious days. "Tell me now," I say. "What aren't you saying about Jasalyn?"

"I had Pretha look into my sister's mind," Brie blurts, shame tinging her cheeks. "Two years ago, when there were no signs of her magic manifesting, I was beginning to worry that Jas would be powerless against our enemies, so I asked Pretha to search her mind and see if she could find any sign of magic. I never told Jas about it because I thought she might be afraid of what Pretha found."

I shake my head. "I don't understand. What kind of power could allow Mordeus to use her to rise from the dead?"

"He doesn't simply want to be alive again," Finn says. "He wants revenge, and he wants power. With his blood magic in place and Jasalyn's gift at his command, he could easily have both."

"How?" I'm losing patience, but I need to understand.

"She's a phoenix, Misha." Brie's expression is grim. "My sister can burn down to ash and rise again, reborn."

My stomach sinks to the floor. "That's an unspeakably rare gift."

Brie nods. "I know. And if Mordeus truly bound their lives together with this blood magic, he could command the power of her phoenix to come back—his spirit in her body."

ACKNOWLEDGMENTS

All the best turns of my career began as moments I was indulging my muse and became new adventures because of reader support. *Beneath These Cursed Stars* exists today only because readers championed *These Hollow Vows* and *These Twisted Bonds*. Whether it was in your local book group, on a Bookstagram page, on TikTok, or just in chatting with your book besties, your support of my debut fantasy series meant that I got to write more, and that's the best gift you could've given me. So thank you for the opportunity to return to this world and these characters that mean so much to me. I am so grateful!

Beneath These Cursed Stars was conceived, written, and revised while I learned to navigate life with the added responsibility of caring for my father, who has dementia, and as our family dealt with the sudden, unexpected death of my sister-in-law. I wouldn't have been able to produce anything new through these struggles if I didn't have so much support at home. Thank you, always, to my husband, Brian, who held my hand and lifted me up even as he grappled with his own grief. Brian, you are the best listener I've ever met, and I feel lucky every day that you're there to hold my hand through the good and the bad. Thank you for being my rock.

Thank you to my kids, Jack and Mary, who have had to sacrifice way too much mom time for their grandfather. You two make me so proud and so lucky to be a mom. You help make home my steadfast safe place to land, and I can only hope I'm always able to do the same for you.

Thank you to my mother, siblings, and in-laws for supporting me through the challenges of this season of life. I wish I could've handled it all with more grace, but I appreciate you standing by my side regardless.

Thank you to my friends for cheering me on. Mira Lyn Kelly and Lisa Kuhne, thank you for believing in my words even when I can't. Thank you to the writers in my Write All the Words Slack group for keeping me company when writing feels lonely. Thanks also to Robin Danek, who understands as only a fellow academic could, just how hard I'm willing to work to never go back there.

To my agent, Dan Mandel, who has my back when I need it. Cheers to over a decade on this journey together!

I owe thanks to the team at HarperTeen, who's helped me make this book what it is today. Special thanks to my editor, Emilia Rhodes, for being a comforting presence through the many changes of the last two years, and especially for pushing me exactly where and when I needed it to make this book something I am truly proud of. Briana Wood, thank you for your notes and perspective and for all your help along the way. Thanks also to the sales and subrights team and the rest of the awesome group responsible for making my vision into a beautiful book available around the world: marketing director Michael D'Angelo, publicist John Sellers, copyeditor Ana Deboo, Chris Kwon and Jenna Stempel in design, production manager Trish McGinley, managing editors Erika West and Mary Magrisso, and proofreader Samantha Hoback.

Finally, dear readers, I want to say I am so grateful to live in a time when it's acceptable, even encouraged, to talk about mental health struggles. These are not new issues for me, but they've been inflamed by circumstance. I'm lucky to have access to therapy and an amazing PCP, but for me, the best processing always comes through story. I relate so profoundly to Jasalyn's struggles and found following her through her journey a source of healing. If you're like me and struggle with depression and anxiety, I hope you'll remember you're not alone. Depression lies. Anxiety deceives. I know they can be so loud at times, but keep going. The sun *will* rise again tomorrow.